THE SKINNY

ADVENTURES OF AMERICA'S

FIRST BULIMIC

BY

RAYNI JOAN

keyhole
publications

Santa Monica, California

First Edition

1 2 3 4 5 6 7 8 9

This is a work of fiction. Except for some details regarding the author's own life, the incidents, names, and characters have been modified to suit the needs of the story. The individuals and events portrayed are composites.

Printed in the United States of America

ISBN: 978-0-9624415-4-7

www.RayniJoan.com

Keyhole Publications
P.O. Box 1064
Santa Monica, CA 90405

To Charlotte and Kate and a better tomorrow for all the girls

ACKNOWLEDGMENTS

I'm grateful to all who have helped bring *The Skinny* into being:

My sister, Ellen D'Acquisto, my friends Marilyn Cohen, Barbara Dulberg, Bev Huntsberger, and my precious daughter-in-law, Caroline Kerpen, all of whom read and commented on early drafts. Terrie Silverman and my colleagues in her writing workshops who listened patiently and offered feedback as I slogged through sections that needed work and sometimes even stood up and improvved scenes. My improv comedy group, and its dedicated leader Brian Hamill, for providing weekly playtime and lots of new playmates, especially theater and dancing pals Elaine Cohen and Alan Cohn, and neighbor Marilyn Brennan.

Mimi Kerpen, an inspiring role model, wonderful grandmother to my kids and great grandmother to Charlotte and Kate – also, of course, many thanks and hugs and kisses to gorgeous Charlotte and Kate themselves...may you and your generation grow up with totally positive, healthy body images! Friends Ronnie Watkins, Bernice Stock, Julie Rich Simon, Phyllis Rosen, Solange Monette, Jill Lewis, Leila Kozak, Susan Hayden, Amy Douglas, Deborah Blossom; my California nieces Tanayi Seabrook and Rachel D'Acquisto – all supportive across time and space. Contessa Rhonda von Sternberg and Chanel Lallouz for their powerful feedback and continued support. Editor extraordinaire Lily Wise, and graphic artist Erin Brubaker.

Thanks to my sons: Dave, for his unflagging optimism, thoughtfulness, and soaring spirit; Phil, whose quiet love I deeply honor and appreciate; Dan, for believing in me and my writing ability and for bringing his wonderful music and poetry to the world...I love you guys dearly.

Thanks beyond measure to my husband, Robert Moskowitz, for being there day in and day out, helping, supporting, loving, and putting up with me in every way. I am truly blessed.

Finally, for all of the above – and more – thanks to my spiritual helpers and guides, always present, always appreciated...all aspects of the ONE.

THE SKINNY

ADVENTURES OF AMERICA'S

FIRST BULIMIC

PREFACE

The Skinny is a fictional version of my personal story, first written almost 40 years ago, and titled *Off the Doors*. Despite the pleas of my wonderful agent at the time, Frances Goldin, who urged me to keep producing, after 26 "encouraging" rejections from top publishers, I burned *Off the Doors* a page at a time and confined my further writing to journals. Back then, my sense of self was weak and sense of shame strong from hiding my addiction. It was either destroy myself or the manuscript, and I opted for survival. Could all the rejections have had anything to do with the complete absence in that breezy adventure story of any mention of an eating disorder? Hmmmm....

Hundred of hours of counseling, along with supportive, loving relationships convinced me to recreate the story, this time allowing my protagonist a lengthy experience with bulimia – coinciding authentically with my own history. I was bulimic from age 12 to age 37, when love for my first baby transformed me. I believe that my eating disorder sprang from feeling isolated, confused, and lonely, and from seeking solace in a twisted cultural image of beauty. I didn't know then that beauty had to spring from the heart. There is no substitute.

Although this story is based on my life, because I filtered events through my imagination, in fairness I must call *The Skinny* a novel.

In a world which continues to celebrate "skinny-ness," eating disorders remain a major affliction for an estimated 8 million Americans, including approximately 1 million men. Fortunately, eating disorders are now recognized and treatable. For anyone just beginning to look for information about healing an eating disorder, in addition to looking into your precious heart, I recommend starting at www.EDreferral.com.

The 26 editors from top publishers who rejected *Off the Doors* 38 years ago all asked to see my next novel. To those 26 editors I say: It's been a mighty long gestation, but finally, here it is.

Rayni Joan
Santa Monica, CA, 2008 (see next page)

P.S. Just to clarify, a *vomitorium* was an ancient Roman system for quickly exiting a stadium and NOT a room designed especially for vomiting.

P.P.S. My fictional alter ego, Rowena Gay Wine, "outs" herself as a bulimic with the first revelatory news article confessing to her own binge-and-purge behavior and analyzing the socio-political impact on women caused by popular but unrealistic body images. My real-life article, originally written for Liberation News Service, is included in the appendix at the end of this volume, reprinted from the front page of *L.A. Free Press*, June 5, 1970.

ONE

It's a Saturday morning, mid 1953, and the Hit Parade is on the radio, blasting Eddie Fisher crooning: "*Oh, my pa-pa, to me he was so wonderful.*" I think of Grandpa and hum along as I sadly and madly chew and snap a mouthful of gum. I'm standing in front of the mirror over the low bureau I share with my sisters, inspecting my new body in the smallest jeans I've ever worn. I'm a fraction of the size I was, but I'd like to be still skinnier so I hold in my stomach and stick out my Marilyn Monroe assets as I brush my unruly chestnut hair into crazy patterns that cover my face. I'm peeking through the hair mask when Daddy charges into the central thoroughfare bedroom and kills the volume. The sudden disruption makes my stomach hurt. This is no wonderful pa-pa. This is the tyrant of my life. I'd like to blast big smelly gas at him but since losing 60 pounds, I don't have that potent weapon anymore. Too bad because now that I force my food up, my sense of smell has been fading in and out, mostly out. It would be so perfect to let loose stinky ones and be immune to the stench. Not that I've ever minded my own farts. They saved my ass from the sensitive-nosed tyrant many times. It's so interesting that vomiting takes away my sense of smell and my flatulence along with the fat. Since I'm the first and only deliberate barfer since the Romans, maybe I should keep track of all the effects of this fabulous new discovery and write a book – except I'll still want it to be a secret. Hmmm. That could be a problem.

Daddy stops near me, mutters a disgusted "Goddamn pig kids," then points to something on the floor. "Pick that scrap up, Weena," he barks. At the moment, he's a bulldog, husky, with large wrinkles.

Slowly, I lay the hairbrush down, turn around and follow his finger. He is pointing to a white speck most humans would need a microscope to even notice on the flowered linoleum. "Not guilty," I say casually, amazed at my boldness. An instant cord of tension arises between us. I continue to chew and snap, careful not to ingest my hair.

He parks himself inches from me, scrunches up his face, narrows his eyes. Raising his voice sharply, he emphasizes each word: "I don't think you heard me, so I'll say it again. Pick it up. Now. And get rid of that goddamn wad of gum while you're at it. You look like a hairy dog crossed with a cow."

I force myself not to laugh although I think that's funny. "I heard you," I declare, eyes fixed on him through the hair veil. For the first time, I

1

notice, even though I'm twelve and he's forty-something, we're the same height. "I meant I'm not the one who dropped it." I shove the hair out of my face and chew on.

I get a quick whiff of his cigarettes and bay rum aftershave, and then the smells vanish.

He slaps me hard across the face. The gum shoots out like a projectile just missing his ear and in the exact same moment, without hesitation, reflexively, my open hand comes up and smashes him back full force. Oops. My heart pounds. I think my handprint on his cheek will be the last sight of my life. For sure, he'll get me now. I stand my ground, ready for anything. Let him kill me. He'll fry in the electric chair.

His color rises, narrowing eyes stare, whites expanding wildly. His nostrils flare, chin juts out. I notice a couple of blackheads on his squashed nose. The muscles on his upper jaws tense as though he wants to bite me. Outraged, beyond words, clenching his teeth, he waves his index finger in my face as he backs me into our little bathroom up against the tub. There's nowhere to go. I have to lean backwards from my waist into the blue plastic shower curtain. This is so stupid it strikes me as funny. My sense of smell returns for a moment and I inhale the unpleasant plastic of the shower curtain, then it's gone. This miniature room is my place of secret empowerment, and it's weird to be stuck here with my crazed father. He resembles the same guy who takes me fishing and plays music with me only now he's possessed. This has happened fairly regularly for as long as I can remember, but it's the first time I've fought back non-gaseously. I didn't mean to, but now I'm glad. I maintain eye contact. Drops of sweat gather on his deep pink forehead, trickle down his cheeks.

"Don't you ever, ever dare to lay a hand on me again or I'll kill you," he hisses, just above a whisper.

I don't believe him. But he never hits me again.

The day after our confrontation, when all of us Wines are at dinner, including my 16-year-old sister Karen and seven-year-old sister Victoria, I tinkle my fork against my glass for their attention.

"Mommy, Daddy, Karen, Victoria," I proclaim before eating a bite. "I have something to announce to all of you."

Daddy looks up suspiciously. Karen chuckles. Mommy keeps passing food. Victoria pays attention.

"I don't want to be called Weena or anything like that ever again. My name is Rowena, and please call me either Rowena, Rowie or possibly Ro. If you call me anything else I'll pretend I didn't hear you. That's it. Now may I have some potatoes, please, Mother?"

"Okay, Rowie," Mommy says and smiles.

"I'm still going to call you Weenie," Karen pipes, then quickly adds, "Only kidding."

"That wasn't funny," Daddy snaps at her. It is the first time I have ever heard him use a negative tone to Karen. Usually this is reserved for me or occasionally, Mommy.

"Sorry," Karen says, eyes down, mouth tight.

"Sorry what?" Daddy continues, his fork down, an unheard of threat hanging in the air. "Sorry who? Speak to your sister, Karen. Rowena has made a very grown-up request and I would like you to be grown-up about it. Kindly address your sister the way I expect you to from now on. Use her name when you tell her you're sorry. I'm waiting."

Karen flushes bright pink. "Sorry, Row E," she blurts out.

"You can do better," Daddy goes on. "Don't be a smartass."

"Sorry, Rowie," Karen says softly.

"Thanks," I say, beaming. I feel like a million bucks.

_ ∞ _

But Daddy doesn't defend me again. Instead, our quarreling escalates. When he rages, I join him at the same decibel level. Not myself anymore, I have a strange sensation that I'm acting for a camera rolling, recording every word and movement except my secret bathroom scenes, which remain off limits. Daddy and I star as antagonists, sparring verbally. I feel far more skilled at it than Mommy has ever been. On the dinner table set, I'm not eating anymore, just filling up. I stuff myself with second and third helpings of everything as the family gossips and chats about humdrum issues.

"Time to take down the storm windows and put up the screens, Buddy," Mommy says at a typical Wine meal. "Pass the butter, please, dear."

"Be nice if I could get some goddamn help with the storms and screens, for Crissake," Daddy says, passing the butter. "Pop used to take care of it with me."

Pop refers to my favorite person in the whole world, my grandpa, whose death a couple of months ago plunged me into despair and triggered my discovery of the ancient Roman barfing technique I'm secretly using to get skinny.

"What do you think about asking my brother Sidney?" Mommy suggests genially.

"What do I think? Aside from your brother being fat, lazy, incompetent and a stupid sonovabitch, what do I think? I think you're dreaming, Pearlie, for Crissake. Your brother's a goddamn slob. He'd just get in the way."

Karen adds, "Oh Daddy, Uncle Sidney would probably be happy to help. You underestimate him."

"No, I don't," Daddy says. "When it comes to work, your uncle's good for nothing."

Mommy's lips quiver. She's on the edge of tears.

"Victoria and I could help, Daddy," I say, shoveling yet another forkful of potatoes into my mouth, close to completely stuffed and excitedly readying for the purge.

Little Victoria nods her pony-tailed head in agreement.

"Don't be stupid," he says. "That's not a job for kids."

At that, I leap into my act. I jump up from my seat right next to him, slam my chair in, and yell angrily, "Don't you call me stupid. I am not stupid. How dare you call me stupid? You might have said something kind about my offer. It was sincere." Then I storm off, straight to the bathroom, lock the door, run the bath so the water can drown out the gagging sounds, and throw up dinner. I'm grateful for the opportunity to get away from the table. Daddy just about always presents me a cue for a similar escape. It is becoming a nightly performance. It amuses me.

Weeks go by like this. One night, as usual, I rise, thrust my chair against the table and erupt. "You did it again, Father. Put me down again. I don't have to sit here and listen to this." My stomach is bursting. I've eaten three helpings of dinner with extra bread and butter and several glasses of milk.

Daddy grabs my wrist.

"Just a minute, young lady," he says. "Sit back down, goddamn it. We have to talk about this."

"What the hell do you mean?" I snarl, panicked inside. I have to find a way to empty my stomach. I stand defiantly. He holds on to my wrist. If only I could get off a nice big fart. I try. Nothing.

"Don't use that kind of language in this house," he says.

"Why the hell not? It's a free country. And anyhow, who the hell do you think I learned from?"

Mommy and Victoria slip away from the table.

"Rowie," groans Karen, getting up and pushing her chair in. "Do you have go through this same scene every night? Enough already."

"Don't blame me, Karen. I didn't start this," I snap.

Daddy clears his throat, wiggles his finger as a signal to Karen. She sits back down.

"Sorry, Daddy," she says sweetly. "May I please be excused?"

"You may, dear," he says. "Run along."

He's hurting my wrist. His demon mask bares itself, flared nostrils, tense jaw, rigid chin, wild eyes. The monster is back. I imitate Karen and him, mocking their saccharine tones.

"Sorry, Daddy. May I please be excused? You may, dear, run along."

He tightens his hold on my wrist.

"Don't you use that sarcastic bullshit tone with me, Rowie, for Crissake. I'd like to know what in the hell you think you're getting away with night after night jumping up and leaving the goddamn table. This is not feeding time at the zoo. You're not fooling me any longer. I've got your goddamn number."

I'm terrified. Am I busted? What will I do? I can't live without my new routine. My stomach throbs. I have to find a way to empty in the next few minutes before the digestive acids go to work and the vomit sours. I tug and yank with the intention of pulling my arm away, but that makes my wrist ache more. I stand there next to my chair staring at him.

Finally, I growl, "What's my number?" My wrist pulsates where he is squeezing it. I think he may be breaking my bone.

"I wasn't born yesterday," he says. "Maybe it's hormonal or a goddamn tapeworm eating you. But it's obvious you're picking fights every night to get out of doing the dinner dishes. You haven't helped your mother in weeks."

Relief floods me. I melt. "Oh, I'm sorry, Daddy. I want to help with the dishes, really I do." He lets go of my wrist. It's swollen and sore. Damn, it's my throw-up hand. No matter, I'm free. I pick up my empty plate and call to my co-conspirator in the kitchen. Mommy knows how I've lost all the weight and has given me the go-ahead, but we haven't talked about it since the night I asked her whether it was okay and she told me the Romans did it so it must be. "Mommy, please leave the dishes for me to dry. I'll dry every night. I'm just attached to my bath right after dinner."

Victoria, who suspects I'm up to something, comes back into the dinette, chimes, "Why don't you take your bath after the dishes are done, sister dear?"

"Because this is my routine, sister dear," I shoot back.

"A pretty odd routine, Ro," says Victoria, raising an eyebrow, as she continues to clear the table. "Hey, Daddy, why don't you ask her the real reason she runs to the bathroom right after dinner?"

Mommy walks in just in time to rescue me. "Now, everyone," she says. "Let's have peace for once. Stop picking on Rowie. She's allowed her oddities."

Victoria mumbles something under her breath and looks disgusted.

Daddy is satisfied. I dash to the bathroom, run the bath, lean over, and, inserting my middle and index fingers into my throat, effortlessly dump a heavy load into the toilet. With my stomach freshly emptied, and my mood elevated, I take a quick dip in the full tub, followed by a shower, which I prefer; then, assuming I smell of soap and toothpaste, ignoring the usual sore throat, pittering heartbeat and slightly swollen glands, I happily skip to the kitchen in my pajamas to dry and put away the dishes. After-dinner baths are now acceptable. I no longer need fight scenes at the table.

– ∞ –

TWO

Before Victoria arrived, Pearl and Buddy Wine, my mismatched parents, Karen Joy - blond, beautiful, asthmatic, and Daddy's pet - and me, of course, Rowena Gay - the brat called Weena - all lived downstairs from Grandma and Grandpa Fine - Mommy's parents - in their two-story Victorian brick on a shady block in Washington Heights, Newburgh New York. A gray-green city of 25,000 dominated by Dupont Chemical and Stroock Fabrics, Newburgh lay in the lush valley of the wide, sparkling Hudson, about an hour and a half, and an eternity, from Manhattan. There's a museum in the old house George Washington used as his headquarters during the American Revolution. GW probably tarried there as long as he did because Newburgh was so oppressive it inspired his continued fight for freedom.

In our working class neighborhood, lush oaks and maples camouflaged deteriorating old houses three seasons of the year, and after autumn's gorgeous color show and late fall's bleakness, snow covered up in winter. Between my parents' constant smoking and Mommy's endless cleaning, our dark ground floor apartment crammed with mismatched furniture smelled of cigarettes, bleach, pine cleanser, and greasy cooking smells, with a whiff now and then of floral Evening in Paris cologne Mommy dabbed behind her ears in an effort at sophistication. Those were smells from before my barfing days when my nose stopped functioning reliably.

Seven months of the year, when they weren't in Florida, Grandma and Grandpa provided a peaceful refuge from my parents' constant civil war - one I got drafted into against my will (on Mommy's side). Just about all grown-ups smoked, and I didn't like the smell much but still looked forward to being old enough to smoke and played pretend smoking with my fingers.

Except for his smoking, and the coughing accompaniment, I loved everything about Gramps: his dark tanned skin, bald head with fringe of white hair, warm brown eyes behind metal framed glasses he was always pushing up because they kept slipping, his Yiddish expressions and thickly accented stories about the *shtetls* of Belarus. Gramps hugged me, smiled, and spoke softly and kindly. He spent most of his day at the treadle Singer mending and tailoring clothing Uncle Sidney brought him from the dry cleaners Gramps himself had owned until his heart attack before I was born. Classical or klezmer music always flowed from the black Bakelite radio near his sewing machine in the

7

sunny bedroom, and when he relaxed in his plaid club chair in the early American living room, he read *The Forward* or listened to the news on the Philco cathedral radio. Gramps also had an old Victrola he had to crank for it to play for ten minutes, and when a record was ending, it would drag and sound silly like a frog swallowing its voice. The Victrola sat inside a walnut cabinet with deep shelves crammed with Jewish music and opera records. When I was little, I burrowed on Gramps's lap, my ear against his chest, and listened to his heartbeat along with the songs. I never got tired of hearing a record wind down. It always made me giggle.

Grandma, with snowy hair and soft round body, loved to cook and bake and was more social than Gramps, frequently going out to Hadassah meetings, mahjong, canasta games and the beauty parlor. I never heard my grandparents raise their voices except to tell funny stories. Mommy said her parents didn't believe in fighting in front of their children, and that's why she and all her brothers had unreal expectations that led to screwy marriages. I didn't like the way Mommy blamed Grandma and Grandpa for her fights with Daddy. After all, I wasn't allowed to blame Karen for our fights.

My grandparents' upstairs apartment was my childhood sanctuary where along with music and hugs, I got plenty of blintzes, knishes, latkes, bananas with cottage cheese and sour cream, brisket, chicken soup, *kneidlach* and matzoh in all forms, stuffed derma, carrot tsimis, seeded rye bread, hot pastrami, corned beef, salami, bologna, tongue, juicy homemade pickles, gefilte fish, kasha varnishkes, chopped liver, mamaliga, babka, marble cake, cherry cheese cake, honey cake, taigelach, rugelach, and tea-drinking slurped through a sugar cube held between the front teeth. No *traif* ever passed through my grandparents' doorway into their kosher home. When people talked about "the man upstairs," or said "heaven" and pointed up, I was sure they referred to my gramps as the man and Grandma's kitchen as heaven. Wasn't that why they were called Fine?

If it weren't for Gram and Gramps I would have believed all married couples fought and acted mean to each other like Mommy and Daddy. Our railroad apartment downstairs was the torture chamber of the house with cursing, bickering, yelling, screaming, belittling, spanking, general humiliation, and meals largely consisting of bacon, ham, pork chops, shrimp, Velveeta cheese, American cheese, Ritz crackers, spaghetti with ketchup, tuna and mayonnaise sandwiches on white or rye bread, Campbell's clam chowder, green or red jello, Mommy's homemade toll house cookies from the recipe on the Nestle's sack, and a large variety of store bought cookies including Mallomars, Oreos, chocolate wafers, Fig Newtons, Royal Lunch milk crackers, shortbread, ginger snaps, vanilla wafers, and Buttercups, not to mention Girl Scout cookies, especially mint, all washed down with plenty of milk which was delivered every other day in bottles. When we were sick, we got Grandma's delicious chicken soup–which was a pretty good reason to be sick. In summer, we rode to a stand for fresh corn, which we drowned in butter, and tomatoes, cucumbers, green onions, and iceberg lettuce for salad Mommy drenched with sour cream.

Every week, year round, Daddy hid boxes of bridge mix, chocolate covered raisins and malted milk balls on a high shelf, and I easily climbed up and pilfered them, just a few at a time. It didn't matter whether I got caught or not because I got spankings anyhow. It's possible Daddy hit me because I was the substitute for the son he never got, and boys had to be toughened by the rod in those days. It felt like such an honor to be the chosen boy figure, I unwittingly cooperated in my torture. At first I think Daddy truly believed he was saving me from spoiling with his strict "spare the rod" discipline. When he overstepped and involved his attached rod, I had no idea why or what was happening and I tuned out. My innate optimism carried me out of my little girl's body, to explore the sky, frolic and play with friendly beings from somewhere, and to connect with them like I couldn't connect with people around me. That was before I got fat and learned to fart on demand.

_ ∞ _

When I was four, Mommy's middle started getting bigger and bigger under tent-like clothing with bows and ribbons I had never seen her wear before. She told me I was going to get a grand surprise before my next birthday so I thought about new roller skates, a bike, or even better, a toy gun like my New York City cousin Ralphie had. I loved listening to Hopalong Cassidy and the Lone Ranger on the radio, and I dreamed of having my own cap pistol or water gun. Guns were exciting! The whole family played a guessing game with me about Mommy's belly, and even though I suspected what was cooking, I enjoyed their attention so I convinced myself they were getting me a present in addition to the new baby.

"Guess again what the surprise is going to be, Weena!" Mommy said giddily one day when her stomach was sticking out like a funny round shelf. She put her finger on her lips to signal Karen to keep a secret. Karen and I sat on either side her on the couch and she wrapped her arms around our shoulders. I was used to Gram and Gramps cuddling me but not Mommy. It felt unfamiliar, but I liked the rare strange warmth. Mommy smelled like flowers and laundry soap. "Come on, Weena. Guess!" Mommy urged.

"A cap pistol?" I answered slyly.

"You're an idiot, Weenie," Karen said. "Girls don't play with guns. And you can't fool me. You know why Mommy has such a fat stomach." She was eight and had fine long blond hair and big eyes the color of the sky. Everyone always said she should be a model. Mommy complained about my frizzy mane, and she was still unsure whether my eyes were gray or blue.

"I know why Mommy's fat," I said, ready with a joke. "She eats lots of cookies and they're fattening."

"No-ooo," Karen sang, and slipped off the couch to sit next to me.

"Play along, Karen dear," Mommy said, throwing her head back and laughing loudly. Her straight black hair flew. "Yes, Weena, in a way you're right. I do eat lots of cookies but that's only part of it. The toy surprise is the other part. A wonderful toy you will love."

"Weenie's a dope," Karen said and secretly pinched me as she ran off to see her best friend, Amanda Slutsky, whose family lived two blocks away on Bay View Terrace. Karen and Amanda hung out a lot together and didn't allow me to play with them unless they played doctor and fooled with my body. I only let them because I had nothing better to do, and anyhow, they mostly tickled me and made me giggle.

"Mommy, Karen pinched me," I whined.

"Tattling is just as bad as pinching, Weena," Mommy scolded, wagging her index finger at me. Then, as an afterthought she called out, "You shouldn't hurt your sister, Karen. It's not nice." But Karen was long gone. I'd have to remember to pinch her back.

Mommy's arm was off me. She lit a cigarette. I got up and from the end table, brought her the large green glass ashtray without her even asking.

"Tell me more about the surprise toy, Mommy," I said.

"Here's a good clue: This is a special miracle because we almost lost this toy."

"You found it again?" I asked.

"Yes, that was the miracle." She blew out smoke and laughed some more. Later I heard her repeat our conversation to Grandma, Grandpa, Daddy, and her friend Sylvia, and they all laughed with her.

Not too long after that, Mommy left to pick up the miracle at the hospital. When she came home empty-handed - no surprise or big belly - she didn't talk to me even to say hello, and she cried non-stop. She lay on her stomach on my bed, kicking and punching the mattress, screaming and carrying on. I watched through the open door from the dinette. Scared and confused, I began to bawl. Why was Mommy so mad at my bed? Where was my present?

Grandpa saw me. I looked up at him, wiped my wet eyes on my sleeve and shrugged questioningly. He took my hand and led me into the living room.

"Mommy's upset because your new baby sister is very sick. God might want her to live with him in the sky."

This confused me even more. I had heard something vague about a new sister. Was she mean like Karen? Did God live in the same place in the sky I visited?

"Pray for her," Grandpa said.

"How exactly do I do that, Gramps?" I asked.

"Just ask God to let her live here. He listens."

God was part of a bad word Daddy said in every other sentence. Once I'd said it and gotten spanked. But I trusted Gramps, so whoever this god-guy was, I asked him to help Mommy stop crying and to let our new miracle sister or whatever it was, live with us, and also to please bring me my toy gun so I could be a cowgirl like Dale Evans.

– ∞ –

When the baby finally came home from the hospital, everyone said the miracle had doubled. First, she was saved from a miscarriage - which I thought was related to an evil teacher in some way because I'd heard about teachers named Miss Something or other, and this had to do with babies so obviously Miss Carriage was a bad person who almost got away with doing something bad to Mommy, maybe broke a baby carriage. When I asked, Mommy laughed. Second miracle was surviving a staph infection at birth. Whatever that was, I was smart enough to guess it was a bad thing. One big messy disappointment.

11

"This baby is destined for greatness," Grandpa said, and everyone repeated that mantra and invoked God a lot.

There was no Dale Evans gun for me. The bald, funny-looking crying thing they named Victoria was supposed to be my present. A sister. I would have liked a gun to fake-shoot her, but I didn't need one because I used my fingers and shot her from a distance. Bang! Bang! She cried and peed and pooped, and everyone fussed over her. Karen held her and even fed her with a bottle. For nine months, I took aim and shot jealousy straight out of my index finger. Bang! Bang! Who needed a gun? Not me. I was angry, and it didn't help that I started getting more spankings, which only made me more furious at the tiny creature. She had upset my world and I hated her. But one day, after she had learned to walk, and she had puffs of fuzzy brown hair on her head, we made eye contact. Her blue eyes twinkled. I thought she was fat and adorable. Almost a year old, little impish Victoria looked at me, grinned, lifted her fingers into a gun and said, "Bang, bang, Weenie." I fell over laughing. It was true love she shot at me, and I reciprocated.

Victoria grew into a magical little kid. She danced and skipped around the apartment accompanying herself with her version of "Habanera" from Bizet's Carmen, music Gramps sometimes played on his Victrola. Her hands flew from above her head to her waist and back again, left and right and left and right, up and down, tirelessly as she sang, " A la-dah-dah. A la-dah-dah. A la-dah-dahda and a la-dah-dah." She danced and sang so seriously that we all had to laugh. Victoria's dancing and singing was fun, and sometimes I followed her around our railroad apartment and danced along klutzily.

– ∞ –

Once, six years old, still sore after a particularly big spanking the night before, upstairs and nestled on Grandpa's lap with my arms around his neck, I asked him a question I'd thought about all day. "Gramps, what would I do without you?"

"Don't say that," he answered sharply, and lit a cigarette. When he pushed my arms away, I felt bereft.

"My parents hate me, Gramps," I went on, even though it was the first time he'd spoken to me so roughly, and my heart ached. I sat up and looked right into his eyes magnified behind the glasses. "You and Gram are the only grownups who love me."

He pushed his glasses up, took a puff, blew out smoke, coughed virulently, turned bright pink, and pushed me away so he could reach into his pocket and pull out his handkerchief. I felt as though his glasses were a transparent wall I couldn't breach. I watched through the wall as slowly, still coughing, Gramps unfolded the big white handkerchief, spit a wad of phlegm into it, then folded it up again and stuck it back in his pocket. He looked at me as though he didn't see me. "Don't talk like that, Ro-ro!" he exclaimed. "Of course your parents love you!"

I shut down and kept my tears inside. Sometimes I wonder how my life would have played out if Gramps had said something like "Don't worry, Ro-ro, I'll be with you forever, even after I'm gone from this old body." Would that have kept me from becoming a twelve-year-old addict the day we buried him?

– ∞ –

Home could have been worse. The roof didn't leak. The furnace shot steam heat through clanging pipes winter mornings like some kind of arrhythmic wake-up music that always fit into my dreams as banging of some sort. When it was banging me, anxiety jolted me up, and I found myself confused, but snug and safe under nice warm blankets. Meals materialized regularly. The clean plate club with its rigid rules beat the starving peasants of Africa by far. Meanwhile fear and insecurity permeated my blood and bones. I was the one whom Daddy always spanked. Never Karen or Victoria. I had to find a way to fight back. If I couldn't have a toy gun, I'd find another weapon. Something nobody would take away from me. I knew it would come to me soon.

– ∞ –

THREE

After living above the family's Fine Cleaners and Dyers for years, Grandma and Grandpa had bought our house in 1927 when Mommy was 13, her brother Benny 18, poised to leave home, and their three older brothers, Phil, Sid, and Jack, already out on their own. Originally a bright single family dwelling built by a medium-prosperous merchant on a sparsely populated block with lots of open meadow and wooded areas, the Fine family used it that way for almost five years. They were tough years after the 1929 crash. Grandpa's tenants in the half dozen duplexes he owned couldn't scrounge up rent, and he had too much heart to evict them. He sold the properties off at a fraction of their value just to get out from under. The new owner did what Grandpa couldn't bear to.

Meanwhile, one shocking day, with no warning, workmen arrived on Overlook Place, trees came down, holes in the ground appeared, and soon new frame houses rose on flanking side lots, walling off fresh air and sunshine. Barricaded in darkness and upset that they hadn't bought the adjacent lots themselves, Gram and Gramps responded by using their small nest egg to remodel. They built a two-story rear addition that stretched beyond the new neighbors' and still left a small backyard. Gramps divided the house into our ground floor railroad flat and, on the second floor, a one bedroom apartment for him and Gram, along with a four room rental unit for income. In this "modernizing" move, he installed an oil furnace, pulled out and covered four fireplaces but left original crown moldings, pressed tin ceilings, hardwood floors, and stained glass over the wide front door.

When Gramps told me that the middle room in our flat, now the "girls' bedroom," had once been the large formal dining room, I imagined my bed was a banquet table and I was served for dinner on a platter, rump up, with an apple in my mouth.

– ∞ –

Clotheslines ran from our back porch to a wild cherry tree in the overgrown yard behind ours. Poisonous to humans, fruit-laden branches hung over much of our yard, and in summer, feasting birds regularly deposited brownish goo on clean, billowing laundry. Before our Bendix, Mommy would have to scrub stains all over again, elbows bent over the washboard at the tub part of the double sink in the kitchen.

In contrast to the cherry tree nuisance behind our house, a tall, sturdy sawtooth oak shaded our façade three seasons of the year. In spring, beneath new chartreuse foliage, I used the heel of my shoe to dig holes in patches of soft dirt, perfect for my solitary marble games. In summer I skated up and down the block and got to know every crack and tilt in the slate slabs of sidewalk. In fall, before Gram and Gramps left for Florida, I collected fallen leaves and acorns, and helped Gramps rake them into a pile in the gutter. I stood close to him and watched acorns sputter and pop in the toasty fire. In winter, I played alone in the front yard under snow or ice-coated branches, and built forts and snow people. I was first in the neighborhood to make a snow-woman with mop hair and snowball breasts, at the tips of which I carefully placed pebble nipples. Mommy giggled, then shielded her eyes when she beheld my icy creation.

"Weena, for heavens sake, what's wrong with you?" Mommy said. "Take those things off the snowman instantly before the neighbors see and call the police!"

"It's a snow-woman, Mommy!" I exclaimed. My nose was dripping, and I didn't care.

"Kids don't make snow-women, Weena. They make snowmen. Wipe your nose."

"That's not fair," I complained, and sniffed.

"Life's not fair," Mommy said and went into the house.

I didn't lop the breasts off. Instead I dressed my snow-woman with an old jacket from the give-away bag in the cellar. Karen and Amanda thought my snow-woman was clever. Karen even cut an orange for us to eat and shaped the peel to look like gorgeous lips for my creation. Later, when Mommy reported to Daddy, I got a spanking for making a dirty snowman. I explained that it wasn't a snowman, it was a snow-woman, and it was made of clean snow and not dirty at all, but they didn't listen. Karen didn't stand up for me, but later she whispered how sorry she was that I got punished for something so neat.

– ∞ –

We were one of the few remaining Jewish families not newly ensconced in a comfortable house on the West Side, and as the Jews moved away, my family acted as though every gentile replacement was sent by the

Cossacks to foment trouble. Grandma taught me that Catholic nuns wore full habits to hide their pregnancies which had resulted from congress with priests. She added conspiratorially, from where do you think all those Catholic orphanages get their children? In the first warm weather of spring, my folks used to sit on our porch and have staring contests with the Polish family directly across the street. It wasn't until I met Richie Gryzbowski in high school, when he transferred from Catholic school, that I knew he existed as a real live boy instead of a symbol full of consonants. He said I was the first Jew he'd ever talked to, and he was surprised to learn I didn't have horns. A smart bunch all of us were.

– ∞ –

Spankings were supposed to remove all traces of evil impulses. I'd already learned to detest Daddy's open hand whacking my bare little tush. With the belt, my butt stung and where the buckle tore my skin, it bled. Plus Daddy did something with his fingers that sort of felt good but also scary and confusing. If I was so bad, why did he want to make me feel good at all?

Every night Daddy came home tired from traveling miles and miles to call on drug stores in three counties. He wholesaled medicine chest products like aspirin tablets, cold cream, Mercurochrome and bandages. Handy things to have around for sore butts. Always an optimist, I'd be delighted to see him, run to greet him and hug him around the legs. Sometimes he'd squat down and throw his arms around his girls in a big friendly hug.

"Were you good girls today?" he'd ask.

"Yes, Daddy," we'd chant.

"Weena was bad again," Mother would say, tsk-ing as she emerged from the kitchen on cue. "She's due a spanking, Buddy. Wait'll you hear what she did this time. Don't tell fibs, Rowena Gay Wine."

Automatically, my heart pounded, stomach wobbled, throat tightened, lips trembled as though they'd slipped a nickel into me somewhere like a carnival game. I hated my body's reaction. I'd have to find a way to get back at them. I had to somehow. I had no idea what I'd done 500 hours ago in the morning so how could I avoid it in the future?

It wasn't always something big like when I went naked to visit Karen at her school, for which I'd gotten the longest spanking ever with Daddy's belt on my tush, legs, arms and back. He made me take all my clothes off for that spanking so I'd remember never to get naked again and publicly shame them.

16

After that, Mommy got mad at me for all kinds of little things like spilling my milk, forgetting to flush the toilet or dropping a piece of something soft like cooked carrot without noticing, then stepping in it and dragging it around a little. I never meant to do these naughty things. They just happened accidentally when I moved around. Mommy said I was a big klutz. Lots of times by evening, I forgot what my infraction was and probably she did too because she rarely reminded me of what I had done, only that it was bad. Sometimes I ran and hid under the bed, but that only made Daddy madder. I watched him from a hundred miles away across the room and quaked. If only I had a toy gun, I fantasized, I could show him how wrong he was. Just like in the cowboy movies. Bang, bang, Daddy, take that! Now you have to stop spanking me! I'd spit on the gun and put it back in the holster.

The ogre had a routine I knew too well. All in slow motion, he took off his dark overcoat and hung it in the dining room closet, put his gray fedora on the shelf, went to wash his hands, and then came for me. He would sit somewhere, usually his big green armchair, stretch me out across his lap with my underpants down around my ankles or all the way off and he'd hit me again and again, hard, sometimes with his looped belt, sometimes just with his hand. When he hit with his hand, he'd make it feel both bad and good, whacking, then rubbing my stinging tush. Sometimes, he wiggled a finger around the place where I wee-weed and that felt both bad and good. If I cried because he hurt me, he'd tell me he'd give me something to really cry about. Often I felt something hard in his pocket which was strange because I never saw him take out a ball or a piece of fruit or anything else that made sense.

_ ∞ _

My first foray into wild imaginary realms occurred after Grandpa taught me that prayers were just fancy requests, like asking parents for a Popsicle. Little kid that I was, at four I begged the bearded god-guy in the sky to save me from spankings, and remembered to say "please" politely. Did Daddy have an instant personality change and spare the rod? Not even close. Instead, God the comedian sent me flying. I zoomed faster than a speeding bullet up to the light fixture and found myself watching from the ceiling as Daddy continued to splay me on his lap and do what he did with his hand and finger. It was a strange and exhilarating experience and fascinated me. Although I could see myself being hit and fingered, I didn't feel like the girl on Buddy's lap. I was disappointed not to be able to see the mysterious hard thing in his

17

pocket because my little girl's body blocked it. Then I had a thought that excited me so much I had to fly down to his lap.

"Is that thing in your pocket a gun?" I asked breathlessly, putting my hand on his pants. I was saving cereal box-tops hoping to have ten thousand to get a Dale Evans cap gun and holster, and I suddenly thought that might be what Daddy had in his pocket.

"Don't be stupid, Weena," Daddy said and slapped my hand away from the hard thing with such force he sent me soaring back to the embossed metal ceiling and my safe bird's eye view. I wondered for years what was in his pocket.

"Daddy, daddy," I exclaimed, when I returned to my body. "I was up on the ceiling! I was! I really was!" I pulled my underpants back on. This was neat! The spanking hardly hurt!

"Goddamn you, Weena," he said sternly, "Pull those goddamn panties back down. Get back across my goddamn knees. Lying will not be tolerated for Crissake."

As he whacked and stroked me again, right then and there, perched like a spider on the light fixture, I decided not to say a word because I didn't want to risk being called a liar again. At least I didn't have to feel the harsh hand and that thing in Daddy's pocket sticking into me anymore. If it wasn't a gun, what was it?

During next night's spanking, I flew straight out of my body to the bluff and picked dandelions and buttercups. With each smack and caress, I plucked a flower and ended up with a nice big bouquet. I made up music in my head and the smacks became drumbeats.

I could even smell the flowers I'd picked and hear boat whistles while I splashed in the cold river water. After that, I branched out and followed the river all the way past Bear Mountain. Little did I know this was just the beginning of wanderings to other planets way up in the sky and lands under the sea. I'd found a way to avoid the conscious experience of being abused by an anger-crazed, weary thirty-year-old man who hated his job and found me a handy outlet for frustration.

I think he might have hit me more when I stopped reacting but I have no way to prove that, and I suppose the opposite argument could be made as well, that he lost interest because I was a limp dishrag. Most importantly, I stopped crying and, although I was powerless to stop the abuse and still struggled to figure out how to stop being bad, at least I enjoyed a new, secret, even fun, life.

– ∞ –

My parents argued all the time. I used to sit at the dinner table in our tiny dining room, listen to the forks and knives clinking against the plates before the inevitable fight began, and stare at Daddy's graceful, well-formed hands. I wanted to touch them, to put my hand in his. But I didn't dare. Instead I stared, fascinated by the gold pinky ring with the Masonic insignia. Sometimes when he hit me, he must have turned the ring around because it branded my bottom with dark red marks that sat inside his handprints. I knew because when he hadn't used the belt and I felt extra sore, I pulled my panties down, stood on the toilet, twisted, and checked my tushy in the medicine chest mirror. It burned when I dabbed it with a cold washcloth. As I got older, I imagined chopping those hands off so he couldn't hit me anymore. I hadn't discovered farting yet. That was still a few years away.

– ∞ –

When Grandma and Grandpa were in Florida I wandered through their cold lonely apartment every day. The place became my playground and stage. I rummaged through the Singer drawers admiring colored bobbins and poking my little fingers into his big silver thimbles. I went through the bedroom closet that smelled of cedar and tobacco and pulled out clothes and hats to try on. There was a long mirror on the outside of the closet door and I'd slip on jackets, dresses and Grandma's funny hats with veils and feathers, stand in her grown-up shoes and pose and sing. I was an appreciative audience for my shows. I pretended I lived in a happy place where things were safe and peaceful. So magical was that upstairs apartment, I never got caught snooping. I carefully restored everything to its proper place. It never occurred to me to recruit Victoria to play dress-up and musical show with me. I guess I was used to my solo act.

– ∞ –

As I grew bigger and bolder, I brought trouble on with my temper. I always meant to control myself, but my momentary tantrums always dominated logic. Slamming the door between the little dining room and our bedroom drove Daddy nuts and for some perverse reason gave me satisfaction. If I'd had a room of my own, I might not have slammed the door, but in our set-up,

19

slamming the door gave me a nanosecond of privacy, separating me from whatever I was fleeing at the moment – usually Daddy – and if I'd made some smart-ass comment, slamming the door served to punctuate my statement dramatically.

Even though Daddy and I had similar tempers, I was way out of my league picking a fight with a grown man. Countless times, after I slammed that door, he'd open it and incensed, follow me, grab me, throw me down on my bed, and make me submit to the spanking ritual. This was different from the spankings Mommy ordered. When she ordered them, he stayed calm and hit me unemotionally, like an executioner carrying out a sentence. When he hit me on his own, he was furious, nostrils flaring with anger, chin jutting out, spittle forming at the corners of his mouth. Even though I took off for the river, I hated him for the spankings, both kinds.

– ∞ –

Small town, working class neighborhood schools demanded uniformity. In first grade, after our very first reading lesson, I delightedly took the book home. Stretched across my bed, I read it through from cover to cover. That was it. One lesson and I knew how to read as though I were remembering rather than learning for the first time. Back in school, I proudly told Miss Sweet about my accomplishment. Like most of the teachers, some sort of secret sorority of spinsters, she was big and shapeless, wore dots of cheek rouge and heavy black oxfords. She wagged her finger at me.

"You bad girl," she said crossly. "These books are never allowed out of the classroom. You took it without permission, and besides, you're supposed to stay with the class. Don't you ever smuggle a book out of school again." I hated her, but in my head I imagined sticking my tongue out at her and later that day, from a safe corner of the cloak room, with nobody watching, I stuck my tongue out at her for a long couple of minutes, maybe ten. I held my thumbs in my ears and waggled my hands at her too.

– ∞ –

I didn't need school's stupid books anyhow. I wrote my own story about a flying baby elephant named Fanta and I read it to Gramps, who was thrilled. He said first graders didn't usually write stories like that, and I was special. Soon, Fanta and I flew all around our neighborhood and sometimes we linked up with Wonder Woman, whom I'd just met in comic books. When I went to bed, Fanta came to me and asked me to go out and play. I felt myself

20

slip out the window or even straight through the wall and up over the trees on our block, around Bay View Terrace, over the bluff, out over the Hudson and back, up to South Junior, over the football field. Along with Wonder Woman, I saw a few other people sleep-flying with their dreams surrounding them. There was one woman a couple of blocks away on Beacon Street who flew surrounded by angels. When I saw her I noticed the shimmery see-through rope attaching her flying body to her sleeping body in her house, and that's when I saw my own broad see-through silver string stretching to my belly button and keeping me connected as I flew. Once I mentioned my night flying with my imaginary elephant friend to Gramps. He paled, said it sounded like I'd created a *golem*, and maybe it wouldn't be such a good idea to tell anyone else because sometimes people got scared of things like that.

"What's a *golem*?" I asked.

"An unreal brainless creature that comes alive," he said. "Like Frankenstein. I think your baby elephant from the story maybe came alive."

"Is that bad?"

He was hemming a pair of pants at the machine. He stopped and looked at me. His usually light-hearted mood became serious. "Good? Bad? Who knows? The rabbis teach us there's a whole other world way far away...." He spread his arms wide and looked up. "We don't know much about it. Except..." He paused for effect. I was following closely. "Except if we go there before we are ready, we don't come back."

"It wasn't just a dream, was it, Gramps?" I shivered.

"Who knows what a dream is, Ro-ro?" he said. In his slight Yiddish inflection, he sang, "Row, Row, Row your boat, gently down the stream. Merrily merrily merrily merrily..."

Together we sang loud, "Life is but a dream!"

"It sounds as though you're dreaming," he said. "It's probably harmless. But, be very careful, dear Ro-ro. Don't get lost out in space."

"Don't worry, Gramps, now I'm friends with Wonder Woman and she brings me home safely."

I didn't tell anyone else about my flying dreams, not even little Victoria. It was a secret between Gramps and me.

– ∞ –

Our city was participating in a scientific experiment to test the effects of fluoride on teeth. Newburgh was one of three cities to have the water supply fluoridated in 1946 and the test continued for ten years. At first, I thought the water had been poisoned. I saw faint puky greenish brown spots that looked alive in it, but no one else seemed to see. No one else saw rainbow colors around people either the way I did. I was teaching myself to stop seeing them so I wouldn't feel so lonesome and odd.

"I'm scared of drinking the water now," I told Grandpa as he sewed on the treadle machine in the sunny bedroom. "I saw monsters in it."

"Ro-ro, you're imagining again," he said. "How could monsters get in the water?"

"I don't know, Gramps, but the water isn't good anymore. It used to be sparkly and happy and now it's dark and yucky. It scares me."

Grandpa moved his sewing machine chair back and to one side so he faced me. He took both my hands and spoke firmly. "Ro-ro, if the water weren't safe, the government wouldn't let us drink it. Stop worrying and just trust it. You're lucky you don't have to go to a well for water every day the way I had to. Drink lots of water and you'll live long and prosper. If you see monsters in the water, make friends with the monsters instead of letting them scare you."

"Really, Gramps? Are you friends with monsters?"

"Yes, Ro-ro, I've made peace with quite a few monsters in my day." He hugged me close and kissed the top of my head.

I made a weak effort to befriend the puky green-brown things, but they weren't friendly so I gave up. Soon I stopped noticing them.

– ∞ –

FOUR

After Amanda's family got a TV set, Karen spent most of her time at her best friend's house. Once in a while, they let me watch Howdy Doody but I had to promise to leave before Captain Video. Fun-loving Mrs. Slutsky used to joke that Karen was her other daughter. Karen flashed her best fake smile when she heard that. Grownups ate that up.

Usually I hung around our house upstairs with Grandpa. Gramps could sew, smoke, listen to the radio and talk to me all at the same time. He told me stories about the *shtetl* where he grew up in Belarus. He told me stories about the boat trip to America and about my four uncles and how they teased Mommy as they were growing up. When Gramps didn't feel like talking, we listened to music together, either WQXR, a classical station from New York, or Yiddish programs on WEVD. He didn't move the record player into the bedroom until a few years later.

When Uncle Sidney breezed in, it was always an interruption. He was cheerful and loud, singing the latest hit parade song, like "One Meatball," or "Cement Mixer, Putty, Putty." He never cared whether we were in the middle of speaking; he'd just barge in and take over the scene. He'd demand the finished tailoring, and deposit the new batch in a pile next to Grandpa. If Gram was home, she would offer him a glass of water, lemonade or iced tea which he'd chug down non-stop, then he'd kiss her on the cheek and take off.

– ∞ –

My most outstanding memory of Uncle Sidney came when I was four and half, hospitalized for a tonsillectomy, and he visited me in the children's ward of St. Luke's Hospital. I was proud of myself for being a big girl and not crying. My parents and the doctors and nurses all promised me ice cream after the operation if I was good. Ice cream was a major treat we usually got at a family outing to Crowley's Dairy. I kept thinking about biting into the bottom of a yummy chocolate ice cream cone, and sucking the ice cream through. I always used to end up with a chocolate mustache Mommy scrubbed off with a napkin.

At the hospital I received scratchy blue pajamas to wear and they itched, so I had taken them off all by myself and lay, head and all, under the covers naked. The sheets were a little scratchy too, but better than the pajamas.

There I lay, daydreaming about chocolate ice cream, still a bit dazed from the ether. My throat hurt from the operation, but I ignored it. I had promised to be good.

"Are you sleeping, sleepyhead?" Uncle Sidney sang gleefully from next to my bed.

"Nooooo, I'm not," I sang from under the covers. It was exciting to have company.

"Come out, come out, then," he sang.

"Surprise!" I shouted and bounded up. I stood in all my naked glory, all grins, freckles, messy pigtails, and joy, a four-year old in a hospital post-surgery.

"Oh my God, didn't you learn anything after your run-away trip to school. Now you get under those covers immediately, you bad girl," Uncle Sidney scolded, staring up at me, quickly glancing behind himself to see whether anyone else had seen my little naked body. "You should be ashamed of yourself. Where are your pajamas? Now you won't get ice cream. Wait till your father hears about this." I dove back under the covers to hide.

He tattled. I didn't get the promised ice cream from my parents. Daddy scolded with his scary demon face and aimed his index finger right at my face. I guess, because of the operation, I dodged a spanking. Funny thing was, I knew how to leave my body and escape a spanking, but the yelling and threatening I had to endure.

– ∞ –

Approaching seven, I was an awkward, lonely bookworm starting second grade. At home, I hardly exchanged words with anyone except Grandpa. Little Victoria hung out down the street at the house of the rabbi's widow with her three-year-old twins, all watched by their grandmother. Their mother, Sylvia Lipton, a schoolteacher, was Mommy's best friend. The only person I liked enough to call my friend was my cousin Ralphie, and he lived in New York City so we rarely spent time together.

Excitement began just after the Jewish holidays in the fall when I found out we were going to spend Thanksgiving together with Aunt Bea, Uncle Benny, and Ralphie at their new house in the Bronx, and not only would I get to visit with Ralphie, but they now had a dog named Scottie I'd finally meet. When Grandma and Grandpa left for Uncle Phil's in Miami in mid November, my life felt as empty as their apartment. The life-raft I clung to was anticipation of Thanksgiving with Ralphie, seeing his new house in the Bronx and playing with the new puppy. It was on my mind day and night.

When the day finally arrived, I woke up early and got dressed in my favorite clothes, dungarees and a red hand-me-down blouse with red pearl buttons. The pants, which rolled up a couple of times at the bottom, were my first long pants that weren't snow pants and I loved them. My whole wardrobe, except for summer shorts was hand-me-down dresses, jumpers, blouses and skirts. I always ended up with scraped knees. Dresses seemed stupid compared with pants. Boys got to wear long pants and do fun stuff and I finally could, too. I fixed myself a bowl of Cheerios with banana and milk, and waited for the rest of the family to get up. I was beside myself with excitement, thinking about Ralphie and Scottie and all the fun we were going to have.

Mommy greeted me with a disapproving look. "You can't wear jeans, Weena, for heaven's sake. It's Thanksgiving," she said. "You look ridiculous. Change your clothes. We have to leave soon. Put on your party dress."

"No!" I said. "I won't. I don't like it. It feels bad. I'm going to play with Ralphie and the puppy so I can't wear that horrid scratchy dress."

"Put on your party dress or stay home," she said, her pointer finger fanning my face.

"I hate my party dress. I want to go like this," I insisted. "Please, Mommy. I have on a pretty blouse. Anyhow, why does it matter what I wear?"

"You are not going like that, period," she said and marched away.

I didn't believe her. The family bustled about getting ready for the trip. Everyone ignored me. I was sure they would change their minds at the last minute. I sat in the green armchair in the living room, near the front door, and waited. Then I moved to the window seat and watched out the window as they all piled into the black Pontiac. I knew they would come in and ask me to get in the car any second. But they didn't. They didn't say goodbye either.

The car pulled away from the curb and I was all alone in the dark apartment, all alone in my dungarees and red blouse. I thought they were just trying to scare me. Surely they would go around the block and return for me. They didn't. A giant wave engulfed me, swallowed me up. I was devastated. I cried and cried. I had nothing to do all day except sleep and dream and cry some more.

For a couple of hours I amused myself in front of Grandma's mirror, but I didn't feel much like singing. I smelled neighbors' turkey dinners and I got hungry and ate Cheerios and lots of rye bread with butter. Later in the afternoon, I dreamed I was with my family in the Bronx wearing my jeans and red blouse only none of them could see me. Ralphie's eyes, magnified behind his thick glasses, drooped as he played chess all alone. He missed me and didn't understand why I wasn't there.

Mommy whispered to Daddy that the turkey was dried out, gravy fat, stuffing over-salted, sweet potatoes canned, mashed potatoes lumpy, peas overcooked, pies store-bought, and next year she would cook. But she smiled and told Aunt Bea the meal was wonderful. I could swear I was there. Scottie saw me and wagged his tail excitedly but my hand went right through his body and I couldn't touch him. He growled at Mommy and that made me grin. In between naps I woke up in my bed and hated them all.

They got home late, and their noise woke me up. My sisters had fallen asleep in the car. Daddy carried Karen in and put her in bed. Mommy did the same with Victoria. I had changed into pajamas when it got dark and went back to bed. I was relieved they were home, but I was still mad, so I pretended to sleep.

Mommy and Daddy were in the dining room.

I heard her say, "I told you she'd be okay."

He said, "I still think it was wrong to leave her home alone."

"Maybe so, but what choice did I have? I suppose you think it would have been better to smack her and force her to change clothes?"

"No, I think you were making too big a deal about what she was wearing. Next time I won't go along with you. I'm sick of your making me the bad guy. You know very well your hero, Dr. Spock, with his fancy childrearing ideas wouldn't approve of what you did."

"You haven't read a word of Dr. Spock so how dare you comment on him. And you don't know the first thing about bringing up girls," she said.

"At least I have a heart," he said. "You're a goddamn ice cube. You told me you hated the way your mother always made you wear frilly clothes when you wanted to dress like your brothers. Now you're doing the same goddamn thing to Weena, and you don't even see yourself. You've turned into a self-absorbed bitch just like your mother."

"As usual, you're crude and vulgar, and you don't know what you're talking about," she said, with a tone of finality that ended the discussion.

Next morning, when I woke up, I thought I'd dreamed not just that conversation, but also, all of Thanksgiving Day because everyone acted as though nothing out of the ordinary had happened. Karen didn't say anything. Victoria didn't say anything. My parents didn't say a word. Nothing. The day dropped out of history. It didn't exist. Truman's victory over Dewey on Election Day held far more importance.

– ∞ –

In contrast to my grandparents' affection for each other, I only saw my parents hug after someone died. When it was Daddy's mother, I was pretty little and it confused me that Mommy acted sad because I knew she hated my other grandmother. She referred to her as her mother-in-law, in a snotty tone, and people seemed to understand it as a curse word.

I always called my father's mother "Grandma Wine" to distinguish her from Mommy's mother who wasn't called "Grandma Fine," but just plain Grandma, the real one who didn't need a last name. Grandma Wine was a frail, bony little woman with a steel gray bun at the nape of her neck and a shapeless flowered dress often covered with an apron. She walked slightly bent forward, and I especially remembered her leaning over our garbage pail, rifling through it and pulling things out triumphantly: a crust of bread, a few drops of apple juice in the bottle or a little cream cheese that could be scraped off the silver wrapper. She and Grandpa Wine lived in Florida so we didn't see much of them, and I knew that was a good thing because both Mommy and Daddy got tense and grumpy when they were around. I barely remember Grandpa Wine at all because he died when I was a baby. But I have a vague recollection of my parents embracing when they found out he'd "passed away." A highly unusual event, the death hug was the only hug they practiced.

Once, when I was sitting on the red metal step stool in a corner of our tiny kitchen, I witnessed a typical Grandma Wine scene.

"You shouldn't vaste," Grandma Wine was saying, carefully pulling potato peels out of the garbage can and shaking her head as she filled a bowl with them. "No vonder my Buddy is unhappy." Then she rinsed the potato peels and set them in a colander in the sink.

Our kitchen was barely big enough for two adults, so she and Mommy kept bumping into each other. Mommy sucked in her breath and stood her full five feet nothing, making her slightly taller than Grandma Wine.

"Momma," she said stiffly, "I must ask you to get out of my kitchen. In your house you do things your way. In my house, I do things my way." Grandma Wine clucked disapprovingly. "Such vaste. Putting potato peels in the gobbage ven you could make mit dem a soup. And milk bottles, you rinse ven they have a little milk yet. Such vaste."

"Out, Momma." Mommy untied Grandma Wine's apron and lifted it over the old woman's head. "Go upstairs and visit with my mother."

Muttering, Grandma Wine left. Mommy wiped her hands on her own apron and groaned. Then she tossed the potato peels back into the garbage angrily. "We will never eat garbage in this house," she announced. "As far as I'm concerned, that woman is garbage."

I imagined Mommy tossing a shrunken Grandma Wine into the garbage pail and banging down the lid. Scary, but so funny I giggled.

Mommy talked to her friend Sylvia over the phone every afternoon and told her everything that was happening. I'd hear her discussing her horrible stingy mother-in-law whenever the hated visit approached. Grandma Wine would stay on the fold-out sofa bed upstairs. There would be more fights than usual. Still, Mommy seemed sad when the old woman died. I couldn't have been more than five or six.

"Mommy, why are you sad that Grandma Wine died?" I asked. "Now she won't be coming here anymore and going through our trash, so why aren't you happy?"

"Don't say terrible things like that," Mommy scolded. She didn't answer my question.

– ∞ –

Mommy only paid attention to me when she thought I was sick or "coming down with something." I usually sat around and did nothing because I was afraid that anything I did would be wrong and I'd get in trouble. But Mommy didn't like my doing nothing either. If we'd had TV back then I probably would've plugged myself in and gotten out of everyone's way.

"Weena, read a book," she'd say. "Ralphie reads sixteen books a week. How can you do nothing?"

So I'd hold a book. As skilled a reader as I was, I was too scared to concentrate most of the time so I moved my eyes over words and daydreamed. I thought about our getting a puppy or kitten but my parents said they were dirty and out of the question. They couldn't stop me from imagining though. I daydreamed constantly. I learned early on that I could escape into my mind and keep secrets there that no one could scold me for because no one would know. Either I hung out upstairs or flopped across Karen's bed which was more comfortable than mine.

One day as I was stretched out pretending to read, a million miles from home and feeling perfectly fine, my throat got dry and I coughed a little. I resisted getting a drink so I could finish my daydream when Mommy decided to feel my forehead. She startled me.

"You're warm," she said anxiously. "I think you're coming down with something. I'm going to take your temperature."

"I only need a drink of water. I'm fine, Mommy," I said, dreading what was coming. Between spankings, enemas and the rectal thermometer, they were butt-crazed in my family.

As I slowly came out of my daydream and focused, I saw her vigorously shaking down that glass butt-stick. Shaking and checking, shaking and checking. She was brandishing a weapon to stab me right in the butt-hole. How come she didn't use that thing on herself? Only the oral thermometer for Mommy and Daddy. I took off running and fled straight upstairs into Grandma's kitchen, and stammered, "L-lock the d-door, lock the door, quickly!"

"I should lock the door?" Puzzled, Grandma moved fast, grabbed the key from its hook, and locked the door, an unheard of action since keys were either lost or decorative, sitting in keyholes flanked by elaborate escutcheons, hanging on a hook somewhere or long gone. Downstairs, only the mysterious little bathroom had a working lock.

"What's wrong?" she asked with concern, inflection rising at the end of each question. "Who's downstairs? One of the neighborhood hooligans, God forbid? Too many goyem around here now. Maybe I should call the police?"

"No, no police. I can't tell you," I said, trembling. Grandma hugged me.

Grandpa came into the kitchen. "What's wrong?" he asked with the same singsong way of speaking.

"Some goy scared our Rifkele," she said, using my Hebrew name for affection.

I heard footsteps on the stairs and I flew into Grandpa's arms.

"Save me. Please save me," I begged.

Mommy barked, "Open this door immediately."

"From your own mother you're running? Oy vei, you did something wrong?" Grandma and Grandpa chimed.

Grandma moved to unlock the door. Mommy stood there, thermometer in hand. By this time, I surely had worked myself into a fever pitch.

"Wait till your father gets home," Mommy snarled. They sure loved to do stuff to my poor little butt.

– ∞ –

Nervous most of the time, I bit my nails so low they often bled. Since Daddy had made it his task to clip his daughters' nails, he must have felt cheated out of a job. Once discovered, he regularly coated my stubs with foul-tasting waterproof paint that was supposed to cure me of the nasty habit. Instead, lips smarting and swelling, I kept gnawing away until Daddy gave up in disgust. Now he wouldn't be bothering me for that torture.

Yes! I thought, dancing in place in our crowded bedroom. I did it! I won a battle.

– ∞ –

The war at home escalated a couple of years after World War II ended. Without consulting Mommy, Daddy quit his long-running sales job and signed over all their down payment money to the latest chapter of his dream, a factory on the waterfront near the Newburgh-Beacon ferry that manufactured ladies' pocketbooks. He'd met a guy in a pinochle game who was looking for a business partner and before the night was through convinced Daddy that manufacturing women's pocketbooks would make them rich.

"Pocketbooks, Pearlie!" he announced, pronouncing it "pockabooks." "We're gonna be rolling in dough."

"What are you, a moron?" Mommy started. "What do you know from pocketbooks? You think you're gonna manufacture them ready made with cash inside?"

It's a wonder the cops didn't show up that night since it was June and with windows open, for sure, the neighbors within the entire square block overheard their ruckus. I hid under the covers as she carried on, crying that he had to go back to his job, he couldn't go into business with a stranger, how could he spend the money they were saving for a house, now they had no health insurance, and she hated him for ruining her life. Daddy barked back that the goddamn signed papers couldn't be unsigned and she should just shut the hell up and join him, she could use her goddamn business school skills for a change so together they could get goddamn rich, stop living with her goddamn parents, and buy their own, really big house over on the good side of town, in Balmville for Crissake.

As the argument went round and round, I got tired of listening and slipped away into a peaceful night flight over the river and farther away to my special glass palace where a beautiful goddess held and comforted me. This Sky-mother looked a lot like a translucent, beatific version of earthy, unhappy Mommy. Laughing joyously, wearing a luminous, gauzy white gown and multiple strands of opalescent pearls, Sky-mother crooned soothing lullabies as she rocked me on her lap. When I woke up next morning, the baking soda and spoon were in the bathroom, a sign my parents had made up. Mommy called it a "doosh." The house felt calm. I closed my eyes and thanked Sky-mother, who smiled broadly. I noticed her teeth had turned to fine pearls.

$$- \infty -$$

Mommy gave up homemaking to keep books for Glorianne Bag Company, Victoria got carted off to nursery school, our house got messy, and bread and butter, potatoes, eggs, canned soups, canned peas, spaghetti with ketchup, and, of course, the usual wide variety of cookies, were frequently all we had in our dinner rotation unless we ate upstairs, which I did often.

Karen always knew how to pacify our parents. She flashed that perfect, dimpled toothpaste ad smile, blinked the bright royal blues, told them exactly what they wanted to hear and then did whatever she wanted to do. Spellbound, they never noticed.

"Listen, Weenie," she whispered in our bedroom one night after I'd gotten a particularly heavy spanking and our parents were carrying on a loud battle about money, "If you're smart, you'll learn to stop being so stubborn. You have to be nicer to Mommy and Daddy. Life's a game and you're losing. Don't show them your true feelings. Just tell them what they want to hear."

"But I don't know what they want to hear," I whispered back.

"Yes, you do."

"No, I don't."

"Just watch me and do what I do."

"I don't have a best friend I can stay with, and I'd rather get spanked than root for the Yankees like you and Daddy," I whispered. "The Dodgers are my team and I'm proud of it."

"You're a stubborn mule."

"Then I guess I should be saying, 'Hee-haw.'"

But I started paying more attention to what Karen did when she was home. She was softer and sweeter than I was, always flirting with Daddy. She even looked like him! I didn't look like either of my parents and I couldn't change that. I definitely wasn't about to flirt with Daddy because I hadn't the personality or the stomach. But the most outstanding action Karen did was occasionally wheeze asthmatically and sometimes turn a ghostly shade of blue, sort of like Daddy's pale eyes. My parents showed great concern when she got that ghost mask and rushed her off to St. Luke's emergency room even in the middle of the night, for adrenaline shots. She was always going for allergy treatments and getting special privileges because they worried about her. That must have been what Karen was trying to tell me, I concluded. So I prayed to the god-guy and, for good measure, to Sky-mother, for asthma to save me.

I remember the day my asthma arrived. On the big old maroon couch, Karen looked pale and pathetic squeezed between Mommy and Daddy who, as usual, smoked madly, filling the small room with smelly cloud swirls. Daddy rubbed her back. Karen wheezed but not so heavily that she needed a shot. I sat unacknowledged in the big green easy chair steps away. Victoria was down the street playing with her friends, the twins, Jessica and Julie Lipton. Silently, I begged for asthma to come to me too so Mommy and Daddy would love me. Then I heard the low whistling from my breath. I was elated.

"Mommy, Daddy, Karen" I announced, smiling inside as I struggled to breathe. "I have asthma too!"

I expected my parents to leap to my side and hold my hand.

"Doesn't sound so bad," Mommy said, without moving from Karen's side. "No," Daddy agreed, blowing smoke toward the ceiling, "Nothing to worry about. Just a mild wheeze. You're fine, Weena."

"I have asthma," I said, coughing, starting to cry.

Just breathe," Daddy ordered, furious. "Push your breath out. You're fine, for Crissake. All we need is more goddamn doctor bills."

– ∞ –

About a week after my failure to get attention with asthma, I came down with a bad stomachache. Grandma and Grandpa were in Florida for the winter, so I couldn't even try to escape my horrid fate, which would be even worse than the rectal thermometer: an enema. My choices were either not to tell Mommy and suffer alone, or tell her and suffer her disgusting treatment. I chose to tell her because at least I would get attention.

In keeping with worshipping the butt, enemas seemed to be my family's answer to all manner of ills. Mommy kept me from school and stayed home from the factory to minister the hated cure-all. Her technique was to sit me on the toilet with the filled red rubber bag on a high hook. She coated the rectal attachment with petroleum jelly, stuck the evil thing in my butthole, then let the water rip, emptying into my colon.

"Hold it as long as you can," she said. "I mean it! Not like last time when you didn't hold it at all."

On this particular day, she left me sitting there with the bathroom and dinette doors open and went to chitchat with one of her friends over the phone. It was impossible not to listen to Mommy's side of the conversation since she was so loud and I had nothing else to do. That was the first time I heard her tell anyone she had decided where I was going to college, the school she had always wanted to attend herself, Barnard College, in New York City. Mommy had made up her mind that her daughters would all get a college education because she didn't. So she's sending me to college in a barnyard, I thought, baffled. Just then, the worst pain I'd ever felt pierced my belly. I screamed in agony and fear. That got her attention, or perhaps her friend heard and asked what it was because I heard her say, "Yes, something's wrong with Weena, I have to go see, I'll call you right back."

I howled. She disconnected me from the enema bag, and leaving me clutching my side, called the doctor, a new one since she owed so much money to the regular one, she was embarrassed to call him. This was a woman, Dr. Edie Amato, and she was due to arrive in an hour. Mommy raced around, hurriedly straightening the apartment up. I just wanted to lie down in my bed, but she made me wash up and get into fresh pajamas, while she changed my sheets, got extra pillows and propped me up nicely. She dusted, vacuumed, picked things up, and made the place look great in minutes. Then she showered, dressed and put make-up on, and by the time the doctor rang the doorbell, it looked like a railroad flat from *Better Homes and Gardens*.

I liked Dr. Amato even though I couldn't stop staring at her dark mustache. She was very gentle with me but spoke firmly with Mommy.

"This child has acute appendicitis. Enemas are extremely dangerous for this condition. She needs surgery immediately."

"But we have no insurance!" Mommy exclaimed. "We're still paying off the hospital for her sister's visits to the emergency room."

"Mrs. Wine, I'm sorry to hear that you are having financial problems, but at this moment, your child is desperately ill and needs an appendectomy. I will be glad to discuss payment arrangements with you privately at another time. Now, tell me, would you like to drive her to the hospital or shall I call an ambulance?"

"I'm sorry, Mommy," I cried, sure this was happening because I had prayed to be sick. Maybe it would be better if I just died and went to the nice glass palace.

"You have nothing to be sorry about," Dr. Amato said gently to me. "I'm going to operate on you. You'll be asleep and won't feel a thing. Everything will be all right. You'll be fine. Have you decided on the transportation, Mrs. Wine?"

Mommy stared at Dr. Amato strangely, then said, "I'll have to call my husband and get him to come home and drive. That way we can save the cost of the ambulance."

"Call him right now, please," said the doctor. "There's no time to spare."

Mommy seemed reluctant to leave me alone with Dr. Amato, but finally went to call Daddy. Dr. Amato got out a Kleenex and gently wiped my tears. Then she patted my hair and smoothed it back.

"My father is going to kill me," I sniffed and began to cry again.

"No one's going to hurt you. I'll take good care of you," she said, and I believed her.

Just as I'd done with the tonsillectomy, I lay in the operating room and breathed ether. I found myself floating by the ceiling looking down on the scene, then shot off into space just as my belly was about to be cut and went farther than usual, to a new unfamiliar place with strange sounds and colors and odd but kindly people.

I awoke from the operation confused. Where was I? A slight ether smell mixed with Lysol lingered. I was lying in some sort of cage or jail in a strange white room. Peering through the bars, I saw my parents, sitting in straight chairs, smoking, and looking anxious. I thought they'd caged me as punishment for the big expense I'd caused, and I knew I'd deserved it. My feet were squished against one end of the cage and my head grazed the other end.

"Mommy and Daddy," I said in my drugged state, "I'm sorry for making you owe more money. I didn't mean to need an operation."

"Don't say that," Mommy said. "It's not your fault. It's your father's fault for leaving his job. We'd still have health insurance if he hadn't quit."

"Shut up, will you?" Daddy said. "Why don't you make yourself useful for a change and go get someone to get our kid out of this goddamn crib. The morons. Putting an eight-year-old in a crib for Crissake."

"Please, Mommy and Daddy, please stop arguing," I said, blinking back tears. "I'm fine. I'm glad it's only a crib. I thought it was a cage. Maybe it costs less than a bed. It's okay. I don't mind." I tried to roll over and felt stabbing in my belly. Then I bumped my head. "Ouch!" I exclaimed.

"Jesus, the kid's a goddamn martyr. For Crissake, will you go!" Daddy snapped at Mommy again. "The kid's right. It is a goddamn cage. Stupid idiots."

"Will you stop yelling and using foul language?" Mommy whispered. "What will people think?" She jumped up to go and fetch help.

When Mommy returned, she brought an apologetic nurse who promised to find me a bed right away. With the nurse nearby, Mommy stuck her head close to the bars of my crib and said rather loudly, "We don't want you to worry about anything, darling. Just get well, sweetheart. We love you. You'll have a nice bed very soon." She blew me a kiss goodbye.Daddy mumbled agreement and said he loved me too. The nurse smiled approvingly. I dozed off in the crib, wondering whether this entire experience was some sort of peculiar dream test. If so, was I passing or failing?

– ∞ –

FIVE

Glorianne Bag Company was poised for take-off when the Korean War intervened. A major order from Penney's, which had elated all of us three months earlier, brought on despair, shame, and failure when Penney's cancelled. The word bankruptcy, spoken in hushed tones, echoed through our house along with I told you so's. The factory closed. I was nine, Karen was twelve and a half, and Victoria was four. Daddy vowed to pay back every penny he owed Mommy's brothers and Gramps, who had finally caved and invested.

"I mean it, Pearlie," said Daddy while he was sitting at the dinette table with Mommy. She had served him coffee and a platter of marble cake, prune, poppy, and cherry Danish pastries, and cinnamon rugelach. It was as though they sat *shiva* for Glorianne's death. They had shooed us kids away so they could talk with the semblance of privacy. Very funny, since we knew they'd end up yelling. My mouth watered as I waited impatiently behind the door.

"I swear to you, Pearlie," he said, chomping on a pastry, "I'll pay the whole goddamn thing back. I don't care about the goddamn bankruptcy."

"That's stupid," Mommy said. "The purpose of bankruptcy is to forgive debts."

"My honor is at stake. I will not give your goddamn Fine family the satisfaction of forgiving my debt for Crissake."

"You've got your own family to think of," she said. "Don't be so stubborn and self-righteous."

He hollered, "Shut your goddamn mouth! Don't tell me what to do!"

"Moron! Self-righteous uneducated imbecile!"

They were off and running. Now they had something new to fight about. I loved them because they were my parents, but I also hated them and longed to get back at them for hurting me. So when Daddy spilled hot coffee on himself and cursed in pain, I smiled as I dashed in and grabbed a couple of pastries.

– ∞ –

After the pocketbook factory failed, Daddy hung around our cramped apartment in his underwear, chain-smoked Camels, yelled, hit me, and generally humiliated us for a week or two while Mommy ferried to work across the river in Beacon for some old accountant who was sweet on her. She didn't say that, but I guessed it from her enigmatic smile. One day, Daddy put on a suit and tie and took off in his Pontiac to drive around his familiar three counties wholesaling radios, TV's, and air conditioners for Emerson. In exchange for the ten thousand dollars Grandma and Grandpa had put into the pocketbook factory – the subject of incessant late-night arguments after it vanished into the bankruptcy hole – Daddy got them an air conditioner for their sweltering upstairs bedroom. At the same time, our miniature downstairs living room received the grand prize, the black and white television set we'd longed for as we'd sat by the cathedral style radio and imagined it transforming into a video screen.

"Why didn't you get two TV's and air conditioners, Daddy?" I asked. "That way we could all watch TV and stay cool too."

"Shut up, Weena," he said, and smacked me across the mouth before I could get out of his way. My buck teeth cut into my upper lip and I tasted blood.

"I hate you!" I yelled and ran away fast enough to avoid another blow.

– ∞ –

A year and a half later, a new trauma occurred, one that was to sink into oblivion for many years to come.

My parents rarely drank alcohol. "Goyem drink. Jews eat," Grandma said. They sipped and dipped the prescribed Passover Manischewitz and occasionally celebrated some special occasion with a shot of schnapps. Dusty bottles of liquor sat on a high shelf of a kitchen cupboard. But one night, after he sold his biggest order for televisions ever, to an upstate hotel, Daddy pulled down a bottle of whiskey and toasted to success quite a few times.

Later that night, something strange awakened me. Karen was at a sleepover at Amanda's. Victoria slept in Karen's bed on the other side of the room. I heard Mommy's loud snoring start up from the back room. I sat up to investigate. Daddy stood near the tri-room (kitchen/our bedroom/their bedroom) doorway winding the alarm clock with the bright kitchen light on him. He was completely naked with a big thick rubber hose-like thing protruding up and out from a dark brush between his legs. My mind tumbled with a confusing mix of terror and curiosity. Wide awake, I bolted down and prayed he hadn't seen me see him. I knew I'd finally seen a real penis, what I knew as a baby-maker. I heard him replace the clock on the kitchen shelf. I expected him to disappear into the back room. Instead he walked over to my bed and stopped. My body stiffened. I didn't move. I heard a low whistle and knew I was wheezing slightly.

"Weena?" he whispered. "Are you awake?"

I smelled tobacco, whiskey and faint Bay rum. He moved closer. Was he going to hit me? He reached out with his hand and stroked my hair. He had never done that before and it felt good and also creepy because I knew he was naked. A cross between a yelp and a sigh escaped from my mouth. I still didn't move.

He turned my head. I kept my eyes shut, praying my eyelids would stop fluttering. He rubbed something smooth against my lips. It was damp and salty. Then he was hovering over me on the bed shoving it into my mouth and down my throat and I gagged and was scared I wouldn't be able to breathe. He whispered to keep quiet, very, very quiet.

"If you stay quiet, I won't hurt you," he said. "I love you. Your daddy's the best salesman in the world. We're celebrating, goddamn it!"

He was crushing my chest. I heard his heart beating and his breath going fast. Then I dashed away to my special magical place with my Sky-mother and I sat in her lap. I was a baby and she was feeding me from her full milky breast and not just the nipple but the whole breast was in my mouth and going in and out and in and out and I wanted to cry out but she kept reminding me to be quiet. She sang to me, Swing Low Sweet Chariot and rocked me and told me everything would be okay. I must have passed out because next thing I knew it was morning and my throat hurt and I knew I'd had a nightmare but I couldn't remember it.

My appetite mysteriously increased. I stuffed myself mostly with bread and butter. My favorites were horn-shaped rolls with salt and seeds, fresh rye bread, and challah, all smeared with plenty of butter. I ate lots of cookies and drank gallons of milk. I expanded into a fat girl. The family called it baby-fat and assured themselves it would melt off as I grew up. Daddy still smacked me whenever he felt I'd transgressed, and his fingers still found my sensitive spot, only now he'd added pinching my bottom hard. He called me Roly, short for Roly-Poly, and Fatso too, like the kids at school. I hated him more than ever. This was when I developed my new weapon, the nastiest, stinkiest farts imaginable, worse than Uncle Benny's, and I learned to control them too so I'd only let them rip around Daddy. I loved my farting ability. It was better than a gun.

"Jesus Kee-rist," he said, the first time I shot one off. Fat as I was, he had me butt-side up on his lap in the big green easy chair, his favorite spanking place. About to hit me, instead he pushed me away. "Get off me, girl. Feh, you laid a stink bomb. What the hell did you eat, a goddamn bucket of beans? Open a goddamn window. Get the hell out of the house. You're a goddamn menace."

"Sorry, Daddy," I cooed, and slinked away, unspanked.

My new weapon kept him away from my butt. Instead he found other places to smack me and used the surprise element to evade my poison gas attacks. But I was fighting back. It felt great.

– ∞ –

Whatever it was, I knew it wasn't punctuation they were talking about when Karen got her period. It came with something called cramps, which I understood were pains. For someone with pains, Karen seemed pretty cheerful so I figured cramps must be unusual pains that didn't hurt. Mommy congratulated her, Grandma slapped her face – an old world superstition – and then hugged her, and Karen herself ran to the telephone to call Amanda and announce, "I got it! Now we both have it!"

– ∞ –

A few months later, when I was nine and a half, soreness in my back and lower abdomen developed. I thought maybe I'd banged into something and forgotten. In the bathroom, shock hit me. I was bleeding! There was blood in the toilet. It was dripping out of me. I was petrified. If my parents saw I'd spilled blood on the floor, I'd be in big trouble. I opened the bathroom door a crack.

"Kaaaaren," I called. "Is Karen here?"

"Karen's not home," Mommy shouted back. "You know very well she always goes to Amanda's Saturday mornings to listen to the Hit Parade."

"Where's Victoria? Victoriaaaaaaaaaaaaa," I hollered.

"She's down the street playing with the twins," she called.

"Please Mommy. Please, Mommy. You come. Come now. I need you to help me right now!"

What was I going to do? Getting Mommy's attention was hard enough when I was in the same room with her. Now she was in the kitchen, two rooms away, not listening to me.

"Mommy," I sang out, trying to sound pleasant so I wouldn't make my parents so angry Daddy would try to hit me. "I swear to God. It's an emergency." I hoped invoking the god-guy would get some serious attention. The kids at school did it.

"Don't swear to God. It won't get me more interested. What's wrong?" she shouted.

"I can't tell you. Just come here, please." It was getting harder to keep my voice happy. She was ignoring me. "Please!" I begged. "Please come now. I need help. I'm scared."

"I'm busy," she shouted. "I'll send your father."

"No!" I shrieked. "You can't!"

I heard her yell, "Buddy, go see what Weena wants. She's in the bathroom fussing about something."

I was sobbing now. How could she send my father? He was going to kill me when he saw the mess I was making. He didn't throw me over his knees anymore, but I hated the way he smacked me across the face, arms or back without warning. I had to anticipate in order to gas-bomb him, and I had no time to slip away and pick flowers.

"What's the problem?" The ogre was at the door.

"I'm bleeding," I said through the narrow crack and sobbed.

"Don't cry," he said gruffly. "Jesus Christ, you're young to have this. Stop crying, goddamn it. There's nothing to cry about. It's normal. Didn't your mother put that goddamn booklet in your drawer for Crissake? I'll be right back with everything you need. We didn't think it would happen so soon, but we're prepared."

I nodded numbly and pulled the door shut. The ogre was the last person in the whole world I wanted to share this disaster with, but at least he wasn't hitting me. So this was the big deal Karen was so excited about. This grossness was it.

Daddy knocked on the door. I cracked it. He opened it all the way and stood there staring at me, a package in his hand, my clean blue plaid dress and panties over his arm. I sat down on the toilet and covered my bottom half with a stained white towel. Then I lifted my butt slightly and laid a killer.

"No, goddamn it, Weena!" He grabbed his nose and held it with his fingers.

I managed to keep from laughing. For a moment I was glad about the blood all over my underpants and corduroys and the tile floor. The fart and blood smells merged. Served him right. He kept holding his nose and spoke as though he had a cold.

"There's a saditary dapkin and a belt in this package," the ogre said. Hilarious. He handed me a brown paper bag. I wondered vaguely why he thought I needed a napkin. I wasn't mussing my face with food. He passed me the clothes and took his fingers off his nose. "And, Weena, this is most important of all." He held up Exhibit A. "Here's a can of deodorant powder. Always, always sprinkle this on the napkin before you put it on. I wish I could give a can of this to every woman on earth. If you don't use powder, you smell disgusting, like a goddamn bloody animal, and everyone can smell you coming. It's even worse than your farts, if you can imagine that."

I stared. Powder a napkin? Was this for real?

"Did you hear me?" He blew his nose, raised his voice, threateningly. "Weena, I asked if you heard me tell you about the deodorant powder? Answer me when I speak to you, goddamn it."

I nodded blobbily. "Yes, Daddy, I heard you."

"Never flush a sanitary napkin. You'd clog the damn toilet. Just fold it over, dirty side in, wrap it in toilet paper and put it in the trash. That's it. Now, get yourself together and clean this goddamn mess up."

– ∞ –

Fifth grade brought other major changes besides menstruation. I loved my teacher, Miss Wheatley. She was about five-six, like Daddy and me, had short, curly white hair, a gravelly voice, and was the kindest teacher I'd ever had. There was something warm and loving about Miss Wheatley, something I didn't feel with the other women in my family, or anywhere in town. She noticed me and treated me so well I might have been teacher's pet except she treated everyone in the class that same way. We would do anything for her. I loved going to school even though kids sometimes made fun of my breasts.

Mommy's icy attitude towards Miss Wheatley puzzled me because she had always lectured me about tolerance and respect for the meanest and most annoying teachers, like horrid Miss Sweet in first grade. It was never much different from year to year. In everything except physical education - which I hated because I was a fat klutz, and my parents said it didn't count anyway – I got the highest grades possible for what I thought was doing nothing but showing up and minding the teacher. School was neutral territory where at least I could follow rules and be safe. Teachers humiliated but they didn't hit.

Since I always got perfect academic marks, I couldn't understand why every report card seemed to please my parents anew. What was the big deal? Daddy embarrassed me by bragging about my grades to Uncle Sidney and I hated that because I thought Daddy was rubbing Uncle Sidney's nose in his son Mitchell's terrible report cards and that seemed mean. But the family judged children by their report cards, so my cousin Mitchell fared badly. I begged Daddy not to even mention report cards to Uncle Sidney, but he always did anyway. He said Mitchell was a goddamn moron and so was Uncle Sidney.

"In fact," his repetitive comedy line went, "If your uncle had another half a brain, he'd be a halfwit." That got him a big fat smelly one I judged he deserved.

But, Miss Wheatley, first teacher I loved, rocked the report card boat, not with the grades I got, which were impeccable, as usual, but with her comments. "Rowena's work is consistently outstanding," she wrote. "She is reading on a 13th grade level. Her classmates respect her ability. But she seems like a lonely and unhappy child. I would like to see her make friends."

"What in hell is this?" Daddy roared. "What nerve this bitch has to write such goddamn crap! Jesus Christ, this is a black mark against our kid. It'll be on her goddamn permanent record. Why, I have a mind to go and see that piece of shit queer pervert cunt right now and give her a piece of my mind. It's none of her goddamn business whether our kid has friends or not, for Crissake."

Mommy reacted differently. "Buddy, watch your language, please. Let's not make a scene with the teacher. Then she might take it out on Weena and write something even worse. No, we have to find Weena a friend so we won't get a comment like that again."

To me, it was all stupid and embarrassing. Miss Wheatley was the first person to notice my loneliness. But I felt it was my fault that I got the messed up report card and upset my parents. I wanted to do the right thing and find a friend so everyone would be happy and calm down. I'd get a hundred friends if necessary to shut them up.

Karen, my goody-goody ghost, beautiful sister, whose life revolved around activities with Amanda – with whom she spent far more time than with me - thought a friend was a no-brainer idea. Amanda's cousin Dorothy, who was my age, had recently moved down the block from us. There were two fifth grade classes at our school, and she was in the other one so I didn't know about her. Karen had mentioned Dorothy to me before, but I'd ignored her. Now I latched onto this as a solution. My parents insisted I call Dorothy instantly and invite her over. No discussion. A Jewish girl my age who lived down the block? Perfect. I went along with getting a friend more to please my parents and the teacher than to end my loneliness. But I was secretly pleased.

_ ∞ _

Dorothy Katz was nine like me - about a head or more shorter like most kids my age, since I was a giant - much skinnier than I was, like everybody, and totally flat-chested, like every other girl except me. She was near-sighted and had to wear thick glasses. Her younger brother, Randy, was the same age as Victoria, but she had no older sister or brother. We exchanged this information right away, and then neither one of us knew what to say or do.

Dorothy's family lived in a small apartment a lot like ours, the kind with one room opening into the next. They had no living or dining room. Their kitchen was where they ate and watched TV. That flowed into a big bedroom Dorothy and Randy shared and next to that was their parent's tiny room, all bed. They had a bathroom in the hall with a gigantic tub on legs. We didn't have a space to play by ourselves. I had no idea what to do with my new friend, but my neighbors soon provided a solution.

_ ∞ _

The little upstairs apartment in our house had recently changed hands and the new tenants were the Fishes, Herm, June, and their chubby daughter Rhoda who was two years younger and almost as fat as me except not as developed. Rhoda went to Catholic school at Sacred Heart and spent more time at her grandmother's than her parents', maybe because her mother had a factory job at Diamond Candle or maybe because, like me, she liked her grandmother better. I didn't understand why June Fish was so friendly to me, but she was pretty and young and I liked her bright clothes so I welcomed her friendliness. I guessed maybe she wanted me to be nice to Rhoda.

One day, she stopped me in the upstairs hall when I was leaving my Saturday morning opera visit with Grandpa. Gramps got up early enough to be back from *shul* in time for WQXR's opera show. I habitually split my radio time between the Hit Parade downstairs and the opera upstairs with Gramps. That day, Gramps and I had just listened to "Turandot" and I was humming "Nessun Dorma," one of my favorite arias, and feeling pretty good. Heading toward the bathroom, which was in the hall, June came out of her apartment, but rather than enter the bathroom, stood and faced me. She looked like a movie star with her long bouncy blond hair covering one eye and curved into a pageboy just below her shoulders. She wore a shiny, green satin robe that showed the outline of her body including her chest, which looked like a couple of large scoops of ice cream with plump blueberries stuck onto them. Was it possible she didn't wear a bra? I blushed and looked away. She had a green book in her hand that matched her robe.

"My husband Herm and I want you to have this book," she said. "Please read it and let us know how you like it, okay?" She smiled and licked her lips. She had shiny orange lipstick on. I thought she looked pretty and I wondered whether I would ever have permission to wear lipstick. "Rowena," she was whispering now and standing so close to me that I could smell her musky perfume. "Rowena," she continued. "Let this be a secret between you, Herm and me, okay?"

"Okay, sure," I said and accepted the hard cover volume. The front was blank but the spine had the title *Love in the Shadows* and a name, B. Pashin.

Intuitively, I took the book straight to a private place in the cellar to examine. The opening scene was about a woman named Nicolette whose cabdriver, Lance, instead of taking her to her destination, drives into the woods, parks, then climbs in back and pulls all her clothes off. He takes off his pants and puts his "big pulsing member" into her mouth. As I read this scene on and on, I broke out in a sweat and quivered with fear, felt my pelvis pounding and then exploding. I had to explore this new, scary, pleasurable, even amazing sensation. I couldn't stop reading. Now I had something to share with my new friend. I hid the book in an old trunk and ran to Dorothy's house to get her and bring her back to share this forbidden treasure.

We took turns reading aloud. This was a whole new vocabulary for us, which we had to discuss thoroughly. From the context, we pretty much worked all the meanings out. We took to reading the book every afternoon after school and debating what we thought was happening. My parents were thrilled that I now had a friend. There would be no nasty comments from Miss Wheatley ruining my report cards now.

Next Saturday around noon, June Fish, in her green satin robe, called me into her apartment. Gramps and I had just listened to "La Boheme" with Victoria De Los Angeles and I was in a sad and romantic mood. "I have a surprise for you," June said, smiling broadly. "Come on in."

In the apartment, Herm was in bed under the covers. Rhoda wasn't home. The place was messy like our apartment only there were beer and wine bottles around which we didn't have downstairs.

"Want a cigarette?" Herm asked. His blond hairy chest stuck out above the covers. He had an anchor tattooed on his shoulder and a couple of side teeth missing.

"I'm not even ten," I said, in case he didn't know.

"I smoked when I was eight. Want to try one?"

"Okay," I said. "I guess so."

He lit two cigarettes and held one up for me. The blanket slipped back and exposed his belly, also hairy. I was pretty sure he had no pajama pants on and felt nervous about his nudity. I had to approach the bed to take the cigarette. I took a puff and coughed. He laughed. "You don't have to smoke it. Give it back to me, I'll put it out."

I handed the cigarette to him, then moved back a little to stand next to the French doors, which separated the living room from their bedroom.

June came in. Her robe was untied and flapping open. I could see she was naked beneath it. Her nudity didn't threaten me as his had, probably because I was used to seeing my sisters and Mommy. Instead, I felt aroused and curious.

"How do you like the book?" she asked. "What have you and your little friend been doing in the cellar?" She laughed.

I blushed.

"Ever read anything like that before?" she asked.

"Never," I said. I was beginning to worry. How did she know we were reading in the cellar? She must have been spying on us.

"Herm and I think you're an attractive girl," she said.

"Me, attractive?" I immediately remembered Aunt Bea's once telling me that I was ugly but I shouldn't worry because she was ugly too and still Uncle Benny married her. "Nobody thinks I'm attractive." My face felt hot. I knew I was too fat and, although I might be considered cute, "attractive" seemed like too grown-up an expression.

45

"No, really. You have a beautiful face and you're... developed." She looked straight at my breasts. "Whose tits are bigger, yours or mine?" With that she slipped out of her robe and stood before me totally naked. Her breasts were perkier than mine, with those perfect huckleberry nipples. I felt something stirring between my legs. "Let's see, dear. I'll help you out of your polo shirt."

"I don't think my parents would like this," I said, crossing my arms in front of me and moving backwards toward the door. Now my face and body were burning. Like Nicolette in the book, I had pounding in my lower abdomen, which in the book was called loins, like chops in a butcher shop. Pounding in the loins sounded like something the butcher might do but there was no butcher in the book, just a taxi driver named Lance, and Dorothy and I had figured out what the pounding felt like because we felt it ourselves when we read the sexy parts of the book. It was like a drum. Boom, boom, boom. I felt it right then and was about to burst out of my body in front of these nice but weird neighbors who treated me as though I were a grownup.

"Don't be shy," June said. "We hear the arguments and the spankings every night. We know you have it hard. Wouldn't you like a little pleasure in your life?"

"I don't know," I said backing up to the door, scared and intrigued at the same time. "I'll have to think about it." There was something, something I couldn't remember and it scared me and angered me, and it stayed out of reach. I knew I didn't want to know about it.

"Herm and I can show you a good time, honey," she said tonguing her upper lip and running her hands along her body, over her breasts and between her legs. "We're real gentle, and we can teach you all about feeling good. We never hit our Rhoda. We don't believe in it, right Herm?"

"Right, baby." He added from the bed. "Listen, here darlin', if you want you can just watch June and me fuck and you don't have to do nothing else but watch. Will you think about it?"

"Okay," I said, and ran out the door. Herm had said a very bad word I knew from the green book.

How can I pass up this opportunity? I thought. This is phenomenally exciting and right in my own house! I went back and knocked on the door shyly. When June answered she was still stark naked. I almost fainted.

"I thought about it," I said, breathlessly, "and my answer is...no." Where had the "no" come from? I had definitely planned to join them.

Shocked, I turned and raced away down the stairs and out the front door. I felt possessed, as though someone else had spoken through me. What was going on?

"Don't worry, you can keep the book," June called after me, and I thought I heard her and Herm laughing devilishly.

For a couple of months, I managed to duck June and Herm by tiptoeing up the stairs to Grandma and Grandpa's and escaping down the back way. I got full relief when June Fish's mother died and they had to move unexpectedly.

A newlywed couple, John and Mary Grimke moved in. We used to hear rhythmic creaking overhead every night and morning. Mommy said the Grimkes had a rocking chair, but I knew exactly what was going on.

– ∞ –

Miss Wheatley lived a few blocks up the hill from us, on Beacon Street. One day, she invited me to her house for milk and cookies after school. I accepted excitedly and told Dorothy right away. "Miss Wheatley invited me to her house! I've never been in a teacher's house. I wonder what it looks like. She said she had a dog and a cat and I could help her walk the dog! Wow!"

"Are you going to tell your parents?" Dorothy asked. She knew Daddy cursed and yelled a lot. The whole block knew.

"I'm afraid they'll say no."

"What if they find out? Aren't you afraid of getting hit?"

"I get hit no matter what I do," I said.

"You poor kid," Dorothy said.

I shrugged. I didn't like her feeling sorry for me but I knew not to tell her about my gas-bombs, and I never let one fly around her.

Miss Wheatley had second thoughts and called one evening to ask permission to have me over. Mommy answered the phone. I heard her stiff tone, and I knew immediately who it was. Agitated, she hung up and turned to me pointing a finger.

"You are never, never to be alone with that woman," she said. "She's dangerous."

"Miss Wheatley dangerous? No, she's not. She's great. What are you talking about?"

"I know what I'm talking about. She's a pervert. She and that Dr. Amato that operated on you. I can't believe I allowed her to touch you. If I ever hear you have gone to that house, I will have her arrested. Is that clear?"

Hurt and confused, I ran off, crying. I knew Mommy was mistaken and I knew, too, there was nothing I could do to change her mind.

– ∞ –

SIX

Grandma and Grandpa had been married for fifty years and they still hugged regularly like sweethearts. We'd had a big party at a restaurant in the Bronx, and I didn't dare complain about the uncomfortable green taffeta dress that rustled weirdly when I moved and made me look like I weighed about a thousand pounds. Daddy asked me to dance and pulled and pushed me around as he crushed me to his body. I knew my face was bright red. My body stiffened like stale bread. I didn't mean to but kept stepping on his toes, and I even slipped a small fart out and pretended it wasn't mine. He told me to relax and poked me a little in the small of my back but that only made me stiffer. Relief flooded me when the music ended. I raced to find Ralphie, whose white shirt was half hanging out of his navy blue pants. We danced a box step, counting as we trod, leaving proper space between us, not like Daddy. Afterwards, we ran around the restaurant threatening other cousins with ice cubes. Our cousin Mitchell wanted us to try bootleg cigarettes and Scotch in the alley but we turned him down. I didn't want Daddy to murder me.

Back at home, after the celebration, I sat at Gram and Gramps' kitchen table, watched them hug by the sink, and felt warm inside. It was good to know all couples weren't enemies like my parents. When I grew up, I decided, I would marry a man just like Grandpa.

– ∞ –

Buddy Wine's birth certificate lists him as Baruch Ofir Wine. His parents, Morris and Minnie Wine, had been Weinbergers before Joshua Benson, a mischievous employee of the United States government's Immigration Department on Ellis Island, said to a young Morris, "Your name is now Wine. Drink and be merry." When his parents named him Baruch, the first word of every Hebrew prayer, meaning Blessed, they expected to call their second boy Barry for short. But the vivacious little fellow, when asked his name at age one, answered "Buh" and his big brother Arnold decided to call him Bud. It stuck and expanded a bit to Buddy.

Bud, a flower that never quite blossoms and blooms, that was Buddy Wine's fate, a guy drunk with dreams. Many years later, it was his wife's hypothesis that Baruch Weinberger would have made it perhaps to Supreme Court Justice, or esteemed Rabbi complete with beard and yarmulke, chanting his name throughout the day, blessed be this and blessed be that, washing hands, eating breakfast, one prayer for fruit, another for bread, yet another for fish or fowl. But Buddy – as a kid trusted friend, pal, loyal comrade, a buddy to good guys, and hooligans alike, easy mark for con artists later on, Buddy, unlike Baruch, had no special angel, no special blessing, and no chance.

He got into plenty of trouble in the schoolyard, jumped headlong into scraps triggered by a slightly raised eyebrow or a curled lip. Quick at doing sums in his head, in class he balked at showing teachers how he arrived at correct answers before any other kid. Who cared as long as the answers were correct? He skipped school often and went fishing or bike riding or hung out smoking cigarettes, looking at girlie rags, and playing cards in Morty Pintchik's basement. With no taste for alcohol, he just watched as Morty got soused on his old man's Scotch and acted foolish. Maybe a bit of Baruch shone through.

The last time he signed his full name Baruch Ofir Wine, he thought good riddance as he signed himself out of high school forever at age sixteen. The guy with that name was somebody else, a different, seriously embarrassing Jewboy. Buddy Wine was a homeboy, a pal's pal, a red blooded American who could go far like the characters in the Horatio Alger, Jr. rags to riches stories.

Next day Buddy went to work delivering flowers. He learned far more than he'd counted on from his third customer, a 35-year-old bleached blond, appropriately named Flora and called Flo. The yellow tea rose bouquet he was bringing Flo contained a Dear Jane card, a break-up letter from her married boyfriend. Flo's delight at seeing the bouquet in the hands of the smiling teenager, with porkpie hat, quickly turned to shock as she read the news and mumbled a few choice epithets for her now ex. Buddy had never heard such language out of a female mouth, and this was a particularly pretty pink rosebud mouth he was in no hurry to take leave of, certainly not before collecting his tip.

"I'm sorry, Ma'am," said Buddy sympathetically and pulled a clean, pressed white handkerchief from his pocket. Flo accepted it and cried into it without even thinking.

"Can I help you, Ma'am?" asked sweet, innocent Buddy, not moving from the porch.

"Come in, young man," Flo said, between sobs. "I'll give you your tip."

He took off his hat and crossed the threshold.

50

"Hold me tight," she said, whimpering, still holding the bouquet, making no move toward her pocketbook.

One thing led to another and soon Buddy found himself inside a pornographic dream, in a four-poster bed with a blond living doll who squeezed his penis between the plumpest breasts he'd ever seen inside or out of a dirty magazine and followed that with an unspeakably pleasurable delight involving the rosebud mouth. How lucky could a guy get on his first day of work, which quickly became his last on that particular job since he stayed and comforted Flo until after darkness fell. Over the next few months, as Buddy flitted from one job to another, his one constant was that four-poster bed. Never had a boy been happier to have quit high school, for this love school offered an unparalleled education, not the disciplined academic variety the Sheldons, Iras, and Harveys were getting on their way to the MD's and CPA's, but the kind most red-blooded sixteen-year-olds could only fantasize about as they furtively tickled the pickle, burped the worm, choked the chicken, basted the turkey, jerked the gherkin and greeted Madame Palm and her five lovely daughters.

Buddy's manly adventures with Flo impregnated him with a sense of self-confidence and pride. When he walked into Acme Wholesale Pharmaceuticals, the sales manager, Irv Prager, liked the kid with the straight posture, easy smile, twinkling eyes, and hired him on the spot. Buddy soon had a closet full of suits, a brand new car, a small apartment of his own off Grand Concourse in the Bronx, and more spending money than any other kid his age from his hometown of Dumont, New Jersey. Although Buddy never acquired a taste for alcohol, he liked the grown-up feel of smoky bars. After Flo, there was no way he could date girls his age, so he gravitated to dance halls and bars, drank celery tonic and Coke and worked out athletically on his mattress with fast girls named Dolly, Babe, and Candy. Irv Prager's instincts had been accurate: this kid could sell cream to a cow and make the cow moo with delight.

Meanwhile, Buddy's parents, Minnie and Morris, tiring of big-city life, sold their cut-rate drug store on Jerome Avenue and their house in Dumont, and bought a similar store with an apartment right upstairs on Water Street in Newburgh, New York, a small town on the banks of the wide, blue Hudson River.

"When we retire to Florida," they promised Buddy, "our store will be yours."

For ten years, Buddy led the Acme sales force and built a reputation as an ace. Meanwhile all the old buddies from high school had graduated from college and professional schools and were settling down with wives and babies. Even his big brother Arnie, with a DDS and office full of impressive dental equipment, had a zaftig wife and two little boys of his own. It's time, old Buddy, he said to himself. Enough of cafeteria food and dance hall floozies. With this mindset, he was working the Newburgh territory he'd requested – more out of duty toward his parents than love for them – when he noticed Pearl Fine for the first time.

He spotted Pearl as she walked, talked, laughed, and goofed with her three friends, coming from high school and heading south across upper Broadway. A petite, raven-haired knockout with straight teeth, fiery dark eyes and creamy olive skin, Pearl had a contentedness and easy laugh so completely opposite from his dour mother that Buddy felt his heart melt and was drawn in right away. Along with girlfriends Sylvia, Tess and Elsie, the delightfully spirited girls were known around town collectively as the Noisy Four.

On a whim, he followed her home to Overlook Place, then poked around a little like one of his True Detective Stories private eye heroes, Sam Spade. As a traveling salesman, Buddy was in town only sporadically and for the next few months, Pearl dominated his dreams. When he next returned it was fall. Pearl's girlfriends had all gone off to college but she, a top student, had to stay in town and face the humiliation of attending Metropolitan Business School because her father refused to send a daughter to college and it never occurred to her to go on her own.

Buddy parked in front of Metropolitan and waited. Pearl came out alone, carrying an armload of books. Her black hair was bobbed, her cheeks rouged, her skin golden, her jaw set, attitude feisty, a result of the raw deal her dad had trapped her with. Buddy, dressed impeccably in new tweed three-piece suit, wool felt Fedora and conservative dark cravat, walked straight up to her.

"Good afternoon. My name is Buddy Wine. I know you are Pearl Fine and have four older brothers named Phil, Jake, Sydney and Benny. I think you're the most beautiful girl I've ever seen and I'd like to drive you home in my new roadster and take you out for dinner on Saturday night. My parents own Wine Cut-Rate Drugs on Water Street. We're a solid, respectable Jewish family. I have a good, steady job with Acme Pharmaceuticals and my intentions are honorable." He bowed low, hat in hand, then swept the hat invitingly toward his shiny black Pontiac with gleaming silver streaks. Astonished, speechless, wide-eyed, flattered, impressed by this dapper, romantic, smiling, charming figure, Pearl stepped gingerly into what would become the nightmare of her life.

During the week that Daddy and Mommy were honeymooning in Niagara Falls, Minnie and Morris Wine accepted an offer from a growing chain of pharmacies they hadn't bothered to mention to Daddy. They had decided to retire to Florida. That's the shocker my parents returned to. That's how their life together began.

Daddy raged and carried on, but it was too late. His parents gave him two hundred dollars, and without conferring with his new young wife, he invested in the first of a series of failed business schemes. He'd gotten excited by a newfangled picture machine for taking small, grainy headshots. It came with a container and trailer that could attach to his car. The whole thing, when screwed together, measured an impressive eight by twelve, the size of a small room. He planned to make his fortune this way and prove to his parents that he didn't need them anyway.

Disappointed and confused, eighteen-year-old Pearl sympathized with her new husband, shared his bitterness toward the Wines, but was skeptical about his hasty choice of the picture machine business. Times were still hard in the mid thirties and two hundred dollars was a lot to risk; but with the deal done, she took off with him. They traveled around from town to town in the Hudson Valley and the Catskill mountains setting up the machine in empty storefronts, printing and distributing leaflets and taking the pennies of country folks in exchange for quick portraits. Pearl added the novelty of color, tinting the photos with colored pencils. Within six months, when she got pregnant with Karen, Mommy refused to live what she termed a gypsy life and, after some stormy scenes, moved back home. That's when my grandparents remodeled the house to make a tenant apartment plus an apartment for the young couple and their baby, just until the kids bought their own place. They correctly predicted Buddy would return to his wife. He arrived a few weeks after Pearl had left him, hungry, hangdog, and ready for yet another try at a business, this time one that couldn't fail, a tavern. He reasoned that Prohibition had only been lifted a couple of years and drinkers were the ultimate repeat customers, thus the tavern business couldn't fail, especially with a wife named Pearl Fine Wine. Just one small catch, start-up money. The bank turned him down since he had no experience running a bar. Asking his folks was out, but he counted on his new in-laws. Except for ritual wine, Grandpa didn't drink, nor did he like the way alcohol destroyed people's lives.

"Jews don't run gin mills," Gramps told Buddy. "Come into the dry cleaning business with me."

"No, thanks, I'll make my own way," replied Buddy, stubbornly.

While he was contemplating how to finance his dream, he ran into an ace salesman, Zaney Kern, he knew from his parents' business, just promoted to sales manager, and Zaney pitched him so skillfully – car mileage allowance, health insurance, bonuses – Buddy signed on the spot to sell pharmaceuticals to drug stores in three counties. Pearl swooned with relief. She thought her dream house was nigh. Later, the pocketbook factory would sentence the family to a life stretch in the downstairs railroad flat.

– ∞ –

SEVEN

When I started noticing boys, Grandpa was the one who encouraged me.

I sat next to Gramps on the porch, in the rockers he had painted grass green. We rocked quietly for a while. My bra cut into my flesh. Why was I so mountainous? Why did I have to be called Fatso, Blimp, Lard-Ass, and Elephant Woman? I pretended not to care, but it killed me inside. I wanted to have a thin waist like other girls my age instead of a 38-incher. I would try not to go inside and snack on bread and butter and cookies.

"I think I have a crush on Dorothy's cousin Paul," I confessed to Gramps. "I haven't told anyone. Do you think I can get him to notice me?"

"Ro-ro," he said. "Whichever boy you choose, if he's smart, will choose you, don't worry. I guarantee it."

"Nobody likes fat girls, Gramps," I said.

"Nonsense," he said. "It's what's inside that counts."

"I don't know, Gramps."

He lit a cigarette and coughed as he smoked.

"Don't worry," he said. "It's baby fat. You'll lose it."

– ∞ –

I wanted to talk to Mommy about boys, but she was never available. When she gave up obsessive housecleaning, her job preoccupied her. I knew she only pretended to listen most of the time. Once in a while she took me shopping. That was a special kind of torture.

"Mommy," I asked one day as we were on our way to buy me a new outfit for a seventh grade party. "How come I'm so huge and everybody else in the family is small?" The car suddenly seemed like a perfect place to have a heart-to-heart conversation.

"You're statuesque," she said. "I don't know where you got your genes, but they're not the same as mine or your father's."

"Am I adopted?" I asked.

She grinned. "Nope, I had all of you girls."

"Could I be part alien?" I asked.

55

"What? You mean from another planet?" I couldn't tell whether she took me seriously or not. She didn't like to take her eyes off the road when she drove.

"Right. Sometimes I think I'm from way far away, like out in the Milky Way. I have weird experiences. I can fly and visit unusual places in my dreams. I'm pretty sure they're real. I see things like glass palaces and crystal rivers and transparent people. I even have teachers there."

"Don't talk like that," she said. "It's crazy talk. Dreams are dreams. You're a beautiful human girl."

"But I'm so big. I hate being so big. The other kids laugh at me. I don't fit in."

"You're not that big," she said. "You're normal. Your classmates are all pigmy midgets. Believe me."

"But how come they're all small, Mommy," I said, not believing her one bit and not liking the term pigmy midget either. "I think they're normal and I'm the giant freak."

"Don't say that," she warned, and added, glancing at me, "I'm a midget, too."

Before we went to the dress department, she took me to somebody called a foundation specialist to get me fitted for a long line bra and girdle.

"My, what a big girl!" said the short, orange-haired woman in black with a yellow cloth measuring tape around her neck.

"She is not big," Mommy said in a huff. "She's just... stocky."

"You can't fool me. You mean fat," I muttered under my breath, looking at my enormous rhino-like image in the mirror growing bigger before my eyes. "Why?" I asked the mirror. "Why am I so huge?"

There was a pattern to my life and it was a very large size. Big was how everyone described me. For quite some time, I could no longer wear Karen's hand-me-downs. Five was Karen's number. She wore size five dresses on her cute, little five-foot nothing figure and size five heels on her petite feet. I wore tent dresses on my elephant body and towered over her in my size ten sneakers. Mommy and Karen, both so much smaller than I, took to dieting constantly on cottage cheese, lettuce, and fruit or tomato juice, rye crisp, and grapes, or whatever the latest fad diet was. When they talked about being good, that meant they'd stuck to their diet. Being bad meant eating something fattening. It seemed that Mommy, Dorothy's mom, Amanda's mom, and everybody's moms, sisters, and aunts were always dieting because suddenly being fat was a very bad thing for a girl to be. Everyone wanted to be thin. Thin meant beautiful. Mommy, Karen, and even little Victoria always tucked in their blouses to show their tiny waists and wore wide elastic belts to cinch them even narrower. Movie stars had big busts and miniscule waists. Ashamed of my broad body, I left all my blouses untucked, and took to leaving on my bulky tan gabardine overcoat even when the weather was warm and dry. Belts were in style, but not for me. I didn't like myself, and I didn't like how I looked.

Grandpa noticed. He seemed tired. It was an unforgettable afternoon. Sweating, I came home for lunch from South Junior, a few blocks away.

"Ro-ro," he said. "It's almost seventy-eight degrees. Spring is here. Why are you wearing your coat?"

"I'm a blimp, Gramps. I feel better in a coat. I hate my body. No boys will ever like me. I want to be little like Karen and my friends."

"Don't say that. You're perfect just the way you are. If you were little, you wouldn't be you. Just be satisfied to be who you are, that's all. Be yourself. Be comfortable."

"I'll try, Gramps," I said, doubting.

"Good girl," he said and gave me a hug and a kiss on the forehead.

Back in school, coat off, I had art class after lunch and my seat by the window gave me a clear view of a Japanese maple I frequently put in my drawings. I was studying the tree carefully when I saw Grandpa sitting jauntily on an upper branch as clearly as I saw my teacher in front of the room. Gramps smiled and waved and then disappeared. Quickly I sketched him into my drawing, and without realizing what I was doing, I created a young version of Gramps with a full head of hair. As Mr. Pelly walked around checking our progress, he stopped by me.

"Rowena, that's special," he said. "I'd like to see you develop it. 'Ghost in a tree.'"

"Thanks, Mr. Pelly. I wish I could draw better."

"Just do what you're doing. There's a special pathos there I admire."

_ ∞ _

Uncle Sidney found Gramps slumped over his sewing machine around the time of my art class. Beethoven's Fifth was on the manual Victrola, the needle scratching at the wide rotating 78 rpm record. Gramps apparently still had a weak pulse but by the time the ambulance arrived, he was gone. They had to get Gram from her Hadassah meeting. I knew something was wrong when I saw Mommy's car parked by our house so early. I broke into a waddling run.

No one had ever spoken to me about death and I couldn't grasp the concept. You were supposed to be sad even when people you didn't like died, like my father's parents. But my dear, beloved Grandpa! How could there be an end to someone so special and what did it mean that I'd seen him wave goodbye in the tree? Was it real? I had the drawing to prove it. I was both awed and dazed when I heard the news, and I didn't come out of the daze during the service at the funeral home or the scene at the cemetery. Witnessing his casket lowered into the ground terrified me. Back home, everyone gathered downstairs but I went upstairs and sat at the Singer. I asked myself how I could possibly carry on without his warm smile and kind words. I sat and thought about my life.

Daddy was selling cars and fantasizing about moneymaking schemes. He and Mommy fought more than ever, and he still picked on me and smacked me around so impulsively I didn't have time to float away or fart. After the last time he hit me, I wrote My Daddy as the heading on a piece of paper, and under it I wrote every curse word I could think of, sex words, scatological words, sacrilegious words. My Daddy, shit, piss, fuck, bitch, bastard, hell, goddamn, Jesus Christ, cunt, pussy, cock, asshole. If I had gotten caught, I would have been mincemeat. Dorothy knew I hated him, and she sympathized. Mommy was getting nicer though. She loved her work. She traveled with her job now, to Colorado, Georgia, California, and even Iceland and Greenland, to help set up automated systems for the Air Force. I was proud of her. She had the most interesting job of all the mothers I knew. When she traveled, I spent most of my time upstairs with Gram and Gramps. My dear, beloved Grandpa whom I would never hug again.

I would have to learn to survive without him, I thought. But then I could swear I smelled his burning cigarette and I glimpsed him sitting near the Victrola. He blew me a kiss! Impossible, I thought. Could it be Gramps wasn't gone? The rabbi had said he was with God now, and I'd seen them lower his coffin in the ground so I was confused. I had surmised that the god-guy, if he really existed, lived up in heaven with Sky-mother, but if Grandpa lived with God up in heaven and was still wandering around the apartment, what or who was in the hole in the ground? I wanted someone to explain this to me, but Grandpa was the only one who ever talked to me about ideas like this and even though I'd seen him, I was scared to talk to him or even tell anyone. What if it was a *golem* and not Grandpa at all? Maybe my drawing was dangerous! I would destroy it first chance I got. I was so confused my whole body ached.

I went out in front of our house and leaned on the oak. A sense of calm filled me. If there had been an opening to crawl inside the trunk or footholds for climbing, I would have stayed in the tree. It offered solace like nothing else. But since it was right on the street, there was to be no lasting relief. When our next-door neighbor, known to us only as the barber's wife, tapped me on the shoulder and offered condolences, I got so startled I flinched, scraped my face against the rough trunk and was suddenly bleeding from a two-inch scratch on the cheek. Muttering "Jesus, Mary, and Joseph," the barber's wife took my hand and led me into her place for first aid and long sugar-coated cookies she called Savoyardi cookies or "baby slippers," which I accepted with trepidation wondering whether she qualified as a stranger since we weren't allowed to go with or accept food from strangers.

"I can tell you're a good eater," she oozed and encouraged me to eat another cookie.

In all the years we'd lived so close, this was the only time I'd ever been inside her house and it fascinated me. I had been taught that gentiles didn't like Jews so we should keep our distance to avoid trouble, and here I was, inside this forbidden place. Such daring distracted me from my grief and the facial gash. Smells of dried flowers tickled my nose. On shelves and tabletops sat dozens of knick-knacks, the things Mommy disparagingly called *tchochkes*, most sitting on colorful crocheted doilies. Tiny shoes, miniature vases, clocks, flowers, thimbles, dolls, angels, statues–all kinds of tiny stuff, in no particular order. Near the front door was a table with candles in tall glasses, also on the same kinds of doilies, beneath a tall sculpture of Jesus on the cross. Before and after washing my face and putting on witch hazel, the barber's wife stood by the sculpture, curtsied, crossed herself, and said a bunch of words I didn't get, very fast. As I was ready to leave, she smiled and told me, "If you remember Jesus loves you, you will be fine."

"I'm Jewish," I mumbled and ran out the door, fearful lest God smite me on the spot.

The lie that I'd gotten scratched from a fall caught on easily since everyone in my family knew what a klutz I was. I didn't mention the barber's wife.

– ∞ –

Downstairs in our tiny living room, Grandma, Mommy, and all her plump, cigar-smoking Fine brothers reminisced and hooted with laughter as they rested their soft, wide bottoms on hard, narrow mourning benches. Cousins, aunts, and men Grandpa and Daddy knew from the Masons, filled the room and spilled into the dinette. Their thick smoke stank, so I stayed out of there. Uncle Sidney was telling a hilarious story about Grandpa's discovery of his sons' moonshine still years ago. I was sure the laughter was disrespectful.

In the little kitchen, pies, cakes, candies, cookies, breads, rolls, and all kinds of casseroles lined the surfaces, which even included the top of the fridge, dish drainer and washing machine. There were baked goods, homemade and store bought, in boxes, bags, and tins, platters and bowls covered with foil, tasty offerings from neighbors and friends, enough for a dozen families. The kitchen was so loaded with food it seemed the whole room might sink into the cellar. I wasn't the least bit hungry, but the louder the laughter, the more furious I became. How dare they laugh! I stood in the doorway between the kitchen and bedroom and thrust a spoon into a large bowl of noodle pudding and shoveled it into my mouth. I barely even noticed the cinnamon and almond flavors. I just stuffed myself as though filling the hole in my heart. When the bowl was empty, I licked the spoon and started in on an apple pie. Like the tears stuck behind my eyes, my stomach was on the verge of bursting through my skin.

I'm going to throw up, I thought and waddled to the bathroom. I locked the door and stood over the toilet. I felt sick, but nothing happened. The laugher from the living room rose. They were enjoying themselves! On a whim, I stuck a couple of fingers into my mouth, down my throat. Brown mush cascaded effortlessly into the toilet. It didn't leave a bad taste like when I vomited from the measles. The cinnamon and apple even tasted good. Full of relief and elated at my discovery, I repeated the secret moves again and again, kitchen to bathroom to kitchen to bathroom. I didn't have to miss Grandpa now. I had found a substitute.

– ∞ –

A month went by. Mommy was back at work and my sisters and I had returned to school. I saw Grandpa a couple more times walking through the house, and thought I smelled his tobacco and sewing machine oil. I ran after him but he didn't seem to see me. The only one who still saw me was my Sky-mother and even she was fading. Right after *shiva* ended, I dreamed I sat on Sky-mother's lap and it was that odd dream again in which I was a baby and she put her breast in and out and in and out of my mouth and then she spilled salty milk down my throat. She got larger and stronger, and we cried together. Feeling pain helps pain subside, she told me, as she stroked my back and hair. That seemed contradictory, but I felt comforted. When I awoke, I longed to connect with Mommy, but she continued to operate in a world apart. I avoided Daddy as much as possible.

One evening, after Mommy got home from work, I sat on the red metal stepstool in a corner of the closet-sized kitchen and witnessed Mommy move robotically as she created dinner. I was steps from her, yet, as usual, she didn't notice me, or if she did, she didn't let on. I wondered, did I still have a visible body?

As I watched Mommy, it struck me how different she looked without a rainbow around her. Fewer trees spoke to me since Grandpa's passing and fewer rainbows appeared around people. Had the colors disappeared? Was Mommy so sad she'd lost her rainbow? What about my friends and teachers? I hadn't even realized I'd seen rainbows until they disappeared. Had vomiting changed my eyesight?

All these thoughts tumbled around my mind like tickets in a raffle drum as I sat watching Mommy's performance as chief cook. Wherever Mommy went in her head, she still managed to effortlessly produce our dinners night after night. She could stand in the middle of the room, and just by whirling reach the refrigerator, sink, and stove and, if she ever chose, me sitting on the stepstool jammed in next to a low corner cabinet with a chipped white porcelain top. I would have enjoyed helping Mommy cook, but she always said there was no room in the kitchen for another cook. "Too many cooks...." she'd say, leaving off "spoil the broth" so she wouldn't be obvious. She hated obviousness.

So I sat idly, waiting for recognition, wondering how to tell her I was steering her meals back up along the path they'd gone down. A month had gone by, and I was beginning to think of food differently, still something tasty, but not nourishment, more like filler, pretend stuff, like props in a play. It was as though my insides were hollow and food plugged up the space. What if the story of internal organs was fake? Had I really had an appendix that was removed? They never showed it to me. When Mommy got a chicken or turkey from the butcher, it was hollow inside, with a bag of giblets that supposedly came from the same bird. Maybe that was a lie. When Victoria fed water to her new doll that peed, the water ran right through her. Why? Because she was empty inside. I felt empty too. I could sense my heart beating, but that could be a trick. My parents lied all the time and so did I. Who could tell what was true and what wasn't? Mommy would routinely say Daddy wasn't home if someone called he didn't want to speak to, and Daddy would do the same for her. Lies were a normal part of life. I had become an accomplished liar so I'd sound like everyone else. It made me feel better and nobody even suspected. What if I'd finally gotten to the truth, that food was a fraud? How come it was bad that so many people in India and Africa were starving, but it was good if Americans and Europeans, especially women, went on diets and got thin? Would I get hit for voicing such odd and heretical thoughts?

Would I even be able to get Mommy's attention long enough to ask her? I didn't even know how to get her attention to ask a minor question – Mommy, do you remember there's the last PTA meeting of the year tomorrow night? This topic seemed huge and confusing. The practice words in my head sounded weird to me. Purposely throwing up? How come I used to think throwing up was nasty just a few weeks ago? I had turned around the most commonly accepted belief: food is supposed to go down and stay down. My new discovery not only empowered me, but it also made sense. Of course, my behavior would be different from everyone else's. I hardly ever agreed with routine things like all girls playing with dolls and wearing dresses. Would Mommy be able to shed light on this for me considering I'd grilled her about other puzzles before from this very place and come away bewildered? Was it important to pretend to go along with the prevailing eating system and continue my new way secretly? Would it be better to skip food altogether? Why eat at all?

If I really had organs that had to be fed and I didn't eat, I could die, but if I ate a lot and threw some of it up, then the rest of it would still be there and I could survive. How would I know whether I was leaving enough to stay alive? Did I want to stay alive? Yes, I wanted to grow up and leave this madhouse where they said they loved me and then told me I was bad and hurt me.

"We know what's best for you," Mommy constantly repeated. Was I terminally bad? Were my secrets bad, like hiding the sex book in the cellar, and now pigging out and throwing up? They felt exciting and bad at the same time. I tried to make sense of it all, but clearly there was something big I was missing. Maybe I was part of an alien race of vomiters, and I was just discovering my true identity. Where would I find my tribe? Who could I talk to about this? Not Dorothy because it would get back to Karen and I could get in trouble. I'd grown estranged from my friend for fear of blurting out my secret, and I avoided her. Gramps would have been the only one. Gram was doing well considering she'd lost the love of her life, maybe because she hadn't lost him completely. I loved her but I wasn't about to raise anything controversial that might upset her.

I sat very still while my mind continued speeding. Maybe Mommy would hug me and tell me to stop throwing up immediately. What would I do then? Feel both comforted and embarrassed? Mommy wasn't a natural hugger. She stiffened when I touched her, not like Sky-mother who, I knew, loved hugging and petting me. Sky-mother's body shone transparently. She had no insides I could see. Maybe I was empty inside like her because I was really her daughter. If I had two mothers, maybe there were two me's also.

I noticed the seams in Mommy's stockings had twisted around her leg and a double run the width of a lasagna noodle went all the way to her toes, her tiny feet now out of stiletto-heeled black pumps and into blue chenille bedroom slippers. Another pair of stockings for the trashcan. I thought nylons were a stupid style and wondered why women didn't just wear long, warm socks in cold weather and go barelegged in summer. Mommy was always bemoaning her tired, sore, little feet but when I suggested she get flats like I wore, she said that was unprofessional and out of the question.

"Better to endure a little discomfort and look right than look wrong," she'd said, pointing her index finger for emphasis. She assured me I'd be able to learn to wear heels with a little practice although, she added, "You don't need the height." This I interpreted to mean that I was a giant freak who always looked wrong.

Since Grandpa's funeral a month ago, except for those great weekend kosher deli lunches, which ended up in the toilet bowl, I skipped lunch altogether. I had taken to eating one plain hardboiled egg for breakfast, then waiting for dinner when I gorged myself and threw most of it up. I filled myself with water during the day when I was hungry. It was too difficult strategically to eat and find a private throw-up spot in the middle of the day unless I was at home.

Even though I felt elevated emptying my stomach–elated, clever, morally superior–there was something strange and scary also, almost as though I personally connected with the lower depths by summoning food up out of my mysterious innards, and flushing it all down to some other shadowy place.

In the middle of chopping onions, Mommy turned her head suddenly, and her blinking, tearing eyes looked my way. She nodded slightly, which I understood meant my presence had registered, so I plunged in, speaking quickly to hide emotion.

"Mommy, is there anything wrong with eating a lot and then sticking your finger in your throat and throwing up?"

"Hmmm," she pondered for a few seconds, dabbed her eyes on her apron, chopping knife still in her hand. She sniffed. There was a black smudge of mascara under one eye and a thin black line of mascara running down the other cheek. "Well, the Romans did it. They had special rooms called vomitoriums, and they all did it so they could keep eating their banquets. It sounds dreadful to me, but I suppose it's okay. Probably would work for getting skinny. If you can do it, more power to you."

"Thanks, Mommy." I jumped down, kissed her on her wet cheek, and pumped my fist in victory as I headed for the bedroom.

– ∞ –

The only one in my family who noticed my new habit was Victoria, who was now seven and more involved than ever in music and dance, with formal lessons in flute and ballet. She was a thin, graceful girl, short like all the other women in the family except me, with long straight sandy hair, usually tied in a ponytail, and a pronounced widow's peak that gave her face a heart shape. One evening we almost collided as I was leaving the bathroom. I knew she'd been spying on me, listening at the bathroom door.

"Are you sick to your stomach, Weena?" she asked. "I thought I heard you throwing up a few times. I think you must be sick because you are sad that Grandpa died. You must miss him."

"I'm not sad, and I don't miss him," I shot back angrily. That didn't feel quite right, but I ignored it. I was reciting my script. "And I'm not sick either. I've learned something cool, but I can't tell you what it is."

Her deep blue eyes widened. "You're making yourself sick, aren't you? I knew it! I'm going to tell Mommy on you."

"Mommy says it's okay. I've already asked her. I'm not really sick. This is different. The Romans did it. So there."

Pony-tailed Victoria stood firm, one hand on her hip, "Then Mommy made a mistake and so did the Romans, whoever they are." She looked up to the right, searching her memory. "Wait a minute, aren't the Romans the ones who made guys fight lions? We saw a movie about that. I'm sure it was the Romans. They had a big place like Yankee Stadium and people watched the lions eat guys. Did Mommy say that was okay too? Weena, think about it, how can it be okay to make yourself sick on purpose? I think you're just throwing up because you're sad. You'd feel better if you talked about it."

"Butt out," I said and gave her a little shove. Actually I wanted to give her a big shove or a punch in the face. She was much too logical for her age. I felt my fists clenching.

"You're only mean because you hurt," she said, stuck her tongue out at me, and danced away.

– ∞ –

EIGHT

Little by little, I learned from experience what came up easily and what didn't budge. Liquids cleared the way, especially warm creamy ones, but chocolate of any kind stuck like glue. Once I ate a bag of Oreos and almost ripped my stomach open struggling to bring them up. My heart pounded, glands swelled, eyes teared, the back of my hand looked like an animal had chomped into it – and still, nothing rose. I gagged again and again, knowing I had all those Oreos lodged in me. They had to come up. They had to. But they didn't. I lay curled up on the tiny bathroom floor berating myself. How could I have been so stupid? Why didn't I know? God, if only you let me get rid of them now, I will never eat Oreos again. Please, I promise! Again I bent over the toilet and gagged. Nothing. I drank warm tap water, shoved my whole hand down my throat, wiggled the fingers around deep inside. Water came up, slightly brown from the Oreos, but nothing solid. How could this be? Beside myself, I prayed to Sky-mother for a solution. Exercise! said a voice in my head. Exercise hard! I had to get out of the bathroom since there was no room in there even to spread my arms. I cracked the door and, certain no one was around, quickly darted straight through the house and out the back door.

In the backyard, I hooked my feet under the decorative molding beneath the porch and did so many sit-ups on my Oreo-filled stomach that I not only ached, I actually felt nauseous. I lost count somewhere around 800, but felt relieved to be using up calories. I decided the Oreo filling must contain glue and vowed once more never to have an Oreo or anything chocolate again. So what if chocolate was my favorite flavor. So what if Oreos were my favorite cookie. I'd sacrifice.

– ∞ –

As I acted out this bizarre ritual day after day, sometimes more than once or twice in a day, I had a big payback. First of all, my ungainly body was shrinking to what I considered a normal range. Secondly, having grown up around random raging, I relished the repetition, familiarity, and security of the new routine. I was in charge now. I had control. Moreover, both overstuffing and anticipation of emptying thrilled me. I could open up my mouth and dump in as much as I wanted of almost anything! More and more and more, I'd stuff and stuff and stuff until there was no more room for anything. Then followed great physical relief of pressure and emotional elation after the purge. The secrecy necessary to carry this out terrified me at times, but it also fed me with satisfaction. I knew something nobody else knew – including Mommy, who, I believed, blocked it out of her mind using classic denial. I felt special, empowered, daring. I got away with something. It was during this time that I shocked and delighted myself by my warrior behavior in smacking Daddy back – with no conscious preplanning. Right after that victory, I strengthened myself further by demanding an end to being called Weena or worse, Weenie. Fresh from a double coup, my attachment to the secret habit was now cemented as never before. I was beginning to sense a tiny, nagging pain as the addiction's hooks dug into me, but I ignored it. How could I possibly give up something which transformed my life?

– ∞ –

Mommy got annual promotions, a result of acing every Civil Service exam she took and taking every one she was eligible for. Her latest job involved traveling, and she returned from a business trip to San Francisco in the most cheerful mood I'd ever seen.

"Hey, Mommy," I kidded, "Did you have an affair in San Francisco?"

She paled, pulled me aside. "My God, is it that obvious?"

"Oh no!" I was horrified. "You did!" I'd been kidding around and she turned it into true confessions. "Does Daddy know?"

She shook her head. Her eyes rolled painfully. "I swear I never did it before," she said. "Tell me, what should I do?" She looked terror stricken.

"Don't ask me, Mommy, you're the one who committed adultery." To soften my harshness, I added, "Don't worry, treat me right and I won't breathe a word."

From then on, Mommy spoke to her friends less and to me more. She noticed me when I sat on the step stool in the kitchen, converted me to pal and confidante. It was a role I both loved and hated. I liked the attention and the bonding, but I still felt uncomfortable with the information about Mommy and sex.

At the time, school bored me so I was supplementing with an ever-expanding variety of library books. Convinced my family was insane, I chose to analyze them by reading the complete works of Sigmund Freud, and I fixated on the concept of phallic symbols.

"Mommy," I said one day from my now visible perch on the stool. "Have you noticed that we're surrounded by phallic symbols everywhere?" I picked up the tall glass saltshaker with silver colored cap. "This is a good example. We pass this thing around at every meal. Isn't that amazing and incestuous?"

Mommy laughed with hilarity and nervousness. "Gimme that," she said, grabbing it out of my hand. "I need it." Giggling, she held the saltshaker in her left hand, gazed at it with a strange moony face, then used the thumb and index fingers of her right hand to stroke it up and down and over the cap. I stared, taken aback. What was she doing? Did this saltshaker really look like a penis? Did she actually touch the real thing? Wasn't it dirty? With two hands around the saltshaker, she sprinkled a bit of salt into the Good Seasons salad dressing she was preparing, then pretended to kiss the saltshaker and handed it back to me. "Your turn," she said.

Dumbfounded, I wasn't about to kiss the saltshaker or even pretend to, but I had started this little game, so I played along and stroked the saltshaker a little, carefully copying her movements. Flushed and giddy, Mommy snatched it back. It didn't feel exciting to me, just odd and funny.

At dinner that night she surreptitiously passed her hand up and down the saltshaker before passing it to Daddy and threw me a furtive look. That began a new craze. She fondled cigarettes, pens, pencils, bananas, cucumbers, carrots, long pretzels, anything vaguely tube-shaped. I mimicked her moves and began to see the whole world as phallic. Weren't arms and legs phallic? Weren't noses and fingers and toes phallic? Everywhere I looked, I saw phallic symbols: hammers, nails, spoons, straws, knives, flashlights, a world of coded Freudian mysteries and delights.

Our private joke went over Victoria's head, and Daddy seemed oblivious, but Karen reacted with horror.

"Are you two perves?" she demanded as Mommy and I finished dishes one evening. I'd just thrown up and was in pajamas and robe, feeling elated, sensuously massaging tall drinking glasses as I dried them. "Nobody else's mother or sister acts like this. I think you're both disgusting and I'm going to move out altogether."

"Leave us your forwarding address," Mommy said, laughing as she caressed the thick handle of a long fork she was washing.

"Mother! Rowie!" Karen insisted. "Stop it! You're scaring me!"

"What are you scared of?" Mommy said. "I've told you before and I'll tell you again because I wish my mother had given me this advice. Don't get married until you've slept around. Remember that. Sex is far more important than love. Love is overrated. Love is blind, but sex opens your eyes. According to the Kinsey Report, ninety-eight percent of Americans have premarital sex. I saw it in *Redbook*. Be smart. Don't be a dumb-dumb like your mother. Women deserve to know what sex is all about before they walk down the aisle and maybe get stuck with a dud."

"With all due respect, Mother dear, you are insane, now I'm sure of it," Karen said, appalled. "And Kinsey too!" As she was storming out, she turned and said to me, "Don't listen to her, Rowie, she's giving you screwy advice."

"Prude!" Mommy called after her and giggled.

For a moment I wondered which one of them was my sister and which my mother. But Mommy quickly diverted my attention.

"Hey Rowie, have you heard the one about the hooker and the Texan?" Mommy asked as she wiped the stove and I finished drying dinner dishes. Of course I hadn't since no one else in the world told me dirty jokes.

"The Texan says to the hooker – and here Mommy did a Texan drawl: 'Ma'am, I've got the biggest dick you've ever seen, bar none.' 'Oh yeah, how big?' the hooker wanted to know. 'Six inches,' he said. 'Six inches! That's average,' the hooker said unimpressed. 'Around, Ma'am?' he drawled, and Mommy echoed the punch line again with a laugh. "Around, Ma'am?" I tittered more because Mommy made it sound comical than because I really found it funny since I had no idea about penis size.

Mommy was still my mother, but suddenly she felt different, not exactly a companion, not exactly a friend, not exactly like anybody else in my world. It wasn't a comfortable or easily defined relationship, but at least now she paid attention to me and didn't sentence me to the ogre's punishments ever again.

– ∞ –

NINE

Dorothy and I moved from duo to trio of friends, joined by a third girl, Greta Rothstein, blond, petite, and pretty. Greta sat next to me in homeroom. One day, I looked over and noticed her perky little strawberry titties had swollen into mid-sized persimmons almost as large as mine. Had that happened overnight? A throbbing wave caught me inside my panties. I looked away, my face flushing. Could anyone tell? What if someone had seen me? What did that mean? Was I queer like my fifth grade teacher Miss Wheatley my parents said was perverted? I liked boys so how come Greta's breasts excited me? Maybe because she was wearing my sweater? Greta was just beginning to date Dorothy's cousin Paul who lived on my block, was in 10th grade and drove his dad's Chevy. I'd had a secret crush on Paul for two years, but never dared elicit romantic feelings from him or, except for Gramps, even mention it anywhere outside my diary because I didn't think any boy would pay attention to a girl as fat as I was. But I wasn't so fat anymore. I thought, maybe Greta excites me because she's close to Paul and he's supposed to be with me instead of her. Later that afternoon, it was an Archie comic that gave me the go-ahead. "All's fair in love and war," Archie said to Reggie. As I read, I experienced my brain illuminating exactly like the light bulbs over these cartoon characters. I would make Paul my boyfriend. I would wear tight sexy clothes and make him notice me. I would experience love at last.

I fixated on winning Paul. Fair, with dark hair and eyes, and an expressive face like a Bassett hound, two years older and almost a head taller, Paul had never noticed me in a romantic way, but I intended to change that. I imagined him kissing me and fondling my breasts. Down in the cellar, I read and reread passages in *Love Among the Shadows* and substituted myself for sexy Nicolette, and this time, Paul for handsome Lance who ravished her. Paul and I both lived on Overlook Place separated by a few houses. Greta lived ten blocks away. I had proximity on my side.

One warm autumn Saturday morning, chore-time, I put on a plaid halter and skimpy blue chambray shorts and, as usual, scrubbed the hall and vestibule floors on my hands and knees. I moved the bucket of water as I worked my way toward the porch, sticking butt and legs out as I went. Paul saw my backside and stopped by to chat, a first. He stood at the bottom of the porch stairs with one foot perched jauntily on the first step. He looked cute in a bright red collar shirt, unbuttoned, cigarette pack expanding chest pocket, and tight Levis. His dark sideburns were clipped short and one straight lock flopped onto his forehead distinguishing him from the greasy boys with slicked-back Elvis hair.

"Hey, Rowie, what are you doing, playing maid?" He lit up a cigarette, offered me one. I refused. My parents would kill me even though they smoked heavily.

"Oh, this is my once a week chore. I'm almost finished. Want to take me for a ride later?"

He hesitated. "I don't know. I'm sort of going with Greta and I don't want to upset her."

"Listen, Paul, Greta is my friend. I like her very much and I don't blame you for liking her. But don't forget, all's fair in love and war. And..." I paused. Could I do this? I took a deep breath and the words came tumbling out. "I've liked you for a long time and I think about you a lot." I wanted to look sexy so I ran the tip of my tongue over my lips the way June Fish used to. I noticed Paul's eyes followed my tongue. He also glanced at my breasts and quickly looked away.

"It is? You do?" He blushed and I thought he looked cuter than ever. Encouraged, I continued.

"Yes, and I want to go for a ride with you tonight, after dark." I tongued my upper lip again. Then I stood up and stretched upwards languidly which I knew would make my breasts look bigger and higher because Nicolette always stretched like that and drove Lance wild. Paul watched me, dazed and dazzled.

"Are you sure?" he asked.

"You have my word," I purred.

"Okay, I'll pick you up at 7:30. But you have to promise to tell Greta yourself. Don't blame me either. Make sure she knows this is your idea."

"Okay, I promise."

Overjoyed, I called Greta and explained the Archie philosophy. She sounded upset with Paul for making a date with me before he broke his date with her, but I told her it was my fault because I fell in love with him and couldn't resist flirting and she should be mad at me but I hoped she wouldn't be because I still wanted her to be my friend and she was so beautiful that she had her pick of boys. I named a few. I must have been persuasive because she relented.

"If it's that important to you, Rowie, go ahead," she said. "But I wish you'd asked me before you made the date."

"I'm sorry, Greta. I didn't mean to hurt you. I care about you a lot." Some kind of shadow flickered and if I hadn't been so excited about Paul, I might have cried, but I put down the receiver thinking about what I would wear for our date.

Paul's dad's Chevy was two-tone green, the same popular color combination as Daddy's Pontiac. He parked behind South Junior and we climbed into the back seat and necked. We kissed and hugged and laughed. I loved feeling pleasure in my body and wanted to stop time and stay in that back seat forever. Was this true love? I told Paul I loved him and he told me he liked me and he probably would love me soon. That hurt me a little but I ignored it. I was with him and that was all that mattered.

The romance lasted six weeks during which I was too preoccupied and elated to binge and throw up and stopped cold without a second thought. I wrote our initials in hearts all over my book covers and felt like a different person, a girl with someone to care about, a girl in love. Thanks to *Seventeen* and Karen's few words of advice, I had boundaries. This was not *Love Among the Shadows* and I wasn't Nicolette. We kept our clothes on. I let his hand slip into my top but not my panties. My hand slipped into his shirt but not his pants. Whatever we felt below we kept private as though our bodies ended at our waists. It was only when he leaned against me in our alley with my back up against our house that I felt the shape of his penis firmly and clearly against my belly. It excited me so much I quivered from head to toe, but it also embarrassed me. On the one hand Mommy had told me to have lots of sex because of the Kinsey report but on the other hand the only information I had about having sex was from a dirty book, so I had an approach and avoidance dilemma. And still something scary I couldn't identify nagged at me. When Paul put his tongue in my mouth, I almost choked from fear and I didn't know why. But I let him anyway.

Once I overheard Daddy telling Mommy he had seen Paul's car or one just like it parked behind South Junior and worried because he saw some activity in the back seat.

She hushed him. "He's a nice Jewish boy. It's all right. Just kid stuff."

One evening around Thanksgiving when Paul couldn't get the car, we sat and talked on my front porch. It was chilly. We wore jackets. He put his arm around my shoulders and I nestled against him.

"I have something important to talk to you about, Rowie," he began, clearing his throat nervously.

"Talk then," I said, slightly worried. Was he going to ask me to go steady? We sort of were steadies even though we didn't call it that.

"Do you know who Susan Levitz is?"

"Yeah, a rich girl from North Junior who wears braces and gets dropped off and picked up from the JCC in a red MG."

"She made me an offer last night."

"You saw her last night?" I pulled away from him. The streetlight brightened the porch enough that we could make eye contact. "I thought you had a headache and were going to bed early."

"I was going to, but Susan called and invited me to a party at her place."

My heart sank. I craved a piece of cake or candy, rye bread with butter and jelly, something sweet.

"Go on."

"Well, it wasn't exactly a party. She was home alone. Amazing place. You should see the hi-fi equipment in that house, Rowie. And the pool, jiminy, it must be nice to have money." He fidgeted with his watch. "Anyways, I'll just tell you straight, she offered to take off her bra and panties if I'd go steady with her. I told her I'd let her know. I figured I'd give you a chance to match her offer because I love you and we know each other and everything."

"Are you serious? She said that?" I thought, he just told me he loves me! But if he loves me, how come this is happening?

"Yeah, she did, but she has pretty small titties, and I really like yours better so I wanted to see what you'd do, I mean in the way of a counter offer. I remembered what you told me in the first place about all's fair in love and war and everything. So, what do you think?"

Bitch! I thought and wondered is this the way love works, like some kind of contest? Did all's fair in love and war mean love was war? I had shot down Greta and now Susan Levitz was taking aim at me. Maybe I should reject love the way my cousin Victor had rejected war. I'd be a conscientious objector to love. Why couldn't things stay the way they were? Why did everything always have to change? And where did sex come in anyway?

"Are you in love with her?" I asked.

"No way, but I guess I could fall in love with her. I fell in love with you after we made out a few times."

"You're in love with me and you'd leave me just like that?" I clicked my fingers.

"Yeah," he said, "Just like that," and clicked also. "If you want me to stay, you know what to do. I didn't have to give you this chance you know."

"I know. I should be grateful and tell you you're wonderful, right?"

He beamed.

"This is what I have to say to you, Paul." I felt a lump in my throat. "Goodbye, Paul, it's been a ball, Paul. See you around." I said it lightly as though I didn't care. I wanted to tell him I loved him but didn't like him anymore. I swallowed my tears, ran into the house, and went straight to the kitchen to fill up. I knew I was going to be insanely jealous of Susan's wardrobe, her parents' fancy home with pool and her Mom's red sports car, but I would find a way to endure. Without a boyfriend, I would have plenty of free time for food mania again. I welcomed my habit. It was familiar and comforting, like an old friend.

– ∞ –

TEN

The following summer, when I was fourteen, I decided to get a job. I rejected camp counselor because I'd have to be a junior counselor and work for tips only. Daddy came to the rescue when he offered to pull strings with a lodge buddy, Marty Gross, and get me work at Marty's pocketbook factory. Mommy went ballistic. She cried and fumed at Daddy, and tearily begged me to reconsider.

"You're better than these people," she said. "They're trash. It could be dangerous for you."

"Mommy," I reasoned. "I think they're just plain ordinary people going to ordinary jobs. You want me to go to college, right? Well, here's a way for me to get paid and put some college money in the bank. Calm down. You're out of control.'

Finally, Mommy wiped her tears. "What am I getting upset about?" she asked rhetorically. "You won't last three days."

I ate two slices of peach and drank two tall glasses of water, a big breakfast for me, and rode my bike a couple of miles to the factory, my bag lunch in the basket hooked onto the handlebars. How I got the energy on so little food is a mystery, but I did it. I left my locked bike out in front and walked through the front door excitedly. This was my first real job. I saw people lined up and got in line with them. I vaguely remembered the time clock from my few visits to my parent's factory, but still I was surprised to learn I had a card with my name on it. Proof that I belonged. Wine, Rowena, right there in a slot in between White, Flo and Zukowsky, Joseph. I felt proud to have my very own card and my very own slot. About thirty people shuffled along, each inserting a card, holding onto it as the clunk sounded, then returning the card to its home slot. They looked a lot older than school kids, and reminded me of the Polish, Irish and Italian neighbors on my block. The men wore jeans and tee shirts and most women wore plain cotton dresses like those I'd always known as housedresses. A few wore jeans or pedal pushers like me. I had a moment of panic, worried I might be putting the card in upside down or backwards and hesitated with my card over the machine. A bleached blond woman right behind me smiled as she pointed to an arrow on the card that showed exactly which end was up. She was missing a front tooth, but her smile was warm and sincere. She smelled like roses.

"The arrow always has to be face up." She read my name. "Hi Rowena, I'm Betty."

"Thanks, Betty," I said as I shyly stuck my card in the time clock and pulled it out feeling smart. "Nice to meet you. My nickname's Rowie."

The factory floor was a large windowless loft filled with rows of vaguely familiar assorted equipment and large sewing machines. Just beneath a high ceiling, pipes and wires formed tubular and stringy sculptures. A hodgepodge olfactory assault of leather, oil, stale cigarette smoke, sweat, dirt, and unrecognizable chemicals briefly met me, all of which reminded me of childhood visits to my parents' monumental business failure, Glorianne Bag – which in my memory blurred into screaming fights about money, spankings I never understood, and delicious Virginia ham sandwiches on seeded rye from Petcher's, a deli near the factory.

I stood inside, near the door, out of the way of people streaming through, and waited for instructions. I was glad I'd worn tan pedal pushers and big tan shirt from when I was heavier, neutral colors to dodge attention. After Mommy's harping about how crude people here were, I didn't want to look sexy. I had to pee, but I thought I'd hold it a little while longer and get settled first. People were taking their places near machines, laughing and joking around, the women putting on smocks, some of the men donning heavy aprons. I just wanted to look shapeless. I heard one of the men yell out, "Who got lucky last night?" and snicker. I wondered whether they'd gone to Bingo.

"Obviously not you, Ace," one of the women said and laughed. Then I figured they played a weekly pinochle game like Daddy.

Marty found me and put his arm around me. He smelled like fruity cologne and cigarettes, and he creeped me out standing so close. He motioned to Betty, only one whose name I knew. She got up from her sewing machine and came over just as the whistle blew and machines started clanging, clinking, clunking and screeching. Marty's yelling added to the mix.

"Betty, this is Rowena. Take her under your wing." She nodded as though we hadn't met.

I shouted to Marty, "Could you call me Rowie, please? I hate my name."

"Whatever, kid." Marty shouted back, his tobacco-stained teeth showing in a lopsided grin that was part sneer.

"Betty, honey," Marty shouted. "Will you show the kid how to put locks on? She's here for the summer to help us out with the Penske order." He pointed to a pile of stiffened black leather rectangles that came up to my shoulders. Then he patted me on the backside. For a split second, I found myself peering down from the pipes by the ceiling. His voice brought me back.

"Good luck, kid," he said, and disappeared.

"How you doin', Rowie?" Betty said, speaking directly into my ear, loud but not shouting. "I got a cousin named Rowena. We call her Winnie. I never heard of nobody named Rowie before. It's different."

"I'm different," I said. "Could you show me where the ladies' room is, please. I have to go badly."

"Break's at ten, honey. You'd better hold on till then."

"I have to go to the bathroom on schedule?"

"You get used to it, hon. It's this way most places. You should go just before the bell and don't drink too much water."

When I returned, Betty was back at her own machine. I tapped her on the shoulder and she walked with me to my station.

"I have a daughter about your age," she said, over the machine noise. "You might know each other. What's your full name?"

"Rowena Gay Wine."

"Oh, yeah, I seen that on the time clock. Wine like the drink."

I nodded.

"I ain't about to forget that. I'll tell Jen tonight. My ma and pa drunk theirselves nearly to death on wine. I vowed I'd never be like them and guess what, I was drinking heavy by the time I was your age. If it wasn't for my hubby, I'd a probably been dead by now. I'm dry and sober twenty years come October."

"Congratulations," I said. "I'm sure it's hard to break habits like that." How well I know, I thought. I'm like a drinker myself, only with food.

She showed me how to use the machine to attach a lock to a piece of leather. With a grave expression, she stressed the importance of getting my fingers out of the way because foot press machines had a high accident rate. I devised a rhythmic reminder. On one, with my right hand I grabbed a leather rectangle from the top of the pile and placed it into a flat slot it slipped right into. On two, I used my left hand to get a gold-colored metal lock piece, with four pointed prongs, and set it into the round hole. On three I removed my fingers and on four, I stepped on the pedal and that big heavy press whomped down and attached the lock.

"Believe me, Rowie," she said. "You'll be doing it in your sleep soon. Just don't daydream. Watch your fingers and you'll be okay."

Betty had twinkly blue eyes and a friendly smile, and I realized Mommy would probably think her missing top front tooth made her look witchy, like a Halloween mask. The bleached blonde teased hair, penciled eyebrows, and dark lipstick I'd only seen on tough girls at school who I didn't know very well and assumed were dumb. I realized if I weren't at the factory, I never would have exchanged two words with Betty, and I probably would have made fun of her looks along with Mommy.

I started in on the pile. Right hand, left hand, remove hand, whomp! Toss into the done pile. Again. Again. Again.

Machines clanged, clinked, whirred, whistled, and screamed. I belonged here. I had a job. I was earning money just like a grownup. It felt great. By 8:30, stuffiness invaded the windowless space even though a few fans blew hot air around. Fluorescent lighting glared. I used my sleeve to wipe my sweating forehead constantly to keep my eyes dry. My clothes clung damply. This was harder than it looked. The repetition wore on me. By break time, my arms ached. I had ten minutes to join the crew in the ladies room, actually two adjoining rooms with no door in between, just a wide opening separating the toilet and sink area from what they called the lounge. Ringed with straight chairs, the lounge quickly converted to a community center with wisecracks, laughter, and cigarette smoke, along with toilet smells and lilac air freshener.

By lunch break, my stomach was growling and my mouth dry. I hadn't drunk all morning. Lunch took place in that same toilet lounge. A large redhaired woman named Flo sprayed floral deodorizer to camouflage toilet smells. I couldn't smell consistently but I heard everyone complaining so I knew the place stank. Betty had saved me a seat next to her. I downed my vegetables fast.

"You're eatin' rabbit food, huh? Whyn't you fix yourself a sandwich, sweetie?" observed Betty. "You on one of them diets?"

"Sort of," I said.

"Can I axe you somethin'?"

"Sure, anything," I said.

"What's a kid like you doing workin' here?"

"Well, Betty," I said. "I think I'm here for the same reason you and everybody else is here, to make some money."

She softened. "Of course. I'm sorry. I just meant...well...I can tell you're smart. I hope you don't plan to work here for the rest of your life, like us."

"I'm only here for the summer. I'm planning on college. That's what I'm saving for."

"Okay, that makes sense. You're all right!" she said.

"Thanks," I mumbled, happy for the acceptance and uncomfortable with a compliment, as usual.

A horn honked outside, three short honks, and Betty's face lit up. She suddenly looked radiant and beautiful, her skin almost translucent. I stared, baffled. What kind of magic was I witnessing? What had transformed her? I had to find out.

"Hey, Betty," someone sang, "It's your honey bunny."

"Bet-teeee," came the chorus of women, laughing, adjusting their clothing, fixing their make-up.

"Betty, what just happened? You look radioactive, in a good way, I said." She glowed mysteriously.

"My husband, Lou, he drives a cab," she said. "Whenever he passes by, he honks three times to let me know he loves me. It's our code. He knows my break times so he tries to come by then so I'll hear him nice and clear. But I hear him even with all the noise on the floor. I can feel him even before he honks. We've been married twenty-one years and we're still honeymoonin'."

"That's so great," I said, awed. "Do you ever fight?"

"We wouldn't be human if we didn't sometimes disagree. But my Lou doesn't believe in hittin' females, thank God. He don't hit me and he don't hit our daughters. We have our little spats but we have a rule never to go to bed mad. We're great at kissin' and makin' up. We don't sweep nothin' under the linoleum. We ain't found nothing worth fightin' and stayin' upset about cause fightin' kills love and we aim to keep it alive and kickin' just like our vows said, till death do us part."

"You're amazing, Betty," I said. "I admire you."

"Thanks, hon," she said. "Like I tell my girls, I wish the same for you."

Betty could teach my parents so much, I thought. Gram and Gramps never fell out of love, but I wondered why my parents stayed perpetually angry at each other. Mommy talked about sex endlessly, but never mentioned love except to put it down. I didn't even understand the difference. I still wondered which came first. Even with her missing tooth, Betty had a happy face. Mommy, with all her teeth intact and regularly tended, usually looked sad or angry but rarely, if ever, happy.

– ∞ –

Next day, Betty told me her daughter Jennifer knew me from South Junior. I had no idea who she was. Betty pulled out her wallet and showed me Jennifer's picture. Bleached blond hair, penciled eyebrows, fuchsia lipstick. A young version of Betty. I recognized her as one of the lower class kids I'd always thought tough and unapproachable. I'd never spoken with her. I felt ashamed and curious about my attitude of superiority. Where had that come from? Wherever it came from I was going to send it back.

I made it through July and August. I even made myself real sandwiches, tuna, peanut butter and jelly, cold cuts, BLT, sandwiches like everyone else's. I packed my lunch in a plastic cooler bag with a chilled can of juice and a piece of fruit. I drank only one glass of water for breakfast, to which I'd added a bowl of shredded wheat with skim milk and fruit. At lunch break, I sat with the other women, ate like them, hated the smell like them, and was proud to keep all my food down. In a ladies' room where everyone sat steps from the stalls, I couldn't take chances throwing up. Even if I could do it silently, unless I twisted around from the waist, they'd probably see my feet turned the wrong way.

It occurred to me that I had just about enough time to read one poem to myself during our short breaks so I began bringing *A Little Treasury of World Poetry* to work, our house's lone volume of poetry, which Grandpa had given me for my twelfth birthday.

"Whatcha readin' there, Professor Rowie?" asked Flo, large, loud, and friendly with a slight Irish brogue. I told her.

"How about readin' a poem out loud to us? We might learn somethin', right girls?"

They cracked up laughing, and agreed. From then on, there were days when 10th century Persian or 19th century Norwegian poems replaced gossip in that stinky toilet room. One day, my throat hurt a little so I asked Betty if she'd mind reading. She chose a Polish poem because she was Polish. For the first time I noticed the reactions on women's faces as they listened to Betty. A couple closed their eyes. I helped Betty with a few words. Everyone clapped when she finished.

"Hey, I've got an idea," Betty said as we stood up to return to our machines. "How about if we take turns readin' a few lines? Rowie can help if we need it. Whaddaya say?" They looked around at each other nervously. "Come on, someone volunteer. If I can read a poem, so can you," Betty said.

Flo raised her hand. "I'll take a chance," she said. "As long as it's a love poem and as long as it's Irish. Anythin' to sweeten our stinkin' breaks."

That began our passing around the poetry book as though it were sacred. We decided to have afternoon poetry sessions and whoever was going to read would practice with me during morning and lunch breaks and read during afternoon break.

Neither of my parents had ever even asked to share a poem with me, nor had my girlfriends. Only Victoria and I had shared poetry from my one treasured volume. Besides poetry, the high point of my day was Lou's honking his taxi's horn declaring his love for Betty, and watching Betty glow. I met Lou one day after work, and it shocked me to see he had bad teeth, long greased Elvis style hair with sideburns and a ducktail like the tough boys I avoided at school, and a big pot belly. He was so sweet and kind, and he had such devotion for Betty, it made me feel I'd discovered a secret of the universe. When Lou stood next to Betty I noticed that their eyes shone and they seemed a little like twins sharing thoughts and feelings and finishing each other's sentences. I felt happy watching them. Would I ever experience anything like that? What did Mommy have against these folks? I knew the answer had to do with a preconceived notion that broadly classified people. I guessed it had to do with making grammatical errors, having missing teeth, living in trailer parks, and dressing a certain way, in clothes that didn't hang quite right, either too tight or too loose. Mommy thought this was low class, but I wished my parents loved each other the way Betty and Lou did, and to hell with trailers, good grammar, and teeth.

On my last day of work, Friday before Labor Day, Betty brought in a home-baked pound cake, fresh strawberries from her garden, and a can of Redi-whip. The ladies surprised me with a goodbye party. I cried as I allowed myself to enjoy the cake and attention. Betty and Flo exchanged conspiratorial glances and Flo sang a da di da da di da drum roll.

"We have a special surprise for you, Rowie," Flo chirped. "Betty?"

Betty held a piece of paper with writing on it and read a line, then passed the paper around. Everyone got a turn reading in sing-song fashion. The women had composed a poem just for me.

We think you are a special girl

Like a diamond or a ruby or a pearl

We thank you for the poetry lessons

You made our breaks into enjoyable seshuns

We wish you good luck in high school and later on in college

We know you will have a good time and graduate and get good knowledge

Roses are red and violets are blue

And we all will miss you.

I overflowed with joy. Filled with emotion, I spontaneously presented the women with the book of poetry. Not since Gramps had I felt this kind of caring. How ironic that Mommy had cried every night about the job's ruining my life. When I proudly showed Mommy the poem, her only reaction was to laugh at the misspelling of "sessions" and the triteness of red roses and blue violets. That saddened me.

In high school, I looked for Jennifer in the hall, found her with her group of girls with teased, dyed hair and heavy make-up, and introduced myself. It felt strange.

"I worked with your mom, Jennifer," I said. "Please say 'hi' to her for me."

She smiled slightly and nodded, and I saw how much she looked like her mother. Then she and her friends went into their General Ed classroom and I walked over to my College Bound classroom, and we hardly ever noticed each other again.

– ∞ –

ELEVEN

Victoria and I worried about Mommy. She had dark circles under her eyes and cried far too easily. She was thirty-eight, and not only did she look puffy and waterlogged, her hair had grayed and her skin matched, snowy like a TV channel with no picture. She looked weary and unhappy, and lay down with headaches frequently. She said her periods were irregular so I urged her – and urged everyone in the family to urge her – to go for a check-up.

Mommy refused to go to the doctor until Karen was in Buffalo at college and Grandma at Uncle Phil's in Florida, both safely shielded from anything unpleasant.

"I don't like anyone making a fuss over me," Mommy said.

The medical consensus was that she needed a D and C, which Mommy explained stood for dilation and curettage.

"It's a scraping," she said. "They'll clean me out, like thorough cleaning the house. It's got to be done once in a while, like it or not, no big deal. Don't worry."

Mommy went into St. Luke's Hospital for a D and C on a Thursday, planning to stay overnight, return home Friday, and have the weekend to recover. I had an odd feeling that things weren't going well.

The hospital had strict rules about kids visiting, so Victoria couldn't join us, but when Daddy and I went to visit Mommy on Thursday evening, we learned she was in the Intensive Care Unit. That news landed like a blow. We tracked down her doctor and he apologized for not calling, told us he'd had to make a hasty decision once he saw she had a pre-cancerous condition overrunning her uterus.

"I take full responsibility," he said. "I saved your mother's life."

The ICU looked like a big, scary dormitory, a line of beds with tubes and beeping gauges and covered unmoving lumps, one of which shockingly was Mommy. We were only allowed to stay for a few minutes and had to agree to speak quietly. I remembered that Gramps arrived dead at this hospital and I immediately felt Mommy was going to die. My throat constricted and tears formed as a nurse led us to her bed. Eyes closed, inside a transparent oxygen tent, Mommy looked smaller than I remembered and totally helpless. Daddy held one of her hands. I went to hold the other hand but an intravenous drip scared me. I didn't want her to die. I stroked her fingers.

Her eyelids fluttered and she struggled to open her eyes but the painkillers were still working. "He had no right," she muttered so we knew she knew. "I never authorized a hysterectomy. This is a terrible time for me to miss work. I have reports due. I should sue the bastard, but I hate lawyers even more than doctors."

Daddy and I laughed briefly. Mommy moved her fingers, but didn't join our nervous laughter. She was obviously fuming, groggy, and in pain. If I hadn't been so scared seeing her like this, I might have asked why she wanted Karen and me to marry a lawyer or doctor if she hated them so much, but I wasn't in the mood to be a smart ass and anyway those kinds of contradictions typified Mommy, so I let it go. I forced a smile and mumbled words of encouragement telling her how lucky she was to avoid something worse, not daring to mention the c-word. Daddy parroted my message. She scoffed and blamed the doctor for not consulting her, then sank into drugged sleep again.

– ∞ –

Back at home, she lay on her side of the double bed and cried constantly. With Karen and Gram gone, and my cooking skills limited to Jello, chocolate pudding, and hard-boiled eggs, we were in trouble. Even though I wasn't throwing up, I still used the tape measure and scale every day and worried about my size. I'd resolved not to balloon up like Mommy and her brothers and the slightest deviation on the scale threw me into starvation mode. Daddy fried eggs and hamburgers a couple of times, but without vegetables or buns. Mostly he acted helpless. We all wanted Mommy to get out of bed and take care of us but she needed us to take care of her. She cried more than ever. We took turns emptying the bedpan and cleaning her up. It grossed me out, but I did it, soon worrying that she was going crazy because she smelled bad, looked witchy and unhappy, and wouldn't get out of bed.

Daddy, Victoria, and I began to eat dinner at Sam and Bill's Diner, and one night, after a big burger and fries, I felt so full and uncomfortable, I was sure I'd gained ten pounds and panicked. The ladies' room drew me magnetically. I told myself it was a one-shot throw-up, the habit had definitely not returned, and I would refuse to allow it back. I meant it. At home, we brought Mommy diner take-out, which wore on her. She barely ate. The dining room table overflowed with mail. Dishes filled the sink. Dust bunnies proliferated unchecked. We never even opened the blinds. Our house had become darker than ever, dreary and sad. Without people yelling at each other, isolation and emptiness ruled. I tiptoed to Mommy's bedside, turned on a lamp, and sat next to her. She'd been dozing lightly and opened her eyes when I sat down. Immediately they filled with tears. I kissed her damp cheek and smelled her sour breath. I was angry at myself for heaving dinner and I was furious at Mommy for staying in bed and burdening us. I imagined yanking her up, rolling her out of bed, throwing cold water on her head, smacking her. But I controlled myself.

"We really need you, Mommy. We hate eating out. You're such a great cook. We need you to get out of this bed."

"I'm sorry, Rowie. I'm having a hard time, feeling old, used up, and good for nothing."

"You're still in your thirties, Mommy. You're definitely not old or used up and you're good for just about everything." Then I added slyly. "Maybe you need another trip to San Francisco?" Why not use all the ammo I had? Her adulterous affair might guilt her into getting up.

She smiled for a split second, followed by a look of alarm. "You're not going to trot that out on me, are you?"

"I don't know, Ma. All I know is you're the mother of this family and you're not taking proper care of yourself the way a mother should. Don't you think it's time for you to stop acting as though your operation was the end of the world? Victoria and I are kids. We need our mother and that means you. What do you think? Don't we deserve our mother back?" I started to cry. "I'm sorry, Mommy, I don't mean to cry," I said. "I hate seeing you lying here weepy all the time. It makes me feel helpless and weird. I know you had a serious operation, but it's like you don't even want to get well. It upsets me."

"You're right, Rowie, I'm being self-indulgent, but I swear to you, I'm not staying in bed to hurt you and Victoria. I truly feel like I'm old and withered and that's the exact same thing as being old and withered."

"No, Mommy, it's not the same thing. You're only feeling old and used up because of your attitude about the operation."

"That's true, Rowie, but a hysterectomy makes a woman old and used up. You don't understand. I'm not a real woman anymore."

"You're not? What are you now, a fake woman?"

"No, don't be silly. I don't have a uterus anymore. I won't get periods anymore."

"For Pete's sake, Mommy, why is that so bad? You have three kids. Were you planning another?"

She sniffed and shook her head. Her gray hair hung in greasy clumps. I wanted to chant Adultery, Adultery, Adultery, but I restrained myself. I was furious and upset and determined to get her up. I went on.

"How long did the doctor say you had to stay in bed? When I had my appendectomy they forced me to walk even though it hurt. You sort of hobbled in when you came home. Now it's been more than three weeks and you haven't gotten out of bed. You've missed your follow-up appointment and you just lie here. Shouldn't you be walking every day?"

"I hate my life, Rowie. I don't want to get out of bed."

"You hate your life and don't want to get out of bed? I don't understand. What does that mean?"

"I've been a terrible, bitchy mother and daughter and wife. The only thing I do well is my job and I don't even have energy to get up and go to work. I don't deserve to live after the way I've neglected my family." Tears again. I held her small chapped hand. Her nails were jagged. I wanted to shake her and scream at her and tell her she was turning into a vegetable, but I contained my rage and fear.

"Mommy, listen, you had surgery and you have to heal. You haven't been terrible and you haven't neglected us. You're the only Mommy we have and we need you." My voice cracked. "We really need you! You take care of us with your job. You take care of us with your meals. We're proud of you. Please please, get out of bed and get well." Did I mean the words or was I lying? Maybe a little of both, I thought.

She asked for a tissue and I brought her some toilet paper since we were all out of tissues but Daddy had bought a huge case of toilet paper he got wholesale, I guess because of all the enemas, and now Mommy wasn't even enema-ing so I knew things were way out of control. She blew her nose and sniffed.

"Please," I begged. "Victoria is scared, Mommy. She's so worried she goes to the Liptons every chance she has and looks at those horrible concentration camp photos. She thinks you're going to die. She's having nightmares."

"I'm so sorry," Mommy said, crying again. "I'll speak to Sylvia about the photos. I'm sorry I've ignored all of you. I've been self-centered. I will try to change, Rowie. I'm sorry I didn't tell you I was proud of you for working so hard all summer and putting away college money and even making friends at the factory. I'm so sorry I nagged you every day. I'm such a bitch. I hate myself."

It scared me to hear her talk like that. I had thrown up my dinner and I suddenly knew I hated myself also. But I didn't hate her despite all the confusing things she'd taught me. I loved her. Still, I didn't want to be changing her disgusting smelly bedpan. At the moment, I didn't care whether she hated herself or loved herself. I wanted her up out of the sweaty bed. She didn't have cancer. She wasn't dying. It was all in her head. I took her hand and held it firmly.

"It's okay, Mommy. Don't worry. Just get well. Start by getting up. You have to force yourself to walk. If you stay in bed one more day, I'm going to ask Daddy to buy diapers for you. I'm scared I'll spill your pee-pee and cocky before I get it to the toilet."

"Oh, I'm so sorry for making you wait on me like this. Thank you, dear. Thank you for talking to me. I've been so lonely. You father doesn't talk to me. I miss Karen, I miss my father, and I probably shouldn't have sent Grandma to Florida. I'm sorry. I will try to get up soon. I promise. I just have no energy, and my legs feel like putty. I'm afraid I'll fall."

"Daddy and I will be right next to you so you won't fall. How about you get up and go to the bathroom and brush your teeth. You'll feel better."

She wept again. "Oh Rowie, I know you're too young to understand. I'm going to have to go through my change of life and I don't want to. The doctor messed me up. He had no right."

"He saved your life, Mommy. Please don't start that again."

"You're right. I should move on. I should get up. I know it."

"Yes! How about right now? I'll get Daddy and we'll help you to the bathroom. It's decided. Don't move. I'll be right back. Daddy's watching stupid wrestling. Better he should flex his own muscles."

She leaned on Daddy and me, and we dragged her to the bathroom. She shut the door. Daddy went back to the TV and I went to get a drink of water. Minutes later, we heard a shriek and flew to the bathroom to help her. We thought she'd fallen.

"Oh my God, I lost fifteen pounds!" she exclaimed. "I'm so excited! Sylvia's gonna be so jealous! I can't wait to try on my clothes. I think my fourteens will fit now." She hobbled to the living room couch by herself, stretched out. "I want you to make a shopping list, Rowie," she said. "I'll dictate and you write. You and Daddy can shop. It's time I taught you to cook."

– ∞ –

TWELVE

Like all my other beginnings, I began high school optimistically, determined to reform my eating madness. Every night I prepared a bag lunch with half a sandwich, and a piece of fruit, and bought a drink at lunchtime.

Newburgh had only one public high school, Newburgh Free Academy, which meant my modest little circle would be joining with all the kids from the wealthy neighborhoods near where the high school was located. I agonized seeing my ex-boyfriend Paul walking around entwined with the girl who I knew took her underwear off for him, Susan Levitz. My luck, Susan sat right in front of me in Latin class. I sometimes imagined bashing her head in or popping an ice pick into her spine like one of Raymond Chandler's killers. My favorite fantasy was unraveling one of her myriad Pringle pastel cashmere twin sets. I'd watch her stand up in her color coordinated Capezios, and I'd snip the yarn and pull, whirling her round and round until she ended up in front of everyone – ankle deep in a pile of pastel yarn – wearing only the infamous small-cup bra and panties I wanted to kill her for taking off. But I acted friendly to her face. It helped that I knew I was the best student in the class without even studying, and my breasts were stupendous. Yes, I was alone now, I philosophized, but I had great brains and boobs.

One of the happiest new beginnings in my life was starting lessons with my new piano teacher, number nine of the line-up of piano teachers I'd endured over the years, and the first one I'd found on my own. To Mommy, piano lessons represented one of the social graces a girl needed to marry well. Every once in a while, Daddy and I used to bang out oldies together on our untuned upright, our happiest moments. He played by ear and it seemed pretty magical to me since I needed sheet music. With financial hardships a constant, Mommy always sought bargains and chose piano teachers based on the best deals she could find even if it meant my switching teachers just when I was adjusting. Karen had out and out refused to take any more lessons at the first teacher switch, but I loved music and didn't balk at the endlessly changing cast. Maybe I was in denial, but I assumed changing piano teachers was like getting new classroom teachers and subs, and I accepted passively.

Around the time I discovered throwing up, age twelve, I had the misfortune to become a student of Mommy's latest bargain teacher, number six, Mrs. Jordan. It was the end of March, a cold, windy day when I took my first lesson with her, and I must have left a mitten on the bus because as it pulled away, I realized too late I only had one mitten. I held the paper with the new teacher's address in my bare right hand and slipped the hand in and out of my pocket, nervously checking the address and trying to keep the hand warm. By the time I rang the doorbell, my hand was chapped, stiff and chilled. I'd never seen a woman fill a doorway the way Mrs. Jordan did. I was five-six and she loomed over me, gruff-voiced with gray hair pulled into a tight bun and big square body encased in tight girdle. Could she be a man in disguise? She pulled me into her house, which opened directly into the living room.

"Quick, get in here. You're letting the cold in," she barked. "Take off your coat and hat and get to work. You're four minutes late. I expect promptness in the future."

"Well, it took a little longer because I didn't know which house it was," I said, rubbing my hands together. My right hand was red and stiff. The teacher before used to make me a cup of hot cocoa on cold days, but here I got no similar hospitality, which was probably why Mommy could save a few cents.

"Your mother said you would bring your Hanon exercises," she said. "Open your book to page 8 and play. Let's go." She clapped her hands a few times.

As I sat down at the piano and moved the bench closer, she turned on a metronome. I explained that the last teacher had me playing Hanon exercises slowly, lifting each finger to develop strength.

"Well, you're here now missy," she said. "Play the scales at a steady clip, like this." She hummed a scale, picked up a ruler, and moved it around like an orchestra leader, clicking with her mouth to the same beat.

I flexed a couple of times then began playing. My stiff right hand couldn't keep the tempo. Suddenly, out of nowhere, whack! Was I having a nightmare? The ruler landed on my right hand, a stinging blow on the knuckles next to the teeth marks from throwing up. I turned and stared at her, tears and questions in my eyes.

"Don't tell me that little tap hurt, missy," she said.

"It did hurt," I mumbled, pressing the back of my hand to my lips. "I don't think you should hit me." I spoke barely audibly.

"Close the book and just play," she said. "A simple C-scale, thumb-two-three-thumb-two-three-four-five."

I followed orders.

"Faster, faster" she said. "No, no, no, not thumb-two-three-four until you do thumb-two-three! Simple fingering. Your mother told me you've been playing for four years." She rapped the edge of a book of music with the ruler and it made a snapping noise that startled me almost as much as hitting me. Her eyes glowed and she smiled lopsidedly. I tried to remember how Mommy had gotten her name. Probably she saw an ad with a coupon. Nobody sane would recommend her. Wait till I tell Mommy about this, I thought. I'll never be back here. But on the way home, I realized Mommy might look at my hands and see the teeth-marks on the back of my right hand. Even though she knew I threw up, she couldn't possibly know how often. So I just said the teacher was horrid and I hated her. For the next few months, I conveniently got sick on Thursdays so I could miss piano lessons. Secretly I thought maybe I was being punished for throwing up and I did my best to play with a minimum of errors. Finally, one afternoon my lesson had been pushed to a later hour and Mommy came to pick me up and met Mrs. Jordan for the first time.

"Why didn't you tell me about her? Mommy asked when we got back to the car. "She's big and scary. I don't believe she was ever married. She may even be, you know, queer."

"I've been telling you for months, Mommy," I said, uncomfortable with the queer label, but kicking myself for not having thought of it myself. "She's horrible and I hate her."

"We'll find you somebody else, dear," Mommy said. "I don't want you returning to that monster. I'll ask around."

Fortunately, Dawn, Mom's hairdresser raved about Tony, a pop teacher, who would give us a special price for half an hour and come to the house to teach me, thereby saving bus fare. Tony, who was originally from a town in New Jersey called West New York, which I thought was hilarious, taught me all the chords to "Stardust." I played the song so well, I got a job playing in the lobby of the Palatine Hotel on Saturday afternoons even though "Stardust" was the only pop song I knew how to play. Mommy said it sounded schmaltzy, but I could tell she liked it by the way she hummed along. I was working on Tony's next selection, "Your Cheatin' Heart," when both Tony and Dawn left their current spouses and ran off to Las Vegas together. Mommy fumed, but quickly found a new hairdresser whose grandmother happened to be a retired music teacher. That's when I began lessons with ancient Mrs. Henning, bent-over, hearing-impaired and ninety-something, who smiled sweetly at everything I played and probably never heard a sound because she didn't give me a word of guidance. I stayed with sweet Mrs. Henning a couple of years, during which I learned very little, but enjoyed her high praise. When she keeled over and landed in a nursing home, Mommy was ready to give up on me and my piano lessons, but I liked playing piano and wasn't ready to quit even if I had to pay for lessons myself.

I found Jimmy's ad in the *Newburgh News*. A Julliard graduate, thin, blond, handsome, sensitive, in his early thirties, Jimmy and I connected instantly. For only three dollars an hour, he gave me great music to play, Mozart, Schubert, Beethoven, in addition to basic exercises I'd gotten from the long line-up of teachers over the years. He sweetly called my rendition of "Stardust" jazzy and cool and said he would have hired me himself. But we agreed to work on classical pieces.

Every Tuesday afternoon, I went straight from school to Jimmy Wilson's home studio on Broadway, a walk of about a mile, rain or shine. As I approached Jimmy's building, I felt exhilarated just anticipating our meeting. How could one person make me so happy? Always beautifully dressed in slacks and colorful shirts and sweaters, Jimmy would greet me with a big smile and a pat on the arm or the back. He was my idea of the perfect man, so easy to be around. I adored him. Finally, I had the right piano teacher.

"You're a natural, Rowie," he said. "Just the way you sit and approach the instrument is so perfect, I'd like to invite all of my students to observe you, not playing, just sitting and getting ready to play. The way you hold your wrists and hands is classic. Just beautiful."

"Thank you," I said, beaming.

"You know," he said, "There's something special about you. When you're here, I feel particularly good. I think you might have had past lives as some kind of healer as well as composer and pianist."

"Past life?" I said, blankly. "What's that?"

"It's based on a theory that we've all lived before. It's called reincarnation. Haven't you heard about Bridey Murphy? Under hypnosis, a woman in Colorado remembered her past life in Ireland. She knew Irish jigs and songs and even streets and neighborhoods in Cork she couldn't have known any other way. They're making a movie about it. Also, a lot of people I know believe Christine Jorgenson was a woman in a past life and that's why she couldn't adjust to being a man and had the operation. In your case, I think you know intuitively how to hold your hands because you've known in the past."

"Well, I've had eight other piano teachers."

"True, but it's more than that. You're a natural. There's something about your connection with music that's very deep. I can feel it. You haven't been trained properly so your playing reflects that, but...I don't know. I'm guessing if you practiced eight to ten hours a day, you'd be able to compete with the best. I mean it. You were a musician before." I shot him an incredulous look. Was he serious? Could I have been Mozart or Beethoven? Chopin, maybe?

"Do you really think I could be good, Jimmy?" I asked.

"You tell me," he said. "How do you feel at the piano?"

"I love how I feel," I said dreamily. "I feel comfortable, sort of like being with my best friend. When I play, I lose track of time and the music becomes part of me. It's a wonderful feeling. I sure wish I played better. Like you, Jimmy. I could listen to you play all day long."

"Thanks," he said and laughed. "I'll bet you and I knew each other in a past life. You have a feel for music, Rowie, a natural talent. You may not be destined for a musical career this time around," he said. "But as long as you enjoy it, it doesn't matter where it leads. Just keep playing and feeling good about it. Don't force anything because then you might get to hate it. Look at me. I thought I'd play at Carnegie Hall but instead I'm on Broadway in Newburgh...."

"I'm sorry," I said, interrupting him.

"...on Broadway in Newburgh, teaching a wonderful girl named Rowie," he said, his blue eyes twinkling. "Rowie, you have to learn to let me finish my sentences. Sure, I miss living in the Village, and traveling around the world, but I don't regret for a minute my career change because if I'd stayed in New York, I wouldn't have met you, and I love having you for a student."

"I love having you for a teacher," I said. "You're the best."

"Okay, enough of our mutual admiration society," he said, smiling. "Let's hear what you've done with Schubert this week."

– ∞ –

Inspired, I practiced daily on our old upright, going over and over sections until I felt I'd progressed, often amazed to find three or four hours had passed. Maybe I could work up to eight to ten hours a day and be a concert pianist! Tuesday became my favorite day because of my piano lesson. Jimmy and I laughed a lot during my lessons, sometimes laughing together at the errors I made. I wasn't even close to playing like him, but I could feel my technique improving.

The first time I got upset over a run of missed notes during a lesson with Jimmy, I couldn't stop apologizing. Sorry, sorry, sorry, I echoed, feeling like a klutz. When I thought I'd messed up, I automatically panicked. I began to cry as I apologized, adding embarrassment to fear. I crumpled forward, feeling like a shameful loser.

"Relax, Rowie. Mistakes aren't bad," he told me, handing me a box of Kleenex. "They're just necessary steps on the way to getting where you want to go. Mistakes guide us to know where to improve. For example, when you miss notes, lots of times it's because the fingering doesn't work and needs changing. See what I mean? We wouldn't know that without the mistakes. They're teachers and we have to welcome them and honor them. Remember that. Now you repeat after me: 'Mistakes are teachers. They help us to learn.'"

I laughed through my tears and repeated, "Mistakes are teachers. They help us to learn. Some of my teachers were mistakes themselves," I said and told Jimmy about mean Mrs. Jordan. He cringed and said it probably wasn't easy being a large woman and we had to feel empathy for her. That was a new point of view for me.

When I thought later about mistakes being teachers, I remembered that Grandpa had taught me to accept mistakes the afternoon he sat on the porch patiently watching me learn to ride my bike. I crashed down over and over, skinned my elbows and knees and kept right on going until I could ride smoothly. But I didn't make the connection with other kinds of mistakes. Mistakes as teachers. Hmmm, I thought, I'd have to tell my parents that one.

Jimmy was far more than a piano teacher. I trusted him and felt happy just thinking about being with him. I had never seen a place like Jimmy's sunny studio on Broadway. The concert grand Steinway had a magnificent mellow tone. Two cornflower blue velvet couches were the most comfortable seats I'd ever sunk into, and I fell instantly in love with the fabulous Persian rug with its intricate red, blue, and gold design and dark blue medallion. The lovely oil paintings of beach scenes he told me a friend of his had painted. I felt completely relaxed in this wonderful open space. I loved going there.

Jimmy never talked down to me or stared at my breasts the way other men did. He had a gentle way of showing me how to improve without criticizing. In just a few months, my playing progressed dramatically. I didn't have to think about the notes my fingers hit. They seemed to move all on their own as though every finger had a little brain inside. I handled complicated chords I'd never imagined I could manage. What joy being able to create such glorious sounds! The music transported me. I gently swayed back and forth rhythmically as I played beautiful music and merged with it. When I hit a snag, Jimmy stopped me, I played the section again, we identified and analyzed the problem, and found a solution. It made perfect sense.

I was practicing extra hard one Monday evening when Mommy interrupted me.

"You might as well stop practicing. Your lessons are over."

"What are you talking about, Mommy?" I asked. "I'm not giving up my piano lessons."

"Your teacher is dead."

My stomach immediately knotted. I felt a lump in my throat.

"Mommy, you're scaring me. Stop saying that."

"He got what he deserved. He must've said something perverted to the wrong guy."

"What?" I stared at Mommy through tears. I couldn't talk.

"Jimmy Wilson was murdered over the weekend. They found his body in an alley next door to a bar."

"No, it must be a mistake. It must be someone else." I said, and resumed playing a loud scherzo, reading Jimmy's notations through tears.

Mommy stuck a folded up newspaper right in front of my face blocking me from reading the music. She could have been sticking a snake in my face. She pointed to a brief article.

"Face reality," she said coldly. "Read between the lines. That man was a disgusting pervert. We were giving three dollars an hour to a queer. Better than that bull dagger creep a few years ago because at least you were safe from this one. He didn't like girls."

I grabbed the newspaper, threw it at her, banged as hard as I could on the keyboard with both hands, slammed the lid down, and crying inconsolably, ran to my bed.

A few minutes later, Mommy came and sat down next to me. I was lying on my stomach with the pillow over my head, my futile attempt at privacy. I had no more tears, just dazed confusion.

"Rowie," she called softly. "Rowie, I want to apologize to you. I was out of line. I'm sorry your teacher was killed."

I rolled over and stared at her. "How could you be so cruel, Mommy?"

"I don't know, Rowie. I don't know. Something came over me. Maybe hormones. That was horrid of me. I went too far. It's just, well, I know how common these perversions are because Kinsey said one in ten men in America...." She shuddered. "But I just can't accept it. It's so repulsive it makes me sick. I'm very sorry I allowed you to study with him. I hope you'll forgive me. At least you've stopped crying. When you cry, it makes me feel terrible."

"I loved Jimmy, Mommy. He was a wonderful teacher. He taught me not just about music, but also about life. Things you don't begin to understand. But it's not your fault. You're ignorant and prejudiced. I'll try to forgive you." I fought back tears. "But I'm still very upset. I'd like to be alone now. Do you mind?"

She stiffened and controlled her rage. Mommy rarely yelled. "I am a liberal. You don't know what prejudice is if you think I'm prejudiced. I'll chalk up your impertinence and name-calling to your shock, Rowie. But I still believe people get what they deserve. A *faygeleh* who walks into a bar on Water Street is asking for trouble."

She patted my hair and I wiped the spot as though she'd soiled me. I wanted to tell her how disgusting I thought she was. My mother actually believed Jimmy deserved to die! My crying upset her! I lived in a crazy house with a crazy woman. My usual solution - puking my guts out - was all I could muster except this time I had a plan.

Pretending to bond with Mommy, I sat with her at the dining room table as we both shoveled in snacks of cheese and crackers, potato chips, or bags of cookies and milk. I knew I could stay thin while she'd balloon back to her fattest and hate herself. I felt satisfaction knowing I was punishing Mommy each time I threw up. Somehow that comforted me.

– ∞ –

The rest of my sophomore year I spent more time at home than in school. What had been minor asthma worsened, compounded by chronic bronchitis. I went to school on Mondays, took all the tests I'd missed, aced them, and stayed home the rest of the week. I did all my schoolwork and much more. I read stacks of library books, lots of fiction and psychology, hoping to figure out the meaning of life. I'd already read the complete works of Freud and now added Adler, Horney, Fromm, fiction by Sinclair Lewis, Harold Robbins, Somerset Maugham, Ayn Rand, just about every novel that hit the bestseller list mixed in with heavy psychological theory. I didn't understand everything I read, but some things jumped out at me like Maslow's hierarchy of needs.

I had food, clothing, and shelter, but I didn't have safety except when my parents were out of the house. I belonged to the Wine family on the surface but I didn't feel like a full member. I had fears and anxieties. I had lots of deficits and Maslow said that was good because if every need were fulfilled, a person would have nowhere to go, nothing to strive for. That helped me a little. I was fulfilling my own needs by staying home from school. My parents didn't care as long as I got good grades. So I schooled myself with no particular direction, just by reading dozens of books and listening to lots of music. It hurt too much to go near the piano. I played Grandpa's opera records as well as our one Broadway show album, "Oklahoma," which I learned by heart.

I danced around the house, ate whole boxes of crackers, drank pots of tea, threw up, ate more, threw up more, read, slept, and put together an isolated existence. Sometimes I visited with Grandma but I told her I was on a diet so she wouldn't try to get me to eat. My parents and my friends thought I was a genius since I got good grades without going to classes. I figured I got good grades because I didn't go to classes. At home alone, it was easier to concentrate and I breezed through the work effortlessly. I didn't have to see Paul and Susan every time I turned around. Paul had filled out and was cuter than ever and it seemed to me that Susan gloated around me, and I hated hating her.

Dorothy and Greta came over at the end of each week to bring assignments and my corrected tests from Mondays and share some gossip, but I had little interest in anyone or anything. I missed Jimmy. I began musing about his life and death.

I thought a lot about Mommy's attitude toward homosexuals. There was an effeminate boy in my class named Stephan and we called him Stephanie - which I was part of initiating, thinking I was funny at the time. Now I thought, so what if he liked boys? So did Jimmy. I hadn't known, but if

I had, would that have changed my feelings for him? I'd reprimanded Mommy, but was I any better? How did people learn to accept others? By getting to know them. The problem was we usually steered clear of people who were different from us. Was my taunting Stephan any different from Mr. Hoenig next door calling me a "dirty Jew bastard" when I was little? Isn't this how Germans allowed millions of their Jewish neighbors to die? What about the horrid things black people endured, slavery, beatings, lynchings? What about the genocide of Indians in both North and South America? Weren't they all related? My dear Grandpa didn't think his daughter Pearl, my mother, deserved a college education because she was female. Daddy's math teacher didn't think he deserved good grades because he had his own faster way of getting answers. What did all these things have in common? They all made people feel bad about themselves. I felt bad about myself because I lied and kept secrets.

Why was weight so important? I had hated being an overweight little kid. Losing fifteen pounds had motivated Mommy to get back to a normal life. Now she was just as fat as before thanks to me and I was right that she'd be miserable about it. She agonized daily. How come no one ever talked about the oppression of fat people? In *Brave New World* by Aldous Huxley, where people had lots of sex the way Mommy said it was going to be in the future, and babies grew in factories, which Mommy rejected as absurd – brain-washing and human engineering insured that fat was as obsolete as motherhood. All classes, Alphas, Betas, Gammas, Deltas, and even moronic Epsilons reacted with shock and hilarity at seeing a fat person as though they were viewing a clown meant to amuse. Were we brainwashed in less overt ways, by Hollywood and advertising images? Why did I become a more valuable commodity when I got thin? I wanted answers.

– ∞ –

One Monday, after school, at the library to exchange my pile of books, I happened upon Sir James Frazier's *The Golden Bough*. The volumes, loaded with descriptions of customs, rituals and practices of ancient people from all around the world, were in the reference section and weren't allowed out of the library. Checking the index, I found a couple of entries for vomiting, which predated the Romans, who I knew ate to excess and then vomited. Frazier wrote about ritual purification related to harvesting the first new corn of the harvest. The Seminole Indians of Florida, in practicing the Green Corn Dance, drank an emetic and purgative, which was supposed to clean their systems of old food to make way for new.

The next day, they ate new green corn, followed by a day of fasting. The fast assured that ordinary food would not pollute the sacred corn. The day after the fast, they feasted. Frazier surmised that these rituals related to the spirits of the food which ancient people worshipped. Fascinated, I read on. When I looked up fat in the index, I found instead a section on ritual fasting of teenaged girls, practices common around the world and related to fear of menstrual blood. Practices included segregation in cold cages, encasement in hammocks, huts, caves and towers, prohibitions on touching the ground or seeing the sun, beatings, and starvation. As I read, my imagination took off. Grandma had smacked Karen in the face when she first menstruated. Daddy had given me deodorant powder in a can, which grew in my imagination to be ten feet tall. Could I be tuning into something far more ancient and expansive than I realized, something from a past life? Maybe throwing up was keeping away evil spirits of some kind? I vowed to pay close attention and learn.

_ ∞ _

One afternoon when Dorothy had come over to bring me schoolwork and keep me company for a while, we were sitting quietly on the big couch in our little living room watching boring TV news headlines, waiting for American Bandstand. For no particular reason, I stood up and threw a punch toward the TV anchorman. At that very moment, he flinched noticeably. His head drew back as though someone had aimed a flying object at him.

"Did you see that?" I excitedly asked Dorothy.

"I did. That's totally weird," Dorothy said. "Can you do it again?"

"I don't know. You try too."

We stood throwing punches toward the TV but nothing happened. Still, I couldn't get that moment out of my head. When I asked my parents about it, they said it was just a meaningless coincidence and I should stop being superstitious and imagining crazy things. But from then on, I was attuned to other strange coincidences. I'd think about speaking to Greta and she'd call seconds later. Or I'd flash on Uncle Jacob who we hardly ever saw and next day he'd arrive for a visit. Once I dreamed about a green sweater and received a green sweater as a gift next day for no reason except that it had been left at the cleaners unclaimed and Uncle Sid brought it to me. No one ever thought there was any importance to any of these coincidences, so I stopped mentioning them, but that didn't mean I stopped paying attention.

One Friday night I dreamed I was sitting in a rocker on a high branch of the oak tree in front of the house when lightning struck and down we toppled, branch, rocker and me. Panicked, I awoke. It was storming outside, heavy thunder and rain. Sweating, heart pounding, filled with an unexplainable ache as though I'd been belly-punched, I cried myself back to sleep. In the morning, oak leaves and branches lay pressed against the window. Struck by lightning during the storm, our beautiful oak tree, which apparently had weakened from some sort of disease, had fallen over and uprooted. When workers removed it and carted it away, the house looked naked and vulnerable. I ached. First Grandpa, then Jimmy, now my tree. Was Death stalking me? Would I be next? I didn't tell anyone about the nightmare. But I wondered, since my parents thought it was superstitious and even crazy to pay attention to things like this, could I be going mad? Did other people have the kind of uncontrollable imagination I had? Did evil spirits have something to do with this? Could I be causing death around me?

I hated feeling sad, scared, and guilty. When I ate a lot and then threw up, my mood instantly improved. Therefore, using simple logic, I continued to pig out, preferably with Mommy, and then threw up. The good mood didn't last as long as I would have liked so I needed to eat and throw up again. And again. And again. Whatever it took, I intended to purge unhappiness from my life.

– ∞ –

Since I'd completed all tests and homework assignments, my teachers promoted me even though I'd missed weeks of attendance. Warm weather lured me out of the house. I walked all over the city, even venturing to Jimmy's building and checking the doorbell and mailbox, which had a new, strange name posted. I decided to get a summer job in a store and went into one after another asking for work. In a children's clothing store a couple of blocks south on Broadway called Kids Stop, the owner, Ira Silver, hired me on the spot for fifty cents above the new minimum wage of a dollar. Now I'd save even more money for college.

– ∞ –

Married and forty, a tall, round, jolly bear of a man, Ira Silver immediately saw me not just as a fifteen year old, but also as a talented business asset. He gave me lessons in his version of selling basics, and I caught on quickly and loved how powerful it made me feel. It didn't occur to me that I had the same kind of job as Daddy.

Ira taught me that people needed guidance. They don't know what's good for them. We help them to be happy. We help them make choices. We sell them satisfaction and happiness. We sell smiles and generosity and good looks and all things good. We lead people where they actually want to go but don't always know it so they need a little push to get there. We provide a service to humanity.

Girls who came in with or without their moms for clothing always gravitated to me, and I patiently let them try on as many outfits as they wanted, cheerfully rearranging them on their hangers afterwards. They began coming in as an activity, with Kids Stop as a destination. Sales increased. I got a raise of twenty-five cents an hour. Ira began talking about a store where he could specialize in preteen girls' gear and call it Teens Stop. Guess who he had in mind to run the place! Yes, me! I loved his appreciation for me. I was still eating and throwing up, but it was just a normal part of my life. No big deal. I had schoolwork, clubs, friends, a job, books, music, and my secret habit. I was a busy girl.

_ ∞ _

As high school progressed, I was popular and a top student. I laughed a lot, joined clubs and then criticized their policies once I was in. I particularly hated what I saw as hypocrisy around me and became an intrepid champion of the underdog known for my outspoken boldness. The world reeked of injustice, so I had plenty of targets for my rage. My unusual views drew both admiration and irritation. I liked annoying others. It set me apart. I still didn't know how to hug like Victoria or flirt like Karen, but I told myself I didn't want anyone close because I had a secret to preserve. So I cultivated rebellious behavior.

_ ∞ _

During the Christmas shopping season, before my sixteenth birthday, as a family favor I worked for my cousin Rosie Fine, in her small department store on upper Broadway near Fullerton Avenue. Mommy told me blood was thicker than water and I had to help Rosie because she had lost money in Daddy's pocketbook factory. Ira Silver at first burned with fury, but later said he would forgive me if I promised never again to leave the store during the holidays. He even hugged me, a big bear hug that felt great. He hugged all the girls who worked for him, but still I felt special.

The Saturday before Christmas, continuous chaos reigned at Rosie's store. Everyone rushed around. From ten in the morning until nine at night, I waited on customers, gift-wrapped, and arranged merchandise, all without a break except to drink water and pee. By the time Mommy picked me up at 9:15, my legs ached, stomach groaned, and brain pounded relentlessly behind my eyes. I envisioned a small snack, couple of aspirin and sleep. The cold weather bit nastily, and I shivered as I climbed into the front seat of Mommy's old Dodge.

"Let's go to Crowley's for ice cream," she chirped.

"No, Mommy, please, let's not. I'm wiped out. Just please take me straight home." I held my head, wishing the pain would stop.

"I'm dying for a chocolate ice cream cone, Rowie," she said.

"I can't believe you're doing this to me, Mommy. Why didn't you get ice cream before picking me up?"

"Because I thought you'd like an ice cream cone after working so hard all day."

"Well, you thought wrong, Mommy. It's eight degrees, and the last thing I want is ice cream. A cup of soup maybe. Won't you please just take me home? I beg you."

"Just one short stop for ice cream and then straight home," she insisted.

I was too tired to fight and too hungry to resist any kind of food.

At Crowley's, Mommy said, "I've changed my mind, I'd like to eat here. I feel like a hot fudge sundae and I can't drive and eat, so I'll have to have it here. I'm so bad."

I surrendered. We sat at a table and I ate a small bowl of butter pecan. Immediately I wanted to throw up, but I was even too tired for that.

We pulled up in front of our house after ten. I felt cold, sweaty, exhausted, bone weary, aching.

I walked in the door of the dark living room, and a flash went off in my face. Someone had taken my picture. "Surprise!" came the loud shout. I was seeing spots so I put my hand up over my eyes. Laughter followed. Lights snapped on. Who were these people stuffed into my little living room and dinette like clowns from a circus taxi? They were a bunch of kids from school I hardly knew, the rich kids, snotty sorority girls, rich boys, plus Dorothy and Greta and a few boys I'd known for years from my neighborhood. Thankfully, Susan Levitz and Paul were not among them or I might have killed either them or myself. The girls were wearing lovely Lanz dresses with layers of crinolines and had perfect make-up, nails, hair and jewelry. The boys sported nice shirts and slacks. None of these kids had holiday jobs. I wanted to fall through the floor, make myself invisible, blank them out. I felt sick. My birthday was in two days, and I could wait.

Mommy was gleeful. "Come along, Rowie, come and wash up and change into a party dress, dear. Daddy and I are making burgers. You didn't suspect a thing, did you? I'm sorry I had to fool you with the ice cream ploy, but they needed more time." She announced to the packed little room how she dragged me to Crowley's. Everyone laughed politely.

She had a whole clean outfit waiting for me, including nylons, stiff dressy heels, a horridly uncomfortable tight and itchy black wool dress I hated, a slip, panty girdle and long line bra that went over the hips known as a waist cincher that should have been called a pincher. She was excited about loaning me her pearls. Pearls from Pearl. I was thinking, she's a shit and I want to give her shit. I want to give all these shits in my living room shit. In the tiny bathroom, on the verge of tears, I perfunctorily washed my underarms and crotch, took a couple of aspirins, and dressed myself in the party gear Mommy thought appropriate. By the time I reappeared in the living room, all of the rich kids were filing out the door, leaving to go to a party in a spacious finished basement where they'd have room to dance.

"Happy birthday, Rowie," they chimed as they marched out.

I was mortified that these kids saw where I lived. Now they knew my family was poor. I wanted to mow them all down with a machine gun so they couldn't be around to bear witness.

A handful of boys and my closest girlfriends were still there. My parents had cooked enough hamburgers for the whole original crew and couldn't believe how the place had emptied out.

Since it was late, before anyone else left, Mommy brought out the requisite cake loaded with candles. She had baked it herself. My wish was for everyone to go home and let me sleep. I blew out the candles and everyone clapped. Someone snapped my picture.

The boys were eager for me to open presents, which had been stacked on the piano. They were snickering as they handed me the biggest one. At last, something exciting, gifts just for me.

"Be sure to get a shot of Rowie's reaction to this," said Phil Pear eagerly. Sammy Field readied his camera. The boys couldn't suppress laughter.

I pulled the paper off, festive red and green like what I'd been using all day long to wrap gifts. It was something heavy, rolled in a layer of newspaper. I eagerly pulled the newspaper off. When I saw it, I was too incredulous to react. I stared at it in silence. Was this really happening? Then it hit me. I burst into tears and ran out of the room to my bed, lay down and sobbed. They had gotten me a painted plaster statue of a fat, old, naked Native American Indian woman with disproportionately gigantic, pendulous breasts hanging down to her bulging stomach. My first reaction was to hit smiling Phil Pear in the head with it, but, as usual, I wimped out from acting on my violent fantasies. Then I thought maybe that was exactly what I looked like. They must have gotten me the statue to send me a message. No wonder Mommy told me to wear cinchers and girdles. I was a fat pig.

I lay on my bed with the pillow on my head but still I heard them calling me. "It was a joke, Rowie!" and "Come back, we're sorry, Rowie." I didn't want to move. My legs, body and head ached more than ever.

Mommy came in and insisted I get up because the party was in my honor and she'd worked all day cleaning and baking and getting ready. Dorothy and Greta came in and sat on the bed and cried with me, apologizing. Victoria came in and sat on the other side of the bed and told me she loved me. The bra and girdle were digging into my body. I felt humiliated, ashamed, exhausted, deformed.

Daddy came in with a shot glass full of bourbon. "Here, Rowie, drink this, for medicinal purposes."

"Daddy," said Victoria, "I can't believe you're giving Rowie liquor! It's illegal."

"Buddy, that's terrible," Mommy said. "Take it away."

"No," I said, to be contrary. "I'll drink it. Thanks, Daddy." I downed it, letting it burn my throat and esophagus. I forced myself to stand up. I stuck a smile on my face and went back out to the living room with my girlfriends. The boys were chowing down burgers, sodas, and cake, banging on the piano, and playing records. "Life is but a dream. Shaboom, Shaboom." They began to apologize for the statue again, now standing tall on the piano, but got stuck in hilarity instead, and doubled over with laugher.

"Shut up, you assholes," Dorothy said.

"You're babies," accused Greta. Phil mimicked a crying baby and got Greta laughing too.

"Laugh if you want to," I said. "I'm not in a party mood. I know some of you mean well and I don't want to seem ungrateful for the party, but I worked a long day, and I'm going to bed now. Good night."

"No, you can't leave, Rowie," someone said. "It's your party."

"Can't I? Watch me." I got up and announced my moves before making them. "I'm turning around now. I'm walking away now. I'm going to open this door to my room and then I'm going to slam it and it's going to be loud and shake the whole house and my dad is going to be angry and I don't care. From the far side of the door, I raised my voice slightly, "Now I'm saying 'Good night.' Good night."

– ∞ –

THIRTEEN

Ira Silver was getting ready to open his new teen store and begged me not to let him down or go running off to help my cousin during busy season since he counted on me. Meanwhile, on a whim, I returned to the Palatine Hotel on Grand Street and talked the manager into hiring me to play background music again. I promised to diversify my repertoire, not that he cared. I hated our old out-of-tune upright and had the brainstorm to get access to a baby grand and get paid for it. I had just discovered jazz and the freedom of improvisation thrilled me. When I listened to Thelonius Monk, Miles Davis, Dizzy Gillespie, and other musical geniuses, I felt stirred like never before. Jazz seemed to fly me to worlds I'd visited as a small child. In a corner of the lobby, flanked by large potted plants which gave me an illusion of safety and privacy, I experimented and discovered I could play just about any song by ear, at least the melody, and by adding a few chords and fooling around with riffs, I found all kinds of thrilling combinations. People came up to me behind the plants and smiled and applauded.

At home, I sat at our scratched, old out of tune upright and improvised. Playing around, I called it, to differentiate it from playing. Daddy hadn't played music with me for a long time, but one day he sat down next to me on the piano stool and soon we were jamming on old song medleys. "A Bicycle Built for Two," "School Days," "My Merry Oldsmobile," "After the Ball." We kept going for hours, laughing, singing, and playing one song after another, all sounding vaguely alike. It wasn't anything like Thelonius Monk, but it was fun.

"You're good at this, Rowie," he said and put his arm around me. I was happy, but I bristled at his touch. Why did my father creep me out?

"You're good at it too, Daddy," I said and, nearly burst with happiness and confusion.

– ∞ –

I stretched time starting in my junior year. I was the new manager of Teens Stop, the small preteen clothing boutique on Water Street Ira Silver had set up with me in mind. I opened the shop after school for a few hours and weekends all day. When I couldn't be there, Teens Stop stayed closed. After our glittering grand opening with pink lemonade, cookies and balloons, young teen and preteen customers continued stopping in, usually dropped off by their mothers who went on with their own shopping while the girls tried on whatever they wanted without their moms pestering. Not only did the shop become a girls' clubhouse, but also the merchandise moved well. My specialty was training bras, training little girls to cover their small macaroon cookie mounds with miniature versions of their mothers' bras, like playing dress-up. I'd watch them, their eyes gleaming excitedly, looking in the mirror in their tiny bras, and I'd tell them how grown-up they looked. I sold dozens and dozens of triple-A bras. I was Ira Silver's heroine, making Teens Stop an overnight success. People thought I was a competent, charming, funny, happy girl. I continued to get top grades and participate in school plays, glee clubs, and sorority. I quit the hotel job, but still played around on our old home piano. I liked the way my family hummed along with me and acted happy when I tinkered with the keys in simple ways.

– ∞ –

Ira and his wife Sophie invited me to their house for dinner one Saturday night after work. They had renovated a turn of the century Victorian on Grand Street with soaring beamed ceilings, gleaming oak floors, exposed brick and white walls adorned with Sophie's paintings, huge splashes of primary colors. I had never seen a space like theirs, open and inviting with soft indirect lighting and comfortable spare furnishings. Their dinner plates were all hand thrown pottery in bright geometric patterns. Sophie was vegetarian and Ira omnivorous. She'd prepared a big green salad and both a bean stew and chicken Marsala, and gave me a choice of entree. I asked for a little taste of both, said I didn't eat much.

"You'll change your mind when you try Sophie's cooking. She's a master," said Ira, rubbing his large middle, reaching for Sophie's expansive bottom. They both seemed okay with their size, which surprised me. I'd never heard either Ira or Sophie talk about dieting, and wondered why since everyone dieted. Mommy and her friends had gone gaga over my calorie free coffee soda invention – instant coffee, saccharine and club soda – which I'd even submitted to Coronet magazine but never got a response. Sophie and Ira were drinking wine, which I knew had to have calories. How strange that they didn't seem to pay the slightest attention to their weight.

Sophie brought a green salad to the table in a curved, high-sided teak bowl. I felt very sorry I'd accepted this invitation. How could I be relaxed? I wanted to stuff myself with this delicious looking food. I was hungry. But I didn't dare. It was a trap and I knew it.

"Really, Sophie, when I say a little, I mean it. Please give me a tiny portion."

"How about some salad, Ro?"

"A little bit," I said, and carefully picked at my food, using the knife to cut the lettuce into the smallest pieces I could. I thought I'd better explain. "I'm really sorry, Sophie," I said, and, it was true, I was sorry I was about to lie. "I was so hungry earlier I couldn't wait and I ate a big sandwich, so my appetite isn't what it should be. I hope you forgive me."

"No problem," she smiled. "I'll give you some to take home in case you get hungry later."

"Great," I said, and I meant it. I liked eating in private so I could do what I wanted afterwards.

Ira and Sophie had invited me to dinner to offer me a full-time job managing a Teens Stop store they proposed to open at a new mall in Poughkeepsie. They thought malls were the future, and they wanted to include me in their plan for continued success and prosperity.

"But I have to go to college," I said, stunned that they would even consider an alternative.

"You can do both," Ira explained. "My brother worked his way through Brooklyn College, and Sophie worked while she went to art school, right honey?"

Sophie nodded.

"We want to be direct," she said, bringing out a chocolate layer cake that made me faint with longing. I didn't dare touch chocolate since the Oreo fiasco. "We think you're a very talented girl, and we're prepared to compensate you handsomely. You will be able to afford a nice apartment and your own car. We want you to join our team, Rowie. It's a ground floor opportunity."

Ira grinned as he took a big bite of chocolate cake and blew Sophie a kiss of approval. He gulped it, downed a tall glass of milk, poured more, and kept grinning. "Rowie, we think you're a phenomenally talented young woman who will go far and we're prepared to reward you the way you deserve, with no prejudice whatsoever to do with your age. We expect you to think it over and we ask that you give us a fair chance. We know how your mom feels about your going to the college of her choice, Rowie, so we advise you to make up your own mind. It's your life, after all, isn't it?"

I felt dizzy. What were these two talking about? My own apartment in Poughkeepsie and a job in retail? Didn't they know my life had a plan? The plan was to go to Barnard. Mommy had spoken to me about going to college since I was conceived, maybe even earlier if that was possible. I couldn't imagine anything else for an instant. My mind simply couldn't consider alternatives, and I was getting uncomfortable with their sales pitch. Still hungry and a bit weak, I thanked Ira and Sophie and got up to go. Ira insisted on driving me home. I accepted. Riding next to him would be a treat.

I could tell he was searching for words I could understand.

"Rowie," he began. "Sophie and I are concerned about you."

"Don't be silly," I interrupted. "Please don't be concerned."

"Well, we care about you. We think you are not eating properly and we're worried you might be getting yourself sick."

I almost fainted. I thought, how can this fat slob have the nerve to tell me I'm not eating properly?

"Ira, I'm fine. Actually, it's funny you should say that because I was thinking that you and Sophie have an eating problem. You're both pretty overweight, wouldn't you agree?"

"I guess I asked for that one, didn't I?" he said, chuckling. "It's not about being fat or thin. It's about being unhappy. Sophie and I want to help you with your body image."

"You two help me with my body image?" I was amazed and scared. I wanted to get out of the car even though I wasn't home yet. "Just because I didn't eat much you think I have a bad body image? I told you I ate dinner before I got to your house. Didn't you believe me? Are you calling me a liar? I don't like that, Ira, I'm telling you right now."

"Oh, Rowie," Ira said. "I'm sorry if I upset you. That's the last thing I wanted."

We were approaching my house. I could feel my face, flushed hot in mortification. I wanted to tell Ira I thought he was a fat pig but I couldn't. What I could do was quit my job! Did I have the nerve?

I got out of the car and held the door open. I imagined what I wanted to say flash before me.

"Ira," I would say. "I'm sorry to tell you, I don't have time for work anymore. I'm much too busy with activities I'll need for my college applications next year. You'll have to find someone else to run Teens Stop. Thanks for everything. Mail me my last check, okay?"

Instead, I thanked him for dinner, told him the Poughkeepsie deal was out of the question, slammed the car door and ran into the house. I was good at my job, and I wasn't going to leave until I was ready, even if the Silvers were onto me.

– ∞ –

The second week of senior year in high school, I heard about the Friday night Hi-Y dances I would have heard about two years before if I hadn't been so focused on my job, schoolwork, and the extra-curricular activities I not only enjoyed, but expected college admissions people to lap up. Along with getting top grades, I was writing for the city paper, acting in school plays, doing a school radio show, and loving every minute because being so busy kept me from remembering the unhappiness of my 'real' life. In spare moments, I'd been to a few Jewish Center Intercity dances, but I was tired of long bus rides to Rochester and Binghamton and thought it was time to visit the Y where so many of my non-Jewish classmates went. Over the dinner dishes on Thursday, already in pajamas and robe, my after-dinner deed accomplished, I asked Mommy for permission to go.

"Jews don't go to the Y," she said. "Especially not on Friday night. Wait for another dance at the Jewish Center. You'll feel more comfortable."

"Come on, Mommy," I said, "You mean you'll feel more comfortable. I am comfortable, which is why I want to go. I've been to lots of Jewish Center dances. I'm ready for a change. It's not as though we're religious."

She wagged her soapy index finger at me, so I knew a lecture was coming.

"Listen to me," she said. "You can fall in love with a gentile or a Jew. Since you're Jewish, it's smart to find a Jewish boy. If you go where there are only gentile boys, you'll be selling yourself short."

"Mommy, I'm not going to Hi-Y to fall in love, I'm only going to dance."

Finger again. "That's what you say now, but what will happen is you'll go, you'll dance with a boy, you'll dance with him again...and again, he'll walk you home, and next thing you know you'll have a *shagitz* boyfriend. That's how it works. I saw it with Karen. Wait and go to a dance at the Jewish Center. You'll do the exact same thing, but with a Jewish boy."

"Come on, Mommy, I want to go to the Hi-Y dance tomorrow. I don't see why it's so important that I go out with only Jewish boys. I think that's prejudiced."

"And on Friday nights, too. It's Shabbos, Rowie, this is the worst possible time to go to a dance with gentiles."

"Oh, please, Mommy, all of a sudden, you're observant? You don't believe in God. You serve bacon and eggs for breakfast. You don't light Shabbos candles. Are you saying on Saturday night it would be all right?"

"I didn't say that."

"Mommy, do you trust me? Because you know very well I could spill that old secret I guessed about San Francisco."

She pulled herself up straight. I could tell by the way her eyes were moving around as she looked up toward the ceiling that she was pondering this. I knew that she knew she had to trust me. I could bust her with Daddy with one word. Adultery.

"Of course I trust you."

"Then trust me to go to a Hi-Y dance."

"All right, you have my blessing, but for heaven's sake, use discretion."

"Yeah, right, Mommy, discretion," I said snottily, gave her a quick kiss on the cheek and bit my tongue so I wouldn't call her hypocrite.

– ∞ –

For the first part of the dance, I felt like a wallflower. The only time I danced was with Dorothy. Boys kept Greta busy every dance. I watched her and other petite girls getting lifted and tossed around during the jitterbug, and I thought what fun they must be having, and I wished I could have fun dancing with a boy too. A slow Johnny Mathis number came on, "Chances Are," and I began watching couples swaying romantically. I was wondering whether I'd ever experience this when I felt a tap on my shoulder. I turned around and there stood the handsomest boy I'd ever seen, grinning down at me from his six feet plus height, asking me to dance. My heart turned upside down as he took my hand and firmly glided me across the floor.

"I'm Skip," he said.

"I'm Rowie," I said.

"I've heard of Zoë, but you're my first Rowie. The prettiest girl in the whole place," he said, and held me closer. What a neat liar, I thought.

We danced silently and I listened to the words. He dipped me at the end and held me tightly and securely.

"I know you," I said as his face brushed mine. "I think we had a past life together."

"In Atlantis," he said, smiling.

I felt my eyes widen. "You know about reincarnation?" I was stunned.

He nodded. "My mom's into Edgar Cayce."

– ∞ –

We danced together for the rest of the evening, fast dances, slow dances. Skip had blond crew cut, all-American boy looks. He asked to walk me home and waited while I went to the girls' bathroom. I could tell my face was flushed with excitement. My friends gathered around and pumped me for information.

"Who is that guy?" asked Greta. "He's gorgeous but he seems old."

"He's in the Air Force. He's an interesting older man, twenty-three. He's planning to go to West Point next year. He knows all about past lives! I'm sure I know him from a long time ago."

"Are you crazy? Your mother will kill you for going out with him. He's obviously not Jewish, he's in the military and he's...he's... all grown up," said Dorothy. "I'm sure he even shaves."

"I don't care," I said. "My mother can't touch me. No other boy ever paid this kind of attention to me. Not even Paul. I think I'm in love. Skip says we know each other from Atlantis. He's teaching me all about a sleeping prophet named Edgar Cayce."

"Is that like 'Casey at the Bat?'" asked Dorothy.

"No," I said. "It's a whole different world, all about psychic stuff and past lives, all the things I've dreamed of and more. Everything my family hates. I love it."

– ∞ –

Skip Christian's real name was John Christian, but I told Mommy his last name was Smith. Why did he have to have that name? What would his parents think if my name were Rowena Gay Jewish? I didn't want to be prejudiced so I focused on him and not his name. Tall, broad-shouldered, and adorable, Skip had peaches and cream skin and baby blue eyes. For the first time ever, I didn't feel huge. He was from Virginia Beach, an airman at Stewart Air Force Base, where Mommy worked, and he intended to be named a candidate to West Point. I let him walk me home and next thing I knew he was my boyfriend. Mommy got that one right.

Skip was so polite and respectful, I knew Mommy liked him despite her misgivings. We dated all that fall and through the winter. Without even realizing it, I stopped throwing up. It seemed normal to eat and digest, speak on the phone to my precious boyfriend daily, and see him on Friday and Saturday nights. I happily juggled our relationship along with schoolwork, job, newspaper column, radio show, and all the preparation for college. We went to dances at the Y Friday nights, movies on Saturdays, and afterwards hung out on our living room couch and made out. We kissed and hugged and spoke endearingly to each other. And we left all our clothes on.

On New Year's Eve we went out with a big crowd of kids to a club with live music. Susan and Paul were there, and I caught Paul staring at Skip with interest. What a burst of satisfaction warmed me! I was wearing a new outfit, the prettiest dress I'd ever owned, soft brown silk with subtle shiny gold threading, sleeveless, low square neckline, fitted to the hips and then flared wide, perfect for dancing. I'd dared to get dressed with no cincher or girdle – Mommy would have *plotzed*. Not to mention I had on new strappy brown high heels and didn't even feel big and klutzy. We danced non-stop, and as I whirled I saw only him, perfectly clearly, in a background of fused, blurry faces and bodies. I was overjoyed and comfortable, believing either I'd found a fellow alien or maybe I wasn't an alien after all. Maybe I was a pretty and lovable girl.

– ∞ –

Our favorite song was "Love Me Tender" sung by Elvis, which we played over and over on my little 45-rpm record player. We set it up in the teeny kitchen and spent many evenings dancing in place, slowly and romantically. Victoria spied on us from the bedroom doorway by the Bendix, but we didn't mind.

Surprisingly, Mommy began lending us her jalopy for our dates, and that gave us a place to make out. I loved kissing, hugging, and stroking, and I was now letting Skip put his hand into my blouse and play with my nipples, and slip his hand under my skirt and into my panties. I moaned and panted with excitement and had giant orgasms without knowing any labels to put on what was happening. Soon Skip started begging me to let him make love to me all the way. But the very idea of seeing or feeling that part of his anatomy I didn't dare even name terrified and embarrassed me.

Here I'd been soaring with pleasure and joy, and suddenly terror intruded. My confusion frightened me. I loved Skip's tall, fit body, perfect musculature, slender waist, graceful hands. I loved his bright mind and the way we freely exchanged ideas about the universe. He'd had psychic experiences and told me more about the life of Edgar Cayce, and brought me a book about him called *There Is a River* by Thomas Sugrue. On the one hand, I found the book astounding. Edgar Cayce had learned the contents of his school books by placing them under his pillow and literally sleeping on them. He could go into trances and diagnose and provide cures for sick people. I believed he was for real. But then the book described how Edgar Cayce was a devout Christian, and I thought maybe Skip was bringing me conversion literature and got scared. In my house, defensiveness against anti-Semitism kept us vigilant and suspicious of Christians, who, Grandma warned, might turn on us at any moment like what happened in the pogroms back in the old country, like the Holocaust under Hitler.

People treated Edgar Cayce like a pariah, suspected of tricksterism, and accused of being a fraud. But those he healed, many whom conventional medicine had given up on, praised him as a miracle worker. Skip said his mother visited the Cayce library in Virginia Beach regularly and attended Cayce study groups. I talked to Skip about some ancient customs I'd learned from *The Golden Bough*. He listened with excitement as I told him about my conversing with trees and punching the TV set and all the other experiences like sensing who was about to call just before the phone rang and flying to other worlds as a child.

"My mother would say you're psychically attuned," Skip said. "You say things I'm thinking. Maybe you were a Delphic oracle in a past life. Maybe you're a healer. I always feel wonderful around you."

"Maybe you're the psychic one," I said. "Maybe you think things even before I do because you're reading my mind."

"Accept your gift, Rowie. Don't run away from it."

"Gift? I don't have a gift. I have a curse." I explained my theory that I'd been a witch in a past life and cast spells on people. I conjectured that Daddy's spankings were his paying me back for hurting him in a past life.

"If you're a witch," Skip said, "then I'm in love with a witch. Maybe I was a toad and your kiss woke me up. Your dad must never lay a hand on you again. I will save you."

"That's okay," I said. "I've saved myself." But I didn't dare tell him how.

– ∞ –

FOURTEEN

I was so scared about Mommy's confiscating the Cayce book that I stashed it in the cellar with the well-worn old porn book and read it secretly. Along with fascinating explanations of Cayce's amazing and mysterious powers, the book made it clear that most people were not ready to accept such phenomena. Cayce was seen as a fraud, yet he maintained his faith and humility even in the face of challenge after challenge from non-believers. According to the book, he simply went to sleep, received information, and spoke it aloud to a secretary who recorded it in a form known as "readings." Not only did he heal people through readings, but he also communicated a system of metaphysical thought derived from ancient mystery schools, which included reincarnation, souls, auras, astrology, thought forms, one God who created it all and Jesus as the true Son of this God. The short chapter that summarized all this overwhelmed me. Instead of getting clear from this infusion of new ideas, I got more confused than ever. Wasn't this just another set of superstitions? As a Jewish kid, I had asked many questions about religion and never gotten a satisfying answer.

Was God like Santa Claus or the tooth fairy, both of whom I knew were my parents right from the beginning? Were my parents then God? How come the Christian god had a son who also was God but there was only supposed to be one god? Who was Jesus anyway? "A man who never guessed he'd get so famous," Mommy once deadpanned. Grandpa said Jesus was a brilliant rabbi whose teachings got changed by politics. What? Jesus was Jewish? So God was a Jew? Wait, who was God again? Gram told me, "You don't need details. Just pray and He'll hear you." According to everyone I asked, God was definitely a He, and probably old, pale-faced, white-haired and whiskered. Sometimes he was called the Lord, which could be that white-haired father Lord God or the son Lord Jesus who had long wild curly black hair and a bushy beard. God Junior had died gruesomely, nailed to a tall wooden cross, because of the sins of everyone else. What an amazing guy to take the rap for everybody! But how could everybody be guilty? And if he'd taken away everybody's sins, how come he'd left such a messed up world? This made no sense whatsoever to me. Such confusion. If someone had given me a coherent story, I might have swallowed it, but instead I continued to ask questions.

What did it mean to be Jewish? Why keep kosher? Grandma and Grandpa had kept separate sets of dishes for dairy, meat and Passover. Just before Passover, they emptied the whole house of anything not kosher for Passover. Even the tiniest bread crumbs had to be swept away. But downstairs in our apartment, it was enough to buy a few boxes of matzoh and get bread out of the house. I'd been to Hebrew school briefly, learned how to decode Hebrew sounds and letters without knowing the meaning of any words except *Baruch Atah Adonai*. In the Orthodox synagogue, girls didn't get Bat Mitzvahs so girls didn't have to go to classes if they didn't like them, and I didn't like them so Mommy was relieved not to spend the money.

We read some Bible stories and colored in pictures. I hated old Abraham for taking his son out to kill him because he heard God's voice telling him to - even though he didn't have to in the end. Would my father kill me? He used to hit me pretty hard. Did God tell him to? No, Mommy gave the orders. Joseph and his coat of many colors was the Bible character I identified with even though I was a girl. He was a good kid and his brothers sold him into slavery and pretended he was killed. What a betrayal. But Joseph got his satisfaction later when he became the Pharoah's prognosticator. So was Edgar Cayce like Joseph? Was I like them? Sometimes I got messages from somewhere. I saw Grandpa in the tree just before he died.

Was I a good Jew? Did I have to stay Jewish? How important was it to fall in love with a Jewish boy? Was I "sinning" being in love with Skip? What did it mean to be Jewish? I liked eating kasha varnishkes and borsht with sour cream and lots of other Jewish food. Would I have to give them up? I liked seders but what I liked best wasn't the ritual stuff - much too long for me - it was the food and visiting with my cousins I hardly ever got to see. I didn't really like going to *shul* because I didn't have clothes as nice as the other girls, and with Grandpa gone, I had no desire to go. What would Mommy think if she knew I had an imaginary Sky-mother I liked better? Was I committing the sin of worshipping idols? If so, did I care? Was I just a bad person, maybe never to belong?

As I read the Cayce book, a strange feeling swept over me, not that Skip had corroborated my normalness, but rather that I'd hooked up with another weirdo alien freak. I'd almost been fooled. I quickly dismissed this scary thought, but felt a residue nagging at me.

At home, Mommy had a mission and a message she advertised non-stop, like commercials on TV, which were growing in popularity. Over and over, this same woman who had lectured me for years to "sleep around" now drilled into me her new message: "I know you'll do the right thing about Skip, Rowie. Remember you could jeopardize your college education if you do the wrong thing. You're a senior in high school. You'll be going to college soon. You could ruin your whole life. Don't do the wrong thing, wrong thing, wrong thing. Do the right thing, right thing, right thing." Her voice echoed in my brain. Right thing, wrong thing. My mother's mixed signals were only part of the confusion. There was something else scaring me, something deeper I couldn't remember. I began to freeze when Skip and I kissed. I preferred conversation.

He and I talked for hours about Edgar Cayce, metaphysics, and reincarnation, decided we'd been souls together in Egypt, Rome, Greece, even the Old West of our country. Skip had been brought up more spiritual than religious, and he was certain there was an organizing power, a Deity of some kind doing the organizing. I told him about my dream experiences in the glass palace with Sky-mother and the little angels, and he understood although in his world it was an Earth-mother and Sky-father. We held each other, silently gazed into each other's eyes, and felt a numinous connection pulling us together, merging us. We told each other we were One Being and felt our hearts melt together. Skip spooked me when he spoke about getting married and living in a sweet house with a white picket fence out in the Virginia countryside, with horses, dogs and a houseful of kids. I couldn't stop Mommy's words from reverberating in my head. I thought how could I be so happy? I couldn't possibly deserve this. I was a bad girl, allowing this older man to touch my private parts. I was so bad. This was wrong. This was going to ruin my life. I wasn't meant to marry a soldier. I was destined for a lawyer, doctor, or PhD. Mommy must just look at me and know I was doing the wrong thing. I had to do the right thing.

One day, after a long and juicy conversation, Skip and I began to make out. He massaged my nipples and kissed me and let his hand stray to my clitoris. I reacted with an orgasm so intense that I ejaculated a flood. I had never heard of female ejaculation and thought this was one more piece of evidence that I was a freak. But Skip liked it. He explained orgasms to me. I'd still totally avoided touching him below the waist.

"That is so beautiful, Rowie," he said. "You're amazing. Please let me make love to you and come inside you, baby. Please. I need you."

"I can't," I said. I was terrified. I knew I wanted to but some colossal block got in the way and threatened me like nothing had ever threatened me before. It was too big and scary to even talk about. It felt as though his penis would kill me, and I had to save my life. I couldn't let myself see or feel or have anything to do with this weapon, and I didn't know exactly why.

Next day when Skip called to arrange our weekend date, I told him I could never see him again. I spoke coldly, all my feelings extinguished.

"What are you talking about, baby?"

"You heard me," I said.

"Rowie, have you gone insane?"

"No, I've gone sane," I said.

"I'm coming over to see you right now," he said and hung up.

I told Mommy I'd broken up with Skip.

"Congratulations, darling," she said. "I always knew you'd do the right thing."

"But I'm so scared, Mommy. He's coming over to see me. I don't know what to do." I began crying.

"Be strong, Rowie. You have your whole life to meet the man of your dreams."

"Skip is the man of my dreams, Mommy," I said. "I'm in love with him. I just know I don't deserve love. There's something wrong with me."

"Don't say that," she said. "That's ridiculous. You're not in love with him. It's just infatuation. He's not in our league. He's in the military for heaven's sake. You'll get over it. It'll be like it never happened."

Skip was ringing the doorbell moments later. He looked serious, anxious, upset.

"Rowie, honey, what's the matter? Did I do something? I'm sorry, baby, if I hurt you. What's going on? Talk to me. Please. I love you." He reached to hug me. I pulled away.

"I have nothing to say to you," I said. "I don't love you. I don't know what love is."

"Rowie, this can't be happening. We're soul mates. Talk to me." He sounded desperate. I looked at him as though he were on another planet, as though there were an expansive distance between us with a transparent wall in between. I was numb. He was a stranger now. I noticed his ears were pointed.

He'd borrowed a green car and left the driver's side door open in his haste to see me. Now, he climbed back in, looking devastated. I stood and watched from planetary remoteness, the only feeling a pressure behind my eyes from unshed tears. He pulled away from the curb. I ran into the house. First I stuffed myself with spaghetti Mommy had cooked, along with slice after slice of bread smeared thickly with butter, then drank warm water and threw it all up. It looked like gooey worms filling the toilet. I went to bed after that, climbed under the covers and felt myself getting progressively weaker. My energy was dwindling, as though my life force flowed out of a hole in my heart.

Mommy came to my bedside and spoke harshly.

"Get out of bed this instant, Rowena Gay Wine," she said. "Cut out this drama. There is nothing wrong with you. I called Dorothy and Greta and told them I was treating you all to a movie. You're going to the movies, do you hear me? Get up now! Cut out this lovesick crap! You did the right thing. Don't be ridiculous. Get up now!"

She pulled the covers off me and kept scolding. Her voice got louder and louder.

"Stop!" I screamed. "Leave me alone! Go away! I hate you!"

"You will get up now, do you hear me? You will get up now! You'll learn who loves you. Only your family can love you! We know what's best for you. Get up out of this bed. Buddy! Buddy! Get in here now! I need help getting our Academy Award winning actress out of bed."

Daddy came in. They both looked mean, like prison guards who were about to haul me off to solitary. He took one of my hands and she took another and they pulled me out of bed, both yelling at me. I tuned out their words, just saw red, scowling faces filled with anger and hatred. I couldn't fight any longer. I went limp. They dragged me into the living room and pushed me into a big soft chair.

Dorothy and Greta showed up. Robotically I got into Daddy's car and went with them to the Ritz to see a movie I didn't watch at all. I cried during the entire show. Afterwards, as we passed the coffee shop hangout, I spotted Skip at the counter looking pale and drawn, smoking a cigarette. He wasn't even a smoker.

"Oh no, there he is!" My heart pounded wildly, my head throbbed, tears streamed down my face. I was petrified I'd run straight into his arms and be lost. In a panic, I ran downstairs to the ladies' restroom and made Greta call my house and get my parents to come and get me at the back door immediately. When she came back after calling, I made her stand outside and wait for them while I hid in the ladies' room. My parents didn't come for an hour because they didn't want to miss a minute of Ed Sullivan. I cried and cried in the bathroom. I was filled with pain, guilt, and confusion.

"Rowie," Dorothy said, as we stood in the small ladies' room. Her eyes looked huge and concerned behind thick lenses. I was sniffing and blowing my nose with rough paper towels, exploding into tears over and over. She patted my back and hugged me. "Rowie, why did you break up with Skip if you're in love with him?"

"I was afraid I'd go all the way," I said.

"But if you love him, what's wrong with it?"

"I could get pregnant and ruin my future." I sniffed.

"You could use protection, you know."

"I don't know about that," I said. "All I know is my mom says it's wrong and I'm scared."

"I think you made a mistake," Dorothy said. "If he was Jewish, your mother wouldn't be so against him. Didn't you tell me your mother said sex was a good thing?"

"She used to say that all the time. But it's not her fault. It's mine. I hate myself."

"Rowie, don't say that."

I exploded. "Goddamn it, I'm sick of people telling me not to say what I want to say. If I hate myself, I can say it. I hate myself, I hate myself, I hate myself."

Greta stuck her head in the door of the ladies room. "Coast is clear and your dad's here," she said. "Around the back. Quick." I ran to the shiny red Pontiac for cover, crying all the way.

– ∞ –

Like déjà vu, or a long-running play, or a stuck record playing over and over boring the hell out of me, the hated addiction was back, stronger than ever. I was eating quarts of ice cream, boxes of crackers and cookies, loaves of bread, dozens of bagels and muffins, pounds of butter, gallons of soda, all of which I forced right up and went back for more. I didn't need a finger anymore, just a slight gag and out cascaded the whole mess, avoiding my taste buds altogether. Mommy bought extra food and asked no questions. But there was never enough. I went through coat pockets for change, emptied my piggy bank, stole a few dollars here and there from Mommy's purse, withdrew some of my college savings. I had to have food. Mommy seemed to leave money forgetfully lying around regularly, which I quickly appropriated. She didn't mention missing it even once. I escalated my favorite pastime of sitting with Mommy at our little dinette table and munching crackers out of a large variety box along with some kind of cheese spread. She kept up with my eating, cracker for cracker. I smeared hers especially heavily with cheese. She shoveled them in one after another, unconsciously, in rhythm with me. She was fatter than ever, wearing tent dresses every day. That gave me enough motivation to put on a happy face in the world. I was miserably unhappy but I sought and found distractions to fool everyone, including myself.

– ∞ –

Since Grandpa's death, Grandma's health had deteriorated. Even avoiding cold winters didn't help. She still got her hair and nails done once a week and cooked kasha varnishkes, brisket, chicken soup, and her other specialties, filling the whole house with aromas I struggled to resist. Somehow vomiting up Gram's meals was sacrilegious. On Sundays, I often sat with her and Victoria and picked a little at my small portion as they ate and Gram told stories of the old country between bites. She recounted her childhood adventures as the youngest of thirteen, the gardens, horses, rules she broke and the pogroms that terrorized their little *shtetl* of Snitkov in Belarus. She told us how she'd had a crush on Grandpa from the time she was Victoria's age and she secretly followed him to America and almost died of pleurisy on the boat. She told us she missed Gramps and was getting ready to join him.

"He waits over there for me now," she said. "He's with the rest of the family. Our parents and brothers and sisters. They're all in a kosher deli. They saved me a seat."

"How do you know, Gram?" I asked. How could people joke about dying? And was I going to face more food issues after I died? No way!

She shrugged. "Do I know how I know? I know what I know I know. How I know I don't know."

– ∞ –

This take on life and death particularly interested me after all the talks with Skip about other dimensions Edgar Cayce had contacted in his sleep states. It comforted me to be with Gram as she spoke easily about what she called "passing over." I myself now seemed less able to contact other realms, unable to fly or even imagine flying. I never saw Sky-mother or angels anymore. The more I devoured and brought food up, the more I seemed to sink into a morass of numbness. Something sticky held me down like walking in boots on spilled molasses. The closest I could get to other dimensions was listening to Gram's stories. Victoria and I both hung out with her whenever we could.

One day she told us of "the man with the black bag" who used to come around every month to "help" women of childbearing age who needed help.

"I wasn't going to have a family large like I grew up in," she said. "*Gevalt*, no, I couldn't because strong like that I wasn't even close enough. We didn't have then the kind of protection that now you have."

"Gram, you used to tell me you miscarried five times. Was that the truth?"

She shook her head. "I had help, Rifkele," she said slyly using my Hebrew name again.

"The man with the black bag?"

She nodded. "He used to travel the Hudson Valley like a saint helping married women like me, already with kids enough. If it hadn't been for him, I'd be long dead. You know why? Because your grandpa and I, we would have killed each other. I wasn't going to sleep with him anymore." She laughed. "I tried all kinds birth control. Herbs and spices, sponges, compresses, counting days, even spells. The only thing, which it worked was to stay away from Grandpa, may he rest in peace. Thanks God for the man with the black bag. He saved our marriage and our lives."

"Wasn't it illegal?" Victoria asked.

"Yes, but this saint, he got away with it. He kept clean and everyone knew he was doing a *mitzvah*. Nowadays, you girls you're lucky, it's a new world. You have all kinds birth control. You can plan now your families."

"Can you tell me about birth control, Gram? I know there's something called a rubber but I don't know about anything else and I don't even know how that thing works."

"Very simple, dahlink. It's a rubber glove for the *shlong*. You're too young to be asking. Just behave and you won't have to worry."

"What's a *shlong*, Gram?" Victoria asked. I was glad because I didn't know either but was too embarrassed to ask.

"Oy, this is what happens when there's no boy in the family. A *shlong* is a man's organ, girls. His, whatchacallit, penis."

"He puts a glove on it?"

"Ask this to your mother. I don't know no more." She waved her hand dismissively.

"It doesn't matter," I said. "I'm never having a family. I'm going to stay single forever."

"Rifkele," Gram said to me. "You'll find a nice boy to marry some day. I'm going to tell you now a secret." I smiled and nodded. "I liked that boy of yours, the *shagitz*, Skipper. I disagreed with your mother about him. I thought he was a mensch. You could have stayed with him and maybe been happy. You should stand up for yourself even if it means disagreeing sometimes with your parents."

"But Gram, he wasn't Jewish."

"*Nisht gehferlekh* – not so terrible," she said in Yiddish and shrugged. "Life, it doesn't always happen like we'd like." She got teary. "I wanted to go before your grandpa, but here I am and there he is. Instead of homemade chicken soup, he has to settle for eating out."

I wanted to get hysterical crying and laughing. Emotions welled up. I thought, great, now she tells me she was on my side with Skip. How stupid I was to reject love! It was love! That's just exactly what I do with food, reject it. If I don't deserve food and I don't deserve love, then I don't deserve life. Maybe I should go with Gram to join Gramps. Except she's telling me there's food over there too. Hell's bells! I can't win.

As though she read my mind, Gram said, "You should live and be happy until eighty-seven years old too, not a day earlier. Girls, listen to Grandma, I'm getting close to saying to you goodbye. Be happy for me. Like when I go to Florida, this is a Florida farther away."

"We don't want you to go, Gram," Victoria said. I agreed. We both were teary.

"It's not so good to hold on, dahlinks. When God calls, we have to listen. You girls, live a good life. Don't fight life and life won't fight you.

Rifkele, eat more, stop with the diet already, thinner don't get, and stop biting your nails." She wrinkled her nose. "They look bad. If you let them grow before I go, I promise I take you to my manicure girl." She held up her perfect raspberry nails. "You are both going to have a good full life. Victoria, *sheyn meydele*, don't expect you'll dance forever, a good brain you've got too, a *Yiddishe kawp*. Rifkele, don't worry. Even if you made mistake with the Skipper, you'll see, there's something good waiting. Take courage. Make, how do we say, careful choices. Gramps and I will look out for you from over there."

_ ∞ _

I had a dream in mid-April. Grandma and Grandpa, holding hands, delivered my Barnard scholarship letter to me, kissed and hugged me, then laughing and flirting with each other, grew younger and younger until they were little kids, and danced away along a path that wound into the mountains. I saw no kosher restaurant.

I knew when I woke up that Gram had gone. She'd died in her sleep, peacefully. Mommy and Daddy hugged. How come the only times in my life I saw them hug was when somebody died? The very same afternoon, I received my acceptance letter from Barnard with a generous financial aid package. My dream reassured me that Gram knew and was happy for me.

_ ∞ _

As usual, during mourning, food arrived and filled every surface in the kitchen. But I wasn't tempted. Sometime when I wasn't looking, I had substituted starvation for eating and vomiting. But I still ate my fingernails and almost drowned myself drinking water.

I got thinner and thinner at the end of senior year. Hunger filled me with virtue. I wore loose clothes so my ribs wouldn't show. I still got high grades and kept up the job and club activities. Somehow I made it through, even giving a commencement address at graduation. I leaned against the podium so I wouldn't fall down. No one seemed to notice. I put on a great act.

_ ∞ _

FIFTEEN

Scholarship students were required to work for the college, which was okay by me, former factory worker at fourteen, store manager two years later. They assigned me to the snack bar at the student center, which got busy at lunchtime selling fresh sandwiches. I had to hurry from English class in the next building to my locker in the student center, grab my salmon polyester uniform and brown hairnet, change in the bathroom, and get to work.

Girls clustered frantically in front of the counter three and four deep, raising hands and voices, competing for attention. I worked with a woman in her sixties, Margaret Kelleher, from Rockaway Beach, who had been making sandwiches for Barnard girls all her adult life. Margaret had a bright pink nose that clashed with our salmon uniforms, brown-stained teeth, lots of wrinkles, an easy laugh, and an uncanny ability to stay calm under intense pressure. While I was in English class, Margaret served a few early birds in between making and wrapping tuna, egg salad, and turkey sandwiches for the rush to come. She and I also made sandwiches to order, on toast or rolls, with tomato, onion, or extra pickles.

"Just take it slow and steady," Margaret said to me, first day, her green eyes twinkling. "These girls bitch and scream every day as though they'll drop dead if they have to wait another minute. Don't take them serious. They all get lunch. If they don't like it here, they can go to Chock Full O' Nuts. They don't get no tuna with lettuce, tomato, onion and mayo on rye toast over there. We're working with sharp knives and we can't afford to rush. I don't think nobody would want a finger sandwich." She held up her left hand. Her thumb was missing the last joint. I winced and mumbled sorry.

The counter was the boundary between madness and calm. Margaret and I moved slowly, steadily, and deliberately. Hungry girls clamored for service. Dorm students from out of town, like me, ate in the dorm cafeteria two buildings away and were oblivious to the busy snack bar scene. In contrast, these students lived at home and commuted to and from school on jammed rush hour trains where pushing ensured survival. They dressed respectably in sweaters and skirts, topped with coats and hats, and carried heavy bags of books, papers, and other supplies for the day while dorm students tended to wear jeans and sweat shirts and carry a couple of notebooks and pens.

126

After the first few days of classes, I began to know the names of some of the girls who sat near me. In English class, Professor Thomas used last names, and had arranged the seating alphabetically so I was in the back row, seated between Miss Weinstein on one side, and Miss Winter on the other. They were both commuters, dressed neatly in pressed and matching clothes. I liked both Naomi Weinstein, petite, with dark curly hair and a thick Brooklyn accent, and Rachel Winter, a tall, lithe blond from Riverdale who was training to be a professional dancer. We began exchanging friendly comments before class, but I never had time to speak after class because I had to run to work.

How thrilled I was to see Rachel and Naomi show up at the snack bar around the third week of classes. They were waving and yelling for attention like everyone else when a space opened and suddenly Rachel was sitting on a stool right in front of me.

"Hi, Rachel!" I said brightly as I assembled a tuna on rye.

She stared at me blankly.

"Rachel, hey, it's me, Rowie Wine, how you doing?"

She said sourly, "Are you going to take my order or what?"

Despite all the commotion, Margaret moved close to me, turned around so her back was to the counter, and said, "Rowie, your mouth is open so wide you could catch flies. Don't take it personal, dear, they don't even recognize their best friends behind this counter. It's the uniform and this thing." She pointed to my hair. I'd forgotten I was wearing a hairnet. Then she patted my arm and grinned. The girls were yelling louder than ever, furious that we had taken a moment to talk to each other.

My pocketbook factory summer had alerted me to separation of people by class and I hated it, although I was grateful for the awareness. Not everyone was so fortunate. My journey from English student to counter girl caused instant image transformation, like an actor assuming an unpopular role and catching hell for it.

Rachel whined for her order and I began making it. A roach scurried across the cutting board just as I was slicing her egg salad on toast in the shadow of the high counter. I laughed out loud as I contemplated slipping it between the bread slices. She'd probably think it was celery. I resisted and eased the sandwich onto a plate, got the drink to complete the order, and took Rachel's money.

"I sit next to you in English," I said, as I handed her the change. "You talked to me twenty minutes ago."

She stared, then grinned. "I didn't recognize you," she said. "You look completely different."

"Yeah, I'm disguised as a worker."

I wanted not to take it personally as Margaret advised, but I didn't succeed. It disturbed me. A few weeks later I got a transfer to the swimming pool, where my job was to give out towels. It was hot, steamy, boring, and smelled of chlorine, but with my face in a book, and no special outfit, my classmates spotted me right away as one of them. I didn't feel like one of them, but at least I could pass successfully.

– ∞ –

I was on Seven Hewitt, a floor of single rooms. It was the first time in my life I had my own room. I was in Room 757, with a window facing the red brick wall of Brooks Hall. The day I moved in, Mommy was horrified about the brick wall, but secretly, I was thrilled. There was a sink in the room and I saw right away the cave effect would give me total privacy.

Slowly, the first week, girls on our floor bonded. I was getting to know Sheryl from Tulsa, Patricia from Boston, Ginny from Richmond, Lydia from Baltimore, and Sara from Tucson. After a conversation in Sheryl's room about T.S. Eliot's poetry, never having heard of T.S. Eliot, I knew for sure every other girl was smarter and more informed than I was. Plus, it didn't take long for me to believe I must have been the only virgin in the bunch.

I spent hours alone in my little room, smoked cigarettes whenever I felt like it, binged, puked into plastic bags, masturbated in front of the mirror, listened to jazz on the radio, stared at the brick wall outside my window, and generally contemplated my life. I suspected if my family said they loved me, it was because of what I had achieved, not because of who I was. They knew nothing about love. Gramps and maybe Gram had been the only ones who cared about me and Gramps didn't respect females all that much so I didn't rate as high as a boy would have. Even though Mommy had been a strong student longing to go to college, Gramps wouldn't send her although he sent her brothers who didn't want to go and eventually all flunked out. That's why Mommy insisted her daughters all go to college and pushed Karen hard when she had no interest. Now Karen was a grateful college senior in upstate New York. I appreciated that on some level but resented that my parents treated me like something they could show off and brag about, sort of like a cushiony green lawn or a Congressional Medal of Honor. I was angry. I'd satisfied Mommy's goal by getting my ass to Barnard. Now, I would put a decisive end to achieving. I would do nothing of merit. I would punish them by getting shitty grades, good enough to pass but poor enough so they couldn't brag. If Mommy or Daddy craved information about my exciting college experience, I'd make up stories to satisfy them. I would tell them exactly what they wanted to hear, all lies. A charade. How delicious!

I had a jolly time inventing stories about a freshman year Mommy would lap up like chocolate sauce. I concocted a Jewish law student named Harvey Bottel, who adored me. Bottel was my little joke because I knew Mommy would ponder my becoming Rowie Wine Bottel. The Bottels were from Orange, New Jersey and had vast apple orchards. Did she suspect anything strange about a family of apple cider Bottels from Orange? No, instead she loved my letters so much she told me she was saving them to publish as *Letters from a Freshman*. My first work of fiction I spent hours writing every day.

I joined no clubs. I did minimum schoolwork. The college had a 1:30 AM curfew and I interpreted that to mean I had to stay out until 1:30 every night. I hung out at the West End Bar, pretended to sip beer, and was proud that no one guessed I was a Barnard girl since Barnard girls were considered snooty and uncool by the drinking crowd. Guys always asked my age and when they learned I was 17, they told me to wait until next year. I had no idea what that meant since I was already drinking beer. Wait for what?

In January of my freshman year, Mommy got her Associate degree from Mid Hudson Extension College, a home study program she'd been taking for years, one course at a time. I took a bus home to Newburgh for the party she was throwing for herself. I spoke to Karen in Buffalo on the phone and she poked fun at Mommy behind her back, for making a big deal of an AA degree and said she definitely wasn't leaving the beginning of her last semester of upstate teachers' college for that, especially because she was student teaching now. But she didn't tell Mommy her real feelings.

Victoria looked great, dressed in a red sweater and black slacks, with that cute lithe dancer's figure. We gave each other big hugs.

"How's Harvey?" Mommy asked, winking, and I winked back. Winks seemed appropriate for a non-existent character. "Why didn't you bring him to the party?"

"He's busy, Mommy. He sends his regards and congratulations. He wishes his mom would go to college. She's a seamstress in a sweat shop."

"Oh dear," Mommy said. "That must be difficult. I hope it's a union shop. The cider business must be slow, eh?"

"Oh, his mother isn't involved in the business. That's his father's family, the Bottels. His mother and father aren't married."

"They're divorced then?"

"Mommy, I'm sorry but I'd rather not talk about it. Just trust me, he's a great guy and he's crazy about me."

"I can't wait to meet him, Rowie. I'm very excited for you."

Being with my insane family for a noisy visit cemented my gratitude for college. I could leave in a few hours! Everyone seemed to be screaming at once, twelve different conversations. A new fill-in-the-blank: restaurant, hairdo, article of clothing, diet, body ache or disease diagnosis. I was more interested in Allen Ginsberg's latest poem, or a new Thelonius Monk record. Had any of these people seen the best minds of their generation destroyed by madness, starving, hysterical, naked, dragging themselves around looking for a heroin fix? Had they any clue?

Uncle Benny and Aunt Bea had flown in from Los Angeles, a big sacrifice since as new Californians, complete with backyard pool, they now wondered how they'd tolerated Eastern winters for forty years. Their son, my cousin Ralphie was a year ahead of me in college, at Antioch in Ohio. We'd grown apart in the last couple of years, but as usual, my aunt and uncle cornered me and filled me in on his long list of achievements I had known about anyway, valedictorian of his class in "the valley," Merit scholar, champion debater, captain of the swim team. They were thrilled that Ralphie was thinking of studying for the rabbinate. I knew Ralph would hate hearing them go on about him the way they did, reciting a laundry list of accomplishments. He'd surprised them by leaving home for college since they were sure he'd go to UCLA. Seeing Aunt Bea and Uncle Benny made me realize how much I missed my cousin. I made up my mind to connect with him again soon.

Everyone commented on how thin I was. Mommy, who was drinking rather heavily, came and put her arm around me and quieted everyone.

"Isn't my Rowie amazing?" she announced, leaning on me. "Look how skinny she got and tell me you're not jealous, I dare you. Remember the fat kid? Can you believe she was a size 18 in fifth grade? Now she could be a model."

"Mommy, please," I said. "You're embarrassing me."

"Now you can get a nice doctor or lawyer, Rowie," shouted Uncle Benny. "Find a Columbia man for yourself."

"She has a future lawyer," Mommy said slyly. "Named Harvey Bottel"

"What kind of a name is Bottel?" roared Uncle Benny.

"Changed from Bottelstein," I said. "Or maybe Bottelwitz, I'm not sure."

The family roared approval and wisecracks.

"Hey Buddy, now that your wife is a college graduate, better watch out or she'll find a doctor or a lawyer to replace you!" quipped Uncle Benny.

"I'm too fat," Mommy said. Everyone laughed.

The strangest part of the party was seeing Daddy in the kitchen cooking burgers and smiling. The only other time I'd seen him do this was my disastrous sweet sixteen party. I sat on the old red metal step stool for a few minutes and kept him company. He kissed me on the cheek, and I smelled alcohol. My heart pounded madly. I felt faint. Something was going on. My parents almost never drank. But why was I so upset? The former ogre's kiss? He seemed pretty harmless now.

"How do I look with an apron on?" Daddy asked, pressing down a burger with his long barbecue spatula. His back was almost up against the refrigerator.

"You look odd, to tell the truth, Daddy," I said. "You smell odd too. Have you and Mommy taken up drinking?"

"Oh Rowie, for Crissake, this is a party," he said. "Have a glass of wine."

"Daddy, I don't drink. Alcohol is all sugar. It's fattening."

"Well, then, may I serve you a burger, my dear?" he asked, removing his burgers carefully from the pan and placing them on a large plate he had given me to hold. They smelled almost enticing.

"No, Daddy, I don't eat much these days, and I never liked meat, so I've given it up altogether."

"Well, you look fantastic! Now you can be a dancer like Victoria."

"What are you saying about me?" Victoria poked her head in from the bedroom doorway. "Are my eyes playing tricks on me, or is my sister Rowie about to devour a whole platter of burgers?"

I blushed. "I don't eat meat. I don't eat very much anymore, Victoria," I said.

She opened her mouth and stuck a finger in, miming throwing up. "No more of this?"

"No more," I lied.

"That's great!" she said. "That was a disgusting habit."

– ∞ –

The following Thursday afternoon, as I sat in our usual seventh floor hangout in Lydia's room, engrossed in a hot conversation about guys and sex, someone called me to the hall phone. It was Mommy on the line.

"I have to see you, Rowie. I'm downstairs. Can I come up to your room?"

"You're here, on a Thursday? That's weird. I'd rather come down to the lounge, Do you mind? That's where visits with parents are supposed to take place." My mind raced. I immediately remembered Grandma and Grandpa were dead and she wouldn't be here if anybody else died, but this was odd. My room was my sanctuary, and I didn't want it invaded by one of the two people in the world I was relieved to have escaped.

"I prefer speaking to you privately," Mommy said. "May I come up, please?"

"I guess so," I said, reluctantly, and hurried to make my bed and straighten up the messy room just as Mommy had taught me. I left the door open and sat down in the neat little cubicle on the easy chair. I hoped she wouldn't smell throw-up from my using the sink.

She walked in hesitantly. She looked bloated and triple chinned in one of her shapeless paisley tent dresses and heels her fat feet bulged from. She must have been at work and taken off early. "Mind if I close the door?" she asked and closed it before I responded. She came over and pecked me on the cheek. I sat expectantly, curious and a little upset with her in my private space.

"Would you like to sit in this chair, Ma?" I asked, not getting up.

"No, don't get up," she said.

She sat on the edge of the bed. I was glad I'd put on the red Bates spread and the throw pillows Mommy had bought me. She patted the cover. The room felt like a cave with a brick wall right outside the window but I didn't turn on the light, so it stayed dim. I waited in silence. What in the world could be so damn important that she interrupted my privacy to come on a weekday? No parents ever visited during the week. I'd fulfilled her damn fantasy getting to this college. Now what?

"I need your advice, Rowie," she said.

"You need my advice?" This was getting stranger and stranger.

"Should I leave your father?"

"That's why you're here? You're asking me if you and Daddy should break up? What the hell?"

I stood and paced the little room. This was the ultimate inappropriateness. I have an insane mother, I thought. Why had I bothered going to her stupid party for that AA degree that took her about a thousand years to get?

"It's your life, Mommy. I can't believe you're asking me." I was astounded. I didn't want to sit still, found myself fidgeting, flashing on ice cream and doughnuts.

"I trust you," she said. "I don't know who else to go to."

"Let's see, Mommy." I counted on my fingers. "You could go to a marriage counselor. Go to a rabbi. Go to a friend or even a shrink. Go to somebody else, anybody else, but not me. How do you expect me to be objective? You and Daddy have been fighting for my entire life. What in God's name is different now?"

She began to cry. "I don't know. This is going to sound stupid, but I think it's because I got a degree. I can't explain it. I'm so sorry, Rowie, it was a mistake to come. I'm sorry I bothered you." She stood up, still whimpering.

"Mommy, sit down." I handed her a tissue box and sat next to her on the bed. I put my arm around her, aware of how pathetic she was. "Please, do whatever you think is right, okay? I'll support whatever your decision is. But it has to be your decision. And Daddy's, of course." I patted her back. "You asked me for advice, Mommy. That's my advice."

"He's impotent, Rowie. He's been impotent for years."

"Oh fuck," I said and didn't excuse myself. I lit a cigarette, and Mommy lit up too. I felt sick to my stomach instantly and thought I might throw up involuntarily. I didn't want to hear any allusion to my father's sexuality ever. I hated Daddy for hurting me every day when I was little, but I hated her too for egging him on.

"Don't tell me this, Ma." I trembled.

I was still a virgin, maybe the only one on my floor. It was one thing to talk about sex in Lydia's room with the girls but quite another to hear this from my own mother.

Why did she have to burden me like this? She'd always burdened me in one damn way or another. I'd thought I'd finally escaped and here she was, violating me and I was allowing it. I remembered that offhand comment I'd made when she'd come from a business trip years ago, saying she looked so happy she must have had an affair in San Francisco, and she freaked out and confessed to me, and from then on I'd become the confidante. I couldn't meet her eyes. She whimpered into her sleeve.

I mumbled, "I'm sorry, Mommy. I had no idea. Isn't there something doctors can do for that?" Just cut the thing off and forget it?

"He tried. He even went to a psychiatrist. You know what the doctor told him? He said I was a castrating woman." She sobbed.

I'd read enough psychology to know the shrink might have nailed that one, but I didn't say so.

"Maybe if you split up, it'll be better for both of you."

"I'm worried about him, Rowie, and I'm tired of worrying about him. He's a grown man. I'm living like a single person so I might just as well be single again."

"Sounds like you made your decision without my advice," I said.

"Victoria thinks I should leave him," she said. "If Karen weren't all the way in Buffalo, I'd go and ask her too. What do you think she'd say?"

I was horror stricken. "You asked Victoria? She's only thirteen, Mommy. Don't you think that was inappropriate?"

"Why? You kids should have something to say. I want our family to be run democratically."

"Mommy, you're the biggest bundle of contradictions in the world. Our family was never democratically run. Anyhow you're not talking about deciding what to make for dinner or what color to paint the living room. This should be between you and Daddy. I can't believe you asked Victoria. You've got a problem."

She began weeping again. "I'm so mixed up, Rowie. I don't know where to turn. I shouldn't have come. Will you forgive me?"

My instinct was to hug her, but we didn't hug in the Wine family so I patted her arm and stayed silent. I could feel emotions zinging through my body. On the verge of tears myself, I controlled. Maybe I could forgive her and maybe not.

"Do you need me to walk you out or can you find your way?" I asked, using Ira Silver's closing technique.

"I know the way," she said, sniffing.

I wish to hell you knew the way, I thought, as I bade her goodbye.

_ ∞ _

SIXTEEN

Daddy moved to a furnished apartment in Yonkers, less than an hour from my school. The first few times he called, it didn't compute that he was my father, living alone in some strange room. I answered his questions curtly. How are you? Fine. How's school? Fine. How's your social life? Fine. He invited me to dinner. I declined. Silence between us embarrassed me. On each call, I quickly told him I had to go, and we hung up. The week of finals, he begged me to have dinner with him after my last exam. Something about his plea sounded so sincere, I relented and accepted. I felt a little as if I were betraying Mommy, and hated dealing with restaurant meals, but I would handle it.

It was like a date. The front desk dorm attendant called my floor to tell me Buddy had arrived. When I got downstairs, I observed him for a moment unnoticed. He looked frail, pale and vulnerable, clutching an unwrapped bouquet of daisies by the stems, as though he'd just picked them. Probably stole them from his landlady's yard or worse, maybe a park. He smiled when he saw me, his face lit up, and he transformed into a boy. I knew in that moment, for the first time, why Mommy had married him. He had turned fifty a week before my birthday half a year ago, and despite his sadness and a few wrinkles, he still had a full head of brown hair and youthful innocence. I wanted to feel good about him, but I still had mixed feelings. Anger ran deep. It was hard to believe this meek little man had terrorized me for years.

"These are for you, Rowie, honey," he said shyly and kissed me on the cheek.

Tears welled up and a lump formed in my throat. I hurried up to my room with the flowers and put them in water. Since I'd started throwing up again, my nose was stuffed all the time and my sense of smell weak. I noticed I couldn't smell the flowers. I blew my nose, checked my eye makeup, felt gratified that I'd dressed carefully in a blue linen sheath.

Daddy drove his sleek, new red Pontiac to the Tip Toe Inn, an old white tablecloth place on Broadway and 86th Street where droopy-faced waiters draped large white napkins over their black-suited forearms. Before we even ordered, Daddy looked at me across the table, tired, honest, sweet, his blue eyes watery.

"I'm sorry for everything," he said, holding eye contact. "I'm very sorry I screwed up so badly. I didn't mean to take my frustrations out on you all those years. I love you and your sisters and your mother more than life itself. Can you ever forgive me, Rowie?"

I burst into a sneeze of tears for about a thousandth of a second, then quickly checked myself, scared the dam would break. I didn't want to cry in public. I forced myself to breathe deeply. There was still something I couldn't remember so how could I forgive him if I didn't know what for. Day after day, year after year he had hurt me, and now it all rolled together into one tiny blink, laden with emotion. What was I blocking?

We reached for each other's hands across the table. At last, I was getting to gently hold the warm hand that had mishandled me so cruelly. I felt his heart and mine melt together.

"I want to forgive you, Daddy," I said, my voice coming out as a whisper. "I don't know whether I can, or exactly what for, but I promise to work on it."

"Thank you, Rowie. I'm so sorry for what I did to you. I must be a monster. If you can't forgive me, I'll understand."

Could I forgive him? I wanted to ask him why, why, why he'd been so mean. I wanted to pound him hard in the chest. But my throat ached. I couldn't talk.

Later, when we tearily hugged goodbye, even though I had the urge to punch him, or kick him, we promised to make this a new beginning and be in touch often.

– ∞ –

Next day, ready a couple of hours before Mommy was scheduled to drive me home, all packed, sitting on my bare mattress leaning against the headboard and smoking a Kent, I vowed to file the present moment in my memory forever. Although I hadn't done well academically, at least I had passed and finished a full year of college. I took in my surroundings – the brick wall just outside the window, the sink, bare walls, basketball-sized frosted light bulb overhead. Except for my motley assortment of bulging luggage, and the vase of Daddy's daisies I intended to take home, the room looked exactly as we'd found it nine months ago. Several girls on my floor had dropped out, but I had made it. I flicked ashes into the seashell I used as ashtray and blew smoke upwards in the dimly lit room. This had been the first room of my life assigned only to me. I had a key. In this room, for the first time ever, I experienced a locked door and privacy. Someone must have thought I deserved it.

"Whoever you are, thank you," I said aloud. "If you're the god-guy listening, I thank you. If you're my Sky-mother, yes, I still remember you. Or my guardian angels, I thank you. If you're Gram and Gramps, I thank you. Thank you, thank you, whoever you are. I'm still messed up, but I've finished a year of college and am truly grateful."

Lydia interrupted my little ceremony with a loud knock on the door.

"Rowie, your dad's downstairs."

"You mean my mom, right?"

"Only if she has a very deep voice."

– ∞ –

"I just wanted to hug you again, Rowie," Daddy said. "I hope you don't mind. Let me take you for a soda."

I threw my arms around him and let him hold me briefly. My body stiffened. Something was wrong. Behind his back, I looked at my watch. "Okay, but we have to be quick, Daddy."

We walked around to a Broadway coffee shop, hand in hand.

"I've been having some chest pain," he said. "Doc tells me it's indigestion. I'm a little worried about it."

"Maybe you should get a second opinion, Daddy."

"Not a bad idea. It's probably nothing. I wanted to tell you last night, but I didn't want you to think I was complaining."

"Oh, Daddy, thank you for telling me. I'm going to call you from home to find out what's going on."

– ∞ –

The funeral was agony. People whispered that Pearlie Fine had murdered Buddy Wine by kicking him out of the house. The presiding rabbi, new in town, hadn't bothered to gather information. He spoke of the good husband, great father, and wonderful provider. With every word, I cringed and wanted to scream and punch him. Daddy was none of those things. He was a screw-up who'd made my early years hell. Yes, he and I had made peace for about ten seconds, and yes, I was grateful, but I was also furious. Hatred and anger overtook me and froze out tears.

Back home, the post-death scene replayed. My aunts and uncles had ordered mountains of corned beef, tongue, pastrami, roast beef, towers of sliced rye bread, vats of potato salad and cole slaw, oceans of fish platters along with sponge cake, honey cake, lemon cake, devil's food cake, and marble cake figuring that neighbors wouldn't be so generous with casseroles the way they had been a year ago when Gram died and six years ago when Gramps died. Mostly guests brought assortments of Barton's chocolates. I attacked the food with the fever of war. I made thick sandwiches and ate until bursting. I knew not to go near the boxes of chocolates that I craved but didn't dare touch. Back and forth, bathroom to kitchen to bathroom I sneaked as though years had taught me nothing but stealth. My throw-up poured into the toilet like hog slop, flushed down along with my feelings, the whole mess safely out of sight. My heart pounded, eyes reddened, glands swelled and I didn't try to cover up. Why not look as though I'd been crying continuously?

– ∞ –

Karen and I rode into the city to retrieve Daddy's belongings and car. On the way home, out of nervousness we got the giggles. As Karen sped us along the Palisades Parkway, I looked through the few things we recovered.

In Daddy's wallet I found a dog-eared paper with a short poem I'd completely forgotten I'd written – a gift to him when he'd gone to the hospital for hernia repair right after he went back to work as a salesman and suddenly had health insurance again. More than eight years ago when I was nine. I read it out loud.

> *Daddy, we all miss you a lot*
> *With you not here, the house goes to pot.*
> *There's no one to yell, "Pick up that scrap."*
> *No one to set the mouse's trap.*
> *But we're all kinda having a lotta fun*
> *Chewing and cracking our bubble gum.*
> *I know you think I'm bad*
> *But I want you to know I love you Dad.*

Karen said, "Jesus, Rowie, he beat the shit out of you and you wrote him we all missed him a lot and you loved him? That's incredible. I don't remember ever seeing this poem. It's hilarious!" She hooted nervously.

"It's not so funny," I said, between giggles. "I thought maybe he'd leave my butt alone when he came out of the hospital."

"He believed it was his duty to discipline you."

"Why me and not you or Victoria?"

"Mommy says he hit me when I was really little. Then I got asthma and he stopped."

"I tried getting asthma. It didn't work." More laughter.

"Victoria was born sick so I guess she was off limits. The princess. That left you to be the punching bag. The bad seed."

I aped a wicked face. "Rowena Gay, the demon child. Hit her or she may hit you. I did hit him finally, and that ended it. Too bad I waited so long. But I was good at farting, remember?"

"You were the champion stinkbomber when you were a baby blimp. Unbelievable. You ate non-stop and laid some of the most potent farts I've ever known a human to create. Dogs, yes. Grown men like Uncle Benny, close. But you could've gotten a prize. Yugh, they were horrible."

"Thank you," I bowed. "Did you realize my farts kept Daddy from spanking my butt?"

"No, I didn't. Brilliant! But before that, when Daddy used to put you over his knee, you hardly ever cried even when he hit you hard. How'd you do that?"

"I don't know. It's a gap in my memory. I had some kind of survival technique I think, like my mind split off. I used to imagine I was picking flowers on the bluff. I'm not sure how it worked, but I hardly felt his blows."

"Split personality? Schizophrenic?"

"Maybe. I don't know. I think it was more of a positive thing. Like I said, for survival."

"Do you still know how to go schizo on demand?"

As I joined Karen in nervous hilarity, it occurred to me that I lived insanely. Eating and puking and eating and puking. Did my secret life qualify me for the white coats? I didn't want to end up in Middletown State Hospital or Bellevue. I vowed to carefully guard my secret, and try like hell to give up the crazy behavior altogether.

_ ∞ _

In August, Mommy received word that her department was decentralizing away from Stewart Air Force Base. She had the choice of moving to Colorado Springs, Marietta, Georgia, or Syracuse, New York. She chose Syracuse. We all hoped a move would be a wonderful way for Victoria and her to get a fresh start.

_ ∞ _

Since I hadn't studied and barely squeaked by my freshman year, I was sure Barnard wouldn't renew my scholarship. Right after the funeral, I wrote a letter to school about Daddy's death, hoping to evoke sympathy for an orphan. Sure enough, they granted me an even larger scholarship, and in the fall, after helping Mommy pack, I returned to Barnard as a sophomore. I was still massively overeating and throwing up, I was still a virgin and still hadn't been able to cry. I'd gained a few pounds so I knew I was safely leaving something to digest. That was good because I didn't feel ready to die. I saw a school psychiatrist for six sessions, with the intention to stop the crazy food thing, but he was a Freudian and never spoke except to say hello and see you next time. I spent the whole hour saying things I thought would make him speak and finally gave up, my secret still intact.

_ ∞ _

As I crossed the Columbia campus the third week back, a tall, broad-shouldered, fair-skinned guy with oily black curls and dark-rimmed glasses blocked my path, his smile almost as big and oily as the rest of him. I couldn't place him.

"I remember you," he said, smiling. "You're 18 now, aren't you?"

"Yes, I've been 18 since last winter," I said, clutching my books to my chest. I felt naked under this guy's piercing gaze through his glasses. Peripherally I noticed people passing us steadily and longed to clutch onto a passerby and keep going. But I stood rooted as though this man were a lion reeling in his prey with his stare.

"I want to take you out," he said. "Are you free this Friday night?"

"I guess so," I said. A low-flying plane roared over Low Library. I thought that was a comical coincidence. He was shouting to be heard now.

"I'll pick you up at 6. Which dorm are you in?"

"Brooks," I shouted back. "But I don't even know your name."

"For shame," he said. "We had such a promising coffee date together last fall. I'm Sy French, like the kiss," he said, grinning widely. "I know you're Rowena Wine from Newburgh and you had a boyfriend in the Air Force. I'm a grad student in the business school and my intentions are strictly dishonorable." He laughed. "So, will I see you at 6, Rowena?"

"Call me Rowie," I said, getting excited. I was embarrassed to be a virgin and I figured he was as good a candidate as any to remedy that. "See you at 6."

He was prompt. I wore my beatnik outfit, dangling silver earrings, black skirt and turtleneck, black tights, black eye liner and white lipstick. I also wore my only black panties and bra.

We went to a Chinese restaurant on Broadway and 111th Street and ordered shrimp chow mein and a noodle dish. He held my hand all the way there and I loved how comforting his warm hand felt. I picked at the food nervously, ate a little more than I wanted. I was hungry and scared, but I knew I was flirting. I downed almost all the tea in the teapot.

"Don't order dessert," he said. "We'll have dessert at my place."

"Excuse me a few moments," I said. "I have to use the ladies' room."

I washed my hands first, then gagged and easily brought up the tiny amount I'd eaten. The warm tea had done its job. Then I sat and peed, flushed, and washed my hands again. I looked in the mirror. With a paper towel, I dabbed at the spreading mascara. Throwing up always gave my eyes a sad, post-crying teary red look and clogged my sinuses. I thought I looked like a ghoul, all skinny in black. I reapplied a layer of white on my lips and went back to Sy. He had taken care of the bill and was ready to go.

Sy's roommate was out of town. They shared a spacious pre-war apartment in an elevator building on 113th Street with an expansive foyer opening into a large living room. Half the long hallway went in one direction to the kitchen, half in the opposite direction to the bedrooms.

"What's for dessert?" I asked, not that I cared. I was just making conversation. Moments of silence unnerved me.

He smirked, pulled me toward him. "You are," he said and moved to kiss me.

"Do you have anything to drink?" I asked as he was mid-lunge. Partly I worried about my breath. Partly I wanted numbing.

He fixed me a strong rum and coke. I dismissed the calories and chugged it down.

We made out a little on the couch, then quickly moved to a dark bedroom he said had been the maid's room, with a bare mattress and box spring. We kissed and stroked each other. That felt pretty good even though I could feel myself beginning to nod out from the drink. I must have passed out briefly and next thing I knew I was shocked to find my hands caressing bare buttocks right over me. The first bare ass I'd ever felt except for my own. Where were my clothes? I was naked but he had a shirt on. He was pumping up and down between my thighs. Was he inside me? I couldn't tell. I lay still. I was finally doing it, and it was boring and nothing like what it was billed to be. Suddenly he stopped, pulled up out of me and groped in the dark for a packet on the nightstand. He ripped it open next to my ear. The sound of ripping filled my head, the room, the universe. I didn't look at exactly what he was up to, but he seemed to be occupied stretching and rolling something.

"I believe in protection," he whispered.

"Thank you," I said, hoping that was the right thing to say, guessing it was that thing I'd heard about that covered the *shlong*: a rubber.

Then he poked himself back in me, and this time I felt it.

"Lift your legs," he ordered.

I did as he said and I felt him even more. It hurt.

He pumped and pumped, up and down, up and down, then shrieked, and collapsed onto me where he lay, unmoving.

"Sy?"

"Yeah?"

"Could you get off me? I can hardly breathe."

"Sorry," he said, and rolled off.

"Here's a towel," he said. I wiped myself in the dark.

He flipped on the light.

"Oh fuck," he exclaimed. "Jesus fucking Christ, why didn't you tell me?"

There was blood everywhere, all over me and him and the towel and the mattress and his shirt. I cried and said that I didn't have my period and didn't know I'd bleed.

"Oh, Jesus," he said, "I thought you told me you'd had a boyfriend in the military.

"I did," I sobbed. "I broke up with him before we did it." I couldn't stop sobbing. "I'm sorry I ruined your mattress," I wailed.

"Forget it. I'll clean it up. The bathroom's there, go take a shower, put your clothes on, and I'll walk you back to school."

I started for the bathroom. He stopped me. "Just one thing, Rowie. Let's be perfectly clear. I don't love you and I don't want you to think, just because we had sex, that you love me. This is not about love. Is that clear?"

I sniffed. "Don't worry, I don't love you." I don't even like you, I thought. Back at the dorm, I looked at myself in the mirror and grinned. I did it, I thought, I did that stupid, overrated thing. I don't look any different, but I'm not a virgin anymore.

– ∞ –

About a week later, sitting alone in the lunchroom and shoveling in my pistachio ice cream, which was all I ever ate for lunch, I stopped cold. A clear voice in my brain told me to pay attention: "The next man who walks into this dining room from the lunch line will be a lover."

In walked a laughing man holding a tray full of lunch. He was delightful looking, a bit taller than average, with a mop of curly brown hair, nice shoulders, straight teeth. He was talking to a short girl I recognized from my Spanish class, Susanna. They sat down together. Perfect. I had Spanish after lunch. I could ask her something about class.

Boldly, I walked over to their table.

"Mind if I sit for a moment, Susanna?" I asked, looking from her to the cute man.

"It's Suzanne," she said. "Professor Sandoval calls me Susanna just to sound authentic." She smiled warmly. "I have a feeling your name isn't Rosita either, is it?" We laughed. "I'm Rowie Wine, as in *vino*. He got Rosita from Rowena."

"I'd like you to meet my cousin Pierre Dreyfus," Suzanne said.

"You two are cousins? How cool!" I offered my hand. Pierre stood and kissed it.

"*Enchanté,* mademoiselle," he said, and added, with an exaggerated French accent, "I am French." Immediately I made the connection to Sy French. My heart dropped. This was weird.

"Pierre," Suzanne said, "Don't overdo it." To me, she said, "Pierre came to New York when he was three. His parents were in the French underground. He has more of a New York accent than a French one."

"Seet down, mademoiselle," Pierre said, pulling out a chair, continuing his game.

I almost sat, but I didn't have time with all that ice cream sitting in my stomach calling me.

"Thanks, I don't have time," I said. I looked right at Pierre and smiled. "I would love to hear more about your parents and the French underground, Pierre."

"I would love to tell you, mademoiselle. Weel you give me your phone number?"

"Yes, but why wait for a phone call? How about meeting this afternoon after class for a coffee?"

"*Mais oui,* mademoiselle. Eet would geev me great *plassir.*"

"Front desk, Brooks Hall, four o'clock."

"Eet's a date."

"See you in class, Suzanne."

– ∞ –

SEVENTEEN

I was flirting so outrageously with Pierre that he invited me to spend Saturday night with him at the apartment of a friend who was out of town. He said he lived with his parents and much younger brother and sister on Riverside Drive. I accepted the invitation. I liked Pierre, especially since he'd dropped the corny accent and told me about his idealistic life plan. He was a senior at Columbia, pre-med, with plans to practice medicine at a clinic he would set up in Haiti to serve poor people.

We ate at a Middle Eastern restaurant in Chelsea near his friend's place. I ordered and polished off what I imagined to be a normal meal except I drank glass after glass of water. After dinner, I excused myself to "powder my nose" and, in the ladies' room, threw most of it up easily, washed up, rinsed my mouth out, put on some coral lipstick, and, elated and excited, returned to Pierre.

The studio apartment was bare except for an open roll-away bed with side-by-side bare twin mattresses partially covered with an army blanket, and a couple of dirty pillows. There was a half-burned candle on the floor stuck on a plate and a torn window shade pulled all the way down. It was a dump. Pierre lit the candle.

"Let's pretend this is our love shack," he said and embraced me.

We undressed and stretched out on one of the narrow beds. I was afraid to move and lay stiffly. Suddenly I wondered whether I would bleed again. I shivered.

Pierre sat up, leaned on one elbow. He pulled the army blanket over us, looked down at my face.

"Rowie, you're not the experienced woman I thought you were. I can't do this tonight. I want to get to know you. I want to court you. I'm going to teach you the art of love. I'll tell you the truth about this apartment. It does belong to someone I know, but he isn't my friend, and he's not out of town. He keeps this and rents it by the hour to classmates. I've never been here before and I'll never be here again. It stinks like a pigsty. I apologize for bringing you here. Let's get dressed, Rowie. We can walk a little and then I'll take you back to your dorm. We have plenty of time before curfew."

By the door of the dorm, he pulled me into the shadows, held me close and kissed me tenderly.

"Rowie, Rowie, there's something very special about you," he said. "You have secrets. That's fine. If you want to tell me I'll listen and if not, I won't ask. Good night, sweet Rowie. We shall meet again soon."

Pierre called every day. He was busy studying and applying to medical schools so we didn't see each other during the week, but we began spending Friday and Saturday nights together, going to movies, concerts, and plays. We held hands, kissed and caressed in the dorm living room near all the other couples doing the same thing.

One Saturday evening, a few months later, close to curfew, we clung to each other in the shadow of a pillar, near the front door of the dorm.

"Rowie, do you have to go in? Can't you stay out with me? I want to play my accordion and sing you love songs. I want to take you home to meet my family. I don't want to let you go tonight."

"I know, Pierre. I feel the same way. I'll tell you what. I'll escape tonight. Let me show you something." I walked him to the back corner of the building where there was a cement parapet. Peering over the wall, we saw a thirty-foot drop to Claremont Avenue below. "This dorm was built into a hillside. If I go out through a window on the first floor and climb along that ledge..." I pointed as best I could in the dark. "I'll come out right here and I can climb over and be safe."

Pierre looked down. "But it's at least a thirty foot drop to the pavement. It's too dangerous."

"Wait for me on Claremont and watch me."

"Why don't you just stay out with me, sweetheart?"

"I could get in trouble that way because we have to sign for overnights in advance. Anyhow, this is an adventure. I'll see you in half an hour." We blew each other kisses and I went inside and signed in.

By two AM, the dorm was locked and quiet. I put on jeans, a heavy white sweater, and sneakers. Totally focused on being with Pierre, I went to the first floor bathroom, opened a window, and peeked out. It seemed like a long way down. There he was leaning against a light pole near 116th Street. I got his attention by tossing my pocketbook down. He looked up with a broad grin and moved under the window, way down below, on the sidewalk. Before I could change my mind, I climbed out onto a narrow ledge, my feet sideways, my body facing the building, my arms hugging the wall. My hands were holding onto an ornamental narrow stone ledge above shoulder level. I tried to keep my head to one side so I could look in the direction I was headed, but I kept forgetting, facing the wall, and bumping my nose. Slowly, slowly, I inched along. I had to pass a dorm supervisor's window. A light was on. I peeked and saw her sitting alone, reading, about three feet from the open window. I took a deep breath and made my way past. She never looked up. Pierre moved along below, his arms outstretched, my purse hanging from his shoulder. Inching, inching, my hands grew sore from the rough stone. Finally, I clambered over the low stone wall to the front of the building. I'd made it! I leaned over and whispered down to Pierre.

"You run and I'll run and we'll meet in the middle." Then I took off toward Broadway and 116th Street. My white sweater was filthy from rubbing against the building, my hands and nose were scraped, and I was wheezing a little. But I was overjoyed.

"Darling, thank God you're safe. Promise me you'll never do that again," Pierre said, hugging me and lifting me off the ground. "If you had fallen, we'd both be dead." He got out his handkerchief. "Spit into this and I'll clean the tip of your nose." I spit and he wiped. My nose stung.

Arms entwined, we took the train a few stops to his parents' place. I washed up while he picked up his accordion and a blanket, packed a chocolate bar and a loaf of crusty French bread. We kissed a few times in the kitchen and headed for Riverside Park.

For the next couple of hours, I received a serenade of French love songs and a feast of bread, chocolate, and kisses. It was my first chocolate since the Oreo fiasco and it tasted incredible. I was falling in love.

Pierre invited me to his senior prom. We still hadn't gone all the way although we were panting for each other. I signed for an overnight at his parents' address. He picked me up and took me in a cab to their apartment. He carried my bag and I carried my gown, an emerald green silk strapless, fitted bodice with a green, black and white print silk chiffon skirt. I had gotten it wholesale through Aunt Bea's brother Marvin who worked in the garment industry. I met Pierre's folks. Maybe because he was totally bald, his father looked old to have such young kids. He grunted hello and went back to reading a French newspaper at the kitchen table. Monette Dreyfus, his mother, was a short, plump woman, sleekly dressed in forest green with a green print silk scarf smartly knotted at the neckline, and elegant gold, diamond, and emerald jewelry that spoke of the family business in the jewelry district. She questioned me closely about my family, what kind of work my father did, what my grandparents did, where my mother lived. I wasn't sure what she was looking for but I was pretty sure she hadn't found it because she didn't look pleased. She did, however, like my gown, and I was glad it was a shade of green she obviously liked.

"Rowie, what jewelry will you wear with this?" she asked and she suddenly took off her earrings. "Here. I want you to borrow these. They will go perfectly with your outfit and your coloring."

"I couldn't, Mrs. Dreyfus. I can see they're emeralds and I'd be afraid I might lose them."

She opened my hand, put the earrings in them, and closed my hand around them. That's when I noticed the number tattooed on her arm.

"Ma, her ears aren't pierced," Pierre said. He opened my hand and gave her back the earrings.

"Thank you anyway," I said, and squeezed her hand.

The Dreyfus apartment had three small bedrooms, a kitchen, living room with dining area, front hall, and one bathroom. I was to sleep on the couch in the living room and keep my bag in Pierre's room.

Pierre's 10-year-old brother, Philippe, and 7-year-old sister, Solange, were watching TV in the living room. They barely looked up until Pierre went and whispered something to them and then each turned attention on me. They were skinny kids with brown curly hair like his.

"Is your father a doctor?" Solange asked me. Pierre told her to be quiet.

"Is he?" she persisted. "My mama and papa want Pierre to marry a doctor's daughter, right Pierre?"

"Don't be silly, Solange. Silly Solange. Silly Solange." Pierre tickled her and she doubled over with giggles.

Somewhere deep inside me, a wound opened. I was a poor girl, daughter of a failure.

The family was going out for the evening, so we would be alone in the apartment until it was time to leave for the dance.

Pierre and I hung out in his room, making out on the bed for a while. I became aroused quickly, but he got up and busied himself setting his tux out. I lay and watched him. He was in his briefs, and suddenly, with shock, I noticed his penis hanging out. I had never seen a full grown, flaccid penis before except in museums, and I couldn't take my eyes off it. It was soft and bouncy, like a fat worm, about five or six inches long. I felt faint with desire, the most overwhelming desire I had ever felt, aching all over.

"Pierre," I said. I reached out my hand. He came over to me and I watched the miracle of soft, bouncy worm transform into long, stiff sausage. My desire burned white-hot, deep within my belly as we made love. It was heavenly, unbelievable, glorious. I orgasmed again and again. He went down on me. I was mad with excitement, noisily coming, ejaculating gallons of wetness onto his bed. He slipped his erect penis between my breasts and it drove me wild. He wanted to show me how to suck it to please him, but I got terrified and then embarrassed about being scared and puzzled about being embarrassed. But he kissed me and didn't seem to mind.

"Thank you, Pierre," I said, hugging and kissing him. "Now I get it. This is why people think sex is so great. It is! I love it and I love you."

I had no interest in going to a prom, but we showered, got dressed and went anyway. I would have stayed happy if there hadn't been food confronting me at the prom. I wasn't sure I'd have a chance to throw up, so I ate a small salad, a bite of chicken, and a couple of peas. Even that seemed excessive, but I managed to hold it down. I wanted more than ever to stay alive. A friend of Pierre's, another pre-med senior named Alan sat at our table with his girlfriend, a hefty, bobbed-nosed Barnard girl named Dana Cohen, who I knew slightly from gym class freshman year.

Pierre introduced me to Alan who introduced us to Dana.

"Rowie, I would like you to meet Dana, the woman of my dreams, daughter of the most famous cardiologist in Boston."

We exchanged greetings and said we sort of knew each other. Pierre was an accomplished dancer, and we had a gorgeous, dreamy evening. Back at his house, the apartment was quiet and dark, with only a night light on. The couch was neatly made into a bed.

Pierre whispered. "Come to bed with me. I'll fix everything up."

He gathered cushions his mom had placed behind the couch and set them up to look like a sleeping body under the covers, then led me to his room. He put all my things in his closet. We made love silently, which was hard for me since it was all new, and my instinct was to be loud. Each time I squealed, he put his hand in my mouth which was better than his dick which would have panicked me. Finally, as light was coming through the windows, we fell asleep.

A knock on his door woke us up. It was eight thirty.

"Quick," he said. "Under the covers." I dived all the way under and scrunched up. I wanted to laugh but felt scared and guilty.

"Where's your girlfriend?" she asked, her voice lilting up at the end of the sentence.

"*Je ne sais pas, maman*," Pierre said.

"I think she's gone," his mother said. "She set it up to look like she's there, but Philippe sat on her and found out it was just cushions. Something is wrong with a girl who would do such a thing."

"Mama, nothing is wrong with her, I love her. She's a good girl. I'm tired, Mama, my love, let me go back to sleep. I adore you. Please. Don't worry. And Philippe should not have sat on her."

"What will I do?" I whispered after Mrs. Dreyfus left. "Your mother thinks I'm nuts."

"Don't worry. They always go out on Sunday anyway. We'll sneak you out."

Back in the dorm, I wrote a thank-you letter to Monette Dreyfus saying I was sorry I had to leave early and I hoped the kids had liked the way I'd set the cushions up as a joke. Lying wasn't as satisfying as it used to be.

– ∞ –

As the semester wore on, Pierre and I spoke regularly. We went out every weekend, signed into hotels as a married couple a few fabulous nights, once made love in the dark shadows leaning against the wall of Barnard Hall, two or three times borrowed a friend's car and made awkward love in the back seat. I settled into a study routine and began getting A's and B's. I threw up less and forced myself to eat meals instead of just desserts. But I couldn't seem to shake the habit entirely. It ruled me mercilessly.

Since Pierre was going to spend Thanksgiving with his family, I invited my classmate from Tucson, Sarah Drew, to come to Syracuse with me for the long weekend. Mommy had sold the Newburgh house when she was transferred to Syracuse. She used the meager proceeds of the sale and Daddy's small life insurance policy to furnish a large second floor apartment in a modest neighborhood with some elegant new pieces, a fruitwood dining set for the large dining room and new beige sectional couch to place around the living room fireplace. Although the apartment was an upstairs duplex, it felt like a mansion to me. Four separate bedrooms with no need to pass through any of them to get to any other. A large eat-in kitchen. Screened-in porch. Bath and a half. This was luxury.

Karen taught third grade in Dewitt, lived at home, and drove a cute new VW bug. Mommy had gotten rid of her old Dodge and was driving the big red Pontiac. Karen looked beautiful. Her hair was long and lightened professionally to a honey blond rather than the peroxide white bangs look she cultivated in high school. She seemed happy with her job and had just had first dates with a doctor and lawyer, both Jewish. Mommy was ecstatic.

My classmate Sarah, a lovely copper-skinned girl with sun-bleached hair, had allergic eczema she'd scratched so much that scabs and redness covered her forearms. I had promised to help keep her from scratching. She walked around the apartment wearing thick gloves.

"I wish I could help you with something too, Rowie," she said as she puffed on a Pall Mall.

"Oh, I'm okay," I said. "No itches at the moment."

Why couldn't I tell her I had a horrid habit? Why couldn't I tell her I longed for help? If I had sores all over my arms, everyone would see my problem. But mine was hidden. If only I'd been born Catholic I could go to confession. But I had no one I could trust. Not one soul. After the Freudian non-talker, I wasn't about to go to another shrink and expend all my energy focusing on getting him to say something. Guilt tormented me. If Sarah could control her scratching for this vacation, I told myself, I would hold down every single thing that I swallowed.

Sarah and I made malteds, ginger snaps, banana shakes, and hot turkey chili with leftovers from our holiday meal. I stuffed myself.

"Do I look Indian?" she asked me as she was stirring the chili. "Not Indian from India, I mean Native American."

"A little, yes, now that you mention it. Your cheekbones are high, your skin is bronze, and your eyes are dark. Are you?"

"I think so. I'm adopted. My mother tells me my lineage is European, but I don't believe her. It kills me not to know. My family is well-to-do and belongs to the country club and all that crap, but I never liked any of that. I relate better to the servants."

"Sarah, do you think there's such a thing as a happy childhood?"

"I don't know. I didn't have one but I want my children to someday."

"I can't imagine having kids. I'm afraid I'd screw them up."

"Yeah, I can see that. I think the answer is to be away from the big cities. I'm going to have a ranch with all kinds of animals, where kids can ride for miles and be close to nature."

"That sounds great. Will you inherit land?"

"Probably. I'm not sure. I want to make my own way. I'm not counting on an inheritance."

"I would if I were you."

"You think that, but you can't really know. Wealth is a mixed bag."

"It is? Tell me how."

"You have to worry about staying rich. It's a burden. Unless you become a dedicated doctor like my mother, you don't feel motivated to find meaningful work. My whole family is alcoholic including my mom. It sucks, Rowie." Cigarette dangling from her lips, she gave me a spoonful of chili to taste. I nodded approval. I was eating non-stop. "I laugh to see people stepping all over each other to climb the ladder to success. You know what I see as success?" I shook my head. "Not scratching my arms, that's success!"

"Your chili is success," I added.

"Yes!" she said. "Staying positive when life sucks, that's success. Have you read Norman Vincent Peale, *The Power of Positive Thinking?*"

"No. Should I?"

"Yes! It's a must. I have it at school. You can borrow it. It's great. I know I'll make my way in life. I'm going to work with Indians, maybe teaching on a reservation."

"It must feel good to know what you want to do with your life."

"Right now my goal is to have healthy skin. No scratching. What do you want right now, Rowie?"

"I want love and affection," I said. "I want to feel loved, and I want to eat healthy."

"So more chili and salads and fewer malteds and cookies. I'll help you with that."

"You're a good friend," I said. "I accept your help."

– ∞ –

EIGHTEEN

I finished sophomore year with A's and B's and decided to be a Spanish major for two reasons: the professors were friendly and kind, and I liked escaping from myself by operating in another language.

I headed to Syracuse for summer vacation. Pierre would be working as a waiter at the Tamarind Hotel in upstate Livingston Manor and we planned to spend as much time as possible together. I got a job in a children's clothing store at a Syracuse mini-mall with the understanding that I would take a long Fourth of July vacation and a few long weekends throughout the summer. They had just acquired a pre-teen line, and my experience impressed them.

Mommy loaned me the red Pontiac for my first trip to visit Pierre. It was still fairly new and shiny and felt flashy and luxurious. I was used to driving Mommy's old stick shift Dodge, and now automatic transmission made driving so mindless that, at one point, I drifted off into a daydream. I imagined Daddy was in the front seat with me, and I made up a pretend conversation with him. He told me he loved me even though I threw my food up, and said it would be good to cut it out for Crissake.

"You're an addict, sweetheart," he said.

"I must get it from you, Daddy," I said, snottily. "You were addicted to hurting me."

"No excuse," he said. "You're not Buddy, you're Rowie." Then he started singing, "Rowie, Rowie Rowie your boat, gently down the stream, Merrily merrily merrily, merrily...." Then, suddenly, he screamed, "Step on the brake, the brake!"

I slammed my foot hard on the power brake and almost merged with the steering wheel. My attention quickly shifted to the red light I was running in downtown Roscoe and a pick-up truck that sailed past so close I could almost smell the driver's breath. My heart pounded. I knew logically it had to have been my own warning voice, but I could have sworn it sounded just like Daddy. Thanks, I said, shakily, just in case, and kept my attention on the road.

At the turnoff sign for the Tamarind, I felt excited and nervous. Pierre had told me to park in the guest parking lot, which I did, proud that the Pontiac fit in perfectly with the other big, sleek cars. I knew Pierre lived with the hired help behind the hotel's fancy façade, in a dilapidated dorm near the main kitchen. I found it easily just by wandering around until I saw ramshackle cabins with broken down porches and lights blazing through torn shades. It was dinnertime when I arrived, and a young woman I figured was a camp counselor told me to look for Pierre in the main dining room.

The dining room intimidated me. I expected unpretentious rustic. This was pretentious Miami Beach. Crystal chandeliers. Marble floors. Blue velvet draperies. My nose opened for a moment and I got the smells of perfume, gefilte fish, chicken soup, roast beef, and tobacco. People wore piles of glitter: diamonds, gold chains, rings, bracelets, pendants, earrings, hair clips. I saw Pierre across the room, just putting down a loaded tray, laughing and flirting with a woman as old as his mother, very tanned, with frosted blond hair, heavy make up, cleavage, and pounds of gold and diamond adornments. Pierre was handsomely dressed in a black tux with white gloves. I felt thrilled to see him, but a little sick, maybe from hunger and instant jealousy.

I had fantasized he'd see me and immediately lift me up high and whirl me around like Fred Astaire with Ginger Rogers. Instead, combination waiter and gigolo, he was doing what was necessary to attract big tips that would help him pay for medical school. I stared across the room like a waif, my stomach rumbling, baggy shorts and top hanging loosely on my body, even though I'd gained a few pounds.

A fiftyish man, with a thin gray mustache, smartly groomed in a formal white jacket, walked straight to me, looked me over quickly. I considered leaving for a moment.

"Can I help you?" he asked. "Are you looking for a particular guest?"

"No, that's okay," I said.

"Who are you?" he demanded. "This dining room is closed to the public. I'll have to ask you to leave." He pointed toward the door. I craned my neck to get Pierre's attention. He saw me and rushed over. He was balancing an empty tray.

"It's okay, Bernie, this is my girlfriend." He leaned over and kissed me, grinning.

"Get her out of here, Pierre. You know better."

Pierre whispered, "Follow me." I followed him through a swinging door. I thought maybe if this boss type saw the Pontiac, he'd treat me better.

The kitchen was a shockingly different scene. Hot, damp, cluttered, filled with sweaty workers in aprons and hairnets engrossed in chopping, washing, fixing salads, huge stoves and counters filled with immense cauldrons of steaming food, humungous frying pans and ovens, stained concrete floors, clanging and yelling in English and Spanish mixing with big band background music from the dining room.

Pierre put the tray down and hugged me.

"You made it!" he said, then he announced to the kitchen help, "This is Rowie, everybody, this is the love of my life!" They smiled and applauded for a couple of seconds. Pierre was clearly happy to see me, and I felt the same about him. I was also tired and uncomfortable attracting attention. An atomosphere of food made me aware of my hunger, which, as usual, I'd denied. Whenever people watched me, I felt fat.

"Do you want me to give you directions to my folks' place?" Pierre asked. "I'm going to be a few hours."

"Your folks are here?"

"I'm sure I told you they rent a bungalow nearby. We've been coming to Livingston Manor for years."

How had I blanked that out? "I hope you don't mind, but I'm tired from driving. Can't I wait for you here, maybe out by the pool?"

"If you really want to. I don't mind. But it's going to take a while for me to finish up here. That's why I thought you could go to my folks' place. Solange would love to see you again."

"Your little sister remembers me?"

"Yes, of course she does, silly."

"She only met me once for about ten seconds."

"Well, she knows I love you, so she loves you too."

"If I don't go to your folks' place, could I go to our hotel?"

"You could. It's not like a real hotel though. It's more like a gingerbread house. He paused and grinned. "The wicked witch's house."

"Pierre! Hurry up! Table ten is ape-shit."

"I gotta run, Rowie baby," he said

Suddenly I noticed the swinging door didn't stop. In and out, in and out, waiters, busboys, full trays, empty trays, pitchers of water, baskets of rolls. When I'd focused on Pierre, I'd missed what was going on around us. We'd made ourselves an island.

He whispered, "Go and warm up the bed for me." He gave me directions. "It's called Lowenthal's. There's a big sign. Tell old lady Lowenthal you're my wife, okay?"

"Do I have to?"

He nodded. "Wicked witch, remember?"

"Got it. I love you, hubby."

"I adore you, wife. See you later."

– ∞ –

I was glad it was so noisy Pierre didn't hear my stomach growling or offer to feed me. Grateful it was still light, I got back in the Pontiac, followed his directions, and drove down the hill to town. The Lowenthal Hotel was right where he said, a two-story frame structure with a small awning in front and parking lot on the side shared with a drug store and a kosher Chinese restaurant. I parked and without even getting my suitcase, went right into Glatt Wok. I resisted over-ordering and got one egg roll and a cup of watery soup, which I devoured on the spot. Since I hadn't eaten properly in a couple of days, I thought I'd better not throw up. Outside, I tossed the empty container and sack in the trash, got my blue bag from the car and headed for the funny little hotel.

Mrs. Lowenthal looked as old as the mountains. Skeletal in a shapeless flower print, with hanging, obviously dyed, thin black hair, a small hump on her upper back, and a long hooked nose, she did resemble a witch. Her mouth was a slice of bright pink that matched long pink manicured fingernails. Her veiny, spotted hand quivered as she handed me the key.

"No cooking in the room," she warned in a croaky voice. "No radio after ten." I nodded. "Don't make a mess because I'm the one cleaning up." I nodded again. "Plumbing's old so don't put nothing in there that don't belong." She narrowed her eyes and looked as though she knew for sure I was a direct threat to her pipes. How did she know? I grabbed the key and hurried upstairs.

Up in the room, I couldn't help myself, I went straight to the toilet and threw up what I estimated to be half the egg roll and soup, flushing as I puked just to make sure I wouldn't stop the toilet up. It worked fine. Then I showered, brushed my teeth, climbed into the double bed, and fell sound asleep.

When Pierre woke me up, it was dark. He wouldn't have to work until eight next morning. We made wild, creative love most of the night. Instead of the usual coitus interruptus, this time, Pierre had special condoms to ejaculate into. He explained that these were French ticklers because they had a little tail on the end that was supposed to be pleasurable. I didn't notice much difference since it was all pleasurable. He had arranged to be picked up in the morning so I could sleep in. We made a plan to meet later for a few hours between lunch and dinner. I told him I wasn't hungry so he shouldn't worry about feeding me. I was glad he didn't hear my stomach rumbling.

When I got up, the bed was empty. Pierre had gone. I was horrified to see the used French tickler like stuffed derma casing on the floor next to the bed. Even though I was supposed to be married, I was still ashamed to have anyone know I'd had sex, especially the old witch. I suddenly had to hide this limp thing, this evidence. I didn't dare flush it for fear of clogging the old plumbing. There was just a small empty, wicker basket for trash. That wouldn't do. Without much thought, I gingerly wrapped the disgusting thing in toilet paper and looked around for a place to put it. I had hung my raincoat on the back of the bathroom door, and now it caught my eye as a solution. I stuck the wad into my coat pocket with the plan to take it with me on this cloudy day and throw it in the trash in the parking lot. But by the time I was ready to leave, the sun was shining. I was wearing khaki Bermuda shorts and a cute little navy top, and I took off for the Tamarind forgetting all about the earlier plan.

This time, when I arrived, the dining room was empty except for the help sitting and eating a late breakfast, laughing, joking, smoking. Pierre was eating a bagel. He grinned, came running to me, and lifted me up just as I'd imagined.

"This is the woman of my dreams," he said again, proudly. I beamed.

"Poor girl," someone said and everyone laughed.

"Sit down, eat something, Rowie. You look weak."

I had one tiny bite of bagel to quiet my stomach, and a cup of black coffee.

After we ate, Pierre and I went out in an old wooden rowboat. The lake was wide and glittering, and I felt the sun beginning to burn me even though it was still fairly early. Later, while he worked lunch, I sat under an umbrella by the pool and read *Marjorie Morningstar*, a romantic novel by Herman Wouk that had been a best seller a few years back. A beautiful, young

Jewish aspiring actress, Marjorie, is madly in love with the artsy, handsome and neurotic Noel Airman. He professes love, yet puts her down, accuses her of being conventional. Part of the action takes place in the same mountain resort area where I was visiting Pierre. Except for her small waist and family money, Marjorie reminded me of myself, willful, independent, and spirited. The story engrossed me. The sun wilted me. Soon, I felt faint and decided to return to our hotel for a nap.

As soon as I got back to the room and saw the raincoat, I remembered what was in the pocket and decided to take it immediately down to the trash. I looked in one pocket and then the other. The only thing in the pocket was one pencil. My heart sank. I pulled it out. It had the imprint of a local kosher butcher shop. I felt my face flush. I was mortified. The witch had emptied my pocket! She'd spied on me and uncovered a secret. I couldn't stay here another minute. Panicked, I phoned the hotel and asked for the dining room. Somehow I got connected to Pierre who sounded out of breath.

"Are you okay?" he asked.

"I have to leave right now," I said. My chest thumped, my brain pounded and I thought if I stayed I might die. I didn't dare tell Pierre what had happened.

"What's going on? Is your family all right?" He sounded alarmed.

"I can't tell you," I said breathlessly. "I just have to leave." Pierre was to have Sunday breakfast off. I had managed to put off visiting his parents until then.

"Rowie, talk to me. What's the matter? Something must have happened. Did I do something to piss you off?"

"No, I love you. You're great. It's me. I can't talk about it."

"Can you wait a little while? I'll come right after lunch. An hour and a half."

"I have to go now."

"Right now? I wish I understood, Rowie. Didn't you enjoy last night? I thought things were going fantastically well."

"I'm sorry," I said.

"I don't get it," he said. "This is not good. Can't you talk to me, Rowie? Please! I love you!"

"You'd be better off not loving me," I said and hung up before I burst into tears.

– ∞ –

I sped back to Syracuse, panicked all the way. All during the ride, I thought about eating but I didn't stop driving. I wanted my favorites, crackers and cheese and doughnuts. I went straight to a Safeway in a strange neighborhood on the other side of town before going home. I knew Mommy and Victoria would be gone for the weekend but I couldn't take a chance I might be seen with all my food packages, maybe by Karen, who had settled on Jonathan Brechner, the stuffy Republican foot doctor for a boyfriend. I bought a couple of boxes of Ritz crackers, a jar of cheese spread, a couple of loaves of bread, a dozen doughnuts, and a gallon of lemonade, swiftly forced all of it down in the car before I left the parking lot, ditched the garbage in a dumpster and, on the edge of exploding, drove straight home.

Karen confronted me as I headed to the bathroom, about to detonate.

"What are you doing back on Saturday?" Karen asked. "What happened? Did something go wrong with you and Pierre?"

I began to cry. "I don't deserve him. I'm unworthy of him," I wailed.

"Rowie," Karen said firmly. "Stop saying that. It's unhealthy. Mommy would flip if she heard you talking like this. Of course you deserve to have a nice boyfriend."

"No, I don't," I said. "I can't talk now. I have to take a bath. Leave me alone."

I locked myself in the bathroom, ran the bath full force, washed up, and took off my clothes. My stomach had risen like a soufflé. I got on my knees and puked, filling the toilet several times over with gooey orange throw up, flushing each time, and then I swabbed the toilet bowl with cleanser and brush, opened the window, very quietly unlocked the bathroom door and stepped into the tub. As usual, my heart pounded and fluttered irregularly. In a few minutes, just as I predicted, Karen knocked.

"Rowie, are you okay?" she called through the door. She sounded concerned. I felt like an asshole for everything I'd said to her.

"I'm fine, Karen. Come in," I sang. Congestion from the crying and throwing up gave me a stuffed sound as though I had a cold.

She poked her head in. "Thank goodness you're okay. Mind if I pee?"

"Not at all," I said. "Wow, this bath feels great. It's good to be home."

"I'm very worried about you, Ro," said Karen, flushing, and briefly gazing in the mirror to examine a microscopic blemish on her beautiful face as she washed her hands. "Maybe you're upset because you're coming down with something."

"You sound like Mommy," I said. "I'm fine."

"You don't sound fine." She pulled the lid down and sat back down on the toilet.

"I'm fine," I insisted. I lathered myself.

"Ro, don't say stuff like you were saying a little while ago. It's bad for you. You're a great person and that French doctor guy is lucky to have you. Wouldn't it be funny if we both married doctors?"

I stared. "I'm not marrying a doctor, Karen. Pierre's better than I am."

"Rowie stop it this minute. What's really going on? Are you pregnant? Do you have the clap? You can tell me."

"For heaven's sake Karen," I yelled. "I am fine! Go away and leave me in peace!"

She got up. "You're not in peace, my dear sister. Jonathan's about to arrive and we're going out to the lake for a couple of days. So, I'll leave you, but seriously, I think you should see a headshrinker. You're acting totally nuts."

"Back to you," I said and gave her a wet middle finger.

I spent the rest of the weekend finishing *Marjorie Morningstar* and was angry and disappointed by the continuing disparagement of women and the cop-out ending. Gutsy, artistic, free spirited Marjorie ends up an orthodox Jewish matron in conservative Westchester County with a house full of kids and no spark of creativity. This would never be me. I resolved never to end up ordinary. Never. Even if it had to be my addiction that marked me as different, at least I wasn't boring.

– ∞ –

Pierre convinced me to make another trip to Livingston Manor. I insisted on staying far away from the Lowenthal Hotel so we stayed at a small motel with stained carpet and lumpy mattress on the outskirts of town. Pierre and I made love a few times, and we had some close moments, but it was never the same as before because he kept asking to talk about what had happened that made me leave abruptly, and I was ashamed to tell him, so I dismissed it as woman stuff. He wasn't buying it.

"I've always guessed you had secrets, Rowie," he said. "And I thought I could accept that. But now I see if we're going to be together, we have to communicate honestly. I want to know what's bothering you so I can help you. I'm a doctor, remember?"

"I'm fine," I kept insisting. "Leave me alone."

"I will," he said. "I will."

– ∞ –

Back at school it was my junior year. John Fitzgerald Kennedy was running for President against Richard Nixon. Pierre was at Downstate Medical School in Brooklyn. I had my nose in a Spanish literature book constantly. Juan Ramon Jimenez, Miguel de Unamuno, Cervantes, Garcia Lorca, Neruda. I fell in love with both *Don Quijote* and the anonymously written picaresque novel *Lazarillo de Tormes*, which the Inquisition had banned because it mocked the Church. Could I live my life having comic adventures and making fun of the system? What fun! I was taking four Spanish lit classes and keeping up in all of them. Operating in a different language seemed to give me a new identity, and even though my elementary Spanish speaking skills made me feel like a five year old, I appreciated getting out of my skin. Gradually, Pierre and I saw less and less of each other until, by October, the relationship had faded to nothing. There was no formal break-up, no bang, no whimper.

I was returning to the dorm one day with a full bag of doughnuts, pretzels, and lemonade, walking on Broadway, daydreaming mindlessly, when I passed a man who looked vaguely familiar with a girl whom I thought I should know as well.

"Hi, Rowie," the man said with a big smile.

I stared, not recognizing him.

"Rowie, it's me, Pierre. How can you not know me? I'd like you to meet Risa Cohen." She was an attractive young woman, as tall as Pierre, with large features except for a tiny upturned nose that didn't quite fit her face. "She's a freshman at Barnard," he said.

"Hi," I said. "You're the daughter of the Boston cardiologist, right?"

"How did you know that?" she asked.

"I know your sister," I said. "You look like her. Nice to meet you. Nice seeing you, Doctor Pierre. So long."

I kept walking. I told myself if I'd had any residue of doubt before that moment, it just vanished instantly. Pierre and I were history. This was the ordinary Marjorie he would marry. Now I wouldn't have anyone meddling in my affairs, and I could fool around with a variety of men without getting close with any of them. Grateful for the bag of food in my arms, I hurried to my room for the quick binge and private ritual I'd quit dozens of times that brought me a few short moments of relief. With one difference: now I began planning the next stage of my life as a picaresque anti-hero.

– ∞ –

NINETEEN

With the 1960 election victory of JFK and his choice of his brother Bobby as Attorney General, our school buzzed with talk of Freedom rides to test the Supreme Court decision calling for integration of interstate travel. I felt a strong pull to get on one of these South-bound buses and seat myself in the back with other whites while our dark skinned sisters and brothers took the front seats. The basic plan was for whites to go wherever signs said "Colored only" and blacks to go into white only areas at stops all along the way to Alabama and Mississippi. I agonized about my eating and throwing up and how I would hide it, and in the end the pull of my habit won. I needed a personal freedom ride to unleash me from the bonds of addiction. I felt sure the world was moving into a wonderful place, bringing true peace and justice for all. If only I could stop eating and vomiting, everything would be perfect.

– ∞ –

Because of my pre-silicone large breasts, in the Marilyn Monroe era, guys hit on me constantly. I had fulfilled Mommy's dream and made it to the college of her choice. Now I would sleep around as she'd counseled years before, living the rest of the fantasy she'd never experienced. I got myself fitted for a diaphragm, bought a tube of contraceptive jelly, and was ready and set for the sexual revolution.

I went out with so many foreigners that I began to deadpan I majored in Spanish and minored in international affairs. I had many adventures. There was an Israeli guy named Avi, a Nigerian named Moiseh, a Swede named Pieter, and a Texan named Billy who might as well have been foreign. There was a law student from Maine, a journalism student from Ohio, and a business student from Vermont. For a while there was a Latin American studies graduate student at Yale I visited on weekends, who rinsed out condoms, hung them on the back of a chair to dry, then powdered and recycled them. Soon I gave up on academic men and began taking the train to the Village, hanging out at the White Horse and Blue Note with bearded musicians and poets who lived in walk-ups, played a lot of jazz, and appreciated my youth and beatnik garb. What I liked about all of them, besides the music, was the casualness of the relationships. I often didn't even have sex with the poets, just drank wine, with them consuming the lion's share and passing out.

I listened attentively to them spout their existential philosophy and then took off when they nodded out. No commitment. With or without sex, I felt like a female Don Juan and began calling myself Dona Juana. Hell, I thought, if guys can do it, I can too. I called myself a liberated woman.

– ∞ –

I was keeping breakfast down since I wanted to live, but I went back to eating ice cream lunches and throwing up. It amazed me that in all these years, with the common dorm bathroom, no one had discovered my secret. It was dawning on me that people saw what they expected to see, what they wanted to see, and what others wanted them to see. Somehow I'd swerved from mainstream perception. Could it be because I'd trained my food to come up, my mind's path also deviated from the norm? Sometimes I looked in the mirror and told myself I was an independent woman having adventures. Other times I felt like a genuine freak trapped in a perpetual sideshow. Why couldn't I stop? What a weakling I was! The more I accused myself of being no good, the more I punished myself with my nasty habit, spinning round and round in a downward spiral, fed by secrecy, shame, and poor nutrition. Sky-mother had left my life and god-guy wasn't around much either.

I finished junior year with a 3.8 average, out of four, my highest so far. Most of the girls I'd started school with had dropped out, disappeared, married, or moved off campus. My dorm scholarship kept me coming back.

My friend Sarah, happily married to a cute artist and living in a walk-up a few blocks away, gave me a copy of *The Power of Positive Thinking*. To a girl who identified as Jewish, it felt scarily Christian, so I just skimmed it and adopted what I could. Rather than use it to normalize my eating, I used it to stay alive.

– ∞ –

Like most normal girls, my sister Karen had a ring and a man. In June after my junior year, she was marrying Jonathan in a reform temple in Syracuse. She called me at school in March and asked me to be her maid of honor.

"What should I wear?" I asked, figuring on a lavender or turquoise taffeta gown I'd never wear again. I'd forgotten how practical Karen was.

"It's not a formal wedding," Karen said. "I'm wearing a white silk dress, not a wedding gown and Jonathan is wearing a suit, not a tux. Just wear whatever you want."

Feeling somewhat outrageous, I dressed the part. I chose a slinky, low-cut, shiny gold sheath and sexy, strappy, gold spikes that made me way taller than every one of my family members and most everyone else at the wedding except the cute, young, lanky Rabbi Luft, who I thought did an impressive job with the ceremony and deserved special thanks I intended to convey. Karen looked radiant and beautiful, in elegant white silk and linen. The Rabbi stole sideways glances at me, and I met his eyes with bold smiles. The reception was in the Jewish Center ballroom, and as soon as I made a toast, before the meal began, my diaphragm and I were off cavorting with lanky Rabbi Luft on the desk of his study downstairs, pleasantly saving myself from having to deal with public consumption of food. With strains of pop music from the D.J. in the background, it didn't surprise me in the least when the Rabbi and I came together with a loud, clear, appropriate, triple stereophonic burst of, "Oh, God! Oh God! Oh God!"

"I hope you don't get the wrong idea," he said, wrinkling his brow moments later, as we retrieved our clothing.

"Hell, no," I said, blowing him a kiss. "I've got only right ideas." I wriggled into the skintight gold outfit.

"I'm engaged," he said. "I don't usually do stuff like this."

"Congratulations," I said. "She's a lucky woman."

"Thank you," he said, zipping his pants. "I'm sorry if I made you miss dinner."

"Oh, that's okay, it's far less caloric feeding my lower mouth." I grinned.

"That's an original way to put it," he said.

I winked, put on fresh lipstick, and went back to the ballroom to dance, thinking I liked that lower mouth line, I'd have to trot it out again.

I briefly hung out with Amanda, Karen's childhood friend. Her husband, an overweight orthodontist, gawked at me, the golden apparition. She brought regards from her cousin Dorothy, now engaged to Paul Schneider's roommate at University of Rochester. Paul and Susan Levitz were engaged too. Greta had been married for two years to the basketball star from Karen's high school class. Gossip about old friends irritated me for some reason, even produced a twinge of, could it be, envy? It all sounded so boring and predictable. No, I had a new and exciting life and, except for family, was ready to slash and burn as many ties with my past as I could. I would operate untied in the world. I would stay free.

– ∞ –

In senior year, I hung out with Lydia, tall, thin, plain brunette, biology major, prisoner of a dorm scholarship, like me. I enrolled in a graduate Latin American lit course across the Street at Columbia with all native speakers. With only baby Spanish to explain complicated concepts, I never once opened my mouth in class. But I was determined to succeed despite overwhelming insecurity. I focused almost all my attention on this course and researched assiduously all semester long to come up with a winning final paper – the course's only requirement along with class attendance. I read piles of books and articles, took reams of notes, and thought long and hard before pulling a thesis together. (Evolution of the word "word" in Pablo Neruda's poetry) Lydia was with me when I got the postcard from the graduate course with a big bold A+.

"It must be a mistake," I said, scared to be happy, and forcing back tears.

"Let's celebrate," said Lydia. "Let's go out to dinner. All these years, we've been eating dorm meals, but we've never gone out to dinner together. Isn't that weird?"

"I'm not hungry," I said without thinking. "Anyway, that's what dates are for."

"Let's have a date with each other!" Lydia said brightly.

"I can't afford it," I said.

"I'll treat," said Lydia. "I've been saving babysitting money."

"Where would we go?"

"What would you like to eat?"

"A big salad?"

"A big salad it is. We'll go to Bunchy's on Amsterdam."

"It feels silly."

"Rowie, enjoy recognition. You worked hard for this grade. You earned it!"

"I did, didn't I?" Now I was crying. "I really did earn it, no tricks. No lies. I worked on it for hours and hours."

"You did, Rowie, you got into it and you did a wonderful job. You can be proud."

"It's the first time I enjoyed my schoolwork since I learned how to read." I couldn't turn off the emotions. "My first grade teacher scolded me for finishing the book after the first lesson. She said I was a bad girl."

Lydia hugged me.

"You have no idea how smart you are, do you?"

"I'm not very smart," I said and more tears came rushing out.

We were still by the mailboxes. A couple of girls we knew saw us in the hall.

"Is everything okay?"

"Rowie just got A+ in a graduate course!" Lydia said. "She's crying with joy."

"Congratulations, Rowie! Celebrate!"

– ∞ –

So we went to Bunchy's, a hip, crowded, noisy student restaurant. I picked at my lettuce and tomato salad. Why did I feel that I wanted to eat pasta, bread, doughnuts, and cookies? Why did I want to fill myself to the brim so I could empty to nothing? My mind zoomed a million miles an hour. Why did Lydia make a big deal of my getting a high grade when she got high grades all the time? I had to study ten times harder, but I was a great actress and made people think I was smart. What if I told the truth about myself? I sort of did by the mailboxes when I admitted to Lydia I knew I was dumb. But maybe, I pondered, I'm not so dumb, just lazy most of the time. I've worked since I was fourteen so I know I'm not always lazy. I wasn't lazy in the graduate course. I worked hard and got rewarded. I never had to work in high school and got top grades. Could it be I'm just badly trained? Could there be hope for me?

Lydia was eating chicken with her hands, obviously enjoying it. She also was delighting in potato salad and coleslaw, eating with gusto.

"I used to love potato salad," I said. "My mom made great potato salad, warm, with mustard and egg. She made good coleslaw too."

"Want some?" asked Lydia.

"I can't. I'm on a diet," I said.

"You don't eat much, do you?" said Lydia. "You're always on a diet. But I'll bet if they had pistachio ice cream, you'd get some. How come you're not afraid of that?"

"Can we not talk about food?" I shot back, irritated.

"I'm sorry," said Lydia. "But you're not fat, you know."

"Thanks a lot," I said sarcastically. I stood up quickly and pushed my chair in roughly. I flashed on the doughnut shop down the street, which would be my next stop. I heard the edge in my voice. "Thanks for listening sensitively and talking about food when I said I didn't want to talk about food, Lydia. You know what? I'm leaving now. I have to get back to school and pack. I'm going to visit my cousin Ralphie in Cambridge tomorrow for a few days. Thanks for the salad."

"Wait, Rowie!" called Lydia. She stood up. "Don't leave. You can pack later. Please, sit down."

I sat. To keep from crying, I twiddled my thumbs, then folded and unfolded a paper napkin.

"You've had a rough time, haven't you?" she said. She kept on eating. "Look, I'm a science major. I've read a bit about nutrition." She waved her hand at me, closed her eyes, shook her head. "I know, I know, you don't want to hear about food. But please listen. I have a hunch your eating habits are getting in the way of your functioning optimally, you know, doing your best. You're a human being, and humans need food. Please, do me a favor and eat a little piece of my chicken and a couple of bites of potato salad. Just to prove you can survive it. I beg you." She took a clean spoon from her place setting and placed the food on my salad plate.

Goose bumps rose all over my body in protest and a fearful voice shouted no, no, no, no, don't. But Lydia smiled and looked hopeful. She seemed to care that I picked up my fork and slowly put the potato salad in my mouth. Potato, celery, onion, mayonnaise. It was so delicious I cried. I ate the piece of chicken also.

"Thanks," said Lydia, smiling.

"Thank you," I said. I was hurting all over. My back and stomached ached, my arms felt heavy, my head pounded. A few tears flowed. "I've got some work to do on my eating habits."

"You're just fine," said Lydia. "We all have crap to deal with. I wish I could stop picking my toenails. I've been doing it since I was six."

169

I smiled. "Really? I couldn't pick mine because you need fingernails to do it and I had none so I learned to curl up like a pretzel and bite my toenails. Can you believe? Once I got started with my teeth, I could pull a big hunk off. Sometimes I still do. Do you spit or eat 'em?"

"Spit. You?"

"I figure they're high in calcium so I eat 'em. Do yours ever bleed?"

She nodded. "Sometimes I pull off whole slices of the nail and it hurts so much I have to pant like an animal to bear it, and then it bleeds so badly I have to wrap it up in tissues or toilet paper and Band-Aids, but with socks on, no one ever knows. It's a winter habit because I like wearing sandals in warm weather. Now our secrets are out. Here I thought I was the only disgusting one."

"Bleeding toenails. Not a very good conversation topic to have at the table, is it?" I said.

Lydia laughed. "Does it really gross you out or is that your mother talking?"

"Wow, I guess it's both my parents. Actually, it doesn't gross me out all that much. I think it's cool that we both screw with our toenails. That's weird that I sound like my parents."

"Yeah, scary, isn't it? I hear my mother's voice coming out of me a lot. I love her, but she's so nuts I can't believe I absorbed her craziness. It's like being brainwashed. I have to listen to myself carefully and make sure it's me talking."

"That's very cool," I said. "I'm going to think about that."

We walked back to the dorm so involved in chatting that I forgot all about stopping for doughnuts.

– ∞ –

TWENTY

Ralphie had a quiet Boston weekend planned. He met me at the train and we rode the T back to Somerville to drop off my bag at his apartment. It was a clear, sunny spring day, and we spent a short time at the art museum and a long time wandering around outdoors. We window shopped around Harvard Square and sat for espresso at a smoky café filled with chess and backgammon players who mindlessly munched on pastries my cells clamored for. I had taken up cigarettes and gum as hunger distraction. I ate breakfasts and salads but still binged and barfed regularly. I hated it.

Ralphie and I walked around Boston Commons and the path along the Charles River where we sat a little and watched skaters, runners, and crew teams practicing snappy, synchronized rowing.

My cousin's face, without thick glasses for the first time in years, seemed naked, his nose a little longer than I'd remembered, his eyes slightly smaller. It was a pleasant, open face, not perfect, but with interesting planes, expressive, even handsome in an offbeat way. Still adjusting to contacts, which had recently come on the market, he tilted his head up a little and his deep brown eyes looked downward giving him a bobbing, puppet-like appearance that took some getting used to. He'd been involved in tennis since high school, and his body was trim and well toned. Ralphie was my age, but he'd skipped a year in junior high so he was in his first year of graduate school at Harvard aiming towards a doctorate in psychology.

"I have a couple of pretty amazing professors," he said as we sat on the grass watching a duck family. "Alpert and Leary, remember those names because they're gonna be famous. They've been experimenting with a substance they believe can totally revolutionize not only psychology, but our whole lives. They're negotiating for a house near school and the new phase of the experiment should be up and running by next fall. I signed on to participate, and I'm pretty excited about it."

"Tell me more. What's the substance? Is it fattening? Can I try some?"

"It's not food, Rowie. It's a drug. It's been around since 1938. They think it's safe, but they plan to be very careful with it just in case and no, you can't. One of the things it may do is mimic psychosis – for a short time only – so that would make it possible to study psychosis in a laboratory situation. If it were available to just anyone, it could be dangerous. The stuff has a long

171

technical name, D-lysergic acid diethylamide, but it's called LSD or just acid for short. It's derived from a fungus that grows on grain plants."

"A fungus among us? Like a mushroom?"

"You're not far off, Rowie. Actually a Swiss chemist named Albert Hoffmann discovered LSD while he was trying to find a blood stimulant. He accidentally swallowed some and had unusual hallucinations. My professors are crazy about the stuff, and they say Aldous Huxley and Allen Ginsberg have taken it and compare it to the mushrooms indigenous people have used for centuries in sacred ceremonies."

"So will you take it too?"

"All the psych grad students will take turns so we can spend some time monitoring each other when we ingest the stuff."

"Sounds wild and a little scary. Do they accept outsiders?"

"Not right now. I had to sign a long document releasing them from liability if I drop dead or go nuts. If you're thinking of coming and joining, forget it unless you want to get a PhD in psych at Harvard."

"That's not gonna happen. I'm a Spanish major, remember?"

– ∞ –

In the evening we went to a party at a friend's. I nibbled carrot and celery sticks and drank wine. Back at the apartment, Ralph made a bed for me on the couch. I hugged him good night and went off to the bathroom to get into my nightgown and brush my teeth. Right next to the bathroom, I noticed the door to another room ajar. Soft sitar music was playing and a candle was the only light. I peeked in. Ralphie hadn't said much about his roommate except that he was a grad student at MIT. He was sitting in a yoga position on the floor, smooth, brown and naked, his eyes closed.

I brushed my teeth, took off my clothes, and before putting on my nightgown, hesitated a moment. I hadn't been with a man in months because I'd been so preoccupied with my Neruda project. What the hell, I thought, this guy will either throw me out or think he's having a wet dream. Just in case, I put my diaphragm in.When I left the bathroom, the door to the roommate's bedroom was still open, the candle flickered, soft music played, and he was just climbing into bed. I stood naked in his doorway and cleared my throat. When he saw me, his face registered fear, shock, lust, awe, happiness, and confusion.

"Mind if I join you?" I asked.

Next morning, I woke up to an empty bed. I stretched, smiled, went to take a shower and get dressed in sweater and jeans. In the living room, I carefully folded the sheets and blankets on the couch.

$$- \infty -$$

Ralphie was in the kitchen making us a peanut butter omelet, his specialty, which he ended up eating all by himself, surprise, surprise. I boiled myself an egg. I had no idea why he didn't say one word at breakfast, just kept his face in the Sunday *New York Times*, which he'd said earlier was a weekly splurge. He finally spoke when we were riding the T to the train station on my way back to New York.

"Rowie, how can you sleep with a stranger?" he demanded.

"All of a sudden your roommate is a stranger?"

He didn't laugh. "Come on, Rowie, he was a stranger to you. How could you do that?"

"Fairly easily," I answered. "I was horny. When I went to the bathroom, Govinda had his door open and there was a nice big bed and a naked man. Or was it a nice naked bed and a big man? Same difference." Still no laughs. "So I climbed in with him. Don't be a prude. We had fun."

"Govinda thinks you're a slut," he said.

"That's comical. He should only know I hadn't been with a man in six months. Some slut. Look, if it bothers you, I won't sleep with him again. No big deal. He wasn't really that great anyway."

"You just said you had fun."

"It's all relative. It was more fun than sleeping alone on the couch. It was an adventure. Look, I figured if he was your housemate, he was okay. Not like a regular stranger. Can we drop it?"

"Only if you'll promise me you won't jump into bed with any of my roommates again. It makes me feel weird."

"Ralphie, are you jealous? You know, the Brits allow first cousins to marry." I winked flirtatiously.

"Rowie, we're like brother and sister. I love you and I can't stand hearing a guy say anything nasty about you. When Govinda called you a slut, I wanted to punch him."

"Wow, that's exciting. Men fighting over me. Thanks for wanting to defend me, Ralphie. I'm sorry I deflated your opinion of me. If it bothers you so much, I'll sleep on the couch by myself next time. But, I must say, Govi could have kicked me out. Believe me, he didn't act as though he minded one bit."

"I'm sure. He's a guy, right? A pretty girl climbing into a guy's bed is a perfect fantasy. But not you, okay?"

"Okay, I've already agreed. So you think I'm pretty?"

"Yes."

"You're just saying that."

"No, Rowie. I mean it. I think you're pretty and so does just about everyone else. Too pretty to be jumping into strangers' beds. You can be afford to be picky, Ro."

"Your mom told me I was ugly when I was a kid so it's ironic that you're telling me I'm pretty."

"My mom is an idiot sometimes. You didn't take her seriously, did you?" He looked into my eyes. "Oh, God, you did. I'm so sorry. It's true that looks aren't so important, and it's what's inside that counts, but you happen to be pretty, maybe even beautiful."

His words fell into an empty compartment somewhere inside me, not fully registering. I had learned a while ago to tune out compliments. I gave a flippant answer.

"Maybe I am picky, Ralphie. Don't you think Govinda is special?" He grimaced. "All right, all right, I'm sorry. I said I wouldn't do it again."

"I appreciate that. One more favor. Could you call me 'Ralph' instead of 'Ralphie'? I'm twenty-one, not ten."

"You got it, Ralph. Correct me if I slip, okay?"

"Okay."

"Do you forgive me my trespass, Ralph?"

"I wish I understood you better, Rowie, but, yes, of course, I forgive you."

– ∞ –

174

TWENTY-ONE

Lydia and I began eating breakfast and lunch together. I'd have small portions of fruit and cereal, a couple of bites of toast, and a cup of tea, and then we'd walk over toward classes even though we were in different classrooms. We met again for lunch and I began to eat a little salad, a few carrot sticks and a half sandwich. I had to skip the ice cream because whenever I ate any, my feet would take me automatically to a toilet to empty my stomach. I rediscovered apples! What pleasure I got from biting into a crisp, juicy apple! I began eating an apple for dessert every day. At first it was hell for me to keep lunch down, but going straight to class with Lydia distracted me.

Dinners still bothered me. I couldn't bring myself to eat Salisbury steak or liver and onions, or any other kind of meat for that matter, and the cooked vegetables were soggy, but there was always an alternative like peanut butter, or yogurt, and I learned to put together breadless sandwiches of peanut butter and apple or banana. I ate slowly, savoring the sweet taste and combination of textures. Sometimes I'd spread peanut butter on bread and eat slice after slice with no control or willpower and then drink coffee or tea and find myself emptying it all into the toilet. At those times, I moved as though I were sleepwalking. I still got an elated feeling from throwing up, but I noticed I was not doing it three or four times a day anymore, but rather three or four times a week. If I stayed away from bakeries and doughnut shops, it was easier. The habit was slowing down. Still, I couldn't muster the nerve to tell either Lydia or Sarah, my closest friends. Shame sabotaged my courage each time I planned to confess, and failure stoked it even more. It was time for me to seek help. I would find a professional.

I asked around and got a referral to a talking psychiatrist. No more silent Freudians for me. This shrink, Emmett Gordon, tall, lean, bald, fidgety, with a nervous laugh, was on 72nd Street off Broadway. He gave me a special rate, which I paid for from my language lab job. I didn't want Mommy or anyone else to know I was in therapy. I went to him every Wednesday afternoon for six weeks and talked in generalities about my childhood before I gathered the nerve to tell him about my throwing up habit. Finally, I took a deep breath and said it aloud: "I overeat huge amounts of food and force myself to vomit." Then I sat in silence waiting for the heavens to send a deadly lightning bolt.

He looked straight at my body, giggled and said, "Congratulations, Miss Wine, I believe you've found an effective weight control technique." Giggle. Giggle.

"What?" I felt as though someone had punched me. "You think it's all right?"

More giggles. "Why, yes, I think it's brilliant."

If I'd been nervy I'd have told him that cutting off his balls would be a good weight control technique too. That is if he had balls. How come I knew forced puking was nuts, but he didn't? I told him I had to leave town so I wouldn't se him again and stumbled out of there. Was I crazy, or was the world insane?

– ∞ –

It rained on graduation day so the Class of '62 convened in the Cathedral of St. John the Divine. Conversation buzzed about engagement rings and June weddings. Lydia and I were among the only ones not flashing rocks. She would be going to medical school in the fall, at Duke, and I had accepted a grant to study comparative literature in Guatemala. My program didn't begin until the following January, and I planned to summer in California and then find something to occupy me for four months in Syracuse. Karen and Jon weren't able to get away from work to be at graduation, but Victoria and Mommy had driven down from Syracuse and were staying over at a hotel. Next day, I would be moving out and driving back upstate with them, leaving Barnard for good.

After the ceremony, we were to lunch with Lydia and her parents, Norm and Phyl. The rain had tapered off to a pleasant, light drizzle, and we all walked over to Broadway together to find a restaurant. Lydia's mom, Phyl, enormous and bovine, moved cautiously, holding on to her frail husband's arm. Just as we turned the corner onto Broadway, the rain picked up again. We were right in front of a Chinese restaurant with a big sign, Welcome Graduates.

"Let's eat here," Mommy said. "At least we can stay dry."

It was the place where I'd dined with Sy French before losing my virginity and bloodying his mattress.

At the table, Mommy was euphoric.

"Do you two know what a Barnard degree is worth?" she asked Lydia and me once we'd sat down.

Lydia laughed. "I don't know, Mrs. Wine, many thousands of dollars, I guess."

Phyl coughed. "Now, honey," she said to Lydia, "it's more than money, it's prestige Mrs. Wine is referring to, don't you think, Norm?"

Her husband nodded. "Right, hon," he said.

"Absolutely," said Mommy, lifting her glass of diet ginger ale for a toast. "Congratulations to the graduates. I'm proud of you. A Barnard degree is like a..."

"A pedigree?" I finished her sentence. "Like a pure bred dog has?"

"Well, I wouldn't want to compare my daughter to a cocker spaniel!" Mommy said, flushing.

"How about a Doberman?" I said and made a warrior face, clenched my fist. "I can now fight my way in the big, bad world."

Victoria spoke up with a mischievous grin. "Even better, you have official papers for breeding now, Rowie."

"Only with the best," said Mommy, beaming.

"Pure Ivy League," said Victoria.

Everyone laughed nervously and shifted their attention to the menu. They ordered what I considered an obscene amount of food. I asked for club soda with a lemon slice.

"Lydia tells me you're going to a banana republic," said Phyl to me, between giant spoonfuls of hot and sour soup. I sipped my soda.

"Rowie has a fellowship," bragged Mommy, slurping her wanton soup as though she hadn't eaten in three months. I watched them all with disgust. "Fulbright funds."

"Why do you want to go to a banana republic?" asked Norm.

"I want to learn to speak Spanish fluently," I said.

"Why don't you just move across town?" said Norm, laughing. "Didn't you see 'West Side Story'?"

"That's enough, Norm," said Phyl. "I'm sure Rowie has her reasons."

"She's going to look for a Latin lover," said Victoria, grinning.

"God forbid," said Mommy, the agnostic.

Victoria continued. "I can see the headline in the Syracuse paper now. "Barnard Graduate Weds Sugar Cane Cutter."

Mommy put down her fork, took a deep breath. "Lydia," she said brightly, "Maybe you could persuade Rowie to go to medical school, like you!"

"I can't stand blood, Mommy, remember?" I said.

"Dear, please don't say 'blood' at the table," Mommy said, making a face. Lydia and I exchanged knowing glances.

"What kind of work would you like to do, Rowie?" asked Norm.

"Truthfully, I'd like to go into advertising," I said. "I think it would be fun to write jingles and songs."

Mommy coughed. "Don't be ridiculous, Rowie. The business world is for shysters and crooks. You're far too good for that. Don't even think about it."

Instantly I was sorry I'd said anything. There was an awkward silence at the table.

Phyl broke the silence. "Rowie, you haven't eaten a thing! What can I serve you?"

"Nothing, thanks," I said. "I'm not hungry."

"Rowie stays nice and skinny, doesn't she?" Mommy said. "I'm so proud of her for that."

Lydia shuddered. I wanted to hide under the table, I was so embarrassed.

Phyl, unfazed, wrinkled her brow. "You have to eat, my dear. You can't just starve yourself. You're quite thin. Are you sure you're well?"

"I'm fine, thank you," I said, almost adding a moo since she looked like a cow.

"She's fine," Mommy echoed brightly.

"She's screwy when it comes to food," Victoria said. "So's my mom."

"Victoria!" Mommy exclaimed. "What a terrible thing to say!"

"Who wants dessert?" asked Norm. "I'm betting my Phyl will get some mango ice cream, right hon?"

"Right hon," she said and kissed him on the cheek. "My Norm knows what I like!" She winked.

"I would like to eat dessert in this restaurant," I exclaimed, suddenly remembering when I was dessert for Sy French.

"You haven't touched dinner and you're eating dessert?" questioned Phyl.

"Hush, Mother," said Lydia and put a finger to her lips.

"I have my reasons," I said and ordered a double scoop of mango ice cream. When the fortune cookies came and we read them out loud, I felt I was getting a personal message. Mine said, "A long journey will save your life."

– ∞ –

TWENTY-TWO

When Ralph suggested we spend the summer together at his folks' place in Los Angeles, I celebrated his genius. I wouldn't be leaving for Guatemala until after the first of the year, and I knew Uncle Benny and Aunt Bea had a grand piano and a pool I'd adore. Mornings, I'd go to Uncle Benny's office to help out, and afternoons, I'd practice jazz riffs, back flips, and work on a tan. Evenings, I'd let Ralph show me L.A. clubs.

My handsome cousin met me at LAX in the blue and silver Bel Air convertible his parents had bought him six years ago when they moved from the Bronx and became California car nuts. An L.A. dream car for a book-centered kid, the Bel Air had sat in their garage next to their everyday Nash Rambler and fancier Nash Ambassador while Ralph drove to college in Ohio in a red Karmen Ghia. Who would have figured, the marathon reader who left Bronx High School of Science, where his peers were all smart, for Van Nuys High where he was a freaky brain, would fall in love with cars? Turned out to be nothing more than a flirtation. In a kind of reverse teenage rebellion, after graduating at the head of his class in both high school and college, in a Harvard PhD Program in psychology, he returned to his roots as an East coast intellectual, broke off the car love affair, and used public transportation – not so difficult in Boston. After a hug and my oohs and ahs over the Bel Air, which Ralph dismissed with a shrug, we set off.

"I've got a bunch of news, not so good," Ralph said, as he maneuvered onto the 405 freeway and into Friday afternoon traffic. He seemed serious, but I didn't want serious.

"Let me guess," I said, lightheartedly, beginning to munch on my allotted peck of dirt the smog provided. I could feel the searing sun as we baked in the open car and made a note to get a hat. "It'll take the rest of the summer to get home?"

"That too," he said. "No, L.A. traffic is normal news. I have seriously bad news. My nana is in the hospital. She has a brain tumor and needs surgery."

His nana was Ceil Frankel, Aunt Bea's mother, a wealthy widow I associated with childhood visits to an elegant and cavernous West End Avenue apartment and a bon voyage party on the Queen Mary with more luggage than I'd ever seen outside a luggage store. Ceil had moved to California after her husband died, while Ralph was still in grade school. I hadn't seen her in more than ten years.

"Ceil has a tumor? I'm sorry," I said. "I hope she makes it. Is it malignant? Is she in pain?"

"She gets bad headaches. That's what drove her to the doctor. Doc doesn't know whether or not it's cancer, but she's seventy-five and brain surgery's serious. He gives odds against her pulling out of this. We haven't told her."

"I hate secrecy and doctors' odds," I said. "They should leave gambling in Vegas where it belongs. If I ever get some life-threatening condition, please do me a favor and inform me. I'll be the first one to think positively. When's your nana's operation?"

"In a couple of days. My mom and Aunt Jeri are completely bonkers. I got in a couple of days ago. Mom and Dad told me I probably got here just in time for Nana's funeral."

"Nonsense," I said, wondering why they hadn't called me. "Haven't they heard there's hope where there's life? They should read Norman Vincent Peale." Actually I had never read all of *The Power of Positive Thinking*. I had meant to, but never got around to it, had just skimmed parts. But I alluded to it freely.

"Rowie, you're such a cockeyed optimist, I love that about you. But Nana is dying. Some Pollyanna religious cliché isn't going to save her life."

"Peale's book is not a cliché, it's a best seller, and she's not dead yet, is she?"

We crept along in silence for a few minutes. Ralph switched on a jazz station. Brubeck's music slightly relaxed my edginess. I was sweating through my light blouse. It was after six and the sun still scorched. I hadn't overeaten or thrown up all day, had even swallowed a bit of wilting salad on the plane. Gimme a medal, Mommy always said when she ate lightly.

"One more piece of news. This one you're not gonna like. I won't be here for very long. I got a grant to study Japanese in Hawaii for the summer. It was an offer I couldn't refuse. I leave in a week, unless I have to stay for the funeral."

My heart sank. I'd be stuck in Los Angeles without Ralph! What the hell would I do all summer? Would I even have come if he'd told me?

"I'm happy for you," I managed to get out. Why couldn't I tell him how shitty I felt? I was incensed for a moment, then felt empty. Suddenly I wanted a bakery or doughnut shop. I longed to stuff myself. Instead I lit a cigarette, swallowing smoke and disappointment. How was it possible for a college graduate to be so unequipped to deal with the slightest adversity? I wondered. Why didn't Barnard require Adversity 101? The course where you learn when life goes sour, pretend it's a Kosher dill.

Ralph pulled open the ashtray. "I'm sorry, Rowie. I know we made plans. I promise to be back in time for our camping trip up the coast."

I grunted.

"Rowie, with your asthma, why are you still smoking?"

"It's better than some of my other vices," I said.

"Yeah, but can they kill you?"

"If I'm lucky. I'll think positively."

"You're a bundle of contradictions."

"So are you."

"I don't blame you for being angry."

"Who's angry?"

– ∞ –

Aunt Bea and her sister Jeri had already ordered a casket and were about to go shopping for black funeral dresses because Bullocks was having a sale. I wanted to shake them both, knock their matching dyed red heads together. They had their mother dead and buried before she had the operation which could save her and they expected would kill her. I was determined to help her to survive, just to show them how wrong they were. My entire summer plans were collapsing. I smoked madly and plotted.

"Rowie," Uncle Benny said solemnly after giving me a tour of the house, which turned out to be a modest North Hollywood stucco, three bedrooms, one bath, with four-car garage they'd expanded for their car mania. Except for a small patio, narrow strip of concrete and tiny cabana, the famous in-ground pool swallowed up the yard, more like a pool with a house than a house with a pool. You could practically jump out the window and land in three feet of water. Uncle Benny didn't count on my fierce reaction to the offer that followed the house and pool tour. "Why don't you go shopping with Bea and Jeri for a funeral dress?" he suggested innocently. "Don't worry, I'll take care of buying it for you. My treat."

I exploded. "Excuse me, Uncle Benny, I don't mean to sound harsh, but I don't understand planning a funeral while there's still hope for survival. I've witnessed pulling funerals together quickly. Why the hell isn't everyone spending time with Ceil instead of going shopping? I'm not even related to her but at least I'm praying for her and thinking positively. She's not dead yet."

"I appreciate your noble thought, darling, but the doctors have given her odds of 100 to 1."

"Well, I'll go for that one shot, Uncle Benny, and I wish you all would too. What if I needed brain surgery? Would you all kill me off ahead of time too?"

"Come on, darling. You're a young girl. It's a lot different with Ceil. She's lived a long life. She's a widow. What does she have to look forward to?"

"God, Uncle Benny, your own sister, my mom, is a widow, Jeri is a widow. I hope they all have a lot more years to look forward to! Are you saying a woman without a husband doesn't deserve to live?"

"Take it easy, Rowie, now you're getting carried away. I've kept Ceil's room overflowing with flowers. I'm not a monster like you think, darling. You've got to remember neither Jeri nor your mom is seventy-five the way Ceil is."

"Well, no matter what her age, I refuse to kill her off in my mind."

"Suit yourself. Do you have something black to wear to the funeral?"

"Don't worry, I'm from New York."

– ∞ –

Ralph dropped me at the hospital on his way to aikido class. Originally I'd planned to learn aikido as part of my self-improvement summer but given the new turn of events, I chose to visit Ceil. I was shaking a little, nervously asking myself why I was so fixated on this mission and why I'd so quickly refused the offer of a new dress. Like a two-year-old, I disagreed reflexively with authority figures. Maybe going shopping was a coping mechanism for Bea and Jeri and not as heartless as I'd judged. Maybe they didn't feel like hanging out with their mother. Mommy had never liked Ceil, described her as imperious and controlling. But then, Mommy never liked rich people, so maybe it was sour grapes.

Uncomfortable but determined, I took a deep breath and entered Ceil's room.

Ceil looked pretty much the same as I remembered. Surrounded by more flowers than the Bronx botanical garden, she was propped up in bed, under the covers from waist down. She whipped off rhinestone-framed glasses. Blotting her lipstick in front of a little mirror set up on her tray table, next to her make-up kit, she looked elegant in a peach satin and beige lace bed jacket, matching nails and lipstick. Her frosted hair, blond on blond, was perfectly in place, her skin pulled taut around the eyes and mouth. I realized the tautness explained why her smile was small and stiff. Did the family have her dead and buried because repeated plastic surgery had left her looking a bit corpse-like? I chuckled to myself at the bad joke. At least the feisty spirit I remembered hadn't been nipped or tucked although she seemed to lack luster. Her eyes didn't sparkle, probably from some combination of tumor, drugs, and depression.

I kissed her on the cheek, caught a whiff of gardenia scent, explained who I was, sent regards from my mother.

"Weena! I wouldn't have recognized you, dear. You used to be enormous. I always thought you had a pretty face buried under the layers. Now you look fabulous, darling. How lovely of you to visit me!" This she mouthed sweetly, then her tone shifted abruptly, and she barked an order: "Sit down!"

I sat. "Yeah," I said, "I'm thin now. It's an obsession. Also I call myself Rowie now. No more Weena. If you wouldn't mind, I'd appreciate your calling me Rowie."

"Rowie, is it? Odd name. You were always an odd one. Anyhow, I approve of your thinness, dear. You were such a horsy girl, but you've come through nicely. Thin is a good obsession. Do you have a boyfriend?"

"Not at the moment," I said, although I would have preferred telling her it was none of her business. It was my idea to visit, so I'd plow through.

"Well, you're young and attractive enough. Keep yourself thin, that's most important. Tell me dear, where are my daughters, floating around the pool? Why didn't they call me today? Why isn't Ralphie here?"

"They'll all try to be here later, Ceil." My nose itched. "Nice flowers."

"I'd rather they skip the damn flowers," she said. "I can't talk to flowers. I see my hairdresser more than I see my daughters."

"Ceil," I said, diving into my mission. "I have a big favor to ask you."

184

She frowned, a small frown since her face didn't have much mobility. "I hope you're not going to ask me for money for some business scheme like your father did. He tried to hit me up years ago to invest in a bar and again later for a factory. I'm glad to say I turned him down."

"I didn't know. Nothing like that." I felt a twinge in my gut, made a note to ask Mommy about this.

"I can't help being suspicious," she said. "I haven't seen you in ten years and you barge into my hospital room where I'm awaiting surgery, and you have the chutzpah to ask for a favor. Now I'm curious, what kind of favor are you looking for?"

I was tempted to apologize and run, but I stayed, feeling a little less sure of myself but plodding on anyhow. "I heard you were scheduled for surgery," I said. "I want you to pull through."

"You want me to pull through? That's the favor? What's it to you? What did my daughters tell you? They think I'm going to croak, don't they? Oh, I know, nobody says a damn thing, they all pussyfoot around it as though I don't know what's going on. I'm not stupid. It's written all over their faces. Those fake smiles. Feh. Do you know they're going to shave my head? Tell Bea and Jeri to stick a decent wig on my head if I drop dead. And if I pull through, I won't even be able to wear a wig for a couple of weeks because of the bandages. Maybe some kind of hat would work. I wish hats would come back. I'd love a good milliner."

"Ceil, I'll bet you can find a milliner to design hats so gorgeous you'll bring them back into fashion by yourself."

"I don't know about that," she said and sipped water. "Would you fluff my pillows?" she snapped and leaned forward to give me access.

I did as she asked. "That okay?"

"A little bit more," she commanded. I repeated what I'd just done, saw no improvement, but she did.

"Now," she said, "tell me again about this favor you're asking."

I spoke slowly and clearly, took her hand, and held eye contact. "The favor I am asking is for you to recover. Then you can wear whatever wig or hat you choose until your hair grows back."

She removed her hand from my grip. "Darling, really, what are you talking about?"

My legs shook, but there was no way I'd back down from this mission.

185

"I'll be direct," I said. "Would you like to pull through, or would you rather die?"

"You do have as much chutzpah as your father," she said. "What kind of question is that? Nobody talks like that. You're supposed to tiptoe around the subject of kicking the bucket. Sure, if I had a choice, I'd like to hang around a while. I have a nice life. A condo in Sherman Oaks. A Tuesday canasta game. And I finally found a good manicurist." She inspected her nails, then narrowed her gaze and scrutinized me. "What makes you think I have a say in this?"

"Two reasons. First, I have a hunch." I smiled. "Do you ever get hunches?"

"I get pretty damn good hunches about business. My husband respected my hunches. I knew to turn your father down, didn't I? For sure I would have lost my shirt with him."

Again with my father. What was it with these insensitive people? I wondered. California smog? Should I mention he was dead? Nah, I'll ignore it unless she brings him up again. "So you know about hunches." I said. "Good. I also think if you believe in yourself, you can make things happen."

She raised her eyebrows slightly, and looked at me with doubt. I went on.

"Let me ask you, do you have a good doctor?"

That perked her up. "Supposedly the best. You know your uncle. He always finds the best of everything when I foot the bill."

"Do you trust him, the doctor, I mean?"

"I suppose. What the hell is this, some kind of *meshuga* game? If you must know, Dr. Rosenberg saved the life of the brother of the President of the United States, so I'd like to think I can trust him to do the same for me."

"Good. That's good." I went on, pulling words from someplace beyond my conscious mind. "So, how do you feel about God? You trust God?"

She raised her eyebrows again. "You're an odd duck, Weena. Always were if my memory serves, even as a fat little kid. You're asking me how I feel about God now, something else most people don't talk about. I don't know why I'm bothering to answer you, but there's something fascinating about this ridiculous inquisition. Get me some fresh water with ice, will you?" I went out to fulfill the order wishing she'd say "please" just once, and call me my name. I brought back a full pitcher of ice water.

"Don't forget, Ceil," I sang, "my name is Rowie now."

"All right, Rowie, you asked me about God. I belong to a temple. I go to High Holiday services. God has been pretty good to me until now. This thing in my head is my first big complaint. I don't know if it's good or bad that it's all in my head."

She laughed stiffly, and I joined her.

"So, if you trust both the doctor and God, would you say you're in good hands?"

She brightened. "Who better than God and the doctor? Maybe they're one and the same?" Her eyes suddenly twinkled.

"That's great, Ceil, that means you have a real shot at making it."

"Thank you, darling! I'll call my travel agent right away. Hand me the phone book on that table, will you? Where should I go? How about Greece for my birthday in August? Will you join me?" I couldn't tell whether she was being snide, but I decided to believe her words. I handed her the phone book.

"Ceil, a trip to Greece sounds fabulous, but August may be a bit premature. How about New Year's? And that's a wonderful invitation, thank you, but I have a fellowship to study in Central America, so I can't go. You're going to have the time of your life. You'll be a new woman. By then, your hair and nails will be back, and the headaches will be gone. I'll bet you'll dance your way through Greece. I'd love to get a postcard from you."

"Darling, you're definitely a *meshugana* but you're also a breath of fresh air. Everyone else comes in here with a long face and phony smiles while they're panting for my money. I wouldn't be surprised if Bea and Benny were already house hunting in the canyon. But you've given me some real hope. I mean it, sweetie."

"They're just worried about you because they love you so much. They can't imagine life without you."

She beamed. I hoped my words were true and not just some made up bullshit to fool us both. I was tempted to ask her to give my regards to my Grandma and Grandpa and Daddy in the event that she died after all, but I didn't want to send a mixed message or mention Daddy again.

I leaned over, semi-hugged and air-kissed her. "I'll see you after the operation," I said. Between her gardenia perfume and the mini-flower shop in there, I wheezed lightly. For a nanosecond, as I was giving my positive thinking

187

lecture to Ceil about healing her tumor, it occurred to me to heal myself. But the moment passed.

Later that evening, as I lay in bed, my mind wandered to Ceil's revelation about Daddy. She spoke so disdainfully of him. It's true he was a shitty provider and rotten father. It gave me a stomach ache just remembering how bad he made me feel most of the time. What a joke that he spent years selling remedies to make people feel better! Mommy used to say he kept that job only because she sat on him and when she got off him for a minute, he leapt into the big fiasco, his pocketbook factory business. After that came the job-hopping, selling appliances and used cars. But whatever he did for a living, Daddy was always ruing his decision to give up the tavern dream, blaming the bank for anti-Semitism, blaming his father-in-law for not trusting him enough to loan him seed money, blaming Mommy for not persuading her father, blaming his parents, blaming bad luck, blaming the kids he had to support, and cursing God for it all. If his tavern had succeeded, how many alcoholics would he have bred?

I realized that Daddy's biggest accomplishment was having a family. Even though he screwed that up too, at least I came into the world. What if I were more like him than I realized? What if my failure to stop eating and puking was linked to Daddy's failure to make a living? No! I screamed to myself. I am me! I don't hurt people. I help people. Somehow, that will make my life meaningful.

– ∞ –

Miracles of miracles, Ceil survived surgery. Astounded, her doctor pronounced an encouraging prognosis. The casket, chosen in advance, was cancelled. I didn't say I told you so once. Even though the black funeral dresses were marked final sale, Jeri and Bea crowed when Bullock's accepted them back for credit. Ralph left for Hawaii, and Aunt Bea went to help Uncle Benny with bookkeeping at the office, a job I originally was supposed to do. Jeri said she was busy even though I knew sending her son Marshall to sleep-away camp had freed her from mommying duties, and she'd probably be busy on the golf course.

When Uncle Benny explained that they could get a stranger to look after Ceil during her convalescence or I could do it – which they would prefer – I agreed to look after her. Ceil would sleep at Jeri's and spend days at Bea's.

She arrived first day home from the hospital shuffling one tiny step at a time, leaning on Jeri who was practically holding her up. Dazed and befuddled, wearing a long, elegant bottle green silk and beige lace nightgown and robe, her head swathed in bandages, Ceil looked like an elegant queen or guru of some esoteric Eastern cult on exotic, spacey drugs. At 7:30 in the morning, just in time for Aunt Bea and Uncle Benny to say hello and goodbye to her after their morning coffee, Jeri, large May's shopping bag in hand, walked her in, deposited her on the couch, plopped the shopping bag down in the kitchen, whispered a few words to Bea out of Ceil's earshot, and took off. Ceil sat and stared vacantly.

"Don't worry, darling," Aunt Bea said to me. She doesn't know what's happening so there's no such thing as a mistake with her." She laughed and added, "You don't have to bathe her. Just use a washcloth on her crevices and holes. Also, I have a great recipe for homemade soup. Mix a can of cream of mushroom with a can of vegetarian vegetable. One of my specialties. She's wearing a diaper right now, and there are more in this bag, but encourage her to use the toilet. Do your best. And just be there to keep her company, dear."

I didn't quite digest the crevices and holes speech and didn't dare ask for clarification.

Ceil's condition was called aphasia, which the doctor said could be short or long term. The presenting symptom was her inability to associate words with corresponding objects. She seemed to have a full inventory of nouns to choose from, but she almost always chose the wrong one. She asked for a pencil, and when I brought the pencil, she scolded me: "No, no, no, a nail file." When I brought the nail file, she got even more frustrated, and yelled, "No, no, no, a flower." I ran out in front and picked a flower, but that wasn't it either. She was beside herself with frustration, unable to communicate the simplest of needs. I kept going, trying comb, clock, telephone, cup, radio, on and on, racing around the house collecting objects for her to look at while she graduated to strange, inhuman screeches that filled the whole place. I tried to teach her the names of objects, but she couldn't retain them.

As we spent more time together, and I calmed down, I discovered a way to get inside her brain's odd system. I'd take a deep breath, shut my eyes, and get an image. Usually, whatever I saw turned out to be what she wanted.

The front section of the living room, next to the picture window, had been designed with a kidney-shaped platform about a foot high, where the original owners had kept a grand piano. Uncle Benny had chosen instead to dine in the kitchen, park his concert grand in the dining room, and make a mini oasis on the platform. There were tubs of all kinds of plants growing wildly around the windows and one chair facing in like a throne. That was the only place Ceil agreed to sit, in a regal, high-backed, maroon velvet chair, her back to the window and plants, her bandaged head alternately teetering and held high, ordering me around in her demented gibberish, and getting frustrated when I occasionally failed to meet her expectations. There were two single beds in my room and Ceil was assigned one for her naps, but she refused to get off the maroon throne. When she nodded out after her sandwich, her head drooping onto her chest, I worried she'd fall out of the chair so I rigged up a couple of leather belts and belted her in. The chair had enough heft to stay in place.

As she slept, I grabbed something small to eat and headed for the grand piano. At the keyboard, I unwound, practiced scales, played with chords, and fooled around with jazz sounds I improvised based on old classic tunes. Sometimes when Ceil started screaming for me, I resented the interruption. I'd bang loud bass chords and go stand in front of her angrily.

"What do you want now, Queenie?" I'd ask, and the guessing game would start. When I felt peaceful, I enjoyed being with Ceil and handled her requests easily. In anger, I had no clue and got frustrated. Sometimes I'd hang out in front of Aunt Bea's open cupboards and refrigerator and search for binge food, lamenting my inability to sneak off to doughnut shops or grocery stores. Ceil and I mirrored each other's frustration. Occasionally, I berated myself for encouraging her to survive, which produced guilt and more binge fantasies. But, who wanted to binge on tuna fish and Campbell's soup? In desperation, I settled for bread and crackers. I was careful not to totally empty packages because then I'd have to deal with empty containers and admit I'd pigged out.

I learned TV was a perfect narcotic. With Ceil parked in front of it, hypnotized into oblivion, I couldn't practice piano because of the noise, but I could binge and purge and read quietly. She had no problem shrieking when she needed help.

The first few days of summer moved along this way. It was warm, but window air conditioners kept the temperature comfortable. Ceil's hair was growing in white and bristly. It turned out her repertory of needs was small, and I had it down. Nail file, hair brush, lipstick, glasses, perfume, tea with milk and two saccharine pills, Chicken of the Sea solid white tuna on rye toast

190

with hard boiled egg and Miracle Whip, no celery, no lettuce. Jeri helped on that one, but still it felt like a coup – as did tweezers and the task of tweezing chin hairs, and the *L.A. Times* obituaries read aloud daily. I didn't exactly clean her crevices and holes although I wiped her mouth and nose when they obviously needed wiping. Apparently the medication she took constipated her, so my leaving the morning diaper on all day wasn't a problem, especially with my defective olfactory sense, injured from all the puking.

On my fourth day, Aunt Bea and Uncle Benny came home to a load in Ceil's diaper. Immediately, they made a big stink over the big stink, opened windows, grimaced endlessly, berated me, and threw me incredulous, dirty looks.

"Oh my God, it smells worse than a public toilet," Aunt Bea said, holding her nose. "Rowie, how can you stand it? Why didn't you change her diaper? What have you been feeding her? It's stronger than your uncle's farts."

"My farts are flowers compared to this," Uncle Benny said, opening the door to the yard. "What's worse, the heat or the stink?"

"Not even close," Aunt Bea said.

"We're very disappointed in you, Rowie," said Uncle Benny.

"I'm sorry," I said. I was scared to mention my impaired sense of smell, for fear they'd send me to a doctor, and I'd be exposed. So instead I allowed them to think I was a slob.

"I'm checking on home care," Aunt Bea said, fanning her face with an envelope. "No," Uncle Benny said. "I'll make the calls, Bea. You clean up your mother."

Ceil's insurance covered home care visits, and the helper was set to arrive next afternoon. Little did anyone in the family guess the depth of relief this would provide me.

It had never occurred to me that the home care aide could be a man. What a delight to open the door and find Tommy Fernandez, muscular, tawny, short, sturdy, and handsome, with loose black curls, dark eyes, and a wonderful smile. He walked right in, quickly managed to guide Ceil to the single bed I couldn't get her to, washed her thoroughly, changed her, spoke softly and gently to her, and won her trust. She snored loudly within minutes.

"You're amazing, Tommy," I said, touching his arm and noting the firmness. "Thank you so much. Would you like a cold drink?" I couldn't take my eyes off this handsome guy. I felt myself grinning.

"Sure, don't mind if I do. I always have a few minutes to spare for a pretty woman." He followed me into the kitchen. "You seem to be taking pretty good care of your grandma."

"Thanks. She's not related to me. She's my aunt's mother. She doesn't remember words so I have to tune in to figure out what she wants."

He grinned. "Honey," he said. "Tell me if I'm wrong. I'm tuning in to you right now, and I think I know what you want."

"Am I that obvious?" I asked, brushing his arm.

"You have beautiful thick hair," he said, running his fingers through my hair. "I'd like to kiss you."

We wasted no time.

Laughing, hugging and kissing, we made our way out of the kitchen to the living room couch, wildly throwing off our clothes as we went. Rummaging around, Tommy pulled a condom from his white pants pocket, and we went at it, this way and that way, panting and sweating with Ceil's snoring in the background. When he left, I insisted he take the dirty diaper and the used condom with him to dispose of far away.

– ∞ –

Uncle Benny had promised to pay me twenty dollars a week for my services. Every Friday evening, with a generous smile, he announced, "It's payday, doll. Hand me your wallet." Then he proceeded to remove and pocket all the bills in there and substitute a crisp twenty. I knew I should say something, or empty my wallet ahead of time, but I was too ashamed and I had the satisfaction of Tommy and my binging, so I told myself I didn't want to rob him of the simple pleasure he got from ripping me off. It seemed unfair that he exploited me, but I laughed and secretly called him a dick. I wondered, could Uncle Benny be blaming me for cheating him out of Ceil's inheritance?

– ∞ –

192

TWENTY-THREE

The last week of August, I said goodbye to Tommy. We both knew it was just a fling. Ceil was ambulatory and out of diapers, the bandages were off, and she was well enough to stay at Jeri's. Ralph came home, and he, his dad, and I took off for our trip to Seattle in Uncle Benny's sleek new Citroën, their fifth car. I had made up my mind, once again, to eat only salads all week and not throw up at all. This time, I told myself, I was serious.

We took the coast highway, with grand vistas of the Pacific giving me new deep gratitude to be alive. I marveled at the beauty of Santa Barbara and Carmel, at the profuseness and variety of plants and colorful flowers. Who knew geraniums could grow into tall, thick walls of hedges instead of constrained little pots? I dreamed of living in this California dream world forever.

We stayed in San Francisco for two days, roaming the hills, the wharf, the various neighborhoods and sights. Our last evening, we dined at the elegant Top of the Mark at the Mark Hopkins Hotel. I was struggling to keep dinner down and wandered out onto the terrace. I had a strange déjà vu and knew instantly that this hotel, the Mark Hopkins, had been the site of Mommy's romantic tryst I'd accidentally stumbled upon years earlier. As I looked out at the city and the bay, it occurred to me that her life hadn't held much romance. Mostly, she and Daddy had a mean-spirited relationship. Not happy and loving like Grandma and Grandpa. I wondered when Mommy and Daddy stopped having sex. Like flipping a switch, the instant I thought about Daddy and sex, I couldn't hold onto my food and rushed to the ladies' room to purge. I couldn't tell whether I threw up involuntarily from nausea or not. All I knew was it triggered a huge disturbance.

_ ∞ _

Next day we checked out of the motel and set off for wine country, the Napa Valley. It was my country, Rowena Wine's country, or Rowena Wine's wine country. All the wineries in the area had tasting rooms, and no one told me until afterward how the ritual went. You were supposed to smell the bouquet, swirl the wine around in your mouth, close your eyes, savor the flavor, and then spit the wine out into a spittoon. I was probably the only one in Napa whose food shot out regularly, and yet in the tasting rooms, I swallowed and kept it all down. We winery-hopped all morning into afternoon. In addition to the wines, Uncle Benny and Ralph enjoyed sampling the many gourmet treats the winery shops offered, pretzels and crackers for dipping into all kinds of interesting sauces, ginger, chocolate, chili, avocado, salty, spicy, sweet, sour, all to entice visitors to buy jars of the sauces and dips to take home. I contemplated pigging out and then puking, but there were too many people around and I didn't know what kind of toilet they had. This hadn't stopped me in the past, so maybe I was getting better. Why couldn't I sample small amounts like a normal person? Why did I have to be an extremist? I thought of buying food I could pig down later, but having earned a grand total of fifty-seven dollars and change from my summer job, I was in no position to shop. Uncle Benny got a thick chocolate sauce for Aunt Bea.

After the sixth winery, I stumbled to the Citroen and promptly fell asleep curled up in the back seat. I woke up disoriented and nauseated with a horrid taste in my mouth.

"Stop the car! Stop the car now!" I pleaded from the back seat. "I'm going to be sick. Hurry."

Ralph was driving and pulled onto the shoulder instantly. We were on a two-lane road surrounded by huge trees. I got out, leaned one hand on the car and bent over. I felt as though I would vomit, but wasn't about to induce vomiting in front of anyone. I immediately spotted a long, wide, striated metal drainpipe on the side of the road, headed right for it. I walked about half the length of it and heaved next to it, wine-purple throw-up, non-induced. Then I made my way to the opening, crawled inside, stretched out in the darkness, and fell asleep.

Loud, tinny banging woke me up.

"Rowie, come out of there!" I heard. "Rowie, are you okay? Say something."

Their voices sounded distant. Who were they? Where was I? Suddenly I knew. I was inside Mommy's womb headed for the birth canal, about to be born. I was scared to come out, scared of what was waiting for me. I wouldn't come out. I would stay inside forever. No one could force me out. There was pounding on the metal, banging right next to my head. I had to put my hands over my ears. I screamed for them to stop. The echo of my own voice reverberated painfully. It got quiet again. My left leg began to itch. I couldn't reach to scratch it. I moved my head enough to push around the pile of dirt and powdery leaves under me. I got a whiff of dust and pine needles and thought for a moment I had to sweep and mop or I'd be in some kind of trouble. Then I realized this was my own private space and I didn't have to clean it. I wanted to get comfortable so I stretched out on my stomach with my arms extended in front of me, my head resting on my right arm.

"Rowie, please!" Ralph's face showed at the opening about ten feet from me. He was speaking softly. "Rowie, I love you. Come out now. You drank too much wine."

"Wine?" I said, stirring a little. Then I remembered. "I am Wine! I am the goddess of wine." I saw myself dancing wildly, in a big Dionysian circle inside a vat of grapes, stomping with every man I'd ever had sex with, starting with the Columbia Business School creep, Sy French, and ending with Tommy, the nurse. We danced ourselves into a swirling mass of color, faster and faster we whirled and whirled, now a formless mass, and then someone hit a button and flushed us all down the toilet. "I see," I said, "I am really Persephone, snatched from my mother and spirited away to the underworld."

I heard a familiar voice from far away.

"Rowie, you drank too much wine, and it's having an effect on your mind. Come out of there. We want you to come out now. Take my hand."

Was that the obstetrician?

"Are you helping me be born?"

"I'm your cousin, Ralph Fine, and I'm helping you get out of a culvert on the side of a road in Humboldt County, in the redwood forest of California. We're on our way to the Seattle World's Fair, remember? Come out, Rowie. Come on out. Take my hand."

"Ralph? How do I know it's really you? Maybe you're just saying that to trick me into coming out, and then you'll capture and hurt me."

"I'm flagging down the next car and getting them to send for the cops, Ralph," I heard Uncle Benny say. "This is ridiculous. I think she needs the white coats."

"I'm handling it, Dad," Ralph asserted. "Do not get the police or any other authorities involved. Go take a walk."

My head hurt, and I had to pee. I knew I had to go down that birth canal and emerge into a world I didn't understand, even though I wanted to lie in the darkness forever. Slowly, on my belly, I inched forward towards the light and Ralph's hand. I had gone in easily, but I must have expanded inside, grown to full term. Moving was difficult, but I had no choice, I was going to be born again, my time had come.

"Atta girl," Ralph said. "Keep pushing forward. You're doing great. Yes, keep moving. Keep moving. You're almost there. Push, Rowie. Reach for my hand. That's it, I've got the tips of your fingers. Don't stop. Keep coming. Good girl."

He entwined his fingers with mine. That felt welcoming. I started crying. I could barely move. I was stuck. Was I destined to be stuck here forever? Would they have to cut me out? Maybe I could be oiled or waxed so I could slip through. After my arms and shoulders squeezed out, my head emerged into the light. Ralph put his arms under my armpits and tugged me the rest of the way.

"Thank God," he said, lifting me to my feet, and hugging me. "You could use a bath, but you're in pretty good shape I'd say. Welcome to the world, dear Rowie. This is like an acid trip. I had no idea wine could be a hallucinogen. Must have something to do with your metabolism. I can't wait to tell Professors Leary and Alpert. I advise you never to go near real hallucinogens. They could kill you. I'd like you to tell me everything you experienced. Don't leave anything out. How do you feel?" He helped me to the car. Uncle Benny approached.

"I'm a little shaky and dizzy, but I'm okay," I said. I looked around. "The trees look different. Greener. What happened?"

"You went nuts is what happened," said Uncle Benny, impatiently, as he climbed into the car. "We lost an hour and a half here. I was beginning to think we'd have to leave you here and pick you up on our way home."

"Dad, cool it," said Ralph. To me, he said, "Ignore the old man. He's being a putz."

"I have to pee," I said. Uncle Benny gasped. "But I promise I'll go right behind that tree." I pointed. My hand trembled.

"I'll walk you part way," Ralph said, and firmly took my elbow.

I knew they both worried I'd climb back into the womb tube, but their worries were unfounded. I was born, out, and ready for a new life. As I looked at the shimmering trees, I saw them smiling at me and I could swear they were whispering a message.

"Ready for love," the trees said. "You are ready for love."

– ∞ –

_ ∞ _

PART TWO

_ ∞ _

TWENTY-FOUR

Before I knew it, Labor Day had passed and I was staying with Mommy in Syracuse, this time just the two of us since Victoria was away at Bennington. Karen and Jonathan lived a building away in the same complex, and my big sister stopped in regularly for a quick visit after her teaching day ended.

"Do you think about getting married, Rowie?" Karen asked one afternoon as she nibbled a butter cookie. "When I was your age I worried." We sat at Mommy's kitchen table over tea. I abstained from cookies so I wouldn't have to run off and vomit.

"You and Mommy are probably more worried about me than I am," I said. "Marriage doesn't interest me. Probably never will. I realize you and Jonathan are happy but to be honest, I'd rather be single than risk having a marriage like Mommy and Daddy's."

"You're the only woman I know who doesn't worry about being an old maid."

"Mommy taught us not to marry young, remember? Finally there's a piece of her advice I can follow."

"Just be careful," Karen said. "Don't let yourself get so old you won't find a husband."

"I can't believe you're telling me this, Karen," I said. "You sound like an old *yenta*."

"I am," she said. "I'm twenty-five, and thank God my worries are over. Jonathan saved me."

I got up from the table. "I hope you're right," I said. "No offense, but as for me, I plan to save myself."

– ∞ –

The school year in Guatemala began in January, so I took a temporary market research job for three months. It was a straightforward assignment. Interview a wide variety of people, and ask them to look at a deck of photo cards of mechanics, professors, factory workers, doctors, and so forth - obvious economic differences - and choose photos of people most likely to watch TV. Since I had no network of acquaintances in Syracuse, I had to tap into Karen's and Mommy's networks. I did most of the interviews in the evenings so I was able to borrow Mommy's car. Otherwise, I took the bus.

For the most part, the results were predictable. Educated people went through the cards with little thought and were sure blue collar folks watched more TV than professionals. Blue-collar folks took their time, thought it through and eventually reached similar conclusions. Big surprise, everyone picked the fat guy in his easy chair with the beer can as the major couch potato.

I had some trouble finding professionals to give me a few minutes for this survey, but through friends of friends, slowly, I neared my quota. Somehow, I had gotten the name of a psychology professor at Syracuse University, Gabriel Friedman, and I reached him on the first try. I assured him this would only take a few minutes, so he agreed, somewhat reluctantly.

His name was on the door, Dr. Gabriel Friedman, Assistant Professor, Psychology. I knocked and he called out a loud "Come in."

I was pleasantly surprised to find a well built man, mid to late twenties, with clear olive skin, wavy brown hair, a slightly crooked nose, and dazzling light brownish, greenish eyes. He'd been leaning back in a swivel chair with his tan suede Hush Puppies up on a messy desk surrounded by books. He stood and motioned me to sit.

Before sitting I introduced myself and shook his firm, warm hand.

I sensed his undivided attention and presence and launched into my spiel, then handed him the cards. As usual, I looked at his ring finger. No wedding ring. He took a quick look at the cards and laughed.

"This is completely unscientific," he said. "It's simple-minded, Rowie."

I loved hearing him say my name.

"Why?"

"Look," he said, and moved around his desk to squat next to my seat. He was wearing brown corduroys and a heather green sweater that matched his eyes. My heart pumped faster. I forced myself to follow his thoughts. "Whoever designed this is obviously looking for results based on class distinction. The premise they want to prove is that there's a quantitative difference in TV habits between more educated and less educated people. But that would be a superficial conclusion."

Going through the cards quickly, he chose every single one, announcing what each one might watch, the women as soap fans, the guys as sports fans, the professionals secretly watching soaps and sports but admitting to watching mostly public broadcasting, and everyone else as open TV watchers. He said the fat guy with the can of beer might work three jobs and collapse in front of the tube an hour a week.

"Let me guess," he said, "You have no place to record qualitative results, right? The kinds of programming people watch are not relevant to this study."

"That's true," I said. "Why is that important?" I had no interest in the cards anymore. This man had a magnetic effect on me. I liked his mind, his looks and his energy. I desired him. Should I put the moves on him right there? What if I put my hand right between his legs? We could get naked and do it in this chair. I'd straddle him, hang on to his shoulders and gallop like a cowgirl. A nice big juicy hard-on to ride. He went on.

"This study is probably funded by an advertising agency to show that commercials should use simple language, aimed at people with only a basic educational level. It's meaningless. I suppose most people you show this to choose the professionals – those surrounded with books – as least likely to watch TV and everyone else as most likely."

He spoke fast, with a slight New York accent. I grooved so much on his voice, I scarcely was able to pay attention to his words.

"You're right," I said. "I like your analysis. But if everyone had the same outlook, I'd be out of a job."

"Sorry, but I think this study is dumb. If I were you I wouldn't waste anyone else's time with it. You might as well make up the results. How are you at creative writing?"

"Are you serious?" I grinned.

"I don't know," he said. "Maybe so. I believe in integrity, but something like this is so lacking in integrity, why take it seriously? Am I maligning your chosen profession?" He handed me back the cards. I began packing them away in their little box.

"Not by a long shot. I just graduated from Barnard in June. I haven't chosen a profession yet. This is just a stop-gap job." I didn't want to tell this man I was leaving town shortly.

He looked at his watch. "A Barnard graduate, eh? Now I don't feel so bad about being truthful. Listen, I don't know about you, but I'm famished.

Since I blew the crap out of your project, can I make it up to you by buying you dinner, or would that be out of line?"

"Wow, thanks, no, it's not out of line, I would love that," I answered, partly mumbling, immediately stressed about eating with this guy, who was both smart and a psychologist. I wondered whether I could avoid ending up in his bed, searched my memory for a picture of the underwear I had put on, hoping it wasn't plain white cotton Lollipops or the torn pink ones I kept forgetting to toss.

"Are you sure? You seem a little flustered. I hope I didn't upset you with my candor. I can be brutally direct. It's my weakness."

"I understand," I said. "I'm pretty direct myself. Maybe it's not just a weakness. Maybe it's also a strength."

"Probably, in moderation," he said. "I like that thought." He looked around the office, packed some papers into his rucksack, and slipped on a brown leather bomber jacket just like my dad used to wear. Then he turned out the light and gently rested his hand on my back as he steered me across campus. Even through my jacket and clothes, I experienced his hand as sizzling.

We walked across campus to a small restaurant on Marshall Street. I ordered a bowl of chicken noodle soup, which inspired me to tell him about Grandma and her cooking and then Grandpa and his starring role in my childhood. Gabriel had grown up in Brooklyn, near Ocean Parkway, also in a nutso Jewish family. He'd had one sister who'd died of polio when she was twelve and he was six, and from then on, his mom's anxiety took over and smothered him. His mother had been a widow for most of his life, and lived with her sister in the same apartment he'd grown up in. They never kept a lock on the bathroom door and for years, both his aunt and mother had insisted on scrutinizing every one of his bowel movements. Even when he was in the city, he refused to stay with them because they wouldn't give up that practice. His mom still expected a call twice a week, a negotiated improvement from every day, and she still threatened to leap from the roof if he skipped check-in. I marveled at the craziness a woman could act out with her child. As we chatted, Gabe reminded me a little of Ralph. I told him about Leary and Alpert and the LSD studies at Harvard. We felt so at ease with each other I didn't even have a problem eating my soup.

Since I had taken the bus to the university area, after dinner, he insisted on driving me home, which meant we had to go over to his place to pick up his little red Renault Dauphin. If he had come on to me, I might have responded, but I controlled my aggressive reflexes even though it had been a few weeks since I'd been with Tommy in L.A.

"Goodnight," I said when we got to Mommy's apartment complex. "Thanks for a wonderful evening."

"I'm the one who should thank you," he said brightly. "What a pleasure to meet a girl who combines looks and intelligence!" I felt both elated and embarrassed by his compliment.

He got out of the car and came around to open the door for me.

"Would you mind a hug?" he asked.

How many guys asked? Usually they moved in on me.

I couldn't remember a hug like that. His whole body melted into mine in the sweetest way, sensual more than sexual and deliciously warm. As though I had known him all my life, Gabriel Friedman felt like family. I knew it was weird, but I had a brief glimpse of life as Gabe's wife with two or three beautiful children. Mommy would approve. Not that it mattered. I gave him my number but I had no intention of mentioning him to her and no intention of following through. I'd been serious when I told Karen I wanted to stay away from marriage. Superficial rolls in the hay were safe. Marriage material I'd avoid like death.

_ ∞ _

Suddenly, I threw myself into nursemaiding once more, this time for Mommy, who was recovering from full mouth gum surgery. She was in agony at the same time the whole country was on highest alert, stocking up on water and groceries as though that was all it would take to survive if the Russians hit us with the nuclear warheads they aimed at us from Cuba. Mommy truly believed we'd be blown away any moment. I marshaled my positive thinking skills to avoid her pessimism.

"Jesus, what an asshole I am," Mommy lamented as she lay on the sectional with an icepack on her jaw, woozy from medication. She spoke out of the side of her mouth with half her usual voice. "What a stupid time to get gum surgery, with the world about to end. I can't believe my timing. That's the story of my life in a nutshell. It figures I'd die like this. What an idiot."

"Mommy, stop it," I said. "We're not gonna die. President Kennedy will take care of us."

"Don't forget, my dear. I work for the Air Force. I know the military mentality. They've been itching to go into Cuba since Castro took over. There are too many of them who don't understand diplomacy, and besides they have lots of expensive toys they'd love to play with. They probably think it'll boost our economy."

"Mommy, relax, we can't die because I have to go to Central America. I clearly see myself there. This will work out somehow."

"I am so stupid," she kept repeating. "I had a feeling I shouldn't have done the whole mouth at once, but I didn't listen. Such a jackass! Give me a poison pill and let me end it now."

Her boss, Air Force Colonel Jim Madison, called to find out how she was. She was in no shape to take the call.

"She's not just in pain from the surgery, Colonel Madison," I said. "She's upset about the world situation."

"Which world situation is that?" he wanted to know. He sounded completely innocent.

"Haven't you been watching the news or reading the papers?" I exclaimed, incredulous. "The Cuban missile crisis!"

"Oh, that," he said nonchalantly. "Don't worry, we're going to blast them into the sea."

Then I joined Mommy in worrying.

– ∞ –

Gabe called three times to ask me out, and each time I told him firmly I was busy. I made the mistake of mentioning him to Karen who was at our place and answered the phone when he called a fourth time. Excited, she immediately began whispering I shouldn't worry, she'd stay with Mommy, and I should go out with him.

"Rowie," he said in his mellifluous sexy voice. "Are you avoiding me? I thought we had sensational rapport. Am I missing something?"

"I like you very much, Gabriel," I choked out. "I hardly know you, but I have a feeling you and I could be close. And I don't want anything to get in the way of my going to Central America."

"You're going to Central America?" He sounded shocked. "When? Why?"

"I'm leaving after the first of the year, and I'm going ostensibly because I have a fellowship, but I know there's another reason."

"What other reason?" Gabriel asked. He sounded disappointed. I found myself getting teary and my emotions surprised me.

"Well, I know this is going to sound crazy, but I'm not sure what the real reason is. I just know there is another reason. That's as far as I've gotten. I'm sorry, Gabriel."

He was silent for a few seconds. In the pause, I could feel him feeling me. Our breathing synchronized. When he spoke, it was with forcefulness.

"Rowie, let's be realistic. Right now the Soviets are building bases for nuclear warheads ninety miles off the coast of Florida. We're meeting it with a naval blockade. Who the hell knows what's going to happen? Let's face it, we could be dust way before New Years. But right now, today, you and I have some kind of feeling for each other. Have dinner with me, Rowie. Ask your sister to keep your mom company. You're entitled to have a life too."

"I'm not who you think I am, Gabriel," I muttered. "I'll disappoint you."

"Rowie, tell you what, I'll let you explain who you are over dinner. I'm eager to learn. This time, I won't take no for an answer. I'll pick you up in an hour and a half. Hopefully we'll still be alive."

– ∞ –

Thanks to the Cuban missile crisis, our romance escalated quickly, and though that tense drama ended with the world intact, our personal worlds had shifted irrevocably

After we'd been together a couple of weeks, the likelihood of missiles taking us out lessened. As we lay in his big bed relaxing by candlelight, Gabe told me there were guidelines he wanted us to follow.

"First, no lying," he said. "Promise me."

"I definitely will not. I've lied all my life. I can't even identify truth anymore."

"No intentional lies then. How's that?"

"How about half truths?"

"Give me an example."

"Food scares me. I feel fat half the time. I hate that I just said what I said. I'm ashamed and I'd like to throw up."

"Jesus, Rowie, you poor kid. That must feel shitty. That's what you call half-truth?"

I shrugged. He sat silently awhile.

"Okay," he said. "Guideline number two. Communication. Can we talk about what you just said?"

I shrugged again. He took my hand and waited silently for me to speak.

"Gabe, I've been screwy with food for at least ten years. I doubt I can unscrew in less."

"Question," Gabe said. "How many shrinks does it take to unscrew a screwball?"

"I give up. How many?"

"Depends on how tightly the screwball's screwed. Depends how much the shrink loves the screwball and loves screwing with the screwball." He walked his hand from my navel up to my breasts and then down, grazing my pubic bone.

"This screwball's tightly screwed, Gabriel. My daddy spanked me a lot and I think there was a sexual element to it. I hated him."

"I may have the perfect cure," Gabe said, and he rolled me onto my stomach. "Will you trust me?"

"I guess so."

He massaged my butt, one cheek and then the other, in a circular motion, and then he smacked me. He interwove sharp slaps with gentle rubs and kisses and penetrating fingers. I could feel the urge to leave my body, but I stayed.

"You're a naughty little girl," he said, and smacked me. "But I love you, pumpkin," and he massaged and slapped, sweet-talked, massaged and slapped, over and over.

I felt myself getting wet, then getting wetter, simultaneously crying, coming and ejaculating a flood. "This is going to heal the wounds," he said. "We're making the boo-boos all better." He said "bet-ter" as though talking to a child. After that, he used long pieces of soft material to tie my legs spread-eagle to the sides of the bed and he handcuffed my hands to the headboard.

"Do you trust me, little girl?" he asked. "Do you trust Daddy?"

"I hate you Daddy," I said. "Bring back Gabriel. Untie me, Gabriel, before I scream and the neighbors call the cops. This is scaring me too much. My father hurt me a lot. I don't remember it all, but it's intense."

"I had a feeling," Gabe said. "I love you. I'll never hurt you."

"I'm scared," I said. "I may never be able to love anyone."

He held me and I cried.

As the holidays and my birthday neared, Mommy, Karen and Victoria began pressuring me to forget going to Guatemala.

"You and Gabe are adorable together," Mommy said. "He'd make a perfect son-in-law. Another doctor. You could do worse."

Karen said, "He's crazy about you, Ro. We all love him. He's the one. It's obvious."

Victoria said, "I'll bet he's great in bed. I can tell because you're glowing, Ro."

Gabe wanted to take me on a Caribbean vacation over his holiday break, but I told him I had to prepare for my year away. He looked grim. For my twenty-second birthday, he got me two dozen red roses and took me to a fancy downtown restaurant where we got our own private alcove.

Before the waiter even brought our menus, he brought a bottle of iced champagne. I knew I could handle only a sip or two. While we toasted to my birthday, he brought our menus, handed one to Gabe, then grinned and handed me mine. "This one is especially for you, miss." He bowed and backed away smiling. Inside, instead of a menu, there was a blown up photo of Gabe on his knees and just above him, in a large word balloon: "Rowena Gay Wine, MARRY ME, PLEASE." Gabe handed me a small purple velvet box and wished me happy birthday.

"I love you," he said. "I want to love you forever."

In the box, lined with pink silk, sat a good-sized diamond solitaire. I stared at it as though it were poison. My mouth felt dry. My heart raced. Gabe took it out and easily slipped it on my ring finger. I felt sick and wanted to leave the restaurant. I couldn't help myself. I cried. How could he spring this on me?

"I adore you, Gabe. But I can't stay in Syracuse. I have to go to Guatemala. There's a contradiction when two neurotics fall in love. We're too crazy to allow ourselves joy. It's too perfect. We need chaos, drama, poor choices, suffering." I laughed.

"Rowie, don't do this to us."

"Gabe, you must have known. I'm not even close to settling down. I'm just discovering love. Mostly, I still despise myself."

"Okay, maybe we haven't burned out enough of the self-hatred, but we're on our way. I predict you'll return, Rowie. One day, after you've traversed the planet searching for some unknown, suddenly you'll know, and you'll return to my arms where you belong. Until then, keep the ring, Rowie, and we'll be engaged."

"I hope you're not saying you'll wait."

"I love you, Rowie. I can be myself with you. I can't imagine marrying anyone else. I want to visit you in Guatemala. I want to introduce you to my mother and my aunt and all the rest of my crazy family. I want you to wear this ring and know how much I love you. If language counts, Central America sounds like an appropriate place to center yourself. Go for it, Rowie. Find your center and then we'll get married."

As unobtrusively as possible, I took off the scary ring, which fit perfectly, slipped it into the case and handed it back to Gabe. I closed my hands around his. Tears streamed down both of our faces. I was embarrassed and wanted to run away.

"The ring is beautiful, Gabe. Thank you for your kindness. But I can't accept it right now. I have a date with destiny."

"Funny you should say that, Rowie, because I believe you and I are *beshert*, destined for each other, and nothing can get in the way of our being together, not your stubbornness or self-loathing, not Guatemala, not time or storms, or wars, not anything except death and maybe not even death. I believe you and I are going to marry and have babies someday. If I had my way, you wouldn't go, but if you'd be unhappy staying, I couldn't live with that."

"Thank you, Gabe."

"Will you promise you'll come back to me?"

"I can't promise because I don't want to make a promise I can't keep. You're the most special man I've ever known, but I'm seriously crazier than you can imagine, my darling, and I have to follow this urge to go thousands of miles away from everything familiar. I'll never forget you and I don't expect you to wait for me because I have no idea whether I'll ever return."

"I'm deeply disappointed, but I respect your honesty, Rowie. Can I at least visit you there?"

"I'm sorry," I said, crying, shaking my head. "I need a clean break."

"I'm sorrier," he said. "You warned me at the beginning, didn't you? I didn't listen."

"Blame Fidel and the Soviets," I said.

"Thank them, you mean. I don't regret one second of our time together. And I caution you, sweetheart, I'm a patient man."

— ∞ —

Journal entry, New Year's 1962-'63: Rowie heard the rain beating relentlessly on the tin roof and found herself wide-awake in the dark cabin. Gabe, she thought, if only Gabe hadn't believed her, hadn't taken her at her word. Why had she driven him away? Why had he respected her wishes instead of demanding a better explanation? She wanted him to tell her he'd wait forever. She wanted him to read her mind instead of listening to her words. She hated her behavior, all contrived to hide her addiction. Manipulation, Victoria called it. Her baby sister saw right through her without knowing nasty details.

"You're a master manipulator, Rowie. Learn to go for what you want and need directly instead of indirectly pulling people's strings. You hurt people who care about you and throw them away as though they don't count. You're fucked up."

Nice. Now Victoria had judged her a bitch, Gabe, the love of her life, had fled at her own request, and she was alone with the rain. How the hell had she ended up in this damp cabin alone for New Year's weekend? Her brother-in-law, Jon, and his podiatrist buddies shared the place and had camped here on the lake for years. Karen thought it would do her good to spend time alone after the break-up. Syracusans expected deep snow since, after all, that's what precipitated around New Years in upstate New York, but freak weather made sense to a woman who considered herself freaky. Late December rain in the Finger Lakes, of course, Rowie thought. There'd be no ice skating or cross country skiing, but at least it wasn't bitter cold, the sleeping bag was toasty, and the remains of a fire in the potbelly stove still gave off heat.

What if the place washed away? What if it slipped into the lake? No matter, the world would be a sweeter place without my craziness, she thought. No one in the world understood how her addiction ruled her. She filled her stomach wildly, madly, like the pounding rain filled her ears. The quantities of food she stuffed disgusted her but nothing could allow her to stop. She'd tried,

God knows. If only she could call Gabe and tell him. Gabe, she'd say, I love you and I'm a freak you can't possibly understand. I'm saving you, darling. If you knew what I did with the beautiful dinners you fed me, you'd hate me for sure. I realize you're a psychologist and maybe you'd try to help me, but I don't know how to tell you the truth. I'm so ashamed. My puddles of old shame merge with constantly new shame, and I drown in oceans of shame and food. Hmmm, she thought, not a bad line. Too bad it's pathetically true. I scribble it in my journal in the dark.

Pitter, pitter, the rain continued, abated slightly. Emptiness crept through her belly and chest, and she regretted not bringing binge provisions to the cabin. Karen had efficiently cleaned the place and the cupboard was bare except for an old can of Budweiser. Rowie disliked the taste of beer. She craved sweet and doughy for her binges, sometimes settled for salty and crunchy. How could she have committed such an oversight? Optimistic, intending to start the New Year with the same resolution as the last ten years, she'd brought two cans of tuna, celery, a tomato, half a dozen eggs, a head of lettuce, a few jugs of water, and three books, *Leaves of Grass*, *Heart of Darkness*, and *A New England Nun* by Mary Wilkins Freeman. Nothing sweet or doughy enough. Only celery for crunch. She laughed, joking to herself about eating Walt Whitman and how Walt would have dug being sucked. Sex jokes hit her funny bone, reminding her she was still alive. Tomorrow at daybreak she could drive to the nearest grocery store and get supplies.

Funny, just before blowing out the candle, she'd opened *Leaves of Grass* to a perfect quote: "Unscrew the locks from the doors! Unscrew the doors themselves from their jambs!" She'd grown up in a world of locked doors and slammed doors and scary doors and imaginary doors she'd dreamed of in imaginary rooms she could hide in. Walt's message hit her anew just as a tree limb fell next to the cabin with a loud thwack. The wind had picked up and was driving the rain again. Snuggled deep inside her sleeping bag, she briefly experienced nestling in her mother's womb. She remembered the way Mommy had held her pregnant belly and assured unborn Rowie she'd be loved and safe, had even sung to her softly while Daddy was hitting naked two-year-old Karen. "I promise you," she'd whispered. "I'll protect you." Beautiful little Karen screamed, whimpered, then wheezed and he had to stop because she turned blue and they had to rush her to the emergency room. He was so scared he never hit Karen again. For some reason, Mommy broke her promise and instigated Rowie's spankings to satisfy Daddy's frustrated spare-the-rod philosophy. Karen periodically had asthma attacks her whole childhood and still needed constant treatment.

The rain continued to pelt the roof as waves of water lashed at the windows. If only she could cry. Who could count all the accumulated spankings, day after day, once, twice, three times a day, building one day at a time, year after year, like unending rain, flooding the river, enveloping the land? Was this the way the Nile Valley became the Fertile Crescent? Could what seemed harmful turn out helpful? Rain hitting the roof was normal and natural, but was it normal and natural for a father to attack a child? How did one define normal and natural? Didn't Walt Whitman advise not to trust anything or anybody unless it came from inside?

Maybe the ugly spankings weren't so terrible. Some kids got broken bones, burns, starvation, isolation. She hated her dad but she loved him too, the way grass loved rain even though sometimes it ended up buried in floodwater. Once she had composed a list of risky words to describe her dad, which would have gotten her minced if he'd caught her. My *dad*, she'd written, *shit, piss, fart, fuck, ass, bastard, bitch, hell, goddamn, jesus christ.* Writing those words gave her enormous satisfaction and she'd smiled as she tore the paper into strips and flushed them down the toilet, an outlaw, undetected. The toilet swallowed her secrets early on.

When Buddy hit her she didn't cry because he said, if she cried, he'd *really* give her something to cry about. Once as he hit her he said he hated hearing her cry because he loved her so much. He'd throw her over his lap and pull down her days-of-the-week panties, pink for Monday, yellow for Tuesday, every day a different color and every day he pulled them down and smack, smack, smack away, and she'd learned to go away, up to the ceiling, out through the roof, down to the river, where water steadily and faithfully flowed, day in and day out. The river comforted her, allowed her to see she too would flow steadily, grow up and pass around the bend, secure, and far from danger. She'd learned to control her tears, leave them safely behind her eyes, and now she couldn't cry, could hardly laugh except salaciously, and couldn't feel pain or joy, just empty numbness. Filling with food and getting rid of it quickly gave her a sense of control and substituted for emotional connection. But now, with no doughnuts, pie, pudding, cookies, cake, bread, ice cream, pretzels or chips, there opened a fissure, a gap, an oversight, an insight, which let Walt's poetry and something else get through.

A small drop of rain fell, then another and another. The roof leaked. She should have known not to trust a Republican podiatrist to rough it, she thought disdainfully. She could move her sleeping bag a few inches to a dry spot. Instead she allowed herself to feel the warm rain on her face and was surprised to taste the salt. She spent the rest of the weekend crying even though the sun came out. Happy New Year, Rowie, she told herself, and smiled as she fixed a tuna and lettuce sandwich.

– ∞ –

TWENTY-FIVE

First stop on the Guatemalan adventure was Washington, DC for five days of orientation meetings at the State Department. The glitch was that nobody there expected me. Luckily I arrived with their official letter so I knew I was sane. The best they could muster was a short brochure on Guatemala for travelers, marked notably by instructions not to drink the water without boiling it first.

"Your hotel and meals are covered and you're free to be a tourist," the smiling young secretary said, as she handed me the thin brochure. "Sorry about the mix-up."

I bought three new composition notebooks and a pack of ballpoints. Rather than visit the Smithsonian or the White House, the Washington Monument or the Lincoln Memorial, rather than go anywhere for fear of ending up in doughnut shops, I stayed in my room, smoked heavily from a carton of cigarettes I'd packed, and madly filled pages with recollections from my life. I wrote about Grandpa and Grandma, Karen and Victoria, Mommy and Daddy, my California trip, Ralph, Gabe, his dreams and mine. I tried to remember every man I'd ever had sex with so I could make a list and have a total. As I wrote names down, I racked my memory to associate faces and cocks, surprising myself because I kept seeing Daddy's face and it creeped me out. I remembered a variety of phallic shapes, sizes, colors and textures, long, short, fat, thin, dark, light, crooked, and all of them reminded me of bludgeons. Creepy. Before Gabe, with all the sexual activity I'd indulged in, I'd never allowed either my hand or mouth near one of those things. That fucking Daddy, I wished I could remember what he'd done to me. I suspected early trauma but couldn't get in touch with it and only partially wanted to. Omitting Skip, the first great love of my life because we hadn't gone all the way, I started with the drunken and bloody encounter with Sy French and ended with Gabe. Along the way I counted Pierre, Rabbi Luft, then a series of ten or twelve - I forgot because they were forgettable - one night stands. Next there were a few beat poets from the Village, a summer fling in Syracuse after my junior year, and in senior year, the Jewish Latin American studies major at Yale who recycled condoms. Ralph's roommate Govinda was on the list and Tommy Fernandez, and, lastly, number twenty-three, Gabe, who I believed loved me. I wrote him an upbeat postcard I'd picked up in the hotel gift shop with a photo of the Washington monument, but I didn't mail it. Better not to encourage him.

In my notebooks, I wrote small, filled the entire hundred pages of the first and started on the second. My words spewed forth. I left the Do Not Disturb sign on the doorknob, room-serviced meals, and left my dirty dishes outside the door. I liked having my own private bathroom where no one would know or care what I did. I didn't have to answer to anyone. I could stay up half the night and sleep as late as I wanted. Wonder of wonders, I surprised myself and didn't throw up once. Not once! How was that possible? Could it be related to writing? I realized when I wrote, time flew by just as it did when I practiced piano. I felt fabulous, productive, excited, and, except for the cigarettes, fairly calm. Never had throwing up or even sex given me such a sense of satisfaction. Sustaining it when I re-entered the world would be the true test. If only I could stop the clock and stay forever holed up, in my pajamas, having meals and new empty notebooks delivered daily to my bubble in room 719!

– ∞ –

I arrived in Guatemala City outfitted in a new look that was more central casting than Central America. It was a conservative corporate image, nubby green and black fitted wool tweed suit, ridiculously expensive even though we got it wholesale from Aunt Bea's brother, Marvin, in the garment district of Manhattan along with a basic little black dress and two other suits, a brown plaid seersucker, and a blue and white striped cotton pin-cord. With a buttery soft, black leather handbag hanging from my shoulder and a new tan leather briefcase clutched in my hand, I looked more like a State Department recruit than a recent college student. I was scared, and the professional image, suit, nylons, heels, and briefcase created a disguise I could confidently hide behind. Although Mommy seriously hoped I'd return and marry Gabe, her second choice was for me to meet a professional Foreign Service man stationed in Central America, soon to be transferred back to the States, but she worried that Foreign Service rarely attracted Jewish men.

– ∞ –

The American cultural attaché, J. Edison Smythe, was slated to meet me at the airport. We deplaned right on the tarmac, into a busy, colorful hubbub of people coming and going in all directions, mostly bronze men wearing straw hats and jabbering in Spanish so fast I could barely catch a familiar phrase even though I could conjugate Spanish verbs perfectly and had even read *Don Quijote* in the original. I stood at the foot of the stairs by the plane, clutched the new briefcase, which held only my newly filled notebooks, and looked around. Where were all these people headed? Why weren't they wearing shoes? The air tasted dusty. A volcano loomed in the distance, a perfect dark triangle, like a child's drawing of a mountain. I didn't see anyone who looked like an American. I stood still, feeling out of place in the scary, chaotic scene.

"Permit me, I will take that, señorita," said a bronze straw-hatted man in Spanish, and yanked the briefcase right out of my hand and started away with it. I did a double take and panicked. Those notebooks held five days of intimate writing I didn't want anyone to see.

"No, you won't." A blond crew-cut giant in a conservative gray suit was right there and forcefully tore the briefcase away. He came toward me shaking his head.

"J. Edison Smythe. Ed to you." He stuck out a hefty hand to shake mine, held onto my briefcase with the other. His Texas accent was unmistakable. "I take it you are Rowena G. Wine." He pronounced my name "wahn."

"Please call me Rowie."

"Lesson number one, Rowie, hold tight to all your belongings or they will sprout wings and fly away, never to be seen again. This is not the USA, Miss Wine. Welcome to Guatemala."

The black limo was waiting, and once we'd retrieved my luggage and passed through customs, we went for our ride to the capital and the house where I had rented a room from the list of approved places the State Department had sent me. There were few other vehicles on the road, just some old open trucks and a couple of rickety buses. I lay back against the soft leather seat and looked out at the activity along the road. I watched a steady line of women and men, barefoot, dressed in brightly colored outfits, many bent forward with immense bundles on their backs held by forehead straps. I would have liked a vest or jacket in some of those beautiful fabrics to wear with jeans.

"So," said Ed Smythe, "We've arranged a teaching job for you at the bi-national center. You start day after tomorrow. Your grant won't be enough to live on. You'll be teaching two English classes."

"I will? I've never taught," I said weakly. "That wasn't mentioned before."

"You'll be fine," he said. "You just have to follow the book. These people won't know the difference. Believe me."

I didn't like the phrase "these people." I shrank into the leather seat and looked again at the foot traffic on the road. I saw a woman squatting. Was she relieving herself? No one seemed surprised. I took the cigarette Ed offered me, and he lit it for me. He was wearing a heavy gold class ring. I always thought people who wore class rings longer than a week were losers. He didn't appeal to me, but I couldn't help noticing his long fingers and wondered what his penis looked like, almost a conditioned reflex of mine.

"So, Rowie, I understand you're going to be studying literature at the university. Tell me, who is your favorite writer?"

"I have lots of favorites," I said. "Lately I've been going through the works of Eugene O'Neill, and I'm awed."

"Oh, yes, I love his novels," said Ed.

"His novels? Which of his novels are your favorites?" I asked, slyly testing him. Or was he testing me? I dismissed that thought because of the loser ring.

"All of 'em, all of 'em," he answered, "How about you?"

"*Desire Under the Elms, Long Day's Journey into Night.*"

"Yes, they're outstanding novels."

That was my introduction to Americans abroad. I instantly lost respect for this ex-Marine from Dallas. Wouldn't a cultural attaché know Eugene O'Neill was a playwright and not a novelist? Who was this guy? I also found myself wondering whether there were any doughnut shops in Guatemala, and then immediately checked myself. In Guatemala, I would continue to normalize. No binging and no vomiting. Not here. I had made it through more than half a week in Washington so I had momentum going. I hated my lack of willpower and was determined to kick the habit. So why at the slightest discomfort did I think of binging? Why hadn't I confronted the cultural attaché gently? Maybe he'd think I was a dope now that I had failed the test of honesty.

The limo driver dropped me and my bags off at the ancient, gated stone house that from the street looked like a door in a brick wall. It opened to two stories of rooms built around a central patio filled with magenta bougainvillea, birds of paradise, oversized rubber plants and banana trees with decaying leaves, a rusty tricycle, battered wooden slide, and balls of several sizes and colors. Everything indoors felt damp and smelled of mold and Lysol.

My hosts, Luz and Paco Nuñez, were at work when I arrived. The Nuñez family took in boarders to help them hold on to the family house. Paco Nuñez had a clerk job in what had been his family's shoe store on 6th Avenue. His wife, Luz, worked as a secretary at the American Embassy – which helped guarantee a steady stream of student boarders paying American rents. Paco and Luz had converted their living room to a bedroom and there they stayed with their two-year-old so they could rent out the three bedrooms upstairs and the little room downstairs assigned to me.

The younger of the two maids, Leticia, about sixteen, holding a toddler's hand, greeted me with a bright smile. She had long black braids, dark almond eyes and light brown skin. The little one was Luz and Paco's three year old, Paquito, who looked up at me with big dark eyes. His skin was fair and features European.

Despite my good intention to stop overeating and throwing up, moments after arriving, I took one look at the bathroom set-up and panicked. It wasn't just the mold. As the house predated indoor plumbing, the one and only bathroom, located between my room and the dining room, had a wall that stopped about two feet short of the 12-foot ceiling. Even if I locked the door, I couldn't extend the wall up to the ceiling. How could I have privacy? I was horrified to see the same kind of semi-wall in my little room, a narrow cell with a cot, small wooden chest of drawers painted chartreuse and matching kid's desk. I immediately hated this space, but had nowhere else to go. I politely asked where the nearest grocery store was. I needed exercise. I needed to binge. I needed to purge. I needed to fuck. I needed something immediately. My skin crawled as though it didn't fit my body anymore.

Leticia's grandmother emerged from the kitchen, wiping her rough brown hands on her white apron, grinning. She had a deeply wrinkled face and no teeth, which made her cheeks sink in.

"Welcome, señorita," she said in Spanish. "This house is your house. My name is Maria Alicia Alonzo, at your service. You have already met my granddaughter Leticia, true?"

"Yes," I said. "Thank you."

"Grandmother," said Leticia, "the señorita wants to know where she can shop. What shall I tell her?"

"First of all, we have food for you if you are hungry. I can happily offer a sandwich. As for shopping, there's a big main market where they sell everything, señorita," Maria gave me directions. It was only six blocks away. Then she admonished Leticia to pay attention to Paquito, who was headed for the plants. Was he going to pee in the bushes?

I changed into beige linen slacks and matching silk blouse and went out toward the market for a walk. I would overcome all challenges, I told myself. I had already learned to have quiet sex, and I could puke quietly in the bathroom with missing wall if I had to, and maybe I wouldn't have to, maybe I could resist, maybe I could be sane instead of a raving maniac. I'd resisted for four whole days so maybe I could sustain it longer, maybe even forever.

A couple of blocks from the house, amid small shops and sporadic traffic, far lighter than traffic I'd always associated with cities, I came upon the binational center Ed Smythe had mentioned, where a job waited for me. I thought that a good sign and ended up getting my room assignment and textbooks.

I met the Nuñezes that evening. The size of an average twelve-year-old American, Paco was thin and slight with fair skin that looked as though he never saw the sun. Luz was his height in heels with the big dark eyes their son had. She wore bright red lipstick and black eyebrow pencil. They acted polite and friendly, but I realized I felt more comfortable with Leticia and Maria.

"Do you wish to have Maria do your laundry?" asked Luz in Spanish.

"How much will that cost?" I asked.

"Twenty a month," said Luz.

"Will Maria get that?" I asked. I heard my caustic tone and wished I'd been more subtle.

Luz looked startled but didn't answer, for right at that moment, little Paquito distracted her. I knew she had planned to make a few bucks without passing anything on and realized I could probably negotiate a fair split between her and Maria. I made a note to bring it up again.

At the dinner table that first night, there was a guest who I knew was there as much to look me over as anything else. Paco's brother Enrique, a surgeon, thirty-five, dark, miniature, wiry, and hairy, had studied medicine at Mt. Sinai in New York and spoke fluent English. To deflect attention away from my picking at the spicy beef, beans and rice, I flirted with him. Wine flowed. We laughed a lot and played footsie under the heavy mahogany table. I instantly felt aroused.

"Let's go for a ride," he said. "I'll give you a tour."

We didn't pass one other car as he drove his Mercedes up a winding road and parked at a lookout point with a panoramic view of the city. Lights twinkled below, above, and out in the distance, as though the starry sky had moved to earth or the city had moved to the sky. I gazed, spellbound. Gabe would love this view, I thought.

"It's beautiful," I said.

"You are beautiful," he said, and he kissed me and patted my hair and kissed me again. Between the view and the kisses and the soft leather seats, I felt like a goddess.

"I want to make love to you," he said.

"I want to make love to you, too."

"You do? Just like that? Oh brother, I love New York! May I take you someplace comfortable?"

"Okay."

We took off for what he called a motel de paso, an upscale, hourly place where I got a quick education in the art of discreet affairs. Enrique pulled his big Mercedes into a dark alley, killed the headlights and rolled down the window. A man dressed in dark clothes and baseball hat appeared immediately, they exchanged a few words and a few bills, then he quickly ran in front of the car with a flashlight and guided us down the alley, into a covered parking stall. Once Enrique parked, I heard a whoosh and clinking, which was the sound of our guide pulling closed what looked and sounded like a silky white shower curtain on a metal rod, enclosing us in a garage area that led directly to our room. The echoing sound of the car doors closing in the small private garage space thrust me back to earth. This was my arrival day in Guatemala and I was in a motel with the first man who flirted with me. What was I doing? How had I lost control so thoroughly?

"Isn't this cool?" he was saying enthusiastically. "I never saw a motel with privacy like this in the States. This is unique. Wives can cheat on their husbands right next door to husbands cheating on them and neither one has to know about the other. That's why it's on a one-way street with no streetlights. Did you notice? Only in a Catholic country."

I nodded. My enthusiasm had waned. I hoped he wasn't married. For all my fooling around, I'd never done it with a married man. He came around and opened the door for me and helped me out. Briefly I thought of asking him to take me home, but I didn't look forward to sleeping in the damp, moldy room and anyway, I thought, this is something new, making love with a man half a foot shorter than I am. This is an adventure, and I am an adventurer.

The room was clean, snug, and even stylish, with walls and ceiling painted deep red-orange, matching tile floor and print throw rugs, coordinated with the bedspread. On simple walnut night tables there were a lamp and ashtray. Two nicely-framed, jungle animal paintings hung on the wall above the bed. In the bathroom, I put in my diaphragm and squealed when I noticed the bidet. I'd only read about them and asked the doctor whether it was safe to use with my diaphragm.

"I have no idea," he said. "I'm a dermatologist. I suppose it's safe. Why not if the diaphragm covers the cervix? A bidet is like a shower, that's all. It's not a douche."

The bidet was more inviting than sex, but at this point, I was committed.

Small, wiry, and hairy, Enrique insisted we leave a light on so he could look at my body. For the first time in years, I found myself up by the ceiling, watching the scene. I had no idea how I'd gotten there. Enrique had a furry back.

"Marry me," he said as we smoked afterward.

"Marry you?" I was too exhausted to think straight but I knew I'd met Enrique only three hours ago. A week earlier I had refused a proposal from an appropriate partner. This guy couldn't be serious. "Marry you?" I heard my echo. "I can't," I said, and I was surprised at what came out. "You're not Jewish," I said.

"You're a Jewess? Wine?"

"Changed from Weinstein at Ellis Island on the whim of an immigration worker."

"I should have known you were a Jewess because you're from New York."

"Yeah, like everyone in New York is Jewish."

"Close," he said. "They're everywhere. But don't worry. For you, I will convert. I have a friend, also a doctor, who is a Jew. I will speak with him."

"Enrique, for heaven's sake. We just met! I'm impressed at your devotion, but I think we have to get to know each other before talking marriage. Don't take it personally, but I have no intention of getting married anytime in the near future if ever."

"You are my perfect woman, Rowena. You are brilliant and beautiful. You are thin like a magazine model but have breasts like ripe melons, and you are a great lover. The women here, they don't do the things you do."

"You don't even know me, Enrique. I'm not brilliant or beautiful and I'm definitely not thin and I'm no great lover." I looked down at my chest and grinned. "Hey, but I'll accept that my breasts are like ripe melons. Nobody ever told me that before. Thanks!"

We made love again. My body was on automatic orgasm. I observed and noticed when Enrique touched my left butt cheek, my breath caught slightly and I slipped outside of my body and the motel room. It felt as though I'd dreamed I was making love while I watched the night sky. I traveled over rainforest, mountains, volcanoes, and lakes. I saw small quiet villages with plain churches and adobe houses built around a square. I saw dark roads and plowed fields in moonlight.

Enrique came loudly, invoking God in Spanish, and I fell back in my body with a thud. He didn't notice, and went back to proposing. I shushed him, reached for my clothes, then remembered the bidet and went to try it out. The warm water soothed deliciously. I wondered why I had to come to an underdeveloped country to experience a bidet. Why didn't we have them back home?

Enrique kept up a conversation from the bedroom. "You're my fantasy woman," he said. "For you I'll move back to New York. I could work at any New York hospital. I only came back because my father died, but my mother, she has her religion and her friends. She doesn't need me anymore. Marry me! I beg you, marry me."

"Enrique," I said, "I'm 22 years old. I just arrived in Guatemala this morning. I don't know anyone here yet. I'll be going to the university, and teaching English. I've never taught before. I have a lot on my mind. If you propose one more time, I swear you'll never see me again."

"All right," he said, gesturing zipping his lips with his hand. "I'll close my mouth tight."

– ∞ –

For the next few days, Enrique dedicated himself to helping me through the ordeal of getting my fellowship money, which I'd heard could take months bogged down in a bureaucratic nightmare. In the evening we visited the motel and during the day, he went with me to the National Palace, sneaking feels here and there, waited with me for the Minister of Education whom, I think, he bribed since I saw them make some sort of exchange.

He drove me to the university campus and walked me through registration. He even invited me to his birthday party at his historic house he shared with his widowed mother and couple of servants. Meeting his mother sounded serious but since he'd kept his word and didn't mention marriage again, I accepted the invitation. I figured I could mingle and practice Spanish. This would be a cultural opportunity, supposedly the reason I was there. His sister-in-law and brother, Luz and Paco, my landlords, were going as well and would drive me in their small, old Ford. The little boy would stay at home with Leticia.

We ran late because Luz had insisted on eating first. She warned me food wouldn't be served until much later. I assured her I was fine. When we arrived, the brown-skinned maid opened the door and greeted us formally. Paco went off to the right and we went to the left. Luz told me to keep my voice down and follow her.

Our destination, it turned out, was a room on the other side of a small living room, probably carved out of what originally was a larger parlor. My jaw dropped as she led me into a chapel, complete with pews and stained glass, only there was no priest, just Mama – I could tell because she had the same face as Enrique and Paco – standing in front and leading the gaggle of praying, chanting, swaying women, all wearing black mantillas over their hair. I stood in the doorway and stared. Luz handed me a mantilla, and, in a daze, I tied it on like a kerchief.

"I don't know any of these prayers," I said low. "I don't like church. I'm not even Catholic. I thought this was supposed to be a party."

A couple of women turned and glowered at us. Mama didn't skip a beat, but she motioned for us to sit down and be quiet.

"It's their version of a party. Just pretend you're content," Luz said, signaling me to sit down next to her in the rear.

We knelt and stood and knelt and stood and knelt again. I thought, wait a second, this isn't so bad, it's a party without food so I don't have to deal with eating, and I'm exercising as a bonus. Soon I could swear they were repeating the same prayers, getting increasingly frenetic.

I felt a bit dizzy and wondered where the men were. Did they have a men's church on the other side of the house? Incense was beginning to choke me. I signaled Luz that I had to pee, and carefully backed out of the room next time everyone was kneeling, thinking how come none of them had to go?

I found the men out on the noisy, smoky patio where colored lights had been rigged up, and several card games were in progress. They were smoking cigars and drinking wine and hard liquor and had bowls of chips and nuts nearby. The maid served them. I walked up to Enrique as he was studying his cards, about to make a play in his poker game, and asked him whether this gender segregation was typical. He put a finger to his lips to quiet me, made his play, then stood up. I scrunched down so he could whisper comfortably in my ear.

"It's a new spin on old customs," he said. "My mother is in love with the church, but she wants to run it her way. It takes her mind off missing my father. Don't preoccupy yourself, dear girl. Soon there will be food and a cake, and I will take you away for some love. Now go back with the women and be a good, quiet girl."

He slapped my butt, and I took off, huffing inside, beginning to wheeze a little, wishing I knew the way home – to the only home I had here. Feeling trapped, I went back to the chapel, where the praying continued. By the time the food was ready, my wheeze was loud enough for me to escape. I told them I was fine, I had pills in my purse. I rejected Enrique's solicitude, and allowed Luz to call a cab.

In the cab I smoked a cigarette which of course made me wheeze even more. I didn't care. I was thinking about being in a foreign country and how I didn't fit in, just as I didn't fit in all my life anywhere. Maybe that's what I came here to learn, I thought. At last, I'm the foreigner I always knew I was. Maybe, at last, I belonged.

– ∞ –

223

TWENTY-SIX

I enjoyed teaching. I liked being the center of attention for thirty-five people. They'd assigned me two beginning classes, given me a textbook, and told me to follow the lessons in the book. I'd lived in New York City for four years of college but had never suspected I'd picked up a New York accent until thirty-five people repeated after me the word "mother" as "mutha." I was teaching them Newyawkese! Horrifying and funny. I wrote that on postcards home only I didn't mail the one to Gabe. I now had half a dozen unmailed postcards to him.

Classes met four nights a week, from six to nine at the Instituto Guatemalteco-Americano, known as the IGA, on Sixth Avenue, a five minute walk from the Nuñez house a couple of blocks over. I used the new schedule as an excuse not to see Enrique. In the smoky teachers' lounge, an interesting collection of Americans gathered. A cute, lanky surfer type from California named Nick found me the third day of school and asked me out. He had straight sandy hair that fell over his forehead and every few minutes, when it reached his eyes, he casually tossed it back. Nick was as relaxed as I was tense. We had immediate chemistry. He invited me on a picnic over the weekend so I could see a bit of the countryside. I accepted with trepidation. What would I do about food? Would I pretend to eat? I had a couple of days until the weekend, so I decided to starve myself to make room for light food the way I'd often done in college. I told the Nuñezes I had a school picnic to attend.

I'd agreed to bring a couple of egg salad sandwiches, which I made myself – to the consternation of all the women in the house who didn't like me in the kitchen – and Nick brought fruit and beer. He looked appealing in his L.A. baseball cap, shorts, tee shirt, and flip flops, behind the wheel of a dusty white pick-up truck. Having been a Brooklyn Dodger fan growing up, I scolded him playfully about rooting for a team of betrayers. But I started getting in touch with real anger, very scary, so I abruptly stopped. I remembered while I was preoccupied being a college freshman, the Dodgers had sneaked out of Brooklyn and moved to Los Angeles. I barely noticed at the time, but when I did, I fumed so much, my anger surprised me. It was a little out of proportion to baseball. What the hell made me so angry? Daddy again? He was dead so how could it be him?

We drove out of the city along a fairly straight road for about twenty minutes – lots of native pedestrians with assorted loads – and then picked up a winding, climbing road surrounded by dense forest and small waterfalls that looked familiar, maybe because I'd flown over them when making love with Enrique. As we got farther from the city, there were fewer people walking and almost no traffic.

Nick turned off onto a dirt road for a few miles and parked near a rustic log cabin in a small clearing at the end of the road. There was a late model Jeep parked next to it. Nick shared this one room cabin with a young Guatemalan named Ricardo Ibarra who sat reading a skin magazine with a bottle of rum. He practically drooled salaciousness. I suspected we'd interrupted his self-pleasuring, said hi from a distance and suggested Nick and I walk. We picnicked next to a mango grove on the bank of a sparkling stream as the sun filtered through the leafy growth. The earth smelled fresh. I was very hungry and ate a whole egg salad sandwich, which kept coming up into my mouth afterwards, embarrassing me. I just swallowed over and over, hoping my breath didn't smell or taste like stomach acid. I'd been noticing lately my food was coming up involuntarily.

"I don't feel so good," I said when it was clear I couldn't control it. "I think I have to throw up."

"Do it, Ro," said Nick. "You'll probably feel better. One egg salad sandwich coming up!" Cute.

I walked a few yards away from him and threw up, no hands. Then I wiped my mouth, rinsed with beer, and was good to go.

He'd had a few beers and obviously didn't mind that I'd thrown up because he kissed me. One thing led to another. We had fabulous sex leaning up against a mango tree and made a drunken decision to go back to the cabin. There was no electricity, and it was quickly growing dark. Ricardo was in bed on the other side of the room, and Nick and I promised we would go right to sleep. But we didn't. When a few grunts and moans escaped, Ricardo cursed, got up and stormed out into the night.

– ∞ –

Next morning, when I got home, I found out, Ricardo wasn't the only one mad at me.

Leticia motioned towards the Nuñezes' bedroom with her head. "They are very angry," she whispered. "I heard them talking. They said bad things, that you are a scandal. They are afraid you will move out, and leave them with an empty room."

"They're right," I said. "I'm moving as soon as I find a place."

"Take me with you, señorita, please take me with you. I will work cheap. I would love to work for you. Don't worry. Even though your country harmed us, I know you personally did not harm us. You are good people. *Buena gente.*"

"How did the United States of America harm you?" I asked innocently.

"Don't you know? Your country made us go back to old inferior ways. Your country - we love your country - but we don't understand why you ejected our president, Jacobo Arbenz, whom we, the Guatemalan people elected freely. We loved him. I was just a little girl, but I remember. My father and my uncle, they got a small piece of land for the first time. The North American United Fruit Company, they cooperated because it was law. It was a very good thing for my people. I remember how happy my father had been until the gringos came - sorry, señorita - and took his land away and he had to go back to his terrible job again."

"I heard the story differently," I said. "I'm sorry."

"Jacobo Arbenz was the one we Guatemalans elected freely and your country had no right to interfere in our domestic matters. My father and my uncle talked about it all the time when they were alive. But you are different, señorita. You are not to blame. You are good. I would like to work for you. I think you would be good to me."

"Leticia, I wouldn't have a clue how to live with a servant."

"I would clean and cook, go to market, and help you out."

"We'll see," I said. "I know how to clean and I'm learning to cook, and I think going to market is fun. Anyway, I don't have another place to live yet. I haven't even started looking."

"You should know, señorita, they are very mad at you. They called you a bad name, something to do with the doctor Enrique and because you were out all night last night and did not call and tell them."

"Thanks, Leticia," I said. I thought, screw them, they're not my parents. I'm a grown woman and I'm finding a way to move out of here pronto. I would have liked helping Leticia out, but there was no way I'd allow someone to hang around invading my private space. She'd figure out in five seconds what I did in secret.

"Have you been to school, Leticia? You're very smart."

"I went to fifth grade, señorita. I read and write," she said proudly. "Please allow me to work for you."

"I'll find something for you," I said. "Maybe you can come and do my laundry if I live someplace with a machine, but don't tell the señora."

She grinned and rolled her eyes. We were conspirators.

_ ∞ _

That evening, in the teachers' lounge, I tinkled a coffee cup with a spoon, got everyone's attention, and made an announcement that I was looking for an apartment. Nick gave me thumbs up from the coffee machine across the room. Lynn Harvey approached me immediately. Lynn was about my age, from Indiana, almost six feet tall, with long blond hair, great clear blue eyes, a slender, almost painfully bony body, and an impish smile that crinkled the corners of her eyes. I'd never seen such a tall woman look impish before. Next to Lynn, I felt petite, which was an accomplishment, considering I'd seen myself as huge all my life in my family of small people. There was so much chatter in the room that just by moving into an empty corner and speaking low, we were able to converse privately. I was glad Nick had enough sense to stay away.

Lynn was looking for a discreet roommate to share her apartment just off Sixth Avenue. After I told her about Nick, Ricardo, Enrique and the Nuñezes, she confided to me about her stressful life. She was having a secret affair with her former college professor, a Guatemalan, whom she'd followed from Indiana where he'd been a visiting professor. Patty, his unsuspecting American wife, was her best friend. Lynn was godmother to their three kids.

"Now I'm scared. I shouldn't have told you," she whispered, knitting her brows. "Please don't tell a soul."

"Believe me, I can keep a secret better than you'll ever imagine."

Her place turned out to be modern, clean, dry, and far more luxurious than any place I'd ever lived. It would be my first grown-up apartment. It was a furnished condo with pale green tile floors throughout, two bedrooms, two bathrooms, living room, dining room, kitchen, breakfast bar, even a tiny maid's room, and my share came to less than I was paying the Nuñezes for the damp semi-walled cell and communal bath. The furniture wasn't fancy, but it was decent and comfortable, and the bedrooms were at opposite ends of the apartment, nice for privacy. Best of all, I had my very own complete bathroom for the first time in my life.

Nick happily agreed to move me, not that I had much stuff. At the Nuñezes, gloom hung heavily. Leticia was the only one around when I was leaving. She hugged me goodbye and again whispered that I should send for her.

"Your sweetheart is very tall and handsome," she said when Nick had carried my bags to the truck.

"He's not my sweetheart," I smiled. "He's just my friend."

– ∞ –

Lynn lent me bedding until I had a chance to shop. Nick helped me make the bed and then pulled me down on it before I'd finished unpacking. We lay close and visited. That felt so much better than making love, it amazed me. I didn't leave my body.

"Rowie, Rowie, what a great little hiding place you've found," he said, holding me. "And safe too. Did you notice the US Marine headquarters are right next door?"

"I had no idea. Really?"

I tore myself away and ran to the hall window. There was an unremarkable brick building next door.

"How do you know the Marines stay there?" I asked.

"It's not exactly a secret."

"May I ask what the Marines are doing here? Is it normal for the Marines to be in a capital city of a small country? The maid over where I lived – you met her – she told me the United States invaded and threw out the President here about seven or eight years ago. Do you know anything about that?"

He was standing behind me.

"Jesus, Rowie, You sound so angry you could be a Commie. Are you?"

"I have no idea. Maybe that's my proper label. I always knew there was something wrong with me."

After we made love, without muffling our groans, we smoked and talked.

"Ricardo was very pissed off at us for screwing while he was in the room."

"He's just jealous," I said.

"I know that," said Nick. "But he's kinda nutty about it. I'm a little worried about him. He has a nasty temper. Why we pick guys like that to work with, I'll never know."

"Work with? Ricardo doesn't teach at the IGA, does he?"

"Oops. No, we do some stuff together. You don't want to know."

We spent every night together for a week, sharing sweet snuggling and lusty, passionate lovemaking. He told me a bit of his secret. Originally, he came to Guatemala with the excuse of crop-dusting, but he was actually flying underground missions for some agency he wasn't at liberty to tell me about, and even telling me that was too much. I didn't ask and he didn't tell. He had to be on call and might be needed at any time to perform his job, for which he was being paid handsomely. Suddenly I was harboring two people's secrets, Lynn's and Nick's. But neither of them knew mine.

Lynn had a strange way with food also. Rail thin, Lynn rarely ate in the apartment, but she baked compulsively. Aromas of cakes and pies constantly filled the apartment – and were strong enough for me to detect. Lynn had a habit of cutting a tiny slice, which I never saw her eat, then leaving the rest on the counter for Nick and me with a little note she attached that said, "Eat me!"

On a Monday after we'd weekended together, Nick disappeared from school, didn't call, and left no word for me. I coped in my usual way, this time stuffing myself with dozens of fresh tortillas, slathered with butter and then enjoying the luxury of throwing up in a toilet I didn't have to share. About ten days later, in the middle of the afternoon, he showed up at the apartment looking tanned and tired.

"Where were you?" I asked. I was leaning up against the wall in our hallway.

Without a word, he leaned against me, making full body contact. Instantly I was aroused. So was he. He kissed me.

"Rowie," he said. "I probably will never see you again. I can't tell you why, but there's a lot of money involved, and I can't say no to this opportunity."

I rubbed my hand on his erection through his khakis. "How about this opportunity?" I asked, pretending I didn't care. I didn't want to care. After all, if I hadn't cared about Gabe, why should I care about this almost-stranger?

Our lovemaking had an edge of desperation. Without thinking about it, as soon as he touched the magic gateway on my ass, I slipped out of my body and observed a group of Marines smoking on the roof next door and talking about sex. Nick didn't miss me, maybe because he wasn't all there either – although if he left as I did, we must have gone in different directions because we hadn't met during my out-of-body wanderings. I thought how strange that I could observe my body making love with a man I hardly knew who was about to walk out of my life. I was in bed with him, acting as though I loved him, and I could probably love him. I liked him. But what was love anyway? Should I tell him I liked him? I thought about Gabe and wondered whether I'd ever talk to anyone about the unconventional sex we'd had. My mind went on and on as I heard my moaning love sounds. My body felt great orgasmic pleasure again and again even though I was more aware than ever that I was detached. It was a strange discovery.

"You're so great in bed," Nick said, sighing as he lit our cigarettes.

"Thanks," I said. "It takes two." I have so many of the right words, I thought. Does anyone know the difference?

"I'm going to miss you," he said.

"No, you're not, kiddo," I said. "You'll be out on some macho cloak and dagger mission."

He insisted he would miss me, so I admitted I'd miss him too. We both felt sad, but we laughed as we hugged farewell. Just like in college, the parade of men was marching through my bones.

– ∞ –

Next day, the doorbell rang, and I innocently opened the door without checking the peephole.

"Ricardo?" I'd slept in the same room with him when I was with Nick weeks ago, but had only seen him briefly. I had a bad feeling about his nasty expression. My instinct was to slam the door, but then I flashed that maybe something had happened to Nick, and Ricardo was here to tell me. Without a phone, I had to receive messages by mail or in person.

"Aren't you going to ask me in?" he demanded. His height, a couple of inches below six feet, surprised me since I'd never seen him standing. He stared straight at my breasts. I wasn't dressed for work yet and I didn't have on a bra, just a loose, short robe.

"No, sorry," I said. "This isn't a good time. Was there some specific reason you came by? Is Nick okay?" I wished Lynn were at home or I had a way to summon the Marines from next door. My knees quivered. Why was I scared? Wasn't he Nick's roommate?

"Nick, Nick, that bastard is gone. Forget about Nick. You should be able to figure out why I'm here, *princesa putita*," he said, and he pushed himself right in, closed the door with his foot, and pressed his body against me. He smelled like rum, cigarettes and sickeningly sweet cologne. Had I heard right? Had he really called me princess whore?

Trapped, my mind raced for a solution. Could I run and lock myself in the bathroom? If I could knee him, could I run outside and get help? He left me no space to move.

"You had some nerve having sex with Nick when I was there," he said, in Spanish.

I could have killed Nick in that moment for persuading me it was okay to stay in the same room with this creep. Why hadn't I insisted on returning home? What the hell part of me attracted these kinds of dangerous situations?

"I'm sorry," I said. "That was ages ago. Would you get away from me now? I can hardly breathe." I pushed him a little and he pressed me back harder. I worried about provoking him too much and forced myself to speak softly. "Nick led me to believe you and he had an understanding so I thought you were cool with me and him being there. Look, I'm sorry, I didn't even know you, so don't take it personally." I spoke in Spanish, hoping he'd appreciate my knowing his language and leave me alone.

"I take it very personally, *putita*," he said and pushed his knee between my legs.

"I'm sorry, but I don't like this. Please get away from me," I said firmly, and began struggling. I wanted to knee him in the balls but didn't know how to free myself. I wondered whether the Marines would hear me if I screamed and come to my rescue but I'd never met them, only eavesdropped when they didn't know I was there. Ricardo pushed his mouth onto my mouth and I turned my head and spit onto the floor. "What the fuck do you think you're doing, you asshole?" I said in English.

"I am doing what you like to do, leetle whore," he said with a thick accent and he shoved me hard against the wall. His broad shoulders were double mine.

I scolded him. "You think I like what you're doing? You're drunk and you're mean and you're calling me a horrible name, and I could call the police and report you."

"Oh you could, could you? My brothers and uncles are policemen and I work for your government. No one's going to arrest me because it's my word against yours. You're an American slut and if you think I've been mean, you will be very surprised because I'll show you mean if you don't cooperate," he said, breathing rum fumes on me. I was calculating how to proceed when he open-handed me across the cheek. "Here is a small sample," he growled, and aimed a small black pistol at my face. Ten years ago, the last time Daddy hit me, I'd hit him back. Now, faced with a gun, my nerve failed. My face stung. My body stiffened with fear. What should I do? If only I'd learned aikido when Ralph offered. I had no idea how to fight someone bigger and stronger than I was. Somehow I kept myself from crying as he shoved the gun into my cheek.

"You know why I'm here," he growled.

I wanted to think there might be a chance I could soften his heart if I let him make love with me. Maybe I'd disarm him completely, convert a bad guy into a good guy. I tried to remember whether I'd ever been forced to have sex. If Daddy had forced me, why couldn't I remember? All I could remember were jumbles of decals from my crib, Jack and Jill holding hands, on their way for a pail of water. Jill wore a pink bonnet and ruffled plaid pinafore and Jack blue and white checkered overalls. Like them, I tripped and tumbled down a steep hill. I was falling, falling and no one was there to catch me. The gun petrified me. I kept thinking he would stuff it in my mouth and shoot me.

"My room is down that way," I said, resigned. He let go of me with a shove and followed close behind. The smell of rum, cologne and fear turned my stomach.

He made me keep the bathroom door open as I put my diaphragm in and took off my robe. Still holding the gun, he managed to get his clothes off and rubbed his balls and penis, uncircumcised and flaccid. On a dark, muscular, hairy body, he wore bright gold jewelry, a thick chain with a heavy cross and medallion that said "San Juan de Dios, Pray for Us" in Spanish and had an image of a monk offering a chalice of wine to a haloed saint. He placed the gun on the dresser next to my hairbrush. Could I grab it and shoot him?

I'd never held a gun since Ralph's cap pistol when I was six. I caught myself choking and realized I had stopped breathing out of fear. He stood next to the bed and glared at me angrily. He still didn't have an erection.

I lay down almost gasping for breath I was so scared. Was this my punishment for leaving Gabe? I could have been married and safe at home now instead of halfway around the world and in danger. This angry hairy guy climbed on top of me, propped on his hands, and rocked up and down like an automaton. His medallion and cross clanked and smacked against my breasts and belly. Yeah, pray for us, Saint John, I thought. A lot of good your religion's doing right now. Ricardo did a one-hand prop and with the other hand kept trying and failing to put his soft penis into me. By flipping his cock around against my genitals, it finally stiffened. Despite the horror, I was aroused and mortified. Did my body think I wanted this man in me? I felt like throwing up and almost laughed at the irony.

I lay like a corpse with a necrophiliac. I said a little silent prayer in case someone happened to be listening. Ricardo reached under me and pinched my behind viciously, tearing at my flesh. I whimpered but stifled tears. Suddenly, the old reflex kicked in, and I whooshed out of my body and had a view of his pimply back. The gun gleamed on the dresser. Never take your eyes off a weapon, I'd read in a detective novel, and I didn't look at anything else.

He blasted into me and cried out noisily. The force catapulted me into my body with a thud. He rolled off me, grinning. My mouth felt cottony. I hated the wetness between my legs. Eyeing the gun with my peripheral vision, I wanted to tell him I was expecting my housemate and her large, muscular, killer boyfriend any minute, but I just calmly said my housemate and her boyfriend were coming to pick me up to do an errand before work and I had to shower and get ready, and did he want a drink of water before he left?

He shook his head no. "Was that good for you?" he asked. "Was it too fast?"

"It wasn't too fast," I said. How could he possibly think it was good? My butt burned. I felt sorry for him, wondered whether he'd ever been with a woman before. The poor bastard, I thought, he doesn't even know he's a rapist.

Finally I was alone. Shaking, I double locked the door and leaned against it. I wondered whether it was my fault, whether I should have challenged him, fought him, killed him, slammed the door in his face. I was horrified that I had to leave the diaphragm in for several hours to make sure the spermacide did its proper ritual murder. Still shivering, I headed straight for a hot shower. Lynn had left an apple pie on the kitchen counter with her usual sliver cut out. Lynn, the skinny compulsive baker, paired with me, the skinny compulsive eater. A match made in lunatic heaven. What was I doing here? I missed Gabe. When I thought about him, the miles dropped away. For once I didn't want to stuff myself. I just wanted to scrub.

– ∞ –

TWENTY-SEVEN

Our living room window looked out on the side entrance to a small theater, which fronted on Sixth Avenue. I began noticing a tall, lean, fair-skinned man, good-looking and sexy in an interesting, craggy way with an uncanny resemblance to my favorite movie star, Gregory Peck. Atticus Finch in Guatemala. This man could defend and protect me! I wanted him. He had dark, slightly wavy hair falling over one side of his forehead, a perpetual cigarette in his hand, and the habit of throwing back his head when he laughed, exposing a couple of gold fillings. He was a little taller than Gabe but had the same loping walk, natural, relaxed, and graceful, similar hair style, only Gabe's was wavier and a lighter shade. My stomach wobbled inside seeing the similarity. I missed a man's loving attention. Had I run away from Gabe's love just to discover love was exactly what I wanted? If I got it again, could I hold onto it? Why would I go for a stranger when I knew Gabe loved me? For the conquest, I told myself. For the experience. For the fun without commitment.

_ ∞ _

Atticus had keys to the theater, and I'd already chosen him as my leading man, so I zeroed in on him. Instead of a couch, Lynn and I had a double bed with lots of pillows in the living room right under the front window - perfect for spying. I stretched out across the bed, chin on a pillow, sill-level eyes glued to the scene on the street from my second floor perch. While I waited for Gregory Peck, I watched people coming and going from headquarters with interest, and I got to recognize the Marines. Since I didn't have to go to work until evening and only took a class at the university once a week, I dedicated myself to the job of tracking the gorgeous actor and soon developed an obsessive crush on him.

He had two co-stars, both young and sexy, both driving late model convertibles, a blonde in a gray BMW and a brunette in a white Corvette. Hollywood meets the Third World. When Gregory kissed each ingenue goodbye, he had a way of running his fingers through her hair and over her cheeks, which I found irresistibly thrilling. I wondered whether the women knew about each other. Was he a cad? I got to know his wardrobe, a sexy gray linen shirt with open lacing at the neck, a white Moroccan shirt, and everything else black turtlenecks which he wore with black pants.

In exchange for my silent acceptance of her affair with her married professor, my roommate Lynn did detective work for me. Gregory turned out to be an Argentinean named Miguel Bono, talented, charming and notorious as opportunist and womanizer, especially interested in those who could help his artistic career. He was broke and courted wealthy women as possible sponsors of his little theater. I didn't have money or a plan, but I told myself I would find a way to make Miguel Bono mine. I fixated on having him at my side. Since the rape, I didn't feel safe, and it embarrassed me to talk about it because I blamed myself. So to get Miguel, I enlisted the help of my old friend, god-guy, the comedian, and any of the helpers from my childhood who might still be around. I had a heart to heart talk with them, and they reminded me that they only helped those who helped themselves. While I was in the midst of plotting, I received an air mail letter from Gabe. My heart thumped. I still couldn't marry him. What did he want from me? I turned it over without opening it, stuck it in a drawer to look at some other time.

A few days later, at a visiting New York Ballet performance of Swan Lake at a municipal theater on Sixth Avenue, during intermission, I spotted Miguel in the lobby. We towered over most of the crowd. I was wearing my highest heels and a long sleeved fitted blue shirtwaist dress in the new wash and wear polyester fabric I'd never worn before. He was alone, dressed all in black, a trench coat over his arm, laughing, smoking, moving around the crowd, injecting a few words here and there. Our gaze met. My heart quickened. I felt sweat pooling under my arms. That was unusual. Ordinarily I didn't sweat heavily. Was I that nervous?

"Hi there, I've seen you so much I feel as though I know you," I said in Spanish, flashing my best smile.

"Really? You've seen me?" I could see he was immediately intrigued and flattered. He was even more handsome up close. Flashing dark eyes. Shiny black hair falling in relaxed waves. Gorgeous.

"Yes, I live across the street from your theater."

His face fell. "Ah, you've seen me in the street, not on stage. You are either European or from the United States, yes?"

"From New York," I said.

"New York! You have connections to the theater in New York?" he asked eagerly.

"Most certainly," I replied quickly, thinking, sure I have connections to the theater - the A train and the IRT.

I excused myself and went to the ladies' room to investigate the creeping underarm dampness. Dark, amoebic stains had spread down the sleeves, sides, front and back, turning the pretty light blue dress into a wet rag. I slipped the top of the dress off and used paper towels to blot the wetness of the fabric and my skin. Intending to hide the soggy mess, I donned my matching blue sweater over the dress and took my seat just as the house lights went out. In the darkness, someone slipped into the seat next to me and startled me by tapping my arm. I turned and there was the gorgeous man aiming his full "You're wonderful" smile right at me! I could no longer pay attention to the dancers. Now, I actually had reason to sweat. My armpits became a virtual fountain. He reached for my hand and intertwined fingers with me. Oh my God, how could this be happening? This was a drama within a drama. His hand felt warm and delicious. What was I doing? I had gotten my wish and now my mind was a mishmash of confusion, made all the worse by the rivulets running down my arms. Would he feel it on his hand? I could only hope the sweater mopped up the dampness.

After the show, Miguel asked permission to walk me home. I was glad when he put his arm around my shoulder rather than holding my hand because my shoulders had escaped the flood and things had gotten so extreme that I knew I was leaving a trail of dripping sweat on the sidewalk. When we got to my house, he laughed and threw his head back. I wondered whether he would've laughed had he known he was in danger of drowning from a human faucet. He leaned me against my front door and kissed me goodnight. My clothing was so soggy there was no way I'd lift my arms to hug him. Did I stink? I stood there, melting into the role of female lead, praying he wouldn't reject me, wondering what kind of lie I could make up about the wetness if he asked. Sweat drenched my sleeves and bodice and dripped steadily from under my cuffs. I could have wrung out my dress and sweater and filled a bucket. What was with this new polyester fabric? I was so wet, I thought if he came upstairs with me, he'd surely think I was a freak, so when he asked whether he could come up, I turned him down. He didn't push it. I let him kiss me a few times and felt like a starlet getting my hair and cheek stroked like his women in the fancy cars. No longer did I have to watch from afar. Now I was in the movie, playing opposite Gregory Peck! He left with a lunch invitation for next day.

Twice that night I had the same nightmare, about a man who was a combination of Miguel, Gabe, Daddy, and Ricardo, the rapist. He kept shoving a big gun in my mouth and when he pulled the trigger, I shot up soaked with sweat. In the morning, relieved to be alive, I showered and went to the market for salad, soup makings, and even ice cream. Back home I got the soup going, then showered again, soaping and rinsing, soaping and rinsing, obsessively.

– ∞ –

At the door, Miguel hugged me and said he respected me for turning him down the night before. My knees wobbled. If only I didn't have to keep secrets, we could have had a good laugh about the polyester. But I walked a tightrope anchored in secrecy. So, I took his hand and led him to the front window so he could fully appreciate the convenient location across from his theater. He appreciated the living room bed even more. I fed him my chicken soup from Grandma's recipe. Lynn had left a fruit pie on the counter for dessert and I fixed him pie a la mode.

It didn't take long for Miguel to move in. Why wouldn't he move in? He had free room and board, including outstanding meals, and a hot woman to sleep with. I had a handsome, sexy lover and protector and could practice speaking Spanish endlessly, even learning to ape an Argentinean sing-song accent. For instance, for the phrase "My name is Rowie," instead of pronouncing the first part "*Me llamo*" as "May Lyahmo," I knew to say "May Zsahmo" as in Zsa Zsa Gabor.

When I asked Miguel questions about politics, he answered me in riddles. He told me about the reign of Juan Peron in Argentina, a Mussolini admirer who won over the masses because he instituted advances like the eight-hour work day, minimum wage and all kinds of social programs. But he insisted on Catholic public education, spent so recklessly the country experienced rampant inflation, and worst of all came down hard on dissidents.

"My father was one of them," Miguel said, his face gloomy. "He was a union organizer and Peron supporter but when he started getting ideas of his own, they came and got him in the middle of the night. We never saw him again, but we heard he was tortured to death."

"My God, I'm so sorry," I said. "I can't imagine such a dreadful thing. Thank goodness I live in a free country."

"Don't be so sure, my love," Miguel said. "You enjoy privileges off the backs of poor campesinos and factory workers around the world."

"What are you talking about?" I asked, my mouth agape. "This sounds like what the maid where I used to live told me. Is my country something other than what I've always believed it to be?"

"You're an innocent, *mi amor*, like so many of your compatriots. Look, I don't want to scare you, so don't even ask me any more about my politics, okay? Just let me put it this way: first and foremost I'm an artist. On the side, I help out people who want to see a more equitable distribution of resources here and everywhere. I'll be spending time out in the countryside now and then, and I may not come home for a couple of days at a time. I don't want you to worry. I play more than one role because I'm an actor. I'm friends with the two daughters of the most powerful politician in Guatemala. We flirt but I stay away from entanglement because I can't afford to mess with their father. They support my work in the theater. So it's crucial they know me only as a struggling actor and director. They know nothing else." He pointed at me, in warning. "You know nothing else. Nothing. *¿Está claro?* Is that clear?"

"*Sí*," I said. "So, that explains the pretty women in nice convertibles?"

He nodded. "I love you," he said. "You're real, not spoiled like them. You have nothing to worry about."

"Okay," I said, remembering Ricardo and Nick. "I don't want to know details."

$-\infty-$

Satisfied, I turned my attention to cooking, cleaning and being a good wifey in between teaching and studying. Why had Miguel appealed to me and Gabe not? The romanticism? The mystery? I'd replaced a familiarly Jewish man who adored me for a man I barely knew. I'd rejected a man my family loved for a man my family would hate. Why? I wouldn't even try to make sense of it. I got two more letters from Gabe and I put them both in the same drawer with the first, unread. I wasn't sure why Gabe's letters threatened me. I didn't want to find out.

$-\infty-$

Lynn didn't mind Miguel's presence. All of us had secrets. I never mentioned my stuffing and barfing - still hadn't told anyone since the New York shrink who approved. I did my thing and carefully kept the toilet bowl clean.

239

With the exception of chocolate, which I still avoided since discovering Oreos didn't come up, Miguel and I scarfed all Lynn's cakes and pies. He'd go across the street to work, and I'd go throw up. Every morning I shopped at the market with the Guatemalan maids and cooked our main meal at lunch, as was the local custom. Just as with my mother, Miguel began thickening around the middle while I stayed mysteriously slender. We settled into our domestic arrangement quickly. I adored him. I knew Mommy would disapprove, and grinned just thinking of her disfavor.

– ∞ –

I was usually conscientious about having my diaphragm in place when we made love, but I wasn't as prudent about using the spermicidal gel, especially in the morning when it meant I had to get up from the warm cuddling when I was feeling totally turned on, remove the diaphragm, wash and dry it and then apply fresh gel. That is how one of his hardy little sperms swam right past my perfectly fitted diaphragm and plunged into one of my cooperative and willing eggs. I knew the moment it happened but I quickly put it out of my mind until I couldn't anymore.

I told myself, if I'd wanted marriage, I would have said yes to Gabe, a man with a doctorate and a secure job who wanted to marry me. At the same time, though I knew Miguel wasn't marriage material, I found myself fantasizing being married to him and having our baby. He had no paying job and was cobbling together productions at the theater by using volunteer actors. He designed the sets, lighting, and music, wrote ad copy, produced, directed, and was general troubleshooter. We had a nebulous plan that included his learning English and going to New York with me. But he said learning a foreign language made him feel ignorant and uncomfortable. I didn't push it since I felt safe staying in Guatemala and stringing him along with my purported New York theater connections. So once I'd confirmed my pregnancy from an over the counter pregnancy test, he inquired discreetly and found an experienced midwife on the outskirts of the city who was known to perform safe, reasonable abortions. I shuddered as I recalled an episode at college when Naomi Fisher almost bled to death after an outrageously costly, illegal abortion. In Guatemala, I learned, abortion wasn't legal, but was openly accepted and not prosecuted. We made arrangements through a local messenger service since neither the midwife nor we had a phone.

The day before our appointment, a messenger came to the apartment with another message, this one to phone Mommy from the messaging center at seven o'clock that evening. Karen and Mommy waited breathlessly at their end, eager to tell me the good news, timed to perfection. Karen was pregnant.

"Congratulations, I'm very happy for you and Jonathan," I said, weeping for my unborn child. How could I dismiss this baby? How could I not? If I had this baby, not only wouldn't it have a father who could support it, but also it would be born to a mother who lied her ass off, stuck her head in toilets, and hated herself. Maybe I should be aborted along with the baby, I thought. Scrape me away. I don't deserve to live.

"Karen, Aunt Rowie is crying from happiness, do you hear her?" Mommy, as usual, unaware of my feelings, had picked up the tears.

"It's just the long distance connection," I lied.

"Oh, Rowie, it's okay to cry. We hope you'll be home for the birth. It'll be next April."

"I don't know when I'm returning," I said. "For now, this is home."

– ∞ –

The night after the abortion, I dreamed I was in a Hollywood movie, playing mother. There was a family around only I couldn't see them. I was alone, standing at the kitchen sink, peeling, slicing, and coring a perfect, round, very large red apple for my family's fruit salad. Out of nowhere Daddy appeared, exaggeratedly big and muscular, like a wrestler. He grabbed the apple from me and forced what was left of it – about half – down my throat. I choked and sputtered but miraculously swallowed it all. Then Daddy took hold of my hair and dragged me away to a deep underground cave. I was petrified. When we reached a wide river filled with floating logs and branches, a ferryman with a raft showed up who looked like a composite of all my boyfriends – I recognized Paul, my junior high beau, Skip, Pierre, Gabe and Miguel. "Help me," I begged them telepathically. "Please rescue me." Daddy heard and cast a spell on the ferryman, transforming him into a nasty, giant frog and knocked him into the water, only it wasn't water, it was vomit.

I woke up in a sweat and threw my arm around Miguel who slept with his back to me.

"I had a nightmare, baby," I said, and he rolled over and held me and patted me. I was slightly tempted to tell him about the vomit addiction that had plagued me for over ten years, but I chickened out. We fell back to sleep entwined.

– ∞ –

Three weeks after the abortion, resuming sex, now on the Pill, I noticed a stench coming from my vagina. Smelly fluid dripped from Miguel's penis. Alarms went off. He found a doctor. Diagnosis: gonorrhea. My reaction: shock, befuddlement, betrayal, humiliation. Miguel admitted he'd been hanging out with a woman who sold sex, but he said he didn't have to pay because they were friends and he liked her very much so he didn't want to call her a hooker. He said she was a revolutionary and was only working as a prostitute for the good of the Guatemalan revolution. Was this the secret it was better I didn't know? Miguel apologized over and over. Was he acting? Horrified and ashamed, he cried and begged forgiveness. He promised he wouldn't see her anymore. When he groveled, I forgave him. I found myself liking his guilt. It empowered me. I even got him to reveal some information about the fledgling revolutionary movement, just enough to make me curious for more.

– ∞ –

One day, at the blanket stall in the indoor portion of the main marketplace, I bumped into an unusual looking man around my age with flaming red hair. We arrived at the same moment, from opposite directions and were so busy looking at the blankets draped high up on the wall that we literally collided. I lost my balance and fell against him once again. We were both embarrassed and apologized in Spanish. Then, in what seemed like a choreographed dance, we both turned and, in the same moment, began speaking to the woman running the stall who observed the whole scene with mild amusement.

Standing next to each other, in stereo Spanish, we pointed to each other and came out with "You go first." It was obvious he was from the United States, not only from his fractured Spanish, but also from amazing, fiery hair. Laughing, we introduced ourselves and instantly created a little dialogue that had us rollicking. We laughed so hard we drew tears.

"I'm Harry Apple, from Boston."

"Rowie Wine, New York. Oh my God, you have an edible name and I have a drinkable name!"

"Not so bad together either," he said. "Apple Wine."

"My mom, Pearl Fine, married my dad, Buddy Wine and became Pearl Fine Wine. If I married you, I'd be Rowie Wine Apple, like Winesap Apple," I said, doubled over laughing.

"Are you calling me a sap?"

"I think we're sharing the sap," I said.

We collapsed into hilarity.

I stopped, looked at his carrot colored hair and gasped. "You poor man, you must get called Red Apple." I couldn't stop giggling. "There used to be a restaurant called Red Apple Rest my folks stopped at all the time on our way home from the city when I was a little kid. They'd get all jazzed about having hot dogs with sauerkraut, and I'd stay in the car and sleep. I'm not sure what made me more uncomfortable, the smell in that place or my family."

"Count your blessings. At least you didn't have to be called a fruit."

"I knew a kid named Phil Pear who was obnoxious. Got me the worst birthday present of my life. Hmmm. Maybe it was all a defense from being called a fruit. I went to college with a Mellon heiress. Wow, we could write a book all about people with fruit names. Let's see, Jack Lemmon, hmm, does John Quincy Adams count?"

"I don't know, is that like saying we're in a 'bananny' republic."

He was smart and quick, and we doubled over in complete silliness there in the aisle of the marketplace next to blankets, across from hats and guitars, surrounded with color, music and aromas of ripe fruit and roasted corn.

Out of the stacks of colors, fabrics, designs and sizes, we both chose the exact blanket, deep red wool with black geometric human figures.

"Tell me the truth, Harry," I said, "Would you have chosen that red blanket if I hadn't?"

"Had my name on it," he said, and we fell into laugher again. Harry had a wide grin, straight teeth, a slightly hooked nose, clear gray eyes, and a shy, adorable laugh. His complexion was clear and creamy, with a handful of freckles on his nose. I found him charming and appealing and immediately thought of Gabe. It was as though Gabe had fallen off a wall like Humpty Dumpty, and splintered into multiple men, all of whom I was attracted to. We felt so at ease with each other that I invited him back to the apartment for coffee and fresh brownies from the batch Lynn had baked in the middle of the night.

"Brownies! I can't refuse brownies. Can we stop and get some milk? I like coffee, but brownies require milk."

I smiled and nodded, feeling a pang of something dark pass through like a ghost cloud. The Oreo shadow, ten years later.

We sat in the living room and chatted non-stop as I drank black coffee and he scarfed brownies and milk. We discovered uncanny parallels in our lives. He was the middle son of three boys just as I was the middle daughter of three girls. His mother had died just after his freshman year at Hobart College, same time as my dad had died. His older brother, whose name was Karl with a "K" like my sister Karen, was married to a woman doctor just like Karen and Jonathan. Here we were, both in Guatemala City. What were the odds of that? It got better. We discovered we shared the exact same birthday, same day, and same year! He showed me his Massachusetts driver's license, and I showed him mine from New York. No wonder we felt like twins. I wondered whether he had any weird eating habits like me, but I didn't dare ask. He seemed pretty normal eating brownies, and he wasn't particularly thin or fat. I wondered whether having sex with him would feel incestuous but quickly put it out of my mind because of Miguel.

Harry was staying at a pension temporarily while waiting for the go-ahead to take off for a village in the mountains where Peace Corps volunteers had been teaching literacy skills. His project was to measure the correlation between literacy and quality of life. He was receiving government funding to live in the village for nine months, working with Peace Corps volunteers and getting to know villagers. He was to keep detailed notes of villagers' attitudes and aspirations and write a report on his findings for an international relief organization, which he hoped to turn into a Masters thesis for a program at New York University. He loved New York and imagined himself living there. New York!

"Any chance you know anybody in theater in New York?" I asked. "Like actors, directors, playwrights or producers? Janitors? Ushers?"

"Hmmm," he said. "I have an uncle in New York in the button business."

"Yeah, and my aunt's brother is in the rag trade. I'm looking for a connection to help Miguel out. He's a dramatic genius."

I went on and on about Miguel, and then Harry told me about Marilena, his maid at the pension.

"I like her," he said, "but I don't think I love her. We don't have much to talk about. She grills me about the States. Her dream is to live in El Paso, Tucson or Los Angeles."

"You'll be leaving her in a week. How's that going to be?"

He thought for a few moments. "I don't like myself for this, but, even though it's been wonderful and exciting being with her, it'll be a relief to leave. I never thought I'd feel that about a pretty girl who throws herself at me willingly."

"I've been bored with lovers," I said. "But I can't imagine ever being bored with Miguel. I love being with him so much. He's like a prize for me."

Right on cue, in walked Miguel, looking sexy and gorgeous with his new three-day-beard look. Harry stood and extended his hand. He was a few inches shorter than Miguel and had to look up at him. I introduced them and switched to Spanish, explained that we'd just met in the market a couple of hours ago. Miguel looked from Harry to me and back again. I knew he was searching for clues to our relationship. I jumped up and kissed my beautiful prized man and put my arm around him.

"Honey," I said. "Don't worry. Harry has a Guatemalan girlfriend, and anyway, he's leaving in a few days, and we'll never see him again." I noticed Miguel raise one eyebrow skeptically. His jealousy excited me.

– ∞ –

A couple of days later, around mid morning, I was leaving for the market just as Harry slipped a note under the door. The open door almost knocked him down.

"I'm so sorry," I said. "I didn't realize you were here."

He rubbed his head and grinned sheepishly. "I guess this looks stupid," he said, picking up the envelope and handing it to me. "The note says I enjoyed meeting you and wanted to let you know I hope we can connect again. I may be coming into the city from time to time and I hope it's okay to come by or look you up at work. If you had a phone, I would have called."

I hesitated.

"Purely as friends and countrymen, of course, Rowie. Is that a problem?"

"No, no, I'm an independent woman," I said quickly. "Yes, sure, you can come by. Mornings after ten are best. Miguel is gone by then. Latin men tend to be jealous even with no grounds, so I'd prefer not to stir anything up."

"No problem, I understand," he said. "I've been dealing with a clash of cultures myself. Marilena is calling me disloyal when she knew all along I had to leave. I locked my door last night, and she unlocked it and came in. That's it for me. I'm only dating American girls from now on."

"Good luck," I said. "Maybe you'll fall in love with someone from the Peace Corps."

"I'm ready for peace," he said.

I locked the apartment door, slipped his note into my purse.

"Walk me to the market? I'd like to ask you something."

"I have about half an hour to spare. If you're still looking for theater connections, sorry, my uncle, the button maker, is still the only one I know in New York."

"It's not that. I was wondering what you think about the U.S. interfering in Guatemala's politics."

"You mean kicking out Arbenz in '54? I don't know details. Do you?"

"Not really, but I know there's a force at work to bring back free elections and land reform."

"A Communist force?"

I shook my head. "They say they don't want the Soviets or Americans or Cubans interfering in their country. They want Guatemala for the Guatemalans. But the problem is they have to get money from somewhere. From what I gather, big American companies like United Fruit and Grace call the shots here. Not that they exactly promote poverty, but if their bottom line means people suffer, tough shit. That opens the door to Communist propaganda and then the Americans can say, 'See, told you so, we have to help fight the Commies, so we'll provide a military solution to keep the country free.' I'm pretty sure there are guerillas in the mountains and jungles who plan to take back the country, and God knows how many of them are independents. They had a taste of reform with Arbenz and they're unhappy now. There are also mercenaries Miguel says are brutally attacking people for organizing, and our government may be involved in paying them or paying the guys who pay them. What do you think is going on?"

"Rowie, I don't think it's a black and white issue. I think there's a gray area. Peace Corps volunteers help people out and that's a good thing. Wouldn't you agree?"

"I would, but Miguel says it's tokenism. He says that building a latrine here and there doesn't materially change the conditions of the people. They deserve land. The maid where I used to live said her life changed when her father and uncle got a little plot to farm under Arbenz. She and her brothers and sisters got shoes for the first time. Now her relatives are working for United Fruit again and are miserable. Will you do me a favor? When you're out in the boonies, will you ask people about the way it was under Arbenz and find out their thinking about the government? I'd like another opinion."

"Sure, that's a great idea," said Harry. "I'll poke around. I'm curious myself."

But I never reconnected with Harry in Guatemala. My grant ended and rather than look for more work, I allowed Miguel to talk me into going back to New York to smooth the way for him to join me. I was hoping he'd forgotten my claim to New York theater connections. He hadn't. He called my bluff. I'd have a couple of months to weasel my way into theater circles. I hated being caught in a lie but was thrilled my Gregory Peck movie star was going to relocate to New York and I would still play female lead.

– ∞ –

TWENTY-EIGHT

I arrived in New Orleans on Monday, February 24th, at four in the afternoon, the first leg of my trip home to New York, and had a layover until six next morning. For a while I nonchalantly walked around the airport, found a newspaper, read a little, did a crossword puzzle, browsed the shops amazed at all the varieties of Louisiana hot sauce, read a little more, got tired, drank black coffee, guzzled water, walked again. Shops closed, and I started getting restless, probably from caffeine and hunger, which, as usual, didn't occur to me. I'd eaten half a slice of pineapple and black coffee for breakfast and another half slice, a couple of bites of lettuce and one forkful of chicken salad for lunch, which I deemed more than enough. I had no credit card, was too broke to go to a hotel, and as my situation sank in, I realized hanging out in the airport all night might not be necessary. Sure enough, there was a flight leaving at two AM, making stops in Atlanta and Washington, DC, and going on to land at LaGuardia at about the time I'd be taking off with my original flight. Delighted with my decision and feeling foolish that I hadn't thought of it earlier, I buoyantly approached the agent at the Eastern ticket counter. He was tall and husky with light, creamy coffee complexion, shock of curly black hair, and unusual gray-green eyes. It was reassuring to see someone cute and boyish I could relate to and flirt with. I greeted him ebulliently, handed him my ticket packet. He took it apart and examined it.

"I'd like to get to New York earlier," I said, as he perused the papers. "Are there any seats on flight 304?"

He handed me back the ticket, looked straight into my eyes. "Yes, there are, but I can't let you on that flight, Miss Wine. You'll have to stick with your original itinerary."

Rage rose instantly. My voice cracked shrilly. "What do you mean? If there are seats, why can't I have one? You're going to make me hang out in this stupid airport all night when I could be on my way home? That isn't right!" I waved the ticket packet madly.

"There's nothing I can do," he said calmly. "I can't let you on that flight."

"I'd like to speak with your manager," I huffed.

"You're speaking with him, Miss Wine. I'm the manager. You can file a formal complaint when you get to New York."

Outraged, I pulled out every argument I could, used logic, emotion, even my female tears to get him to allow me on that plane. He was made of stone, apparently, and absolutely refused. He didn't even apologize or explain. Helpless to get what I wanted, I stormed away. I resisted vending machine candy – easy because it was all chocolate and that hadn't tempted me since the Oreo trauma. If there had been a pizzeria or doughnut shop open, I would have indulged recklessly, but instead I stopped in a restaurant for a few more glasses of water. An Agatha Christie someone had left behind got me through the night. Between the book, anger, exhaustion, and hunger pang denial, I was too fogged to notice anything else.

By the time I arrived at LaGuardia, even though I'd napped on the plane, I drooped with exhaustion. I caught a shuttle to Port Authority and a bus to Vails Gate, a suburb of Newburgh, where Mommy now rented what had been a Revolutionary War hunting lodge, a two-hundred-year-old, rustic, historic frame cottage she was thrilled to have found and had written me all about. Another place George Washington was purported to have slept. I had never seen it since she'd been living in Syracuse when I left fourteen months earlier. I'd meant to call her from the bus station but skipped it and waited to phone from the suburban Mom and Pop convenience store where the bus stopped.

"I'm here, at Al & Mabel's store, Mommy. Please come pick me up."

She got so blubberingly hysterical when she heard my voice, she couldn't speak coherently.

"What's wrong, Ma? I thought you'd be happy to hear from me."

"You have no idea how happy I am, Rowie, darling," she sobbed. "Thank God, you're okay. We were terrified you'd been on the other flight. I'll be right there to pick you up as soon as I call Karen, Victoria, Aunt Bea, Ralphie, and Sylvia."

"Mommy, wait, don't hang up, what are you talking about? What other flight? I was up all night, I'm really tired and there's no place to sit down here. Can't you wait and call the family gossip network after you pick me up? Please don't make me stand here."

"This is not gossip, Rowie. We've been scared to death. Why didn't you call earlier? Don't you know? There was a plane crash around two in the morning in the lake in New Orleans. A flight to New York. Oh my God, I'm so relieved. I have to call your sisters. I'll call the others later although by then word will be out, I suppose. I'd rather tell them myself, but don't worry, I'll be there soon."

A huge "PLANE CRASH!" headline screamed from the front page of the Daily News. I bought a paper. The flight I'd tried to fight my way onto had crashed into Lake Pontchartrain shortly after take-off and killed every passenger and crewmember aboard. I'd begged to be on that plane. Reeling and dazed, I spent the last of my cash on my usual medicine, a large box of glazed doughnuts. I pulled a sweater out of my suitcase to make room and smushed in the doughnuts, hidden for later when I'd surely need them. Even crushed and crumbly, they would do the trick.

So who was the ticket agent? How had he known? Had he known? Why was I supposed to live? Did I have some special mission? Why wasn't the flight cancelled? What about the other passengers? Why wasn't I dead and buried in the lake and finished with all the problems of my life? My mind overflowed with questions I couldn't answer. Shouldn't I tell somebody official? If only I'd paid attention to his name. He'd said I should file a report. Was that code?

After admiring Mommy's new Volkswagen bug, I put my bags into the trunk under the hood, distracted that the engine was where I expected the trunk to be. "Very cool," I said. I turned down the offer to drive and then explained what had happened and asked her opinion about the ticket agent.

"Don't make a whole *tsimmes* out of it," she said after a quick hug and peck on my cheek. Her eyes were still red, but the tears were history. "Just thank God you're alive, dear. It wasn't your time."

"Ma, don't you find it just a teensy bit hypocritical to thank God when you don't believe in God?"

"It's just an expression, Rowie, for heaven's sake. And who knows? If it was God that saved your life, who am I to question? So sue me, call me *pisher* if I say thanks, just in case."

"Oh Ma," I said. "You're so funny. Still the befuddled queen of double messages."

Mommy chattered about this and that and didn't even realize my mind was somewhere else. I wondered about the ticket agent and God. Maybe it'd been a huge mistake! Or had been random and had nothing to do with any divine being? After all, why would a god want someone as nuts as me around? But then I thought I'd better do like Mommy and say thanks just in case. Hey,

I said silently, if you're there or here, in whatever wild and weird form that is not an old man with a beard up in the sky, please give me a sign. Or was this plane crash a very big sign you just gave me? I'm so confused.

"I've made matzo ball soup," Mommy said. "Glad you're here to eat it, dear. You will have some, won't you?" She turned into an almost hidden driveway. "My wonderful old house is about half a mile up this dirt road. Isn't this amazing? Wait till you see the place. You'll love it!"

– ∞ –

She was right. The two-hundred year old rustic dwelling was charming with original fireplace and oven, beamed ceilings and wide plank floors finished in a warm honey tone. I felt a pang of bitterness that I'd grown up in such a tiny crowded dump and now, with her family gone, Mommy had space.

As soon as the house tour ended, I collapsed into a comfortable bed in the roomy downstairs guest bedroom and allowed Mommy to wait on me. It slowly sank in that I had escaped dying in a plane crash. Why? I ate a cracker, a cup of chicken broth, a couple of pieces of cooked carrot, figured it at around four hundred calories, maybe more since the soup gleamed with fat, drank three glasses of water, and slept for hours, getting up just to shuffle across the wide pine planks to the bathroom and back to bed again. I was keenly aware of the box of doughnuts, carefully stashed in an upstairs dresser under sweaters. If I could keep the chicken soup dinner down, maybe I was cured and would never eat boxes of doughnuts again.

For two days, Miguel, Lynn, and fellow teachers at the binational institute in Guatemala worried that I'd gone down in the plane crash. All they knew was I was on my way from New Orleans to New York and they hadn't heard from me. In a panic, Miguel finally got a call through. I dragged myself up long enough to let him know I was alive. Funny I didn't feel so alive. How strange that so many people cared whether I lived or died! Gabe would have worried too if he'd known. Why did people care more about me than I did about myself? In Mommy's historic cottage, I repeated a piece of my own history, slid into a deep funk, and there I rested.

– ∞ –

In early April, Karen gave birth to a daughter, Eliza. Managing to skirt a spring snowstorm, Mommy and I peacefully survived the four-hour trip from Newburgh to Syracuse in her red Volkswagen bug, excited at becoming

Grandma and Aunt Rowie. Baby Eliza had arrived late on Thursday, April 2, and we'd waited until Saturday to leave so Mommy could clear her desk to prepare for taking the next week off and also get to her regular Friday evening beauty parlor wash and set. We timed the trip in conjunction with opera from the Met on the car radio – "Don Giovanni" – but unfortunately lost the signal an hour from home. Mommy didn't complain when I switched to the top forty hit parade, not my favorite music, but done slyly with intent to rankle. When it didn't have that effect, I switched the radio off and forgot about irritating her. I liked being behind the wheel on the open highway. Staying close enough to the speed limit that I didn't have to worry about state troopers or Mommy's interference, I mindlessly hummed familiar arias from "Don Giovanni." When I realized that every other Volkswagen bug on the road honked hello, I began honking too, and determined to get myself one of these friendly little cars.

Mommy went into a long tale about how guilty she felt buying a German car, how she knew her parents must be turning over in their graves, how many of her coworkers loved their Volksie bugs, and even though it struggled to go uphill, did I notice how little gas it used compared to the big Pontiac we used to have? Preoccupied with our excitement over the baby, and proud of the healthful home-packed snacks of apple slices, carrot and celery sticks, and farmer cheese with caraway seeds that kept us feeling like good girls, we stuck with our usual topics – diets, recipes, Volkswagens, and politics. She didn't mention Gabe once. She and my sisters must have made a pact because I'd spoken with both Victoria and Karen over the phone, and they hadn't mentioned him either. Why did this bother me? I should have been grateful they weren't meddling. Why did I feel, as we got closer to Syracuse, the distance between Gabe and me shrank? My family drew me to Syracuse, my sisters and new niece, not Gabriel. Not Gabriel. Not Gabriel. I drummed it into my head. Now it was Miguel I loved. Miguel. Miguel. Miguel.

I hadn't seen either of my sisters since before going to Central America over a year ago, and looked forward to our visit. I'd spoken by phone with Victoria at Bennington a couple of times since I got home. I adored her but walked on eggshells around her ever since her childhood truth detector gauged my secrets. I was pretty sure she had no reason to believe I still had the old puke habit, but I would have to be cautious. The trick with Victoria was to distract her. This weekend looked safe, since she'd be preoccupied writing a paper. I'd have to be careful at night though because she and I were sharing a room at Jon's mom's house and sleepovers could get intimate. I'd have to ask her lots of questions about her life and tire her out.

We arrived at Karen's place just as the snow started falling and took it as an omen for a lucky weekend. As soon as we got our bags and the cooler inside and hugged all round, we peeked in on the sleeping baby. Then Mommy retired to the kitchen to make chicken soup. Becoming a Grandma evidently inspired her to produce Jewish food.

$$- \infty -$$

Later, we sat around on the tropical print couches in Karen's living room, an archetypal circle of women gathered around new mother and sweet, tiny infant in rocker. We continued to fuss over baby Eliza, taking turns holding her, and grooving over the miracle of life. My big sister looked tired, but radiant. Victoria was semi-attentive, face in and out of a book and yellow pad she scribbled notes on, her face hidden behind a curtain of hair. She dressed all in black, beatnik style, just as I'd favored since college, complete with silver bangle earrings I'd given her for her eighteenth birthday. I wore similar ones only I'd pierced my ears in Guatemala - heated a needle, downed a tall glass of tequila, and punctured my lobes. No big deal.

"Hey, Ro, you pierced your ears!" Victoria said. "Cool! I gotta do that too. There's a girl in my dorm who does it if we provide the studs. You've inspired me."

"Nothing to it," I said and stood to stretch way up toward the ceiling.

"You're so skinny!" Karen exclaimed. Victoria echoed her.

"Are you saying I was fat before I went to Guatemala?" I asked. I hated this topic.

"You were never fat," Mommy said, lying with enthusiasm. "But now, you're thinner than ever. I'm so jealous. Ask her about the new boyfriend, girls. Maybe you can pull info from her she hides from me."

"Better yet," I said, sitting down again, infuriated, "I'll tell you all about what's going on politically which I'm sure you don't hear about on the evening news." I launched into a long harangue about W.R. Grace and United Fruit and the way our government overthrew Arbenz and the need for land reform in Guatemala.

"Rowie," Karen said grinning, when I came up for air, "It sounds like you've moved from liberal to Communist."

Victoria chimed in. "My sister, the Commie pinko. Sweet. You want to go to Cuba? I'll go with you. I love Fidel."

I reacted instantly. "That's unfair, you guys. I'm not jumping on the bandwagon for Fidel, but I am going to watch with an open mind to see how Cuba turns out. Just because I'm in favor of a nation's self-determination, that doesn't make me a Soviet-style Communist. I'm a loyal American and you know it. I love our country. I just hate what our government is doing. Did you know that students who demonstrated against the new military leaders in Guatemala were tear-gassed? Are you aware that the U.S. is supporting the bastards who gas students? Probably an American company is selling them the tear gas. I'll bet you didn't even see a thing on TV or in the papers about it, right?"

"Calm down, dear," Mommy said. "You're getting carried away, as usual. Students have been demonstrating for years everywhere but here – which I would like to see change, and I think with the Civil Rights Movement it's finally shifting. You act as though nothing exists until Rowena Gay Wine discovers it. We've talked about this before. Don't go to extremes, dear. You're so angry! Get some perspective."

She was right. I was angry, and I didn't know how to get perspective. I noticed no one answered my comment about seeing this political information on the news.

"I'm serious, Rowie," said Victoria, ignoring Mommy's remarks. "I'd love to go to Cuba. Why are you so defensive? I like Communists. I think they're cool."

I skipped asking Victoria if she thought Stalin was cool. My nerves crackled.

Karen gazed at us, from one to another, wide-eyed, like watching a tennis match. Then she spoke to me. "I think you cleverly changed the subject, Rowie. No fair. Now, we insist you tell us about your new boyfriend." She attached Eliza to her other breast, as smoothly as she steered the conversation back.

I blushed. "He looks like a movie actor," I said, caught off guard. I hadn't planned to talk about him at all, but when I did, it comforted me. "He's gorgeous."

"That's wonderful, dear, but does he have prospects? Will he offer security? Is he an educated man?" asked Mommy. "I wish he'd speak English when I answer the phone."

"No, Mommy, he's a bum and high school dropout, like Daddy was," I mumbled under my breath.

"I missed that, dear," said Mommy. "Speak up."

"You were supposed to miss that, Mom," said Victoria.

"Why won't your sister talk to me about this boyfriend of hers? I don't get it."

"Mommy," I said, choosing my words carefully, "I am in love with Miguel. I am choosing to be with him. He has intelligence, talent, and good looks. You will meet him in a few weeks. Meanwhile, I do not want to discuss him. So let's all just shut up."

"Well, pardon me for living," Mommy huffed, helping herself to a chocolate from the open box on the coffee table. She slammed the lid on the box and carried it toward the kitchen. She turned around. "Ever since you got home, you've refused to tell me about this Miguel. It's frustrating. He called a couple of times, and I thought it was a wrong number. The boyfriend can't speak a word of English, but he's coming to live in New York. So where will you live, in Spanish Harlem? Maybe on Avenue D? My daughter, a Barnard graduate, living in a slum. I can't stand it. It isn't fair, Rowie. Especially since Gabriel is still single. There, I finally said it. I vowed not to, but I had to. He called Karen and asked about you. Tell her, Karen. Rowie, you're driving me to be bad and eat these goddamn chocolates. You know what I think? Obviously, you're ashamed of your new boyfriend. Otherwise you'd tell us about him. I feel like calling Gabriel myself."

"Come on, you guys, you promised me peace," Karen said. "Ma, I wish you hadn't mentioned the unmentionable. We had a deal about that. I'm sorry, Ro."

"I'm sorry too, okay?" I said, feeling a familiar knot deep in my belly. I was furious. As I suspected, they had a conspiracy of silence about Gabe. So he asked about me. Should I call him? No, my life was with Miguel now. So what if Miguel didn't speak English. It wouldn't kill Mommy to learn a few words of Spanish. They'd never understand his genius. Why did I even bother coming home to the States? What was home? Mommy's place didn't feel like home. No place felt like home. I sighed. "Miguel and I are going to live in the Village,

Mommy. Don't worry, it's a safe neighborhood. Now, please, let's not fight. Gabe and I are history. You can't change that. Furthermore, I'm not responsible for what you eat, and you know it. That's insane. You stop and I'll stop, okay?" I forced myself to sound calm. "Karen's right, we promised her peace."

Fuming, confused by my excitement at the mention of Gabe, I purposely, silently focused on Karen nursing the baby. Watching the sucking infant and glowing mother, again I felt intensely aware of the connection between food and love. So this was where it began, I thought.

"Ma, sit down with us. Relax," Karen said. "You're making me jumpy. This is a rare chance for us all to visit."

"Are you sure you don't want a bowl of chicken soup, Karen? You need extra calories now. You're not hungry?"

"Ma, I'm fine, really. Sit down, please."

"I'd love your soup, Mom," Victoria said, "it smells amazing. But I'd like to finish annotating this story first. I have to do a great job on my "Lottery" paper because I baby-sit for Shirley Jackson's kids. She's the first author I've ever known personally. I thought she was normal until I read this weird story. Brilliant but definitely weird. Soup in about an hour, okay? Skim the fat, would you?"

"I'll take from where it's boiling. Tomorrow I'll skim the fat from what's left over. I made it just like Grandma's. Drink, Karen. You have to drink plenty of water when you nurse."

"I have water, Ma. I'm fine. Sit down. Please!"

"You should drink like Rowie. She knows how to drink water. Tell them about the water in Guatemala, Rowie."

"I was a compliant daughter. I boiled it and then refrigerated it just like my mommy told me."

Pearl beamed.

When Karen handed me the baby to burp, I was scared, but I took her anyway. Would I drop her? She was so tiny and fragile! Was that a crazy thought? There was an air of ancient wisdom about her. After she burped, a big, juicy one, I cradled her and watched her face. Transfixed, I saw her face morph into one face after another, women's faces, men's faces, monster faces, young, old, regal, poor, deformed, a parade of unfamiliar faces and then, among them, unmistakable, Grandpa's face! It passed so quickly I did a double take and all the morphing stopped. Baby Eliza was herself again. I had a strange infinity feeling in my stomach, the same ache, similar to hunger, that came whenever I thought of abstractions I didn't quite understand.

"Did any of you see that?" I asked in a hushed tone.

"See what? Rowie, you look odd and inscrutable," said Karen. "What happened?"

"It's nothing," I said, blinking. "I must be imagining."

"Imagining what?"

"For an instant, Eliza looked like Grandpa."

"I've noticed that too, Ro. I'm so glad she was named for Gramps. Around the eyes, right?"

"Yeah," I said. I was too embarrassed by what I thought I'd seen to share.

"That's it?"

I nodded. I didn't dare say Grandpa's whole face replaced Eliza's along with one after another I didn't recognize in an instantaneous film sequence through something like a dimensional portal. What the hell was this? Past lives? Why monsters? Was it only my imagination? Was this a sign from god-guy? How could I tell? Whom could I tell? I felt puzzled, a little scared, and honored too, as though chosen for this special experience. Saved from the plane crash, and now this. I remembered Edgar Cayce, the simple Kentucky farm boy who in his sleep became a psychic healer. So what if my family thought it better to avoid these kinds of unexplainable phenomena, which they lumped into a category called "Superstitious Thinking." I wasn't about to talk about the way I slipped out of my body at critical moments or this incredible morphing. I'd talk to the baby! Maybe she'd understand since she's the one who morphed. I closed my eyes and concentrated, but what I expected to say changed.

"Please be sane with food, little Eliza," I heard myself communicate. I could swear her response was, "You too, Auntie Ro-Ro." Could I be sane with food? How was it possible for this baby to know my secret? Was Ro-Ro just baby-talk or coincidence because Grandpa called me Ro-Ro? I thought, I'm hearing voices. I must be losing my mind. Am I certifiable? I sat tensely.

Mommy sat and immediately started reminiscing about us when we were babies. I listened carefully as I continued to cradle my baby niece.

"Rowie, you screamed so loud the whole neighborhood must have thought I was starving you," Mommy told us. She chuckled. "She was nothing like you, Karen, or you, Victoria. You two were good eaters. But you, Rowie, you were another story. I didn't know how to cope with you. One bottle was never enough for you. You'd scream and scream as though you were being tortured. It took two whole bottles to shut you up. You were such a pig, it was embarrassing."

I felt my face reddening. I hated being called a pig, probably because I knew I was a pig. I also hated reacting uncontrollably as though I had hundreds of buttons right down the front of me, each one easily pushed. "Why didn't you pick me up, Mommy?" I asked. I hated the shrill edge in my voice. "Maybe that's all I wanted, just love, the one thing I didn't get." My heart pounded. Rage rose. Eliza fussed so I handed her back to Karen.

Victoria groaned. "C'mon, Mother, how can you call an infant a pig?"

Karen gave Victoria and me a warning look. What was happening to the peaceful visit? Mommy answered easily.

"Stop attacking me, you girls. Rowie, you know very well you were loved. Victoria, I can call Rowie a pig because Rowie was a pig, an insatiably hungry baby." She looked at me and continued. "As soon as you got a second bottle, you were fine, Rowie. You needed to eat to grow fast. It's no secret that you were always big for your age. You still are big, tall I mean. Karen and Victoria, you two were always petite shrimps like me. Not that I'm petite anymore. Speaking of pigs, I'm a fat pig now that I've gained thirty pounds. Did I tell you I'm planning to go to Weight Watchers? I saw the woman who started it on the Tonight Show and I could swear she's Jewish. Jean Naiditch. Do you think that's a Jewish name? She's gonna make a mint with that business idea. Why didn't I think of it?"

"Mommy, you're not fat," I said, unsure whether I believed it or not. She wasn't thin, but she wasn't obese like I felt, either. "I hate hearing you say that as much as I hate being called big. I'm five-six for heaven's sake. That is not big."

"Oh, Rowie, you should be happy to be statuesque. Anyhow, now you're so skinny you could be a model except for your ample chest, you lucky thing. Your size eights swim on you. Don't make a face at me! But thank you for saying I'm not fat. I feel like a disgusting slob."

– ∞ –

TWENTY-NINE

Mommy had used one of her code words, statuesque, which I knew meant I was grossly fat. So what if they thought I was thin, so what if I'd just discovered the holiness of food, so what if I willed never to overeat or throw up ever again. The insight vanished, replaced by the compulsion creeping into my body, right below the navel. Could I resist this time? Could I ever resist? I wanted to, but it took me over. It started with a tiny ache in my stomach, the size of a pea, right there in the same spot where I felt god-guy, right in my middle, halfway between my front and back, inches beneath my belly button, embedded there. It was a small ache, like hunger, not just for food, but for relief from intolerable pressure building inside me. Ripples spread from that single spot out into the rest of my body. A roaring train of need, desire, weight, emptiness. "I need a walk," I said. "I have to think. The snow is beautiful." I smiled. Let them believe I was thinking about Gabe. Let them believe whatever they wanted as long as they didn't know the truth.

No one asked to go with me. Good. If one of them had, I'd have said I had to be alone. I packed my sunglasses and wallet in my green loden coat pocket so I wouldn't need a purse, pulled on boots, covered my thick hair with Jonathan's dorky khaki hat with big visor and furry ear flaps, donned my own green scarf and mittens, resisted the urge to slam the door, and braved thickly falling snow to trudge a few blocks to Sal's, a neighborhood Italian restaurant I remembered from college vacations I'd spent in Syracuse during years when Mommy lived here.

Did Gabe know about Sal's? I didn't think so, he hung out by the university. Just in case, I pulled the hat brim down low, wrapped and tucked the green wool scarf around my head and face to warm the frigid air and stave off wheezing. In the waning light of late afternoon, I made my way through the April snowstorm feeling like an April snowstorm myself, a turbulent misfit, a misshapen, giant snowflake.

It occurred to me as I passed through wind and snow that I was infected with food madness like a virus. It ate me. Devoured by food, that was funny. I'd remember to write it in my journal, the only place in the world I knew of with information about this peculiar addiction, and all written by me. Was there anyone else suffering from this same insanity, filling the emptiness, then emptying the fullness, still feeling jubilant for a while, like celebrating and partying, drunk without drinking a drop? Was there another girl somewhere thinking she was alone, or was I the only one in the whole world who knew about this strange secret, which shamed me and thrilled me?

If I walked into Sal's, would I have the nerve to do my exaggerated eating with people watching me? I wouldn't know until I faced the moment. There was still time to resist. Would I? Could I? I had to think of a way to make this work because if I didn't, I couldn't survive. It was a matter of life and death. But, what if someone I knew were in there? Would they call the white coats? An answer came to me. I would pretend I was someone named Harriet Fishbaum if anyone asked. The name popped into my head. They might say I looked just like a woman they knew named Rowena Gay Wine and I'd say people always said I looked like someone else. I just had one of those familiar faces.

Just a little way to go, through a small snowy playground, where eery white monsters like aliens, replaced play equipment and benches.

Sal's looked exactly as I'd remembered, small red and green neon sign in a dark, steamy window filled with long trains of dusty philodendrons. I whipped out what I thought of as Harriet Fishbaum's sunglasses and put them on just before entering. Dean Martin was singing over their hi-fi system. "When the moon meets your eye like a big pizza pie, that's amore." Unwinding the damp scarf, I went straight to the rest room to make sure the toilet was working. Good, I'd remembered right, it was a onesy with a lock, no individual stalls. The linoleum floor had been mopped and was fairly clean, but there were dark hairs in the sink and on the bar of soap that turned my stomach. I'd take care of them later. What counted was that the toilet flushed.

Back in the dining room, Harriet left on the dark glasses and wet hat, pulled the visor lower to hide as much face as possible, took off all the rest of the wet things and looked around for a place to sit. The place was almost deserted. She chose a dim corner booth, threw her wet things, smelling now of wet wool, onto the empty seat and sat down across from them. Doing this in public was new and risky. Was anyone watching? It didn't matter, I wasn't myself anymore, I was Harriet Fishbaum, and Harriet didn't give a shit what people thought, only Rowie cared.

A waitress approached. Rather than look at her, I pointed to what I wanted on the menu as I spoke. I ordered an extra-large pizza with double cheese, mushrooms, onions and broccoli, an order of garlic bread, and a pitcher of root beer. I needed plenty of liquid to lube the food properly. Warm water was best, but soda would do.

"To go?" asked the chubby waitress, grinning and chewing gum. "You want a large bottle of root beer?" She seemed friendly and uninvolved, but I imagined she was stifling laughter when she looked at Harriet's weird get-up. She was a teenager in white sneakers and low socks, short black skirt, white tee, and gold chain with gold charm that spelled out Jo-Anne. Harriet shivered just looking at her scanty outfit. Jo-Anne chewed gum with her mouth open as she wrote on the order pad and then waited expectantly for a reply. I wanted to say something snotty like "No, not to go. For here, dummy. Did I say 'to go'? Would I be sitting down at a table if my order was to go?" But my heart suddenly pounded with fear and I heard a sweet voice coming from my mouth: "How did you guess, Jo-Anne? Yes, to go. Yes, thank you, I'll take the large bottle of root beer if you would. And bring me a cup of hot tea while I'm waiting, please. And an extra plastic bag if you don't mind."

I reneged, chickened out, couldn't go through with a public binge, even in disguise. Too risky.

I sat and folded and unfolded two paper napkins as I waited for the food, on edge, vigilant and energized just anticipating the binge. Frank Sinatra sang over speakers, "Taller than the tallest tree is, that's how it's got to feel." My hands trembled and I hoped I'd manage to move the teacup from the saucer to my mouth. I got tremors like this frequently and couldn't lift a spoonful of soup without spilling it. I breathed deeply and my hand steadied. Important to fill with liquids to ease the exit route. The plastic bag would have to do. I could plead indigestion if anyone asked. Frank sang, "Awwwll the way. Awwl the way." Did Miguel love me all the way? Gabe did. Gabe would have spent the rest of his life with me. Why couldn't I love myself even part of the way?

As I left Sal's with my order, Old Blue Eyes was still singing, "Who knows where the road will lead us, only a fool would say." I hummed along with the last line, "But if you'll let me love you, it's for sure I'm gonna love you all the way, all the way." I knew I was singing to myself, and a wave of sadness swept over me. What was love anyway? Did I ever know? How could I be so confused? Not important, baby, I said under my breath. Help is on the way. Fabulous pizza now and soon gorgeous Miguelito on the way, to play love scenes with you.

Out in the cold again, I headed for the deserted playground. Using the pizza box, I cleared snow from a bench trees blocked from streetlights, then sat on the extra plastic bag to stay relatively dry. The snow provided plenty of light, and I doubted anyone would be moseying along in this weather. If so, I'd come up with a good lie, tell them I was fulfilling a dare and there was a camera hidden in that tree, and I'd point.

I went through the garlic bread first, lickety-split, washing it down with soda before turning to the pizza. I played a game with the pizza slices, wolfing each one down fast enough to avoid getting watery from snow. Like I cared. The first slice burned the roof of my mouth. How could it stay so hot in a snowstorm? Steam pouring off the pizza fogged the sunglasses so I removed them. It was dark anyway. My mouth filled with warm flavors and textures, oily, squishy, crunchy. I closed my eyes for a few seconds and chewed and swallowed, chewed and swallowed, drank root beer, ridiculously cold, and chewed and swallowed, filling the hole in my belly, filling the hole in my heart. This was my first playground binge and it seemed fitting although I couldn't remember why. I lifted each soft slice, each cooler and wetter than the one before, doubled it over from front to back so it wouldn't catch snow as easily, and devoured slice after slice in a dream-like state, the flavors barely registering, chewing cud, chewing gum, chewing my tongue, teeth, brains. I felt stuffed and chilled, forced down more soda. Water worked better since it lacked the bloat effect and it didn't cost like soft drinks either. I wanted to save for Miguel and me, but a large portion of my paycheck went for food.

About to explode, I stood up, opened the plastic bag I'd been sitting on, caught some snow in my hand and wiped off on a napkin, then stuck my head in the bag, gagged a couple of times and let loose. When the binge was this big, I didn't need fingers, but I wanted them clean just in case. With satisfaction, I watched the white bag fill with a flood of puke, like a tomato red waterfall, the dough turned into thin paste by the soda, all speckled with small pieces of mushroom and broccoli and yards of gooey cheese.

I loved the way I could taste the food on the way out if I threw up before stomach acid went to work. That kept the sour smell to a minimum. I loved eating and eating and letting go. It was special, like winning a jackpot or beating the system. I tied the full bag, careful to hold it at a distance in case it burst, found a trash basket and used snow and napkins to wash up hands and face. Freezing, burning, insane, but it worked.

As always, I felt euphoric and intoxicated, even pretty although I'd seen myself in mirrors enough to know my eyes were rimmed red, nose was stuffed, glands swollen, and I looked as though I had a raging cold. I adored this high even with those symptoms. Would anyone at home be able to tell what I'd just done? No matter. I could blame my stuffed nose and runny eyes on the weather.

I started back to Karen's apartment, planning to report I'd had a bite to eat and wasn't hungry for dinner. Immediately, my mind turned to food. What could I eat next? Was there a doughnut shop nearby? Why hadn't I ordered a sweet dessert?

– ∞ –

Back at Karen's, I went straight to the bathroom and washed up again. My throat felt the usual post-throw-up soreness, glands swollen, eyes tearing. I inspected myself in the mirror, saw cheeks rouged from cold, hair flat from hat and scarf, expression cheerless. I made faces in the mirror, told myself I hate you a few times then practiced smiling so no one would guess what went on inside me. I rinsed with Karen's mouthwash, finger-fluffed my hair, and emerged determined to connect with baby Eliza. This perfect miniature human drew me, fascinated me.

Karen was burping her and happily handed her over. I walked with her, swayed with her, moved her gently up and down, felt her breathing and began to have a strange sense that she had a message for me. How was that possible? The bassinet was set up in the master bedroom, but I bounced us into the nursery for privacy. A private meeting with a newborn! Maybe I had lost my sanity.

Silently I spoke with her. "Eliza, welcome to the world, dear beautiful one. Did you know my child who existed for a blink? Did you know your cousin whose muscousy body I discharged like blowing snot out my nose? Did you know her? I'm asking because I'm so sorry. Can I explain? I think I'm too nuts to mother, and I wanted to spare my baby. I meant well. That's the truth. I'm naming my baby True because I'm a liar but now, for once, I'm telling a true story, and I'd like to from now on. Did you know your cousin True?"

I imagined baby Eliza answered me. In my mind, I heard a sweet voice. "Yes, Auntie, I know True. She forgives you, dear Auntie Ro."

I had to sit. Was I hallucinating? I rocked in the upholstered rocker and listened, sensing it didn't matter where the voice came from even if it were just a message from me to myself.

"Look, Auntie. Look into the upper Southeast corner of the room, up by the ceiling. Everyone who loves you greets you."

I hadn't the slightest idea which direction Southeast was, but apparently I chose right because there they shone, as though beamed by a projector, radiant gorgeous heads that smiled at me. My personal Mt. Rushmore. They lined up across the ceiling: Grandpa, Grandma, Daddy, and my piano teacher, Jimmy! A couple of weak images next to Daddy I identified as his parents, Grandma and Grandpa Wine. Weeping with joy, I thanked Eliza who was stretched across my shoulder, eyes tight shut.

Could I tell anyone about this?

"Auntie, listen carefully to a message."

My attention heightened.

"Stop. Sanctify. Harmonize."

That was the message?

"Oh, there you two are, we were wondering where you disappeared to." Mommy walked in. "Great, she's asleep. What a good auntie you are! Now, I'll take my granddaughter and put her to bed." I handed her to Mommy. She left the room, humming.

Stop. Sanctify. Harmonize. What the hell did that mean?

I pondered the message for a long time.

Was it real?

Was I temporarily mad from hunger? Was I suffering from puking and abortion guilt? How could I mention this to anyone? Who would believe me? What did those three words mean? "Stop" could mean stop my addiction, stop lying, stop obsessing, stop being mean to my mother. "Sanctify." Make holy? Make what holy? Hadn't I just epiphanized that food was holy and then gone and desecrated the insight by pigging out and puking? What about "harmonize?" Make peace? Make music? Forgive myself. Get along with food? Every interpretation of the message came back to the same bottom line. I had to reform. I would go cold turkey. This was it. Finito. I would kick the habit.

– ∞ –

I used my willpower to stop throwing up. But I had no idea why I ate so much in the first place and immediately began to eat everything in sight. Cake, cookies, ice cream, pasta dishes, whole crusty Italian breads and seeded rye breads with gobs of butter. Soups. Stews. Casseroles. Roasts. Food comforted me. I loved and hated stuffing myself. I threw out Mommy's scale and covered the mirror in my bedroom. I sank into denial. I bought a couple of black skirts with elastic waists and full, loose tops. Never clear about my size, I continued to tune out my body. I indulged in marathon cooking and eating obsessively, madly, continuously, and I kept it all down.

Miguel would be arriving in a couple of months. Some days I thought when he arrived, we would move to the Village, and I'd work to support him while he learned English and waited to be discovered. Other days, I thought he'd never show up, and if he did, he'd find me repulsive and go away again. These thoughts I drowned in chocolate ice cream sodas. Meanwhile I saved what I could for the big move by substitute teaching at Newburgh Free Academy, NFA, the high school I'd graduated from six years earlier. I dressed in my new black outfits every day, with scarves and jewelry borrowed from Mommy. She lent me her Volksie and carpooled to work with a colleague.

Since I had no friends locally anymore, I spent my spare time alone or with Mommy. We engulfed ourselves in gastronomy. We ate out and experimented with a variety of ethnic cuisines, bought cookbooks, shopped for ingredients at specialty food stores, cooked together, ate huge portions, and talked into the night about recipes. Even though I wasn't throwing up anymore, I didn't dare mention anything about it, because it still shamed me. Only with reluctance did I talk about Miguel.

"Mommy," I said, one evening as we got ready for dessert after our main course of burgundy-baked brisket with new potatoes, butternut squash, carrots, apricots and prunes. Already stuffed, we now glommed dark chocolate cherry mousse I'd made from a recipe in the *New York Times*. "I know you're eager to hear about Miguel, but I'm afraid to tell you because I'm scared you'll criticize me."

"I'm sorry, dear," she said, her spoon in the big bowl. "I don't mean to hurt you. I only have your best interest at heart. Oh, Rowie, this mousse is so scrumptious, I'm *plotzing*. I won't criticize your cooking, that's for sure and as for any other criticism, I think you should feel lucky that I care enough to interfere."

Lucky? Lucky? For a moment I wanted to scream and choke her to death. But the incredible mousse I produced from dark Belgian chocolate, brandy, butter, sugar and heavy cream, rendered me noncombative. "Oh God, Mommy," I said, licking my lips. "It's outrageous, isn't it? It's the cream. Listen, I understand you think it's a good thing to criticize and give me your point of view, but I'm not a little girl anymore, and I have to be free to make my mistakes."

"Yes, but what's so terrible about having someone older and wiser who loves you giving you advice so maybe you won't make so many mistakes?"

"Mommy, if I ask you for advice, that's one thing. You're always offering advice I don't ask for, then you get upset when I don't follow it."

She stopped scraping the bowl and stared at me. Chocolate ringed her mouth. I wiped it with her napkin. Her eyes softened and filled with tears. "I've been a terrible mother, haven't I?"

"I hate when you say that, Mommy. It feels as though you want me to disagree. I don't have anyone to compare you with. You're my only Mommy experience. I suppose you did the best you could." I took her hand, so much smaller than mine. Tears welled in my eyes also. Next, we'll bring in violins, I thought. This is too soupy for me. I let go of her hand and swiped my finger around the remaining specks of mousse. I was so engorged I could hardly move.

"Thank you for saying that, Rowie dear." She dabbed her tears with a clean end of the chocolaty paper napkin. I handed her a clean napkin. "When it became clear that your father was a dreamer who didn't know how to be steady and reliable, I realized I would have to support the family." Violins played in my head. She continued. "I was angry and determined, and I focused on my career. More than anything, I wanted to make sure my girls didn't screw up the way I did, marrying too young, a man who was confused, who didn't have a solid profession. I was a baby with stars in my eyes. What scares me about you is seeing you with stars in your eyes too. I love you, Rowie. When I thought you'd gone down in that plane crash, I felt as though I'd lost an arm or a leg. I ached. That's when I knew how much I loved you."

"I love you too, Mommy," I said.

We cried, blew our noses with napkins and laughed. When I looked at Mommy, I noticed a grid of crisscrossing wrinkles around her eyes and lips.

"So tell me, do you realize you have stars in your eyes about this Gregory Peck look-alike?"

"Maybe a little."

"A little's not so terrible, I guess."

I cleared the table. I felt stuffed and uncomfortable.

"Rowie," Mommy said, using an emery board to sweep tablecloth crumbs into her hands. "Tomorrow I'm going on a diet and I want you to join me. You've puffed up from all these gourmet meals. Let's get skinny together."

"Diet? No way. I hate diets. I don't want to think about dieting. Do what you want, but don't pull me into it." I was on the verge of telling her my whole crazy food story, but I muzzled myself. Even though I felt we were more harmonious than we'd been in years, there was still a wall of pain between us. Mostly I didn't allow myself to acknowledge it because when I did, even fleetingly, my throat, belly and, especially, my chest tightened and I wheezed. This felt so familiar. Just as Daddy did, Mommy had finally told me she loved me, and for a moment I felt my broken heart. But not for long. It was far too painful to sustain. My overstuffed belly enveloped me in a different kind of pain. I numbed with Alka-Seltzer, lay down, and drifted off to dreamland.

– ∞ –

THIRTY

Miguel and I set up housekeeping at 29 Jones Street in Greenwich Village, in a furnished ground floor studio so narrow he could stretch his long arms out wide and just about touch both side walls. No matter. Our cozy, private nest thrilled us. I got a nine-to-five as investigator for the Department of Welfare, with a Spanish-speaking territory on the Lower East Side. I ingratiated myself with the Welfare clients and sent them extra money the only way I could, by approving new mattresses. Hundreds of new mattress requisitions passed through my caseload. It didn't take long for me to understand that mattress money wasn't the answer. People needed training and jobs, neither of which I could provide.

Meanwhile, Miguel and I would be able make our rent. Grateful to have a paycheck and a man, I ate lightly, lost extra pounds, and maintained my weight comfortably. Miguel's reaction to my chunky body had shocked me. He'd smiled and called me "*gordita* – little fat one. "Now I know for sure you've been faithful," he'd said with assurance. "I will make love to you so much, you'll get your tiny body back quickly." I got rid of the elastic waists and fit into my old wardrobe again. Without a scale, I secretly measured myself in the locked bathroom every morning just to be sure I didn't expand. Once in a while after a particularly big meal, I quietly threw up. The secrecy felt slightly crazy but that didn't stop me. It wasn't only the food. The closeness of a relationship scared and confused me. I had an adorable boyfriend who was devoted to me. But it wasn't enough. Did it bother me that he and Mommy hated each other? He spoke no English and she was outraged. "She's a frustrated woman," Miguel said. "When is the last time she got laid?" She thought him an empty pretty face with no prospects, a gigolo parasite who would break my heart. I didn't tell her she'd done that years ago.

Miguel eagerly awaited my theater connections. I bought time by claiming I couldn't find my school friends, and even if I could, how was I supposed to introduce him before he learned English? I found half a dozen English classes in the neighborhood, listed them separately, drew maps, and gave him the information and registration money. The many choices overwhelmed him and he didn't go. That pleased me. As long as he stayed away from English, I could stretch out my lie. I liked my fantasy. I liked being in love.

In summer, we went to concerts in parks, took endless walks around the Village, down to the Battery, over to the piers, up to Times Square. We caught the train to Coney Island and the Bronx, walked on beaches and went to street fairs. Miguel auditioned for a part in a Puerto Rican theater company, didn't get it, and criticized them endlessly.

In fall, we rented a car and drove to Vermont to see the peak foliage and visit Victoria at Bennington. Miguel had no driver's license so I drove. He smoked and pouted a lot, barely looked at the breathtaking nuances - golds, reds, oranges, purples - colorful leaves, pumpkins, cider, flint corn. I'd missed autumn when I was in Guatemala, and was overjoyed to see it again.

Foliage at the Bennington campus continued to dazzle me. Miguel said the leaves smelled of death and decay. Oops. I was inspired, and he was gloomy. I couldn't pull him out of his sinkhole. Victoria and I walked together. Miguel strayed off alone to smoke.

"Aren't you tired of him yet?" she asked.

"Victoria!" I was shocked. "He's the love of my life. How can you say that?"

"I give you the winter of discontent, and he'll be gone."

"Why do you say that? You don't even know him."

"I know you. You're not yourself. You're in a fantasy bubble. And anyone can see Miguel is unhappy and dissatisfied. How come he still doesn't speak English?"

"He knows a few words. He can say, 'Gimme a packa Weenston,' or 'One es-slice, please.'" I thought that was hilarious.

"I'm impressed."

"All right his language skills suck. I don't care. I love him."

"All I can say is enjoy it while you can. He must be one fabulous fuck to have you so hypnotized."

"Screw you, Victoria! You're talking about the man I'm going to marry."

"Why would you want to? So you could keep on supporting him? He's a gigolo, face it."

"I hate you, Victoria."

"I'll take that to mean you hate the truth, Rowie. This man's a parasite. Wake up, Ro! You deserve better."

"I'm leaving now. Don't expect me to call or write until you apologize."

– ∞ –

When the weather got cold, Miguel needed a winter coat, so I cheerily led him to a used clothing store on First Avenue. He ended up selecting a shabby charcoal gray wool short coat, but on him anything would look good. He turned the collar up for effect.

Every day after work, he met me at the West 4th Street subway stop and often we ate pizza before walking home arm in arm to our narrow studio. One evening, as we passed an attractive woman on Sixth Avenue, Miguel nodded hello to her. I picked up a flash of electricity between them.

"Who's she?" I asked, doing my best to sound casual.

"She lives on Greenwich Avenue," he said.

"You know where she lives? What's her name? How do you know her? Do you sleep with her?" The questions spilled out of me on their own power.

"Her name is Rosalia. As a matter of fact, yes, I know her intimately." We stopped right under the Waverly Theater marquee. We faced each other.

"You sonovabitch! I go out to work and you screw around. You goddamn bastard. I hate you."

"I'm sorry, Ro," he said quietly. "You cannot imagine what it feels like not to work. I've grown soft and fat. You support me. My manhood is weakening. She is Latina, an artist, a painter, from Mexico. She is healthy. I did not mean to deceive you."

I could feel my cheeks flaming red, my stomach knotted, my whole body on fire. A storm of humiliation mingled with flashes of logic and understanding. I was confused.

"I love you," he said. "But I must leave New York."

"I'll come with you. We can move to Los Angeles. You can be in the movies."

"Yes, I suppose you have connections there?"

He knew. I was busted.

There under the marquee, speaking Spanish, as agonized as I felt, I was aware of the scene, the man with Hollywood good looks, so tall, great bone structure, strong jaw, jet black hair, clear blue eyes. Such intensity. Such sex appeal. I loved being his partner. He validated me. I hated him for betraying me, but I didn't care. I had done whatever I had to in the first place to get him, and now, I wanted him to stay. My feelings were no lie. I forgave him instantly.

"Let's go home and make love. No woman can love you as I do."

He grinned. "Mi *gringa judía de Nueva York.* You are good, Rowie. I believe you really do love me. I can't figure out why." He swept me into his arms, right there under the Waverly Marquee, and kissed me, long and dramatic.

A small audience gathered, hooted, whistled, shouted, "Get a room!"

"I will marry you someday, my love," he whispered.

"We are married, spiritually," I answered, starry-eyed.

He stayed for ten more days. I bought him a one-way plane ticket to Mexico City, gave him two weeks of my salary, and he left, eight months after he arrived. It was a wrap. But I wasn't ready to let go.

– ∞ –

My first stop, after I put Miguel in a cab bound for the airport, was the Jon Vie French pastry shop. I remembered the ritual, buying cakes and tarts and announcing each was for this or that uncle and aunt. Like the clerk cared. All the way home, as I carried the big bakery box, I felt like a thief, an outlaw, separated from everyone else by my nasty, insane intentions. I was horrified to see a neighbor on the front stoop, Lottie, an ancient, shapeless yenta from across the hall who always smelled of gin, dressed shabbily, and could easily have passed for homeless. Her dentures were out and her fallen mouth looked as though she was about to swallow her cheeks. She had thick gray roots poking out of a mix of brown, platinum, and yellow greasy strings hanging to her shoulders. Lottie sat and smoked, elbows on thighs, observing the world.

"Gonna invite me to the birthday party?" she grinned, pointing to the bakery box.

It hadn't occurred to me that anyone would comment on the huge and now growing bakery box.

I blushed. "Oh, my husband is away visiting his family in Argentina so I'm going to send them these pastries. I have to pack them."

"Too bad," she said. "I hope he comes back. You have to be careful of the handsome ones. They're heartbreakers. I know from experience."

271

I hurried inside. Would I end up like that, gumming my doughnuts? I made a note never to bring a bakery box home again.

The pastries didn't satisfy me as they had in the past. I ate a few, washed down with warm tea and tossed most of them straight in the garbage. But a couple of hours later, I fished them out like my father's mother used to, stuffed them down, barfed, and then felt worse than ever about myself. I tried to make up for it by creating romance. I lit candles, put on soft music, lay on the bed, and stroked myself. Afterwards, when I began a love letter to Miguel, I shocked myself by starting it "Dear Gabe." Where had I dredged that up from?

For a few weeks, my darling wrote me regularly, from Mexico, sweet, funny, tender letters written on thin parchment, powerful mood elevators with grammatical errors I tried to ignore. How could my Spanish grammar be better than his? He always began with "My precious, beloved wife, Roi." So what if he couldn't spell my name. When I found an airmail envelope in my mailbox, my heart ascended instantaneously, and I seemed to defy laws of matter and walk through the wall to our apartment. He was staying with an old friend and her mother, and I was glad I had the return address. Suddenly, letters stopped arriving, no explanation. Days, weeks, months passed. How could this be?

I decided he was working to establish himself and would send for me as soon as he had success. I remained devoted, lived in the same apartment, kept the same job, and saved money from every paycheck. To fill long hours of loneliness, I involved myself in political activism. Miguel was a revolutionary. Everything I did I measured with this yardstick: What would Miguel say?

I thought the 1954 coup ousting Arbenz in Guatemala had gone so smoothly, it must have inspired our leaders to have a go at Indochina. There were a growing number of advisors in Vietnam, now joined by troops. The Vietnamese were interested in sovereignty, and the United States like the French before, meddled in their internal affairs. I saw an immediate parallel with what I'd personally found out our country had done in Guatemala, and I shared my opinions with anyone who would listen. Victoria was a member of Students for a Democratic Society at Bennington. Without much explanation about Miguel and me, I called her regularly. She didn't gloat or ask for details. Together, via telephone and mail, we wrote leaflets, which I distributed in front of the welfare center where I worked.

"U.S. out of Vietnam!" I shouted to passers-by. I arrived forty minutes early and stayed late every day to distribute leaflets and engage my fellow workers and passersby in conversation. Some took leaflets and dropped them directly in the trash on the corner. Most of them ignored me. Quite a few who stopped said they had not heard of Vietnam and had no idea where it was. I began bringing a map so I could show them. I talked about the coup in Guatemala. People knew even less about that.

The administrator in charge of the Welfare Center, Harriet Kleinman, called me in, waved one of my leaflets, and warned me to stop political activism on office property. I pointed out that I was careful to stand in the street in front of the building so I violated no law.

"We'll be watching you," she said. "If you step over the line, you'll lose your job."

"Thanks for the warning, Harriet," I said affably, and added, "I hope you pay attention to what the leaflet says. If you have questions, I'll be glad to answer them – over a cup of coffee, maybe?"

"Just get out," she said, "and don't push your luck."

In April of 1965, SDS sponsored a march on Washington to protest what was not being called a "war" in Vietnam. It was a "conflict." We expected a couple of thousand people and were astonished as busload after busload of protesters pulled up bringing ten times that many, mostly college kids, many wearing bright tie dyed shirts, love beads, headbands. It felt festive. We sang folk songs, union songs, freedom songs. We sang, "I ain't gonna study war no more," and "We shall overcome." The sun was shining. The spirit of camaraderie was high. Victoria and I found each other and hugged and danced around, thrilled by the turnout. She was excited and pleased that Miguel was gone, and I ignored her conviction that he wasn't returning.

A cause I could throw myself into met my needs. I was lonely, back to perfunctory eating and puking at least once every day, engaged in a fantasy that Miguel would return or I would find him. Tenaciously, I clung to my dream. Hadn't he said he would marry me one day? I bought a little fake diamond ring at a Village swap meet so I didn't have to keep making excuses to men who asked me out. I dreamed I'd pick up Miguel's trail and show up wherever he was and he wouldn't be able to resist me, especially now that I could tell him about my new activism. I'd wear a black or red beret and an army jacket, and if I became a famous revolutionary like Che, Miguel would read about me and swoop in to stand by my side in the struggle.

All summer, I went to mini-demonstrations around the city after work and on weekends, never paying attention to who was organizing these protests but happy to have an outlet for my frustrations. I'd often join folks on the podium and add my message about what I saw in Guatemala and how what was happening in Vietnam was the same thing. I was a horny woman turned fiery speaker.

In Union Square Park I stood at the mic with its screechy feedback and railed. "How many of you know what happened in Guatemala in 1954? How many of you know where Guatemala is? Are you aware that a popularly elected president of Guatemala was ousted by our government because our leaders didn't like his politics? Do you know why our leaders didn't like his politics? Because the United Fruit Company and W.R. Grace Company didn't like his politics. Do you know why United Fruit and Grace didn't like his politics? Because Arbenz was a man of the people who stuck to his promises and nationalized some of the land holdings of the large corporations and gave small parcels to poor people to farm. These parcels weren't even prime land, not even land upon which anything was happening. Yet, the principle of giving land to campesinos was unacceptable to United Fruit and Grace and they pressured the United States to engineer a coup d'etat. That makes our beautiful country colonialists. Imperialists. Now think of what is happening in Vietnam. Do you know about the war for liberation the Vietnamese people have been waging for years? Educate yourselves because we are America. The United States of America is you and I. If we don't know what's going on, how can we speak intelligently to our elected officials?" I went on and on. People responded when I spoke. I loved the attention. I felt the small crowds listening to me and I spoke into their listening and I merged with them. This nurtured me in a way I had never felt before except during school plays. Occasionally I had the urge to pick up the phone and call Gabe, but I resisted.

– ∞ –

In the fall, a stroke of luck brought me another cause, this one closer to home. The Social Service Employees Union called for a strike of Welfare workers. We were asking for higher pay and better working conditions since we had to go into poor neighborhoods and run down, dangerous buildings routinely to make home visits.

I was the loudest one on the picket line.

"No contract, no work!" I'd yell, over and over, as I circled with my coworkers on the picket line. Protesting suited me, released some of my frustration. I was used to getting to the office early for anti-war leafleting, and now I leafleted again, this time about the strike. I was relentless with people who crossed the picket line.

"Scab!" I'd scream bitterly. "Betrayer! I hope you're up all night with your guilt, you rotten fink!"

After three weeks of circling and yelling in chilly weather, we won a pay raise. The city would need several months to get our retroactive winnings to us.

Right after the strike, a new guy came to work in my unit, placed in the seat next to me. We sat in open rows at long tables. He was tall and skinny, with a strawberry blond crew cut, lots of freckles, an upturned nose and a goofy grin. He introduced himself as ex-Marine from Dallas, Joe Bob Allen, whose former job had been venereal disease investigator. I found him a strange addition. First of all, his name sounded like a cartoon joke or a mother calling three kids to dinner. Secondly, most of the people at the Welfare Center were either social worker types, very liberal, or artists who couldn't get other jobs, also very liberal. Joe Bob didn't fit the profile. Someone assigned him to be a trainee of mine even though I had no experience training, nor was training a part of my job description. I was lonely, so I didn't mind the company. Joe Bob came with me into the field when I made home visits to clients, he took me out to lunch and insisted on paying, and he was a willing listener to all my political tirades, even encouraged me to talk.

With Miguel gone, I paid more attention to my work. I concluded that the Welfare system encouraged dependency and just about every client on my caseload would have preferred a job and independence. Why weren't we giving out fishing poles instead of bony fish?

"You're smart," Joe Bob drawled over a cheeseburger and fries lunch.

"I'm Jewish," I said, laughing, chomping my green salad.

"Are you really Jewish? I've never met so many Jewish people in my life as I have here in New York. Y'all are different, aren't you?"

"Different how?"

"You think different and you act different."

"Here's what I think about that, Joe Bob. I grew up next door to a man who hated me just because I was Jewish. I didn't understand that. It made me see myself as separated from other kids and that made me feel different. But that wasn't anything real, it was just an illusion because if I'd grown up

275

among Jews, I wouldn't have felt different. See? What you perceive is programmed from your experience. It's illusory."

He grinned. "I never met anyone who said things like that. That's what I mean. You're different."

"Joe Bob, you didn't hear a word I said. People aren't so different from each other. I see my clients. Most of them are Puerto Rican mothers. They want good lives. They'd like to live in a nice place, have enough to eat, send their kids to school dressed decently..."

"And have you and me pay for it, right?" He grinned.

"They'd like to be independent. It's not so easy. The women want to stay home and take care of their kids, but I know some of them could watch other kids too and make a living that way. They hate depending on the government and having to be investigated for eligibility. Most of them live in fear of losing their benefits. They have no control over their lives, and they hate that."

"Why do they have so many babies?"

"Joe Bob, all Welfare mothers don't have a lot of babies. Are you baiting me? I'm getting the feeling you're baiting me. You know I can go on and on about my convictions."

"You do have convictions, don't you?"

"Damn right I do. I have a strong sense of right and wrong. I recognize that there are plenty of wrongs in the world, and I'm doing my small part to right them."

"So I gather," Joe Bob said and grinned devilishly.

Joe Bob was never romantic, for which I was grateful.

– ∞ –

When Victoria got into graduate school at Penn in Philadelphia, she began lobbying for me to move to Philly and live with her.

"In my humble opinion it's unhealthy of you to stay in that apartment and cling to the Miguel dream. He's not coming back, Rowie. Accept reality."

"He's still in my reality. If the mountain won't come to me, I'll have to go to it," I said.

"All well and good, Miss Mohammed, but where the hell will you go to locate that frigging Argentine mountain? Number one Latin America? Worse, what if you find him shacked up with some beautiful rich woman? I don't want to see you hurt, Rowie. Give it up. Come to Philadelphia. I'm sure you can find a job here. And there are plenty of men who would be happy to distract you."

"I'll compromise," I said. "I just read about the National Teacher Corps, like the Peace Corps only the projects are in inner city schools and they pay you to get a Masters in Education at the same time. There's a program starting in September in North Philadelphia affiliated with Temple. I'll apply. Meanwhile, I'll plan to head for Mexico where I think Miguel went. His first letters have a return address of the friends where he stayed in Mexico City. I'll go look there. At least I can get closure and have a vacation. If I get into the Teacher Corps, I'll come back and move in with you. If not, I'll decide where to go. Does that sound grown-up?"

"Do you want my true opinion? Because I think a grown-up would make a phone call to the friends instead of just showing up," Victoria said. "Don't you think if Miguel wanted you to find him, you'd know it? You've swallowed this guy's bullshit line and you can't get him out of your system. I'm worried that you're chasing a fantasy and humiliating yourself, Ro. You're better than that."

"So I eat some humble pie," I said, and immediately wondered why love metaphors were all about food. I didn't tell Victoria, but I told myself, if I'd really swallowed Miguel's bullshit, one thing I knew how to do was throw it right back up again. So why was I holding on?

The same day I got my acceptance into the Teacher Corps, we received notice that our retroactive pay raises would be arriving in two weeks, at the end of June. I had made up my mind to resign as soon as I got the money and go to look for Miguel. I turned in my resignation, effective, coincidentally, on the big payday.

"Are you giving up your apartment?" Joe Bob wanted to know.

"Yes, I am," I said. "I don't know how long I'll be gone."

"Can I take a look at it because I might want to rent it?"

"Really? It's pretty narrow. You can probably do better if you look around."

"Can I come look at it tonight after work?"

"Okay, if you really want to."

So Joe Bob went home with me, took a long look around, grinned goofily, and said it was the perfect place for him and he'd seriously consider it.

I had a strong feeling he had an ulterior motive, but he didn't come on to me, and I couldn't think of any other reason he'd want to see the apartment. My back pay came to a few thousand dollars, and together with my savings, I was ready to go on a manhunt for my man. Joe Bob was awfully interested in my trip. He wanted to know who I would be staying with, what my intentions were, how long I'd be there, and on and on. I patiently told him the truth. I was going to search for my long lost boyfriend, and that was that. I knew no one in Mexico, I had no place to stay yet and didn't know how long I'd be there. I figured Mexico City was large and had many hotels and I would find a place to stay, settle in, and then go to visit Miguel's friends, the only lead I had.

Joe Bob insisted on taking me to the airport so he could help me with my bags. Just before I boarded, he bought me an oversized decorating magazine, which I had no interest in.

"Airplane reading," he said. "Good luck, Rowena."

"Rowena? Should I call you Joseph Robert?"

He grinned. "That's not my name, Rowie. What you see is what you get with me."

"You're a strange one, Joe Bob. Thanks for the ride to the airport. See ya."

– ∞ –

THIRTY-ONE

As soon as the flight was airborne, the steward came over and asked about the big magazine I was leafing through. I was sitting next to the window, and had my row all to myself, so he leaned in to talk.

"Are you a decorator, señorita?"

"No, I'm not. Are you? Because if you'd like this magazine, you're welcome to it."

"Oh no, just wondering. I thought perhaps you were going to Mexico on business, going to decorate the President's living room." He winked. "May I interest you in a drink, on the house, to celebrate your trip to Mexico?"

"Special for me, even though I'm not going first class?"

"Yes, I can't help it, when I see a pretty woman, I get the desire to give special favors. I'm Osvaldo, by the way."

"Hi Osvaldo, I'm Rowie. That's 'Ro' as in Rosa and 'wee' as in French for 'yes.'"

"Ah, I like the 'yes' part! Does that mean you accept a drink? How about a margarita?"

"Better a Cuba libre."

"Very good, at your service, Señorita Rowie. I shall return in a moment with your Cuba libre."

In Guatemala, I'd learned to drink Cuba libres, Coke with rum and lime, caloric but delicious. Besides, I was a radical now. Miguel would approve.

I was enjoying this flirtation very much. It had been a long time since I'd been open to a man. It didn't take much to get me feeling the effects of the alcohol. Osvaldo was tall and broad-shouldered, a little chunky, with dark, curly hair, mocha skin, and beautiful Aztec high cheekbones. He looked dashing in his navy blue steward uniform with gold buttons.

I snoozed a while, and when I woke up, there was Osvaldo with a beverage cart.

"Regular coffee, Rowie?"

"I prefer black," I said.

"Rowie," he said, a little while later, sitting down next to me in the dark, "I have a big favor to ask you."

"Sure, what?"

He leaned close and spoke low.

"Americans like you can take anything through customs with no problem. For me, a Mexican, it is problematic. I have a new pair of ice skates for my sister. Would you mind taking the package through customs? I will meet you in a few minutes by the international monetary exchange counter to pick up the skates. I would so much appreciate it."

My first instinct was that it was a weird request, but he seemed nice enough, so I agreed, and he brought me the package, slipped it onto the seat next to me and I put it on the floor.

I glided through customs pretty quickly. To my relief, there really were skates in the package, which the inspector barely glanced at. I got to my rendezvous spot with Osvaldo at a few minutes before eight in the evening. After twenty minutes of standing there I started thinking about leaving, skates and all. I planned to grab a cab and go to find a room. I was tired and irritated. But I waited. Eight-thirty. Eight forty-five. What the hell? I started thinking if I left with the package, I could be arrested for stealing, or who knew, maybe there were drugs hidden in there. So I thought of ditching the package, but then I worried someone might see me, and I kept thinking this guy was going to show up. Just as I was about to give up, at nine-fifteen, he showed up full of apologies.

"I'll make it up to you. I'll drive you to where you are staying. My car is in the garage. It's no problem."

"The only problem is I don't have a place to stay. I have to find a hotel room. I had planned to take a cab."

"You really don't have a place to stay? I'll help you find a room. Come with me."

He drove a new Chrysler, elegant with leather interior. Wow, airplane stewards must make good money, I thought. We drove to one hotel after another. No rooms. No vacancy. Conventions in town. It was getting close to eleven when Osvaldo pulled into a swanky place where they had only what they called a Presidential suite for three hundred dollars. I was so exhausted, I pulled out my travelers checks and signed them over. This would make a dent in my finances, but I couldn't stay in the street. I'd find an inexpensive pension next day. Osvaldo went with me to the room.

"I accompany you just to be sure you will be safe, Miss Rowie."

There was a carpeted living room with big TV, kitchenette with bar, big bedroom with king size bed, roomy dressing room and two baths. Not particularly presidential, but not bad either.

"Do you want to stay with me?" I asked.

"You are serious?"

"Yes. Are you surprised?"

"Yes, I am. Well, to be honest, I was hoping it would work out this way. Thank you! I accept your invitation. I will get my bag and park in the hotel garage. And I have to make a phone call. I live with my mother. She expects me. Otherwise I would have invited you to my home."

"Your mother?" I laughed. Might as well believe he was a good son rather than a bad husband. "Sure, there's the phone."

"I'll call from the lobby. Back shortly."

I hugged him. He was solid muscle.

"Thanks," I said. "You've been a great help."

We made love in the big presidential bed, tired as we both were. He was an okay lover, very verbal, asking me what I liked, what I wanted, was this good and was that good. It made me stay in my body. I hadn't been with a man since Miguel, and I felt even though the purpose of my trip was to find my man, maybe by sleeping with somebody else, I was breaking the spell I'd cast on myself.

"Are you really here to look for your boyfriend?" asked Osvaldo as I was drifting off in his arms.

"Yes," I mumbled. "Sounds pretty crazy I guess, considering here I am with you."

"I'm glad you are," he said.

"Me, too."

"Tomorrow, if you would like I'll help you find a place to live."

"Really? Thanks. That's incredible."

"I think I know the perfect place."

"Tell me in the morning."

"Okay. Good night, Rowie."

"G'night, Osvaldo, Wizard of Oz."

– ∞ –

The morning sun poured through the big windows. Osvaldo was just hanging up the phone when I walked sleepily into the living room.

"I was right! The place is available. Someone I know used to live there. We can see it this morning. Guess where it is, Rowie, on New York Avenue! Isn't that poetic? Here's coffee I ordered from Room Service. I'll take you to see your new home as soon as you are ready."

"Wow," I said, still waking up, "That's amazing. Thank you. Tell me about the New York place."

"It's a room and bath in a beautiful private house belonging to a doctor who has seen better days. They tell me there is one other boarder, a woman your age who works for the American Embassy. It is a good area, very reasonably priced, and convenient to everything since the bus stops on the corner. It will cost you for a month half what you paid for this room for one night. By the way, I have decided to share the cost of the room with you. I would pay for the whole thing, but I cannot afford it on my little airline salary." He grinned.

"That's very generous of you and not necessary. It's my own fault I didn't make a reservation at a hotel in advance."

Osvaldo insisted, and the cash he gave me was exactly what I needed to pay the rent for my new room, which turned out to be quiet, bright, and clean, with its own adjoining yellow tile bathroom. The entry hall and staircase were dark and strangely hushed, heavy with mystery as though everything there – banister, steps, carpet, the air itself – bore secrets. But I didn't have to live in the hall, so I didn't care. Something with the doctor, I figured. Malpractice maybe. A scandal of some sort that didn't pertain to me in the slightest. Everything was unfolding so smoothly, I was thrilled.

"No cooking, no smoking, and no visitors," my landlady, Señora Campos, said with little emotion in Spanish. She dressed all in gray and wore no make-up. "We have a strict policy in this house. You may receive occasional phone calls, and make local calls, but you must be prepared to pay for any long distance. Absolutely no visitors in your room."

"Okay," I said, and paid the one fifty rent for one month. For five dollars a day, who cared about the rules? I'd quit smoking a few months ago anyhow. It would be under twenty-five a day even if I stayed for just one week. I didn't have to cook - I'd grab a little taco somewhere when I couldn't bear the hunger - and I was just as happy not to have men in my room. The important thing was having that private bathroom. Of course, I was not going to throw up, but just in case, there it was. I thanked Osvaldo, and sent him on his way.

I'd remembered to get a map at the hotel, so next morning I took off for Miguel's friends in Colonia Roma, Fabiana and her mother, Eugenia. I'd written them a short note from New York letting them know I might be arriving. For a peso, I caught a roving car, something like a gypsy cab in New York, only shared, and I made my way around the city easily, with the help of many cooperative and friendly people.

Fabiana and Eugenia lived in a three-story apartment house in a modest area of yellow stucco buildings with outdoor staircases. Because of the set-up I was able to go right to their door and ring the bell.

Fabiana was at work but her mother answered the door. She had both European and Indian features, short and very heavy, with dyed black hair, a wrinkled, kindly broad face and high cheekbones. She was smoking a brown cigarette.

"Oh, yes, the girl from New York. Miguelito told us all about you. Come in, come in, please. My house is your house."

The apartment was as dark as the furniture, big antique pieces, a nice china cabinet, grandfather clock and a dark maroon couch like my grandmother's, with crocheted white antimacassars. We sat at the rectangular white metal kitchen table as Eugenia made coffee.

They had neither seen nor heard from Miguel in months.

"Something tells me he went to Spain," said Eugenia. "He talked about it. He didn't want to return to Guatemala, nor to Argentina and he wanted to live where he could speak the language."

"Any idea where in Spain?"

"My dear girl, no idea. It's a dead end for you, you should know."

"Why?" I felt hungry all of a sudden, hungry enough to eat a couple of loaves of bread smeared thick with butter. I fought back tears.

"He told us you were special, and he loved you."

"He did?"

"Yes, but he knew he couldn't be with you. It saddened him."

"But, why not, if he really loved me?"

She poured my coffee. I motioned that I didn't take sugar or cream. I accepted one of her brown cigarettes, choked a little and kept smoking anyway even though it tasted bitter.

"Miguel is the kind of man who needs a woman who – how shall I put it? – a woman who takes care of him royally."

"You mean a rich woman?"

"Yes. There are men like that. He wants something in return for loving. He does not wish to give himself freely."

"What about love?"

"What about love? Overrated. Superb for short-term romance. For marriage, better an arranged match between strangers who agree to make it work. Not just any strangers, but people with common values and interests who make a business arrangement. Love grows. Arrangements are more secure for the long run. This I have concluded, although I myself have never married."

Interesting, I thought. An unmarried woman with a daughter. Quite a no-no back home.

"What did Miguel give you that you liked?" Eugenia asked me.

Fabiana charged into the kitchen just then, a tall, broad, exotic looking woman, tanned, with long blond hair, blue eyes, high cheek bones, and effervescent energy that lit up the room. She looked like a cross between a Swede and an Aztec. It hadn't occurred to me until that moment that she and Miguel might have been lovers. I dismissed the thought quickly.

"Ma, wait, don't tell me, you're about to get out your card deck and give an unsolicited reading." She kissed her mother on the cheek. "Don't I always tell you not to meddle?" She turned to me and spoke in barely accented English. "Hi, you must be Rowie. I'm Fabiana." She hugged me, a big, warm, solid hug. "I hope my mom hasn't upset you. She has fixed ideas about some things."

"Speak Spanish!" said Eugenia.

"One moment, Mommy," said Fabiana. "What did my mother tell you?"

"She told me I should give up on Miguel. Do you agree?"

Fabiana let out a loud sigh and sat at the table. She lit a filtered cigarette.

"Miguel really loved you," she said. "He surprised himself. He doesn't love easily."

I wondered what it meant to love easily.

Eugenia got up and poured a cup of coffee for her daughter. She scowled in frustration.

"It's complicated," said Fabiana.

"Do you know where he is?" I asked.

"We think he is in Europe."

"I told her," said Eugenia, in Spanish. "Not the whole story."

Fabiana took a deep drag on her cigarette. "All right, I'll tell you this. You won't be happy if you find him. He's with a Spanish woman who has a good deal of wealth. She has agreed to sponsor him, and he is going to develop his creative genius further. That's our Miguel. He's determined to be world famous and he now has found a way. He may already have married her. I'm sorry."

At that moment all I could think of was how glad I was to have slept with a new man the night before. For months and months in New York, I'd nursed a delusion. I felt deflated, lost. Couldn't he at least have written me the truth so I could have gone on with my life? How had I misjudged him? Not hard to understand, you idiot, I told myself. You lied from the beginning! What did you expect? It was a fantasy relationship based on a lie. He was a watered down, prettied-up Gabe. Gabe was going to uncover something you didn't want to see. You chose to be blind, and you got blind-sided.

"I am going to stay in Mexico for a while," I whispered, my voice catching. Was asthma returning? "I wonder whether you could help me find a job."

– ∞ –

On Fabiana's corner, there was a vendor selling woven basket tote bags, and I went straight to her and bought one large enough to hold a side of beef. Grimly determined, I headed for a grocery store, walked around the aisles choosing sugary cookies and pastries and a couple of bottles of lemonade. Excited about my plan, I secured the purchases in the tote bag, and headed back to New York Avenue. In my room, behind a locked door, wheezing slightly, I took off all my clothes, spread a towel on the bed to catch crumbs, lined up the packages on the towel and the bottles of lemonade on the night table. I heard a little voice asking, "Are you really going through with this?" I nodded. Part of me wanted to interrupt the process, but I was unstoppable. My energy shifted. Transformed into a wild animal, I tore into the packaging with my teeth, devoured everything in sight, downed all the lemonade, then kneeled by the toilet, stuck two fingers in my throat and watched the cascade. Satisfied that I'd gotten it all, I calmed the animal wildness, showered, dressed, hid all the packaging in my tote bag so the garbage wouldn't give me away, dumped the crumbs into the bathtub and returned to normalcy just in time to answer a knock on the door.

"Hi, I'm Lupe. I live in the room across the hall. I stay with my boyfriend most of the time, but since I'm around today, I wanted to meet you. I work at the American Embassy, and I love Americans. Would you like to go out for a coffee?"

A plumpish girl around thirty, a few inches shorter than me, with short, permed black hair, dark eyes and thin lips with bright magenta lipstick, Lupe was wearing a stylish beige linen pants suit and matching silk shell. She was smiling broadly, but there was something about her I didn't trust.

"Nice to meet you, Lupe. I don't feel like going out right now. Another time, maybe?"

"Do you have a cold? You seem stuffed up and your eyes are red."

"Just allergies," I said, embarrassed that she noticed.

"Well, would you like to hang out in my room while I sort through my clothes? I just got back from a Texas shopping trip and I have to figure out where I'm going to put the new stuff. I have a clothes addiction."

"Okay, I'd like to see how your room compares with mine," I said. "I'll come over for a few minutes."

Lupe's front room was noisier than mine, because of street traffic, but it was about the same size and had an identical yellow tile bathroom. Dresses, skirts, sweaters and blouses were hanging or strewn everywhere. The bed and chair were layered with more clothing than a clothing store, piles and piles, all of it black, brown, gray, navy or beige. No pastels, no prints, no bright colors. Dresses hung from the curtain rods. She began folding and sorting. There was no place to sit so I leaned against the door as we talked.

"I have to figure out whom to give this stuff to," she said. "I don't wear clothing more than once. It saves on dry cleaning." She laughed. "Too bad we're not the same size."

"Well..." I was too polite to say I was glad I wasn't fat and she picked right up on it.

"I mean I wish I were your size."

"Are you serious about wearing things only once?" I wanted to know. I had a few favorite outfits and wore them until they shredded. It took me a while to get used to a new article of clothing.

"Yes, I'm serious," she said. "It's a sickness. I have no control over it. It doesn't apply to underwear, only stuff that shows."

"How can you possibly afford to keep getting new clothes? Three hundred and sixty-five different outfits a year. That's a lot."

"Oh, more than that. Sometimes I have to change three times a day. My father still gives me an allowance, and I shop in Texas. It's cheaper."

"It's a new one for me," I said. "Do you ever forget and wear the same thing over again?"

"No, because I leave the tags on everything until it's time to get dressed. That's how I know. I'm very strict about tags."

"So when you go on a trip to Texas, do you leave your old clothes there and bring back new ones?"

"Pretty much. The chambermaids all love me."

This conversation was making me increasingly uncomfortable. I wanted to run out, but instead I changed the subject.

"Do you know Osvaldo?" I asked. "He got me this room."

"Of course," she said. "We used to work together. He worked for the Embassy until last year. He may still do some part-time stuff."

She was cutting tags off clothing as she packed an empty suitcase. They fluttered into a colorful pile on the pale green carpet. "He's a nice guy. Do you like him?"

I had a moment of terror in which a shadow passed through me. I felt lonesome, scared, hungry, crazy. But I showed nothing.

"He's okay as a fill-in type guy. He got me this room." A liar like me. Sonovabitch. I was set up.

She laughed. "Well, I hope you are having a good time together even if it's temporary. So, what brings you to Mexico City?"

"Nothing in particular. Just exploring."

"Do you know people here?'

"I have a couple of contacts. Nobody I knew before."

"Who would that be?"

"Just friends of friends."

"How long will you be staying?"

"I don't know."

"So this isn't just a vacation?"

"It is and it isn't."

Now she was stuffing newly untagged things into her suitcase.

"You're full of mystery, aren't you, Miss American girl?"

"I hope so," I said, and grinned. "I gotta go." Why the hell were these people so interested in me? I wondered. She hugged me and kissed both cheeks. "Have fun and be good," she said. "Give my regards to Ozzy if you decide to see him again."

Don't count on it, baby, I thought. No one can be trusted. No one.

In my room, I locked the door, flopped onto the bed, and burst into tears. In one day, I'd accomplished my mission. Now what? If only I'd married Gabe, I wouldn't be in this pickle. No, but you'd be in another, a little voice said. Can you learn to process bite-size pieces of experience instead of overstuffing?

– ∞ –

THIRTY-TWO

Next day at an American style coffee shop downtown, I allowed myself half a buttered bagel, a poached egg, small fresh orange juice, and coffee. The food immediately threatened to come up, as my body seemed to have adopted reverse peristalsis as a norm, but I focused and managed to keep it down. I'd topple over if I didn't nourish myself. While I waited in line to pay, I felt someone staring at my neck, and turned around. He looked familiar, twenty something like me, a little taller, beard, glasses, balding, sturdily built, jeans and backpack. My eyes looked up to the right as I looked inward, searching through memory files. I almost had it.

"Hi," I said. "New York?"

"Is it that obvious?" he asked.

"Lucky guess. Wait. Columbia Law?"

"You're scary."

"I went to Barnard. I'm pretty sure I saw you around. I used to study at the law library."

"Oh good. I'm relieved. I thought you were a witch. Arnie Greenbaum."

"Rowie Wine." We shook hands.

"Do we know each other?" he asked. He crinkled his forehead and I noticed his eyes pointing upward to his right. He was searching his memory – probably wondered whether we'd fucked each other.

"Maybe you attended meetings of my coven?"

"I don't recall," he said. His brows wrinkled with worry.

"Joke," I clued him and watched him hit himself in the head and laugh. I paid for my breakfast and waited for him by the front door although I wasn't sure why.

"Would you like to travel together?" he asked me. "I'm going to Cuernavaca, Taos, and Acapulco tomorrow on the bus. I have reservations."

"Reservations about traveling with me or room reservations?" I quipped.

"You don't need reservations for the bus."

We arranged to meet at the bus station next afternoon.

What the hell was I doing, off and running again, back to the same old insane pattern of impulsivity? I didn't even like this guy. There was something about him that rubbed me the wrong way. Too geeky? Too serious? Or too normal?

During the bus trip, we exchanged a few stories about Columbia, and it was pleasant enough. In Cuernavaca, we wandered around town, checked out art galleries, shops, the market, ate at a charming restaurant where I insisted on splitting the bill even though I just picked at the food. In our hotel room, there were two queen beds. He had undressed and climbed into one. He reeked of bay rum, which my dad had used, only my dad used it lightly, and Arnie must have bathed in it. I put on a granny nightgown, climbed into the other bed, and turned out the light.

"Good night, Arnie," I said.

"Aren't you going to sleep with me?" he whined.

"I didn't know that was part of the arrangement," I said, much to my satisfaction.

"It was understood," he said. "I asked if you wanted to travel with me and you said you did."

"Yes, and I am traveling with you. Since when does traveling together mean sleeping together? I hardly know you. You mean you actually expected to have sex with me?" I made myself sound indignant.

"I did. I'm sorry. I misjudged you. Can I kiss you goodnight?"

"I can't stand the smelly stuff you put on. It's making me nauseous."

"I'm glad you told me. I'll get up and take another shower."

"Good, do that."

I was just falling asleep when he crawled in next to me. Spooning felt cozy, so I didn't object, but I didn't encourage him either. In the morning, he rubbed his hardon against my leg and begged to make love to me. Begging wasn't my thing. I had to get away.

"See you in Acapulco," I said after showering and dressing in the bathroom. "I'm skipping Taos. I want to go to the beach."

"Please forgive me, Rowie. I'm so sorry I was aggressive. Don't go. I like you. I'd like to take you to breakfast."

"Okay, thanks," I said. "I'll have a little something. But it's time for me to push on." I thought, Mommy would like this man. Is that why he repels me?

"Everything is booked in Acapulco," he said. "This is a holiday weekend for Mexicans. You're going to have a tough time finding a room. I promise I'll behave if you stay with me."

"I'll take my chances," I said, hoisting my pack. "I need my own space."

– ∞ –

After rejections from every Acapulco hotel, motel, pension and guesthouse with a telephone, I sat on a bench near the Isabella Hotel and stared at a gently swaying palm tree. Every rental car in town was taken. A friendly hotel clerk had slipped me a list of unauthorized room rentals with addresses but no phone numbers. I was about to call a cab and go around checking them out when, for the helluvit, I stopped and prayed for a little help. Are you listening, god-guy? Are you listening, angels? Whoever you are, you who saved me from the plane crash, please do your thing and find me a safe room in Acapulco.

Just then an orange Volvo station wagon pulled up filled with teenaged boys who'd spotted me and were flirting madly. I smiled. They conferred. The appointed one, a tall skinny kid with a fuzzy mustache and dark brown hair, jumped out and nervously approached me.

"Hola, hermosa," he said, grinning. "Would you like to take a ride?"

"Do you think I'm crazy, sonny?" I said. "My mother taught me not to ride with strangers. I'm a tourist and college graduate, not a street woman. How old are you?"

"Oops, sorry," he said. "I'm twenty-one. Well, almost. How old are you?"

"Twenty-five."

"I like older women." He sat down on the bench next to me. His friends gaped and giggled. "You're an American, aren't you?" I nodded. "You're staying at the Isabella?"

"Funny you should ask. I need to find a place. If you kids are well-behaved gentlemen, I'll allow you to help me find a safe, clean room. I have a list of places that don't have phones. Would you guys mind driving me around?"

"We would love to, pretty woman."

"Cut the pretty woman bullshit. I have a name. Call me Ro."

"I'm Gilberto Suarez de Peña at your service. I'll talk to my friends." He went off to confer.

Am I nuts? I wondered. Can I trust five high school kids?

"We are all staying with our parents, but we will help you find a room." Gilberto rolled his eyes and raised his eyebrows questioningly. "If we find you a room, can I stay with you?"

"Just you?"

"Honest, just me."

"No funny stuff?"

"I promise."

"I'll consider it."

The boys were from Mexico City, but they knew Acapulco because their folks had vacation homes there. They were good kids, silly and cute, and they drove me all around checking out places on the list. Booked. Booked. Booked. It was getting later and later. When the boys stopped for tacos, I ordered one, and ate about half. It got dark, and we were still driving around. The last place on the list was a modest stucco on a street where all the houses looked alike.

"Sorry," the woman of the house said. "Our room is occupied."

I was so tired and disappointed I burst into tears.

"No!" I said. "There must be a place! I've tried everywhere. I can't sleep in the street."

"I'll talk to my neighbors," she said sympathetically and headed down the street. I followed as she rang the doorbell a few houses down. A dog yapped non-stop. The door opened slightly. A thirty-something couple came outside, the man holding a noisy beagle by the collar, the woman holding a baby. A gaggle of kids watched wide-eyed from the front window. My advocate introduced Felipe and Dora and told them my sad story. The beagle barked and wagged. Felipe shushed him. A girl around ten opened the door to ask a question, and a white cat darted out. Pandemonium unleashed. Five kids tumbled onto the front lawn. The parents scolded, baby cried, beagle barked, kids yelled. The boys in the car laughed loudly, and I realized they'd moved the car up. Other neighbors came out to investigate. I hated bedlam like this, but I needed to stay here and had to win these people over.

The cat seemed to be ensconced behind a nearby bush.

"Blanquita isn't supposed to be out until she finishes her medicine," the oldest girl explained, sobbing, and apologized repeatedly.

The kids and I squatted by the cat's bush. I rubbed my thumb and index finger together. The cat put one paw forward. I saw in the lamplight that she had yellow eyes and black markings on her chin. Five kids reached for her madly, and she cowered. I managed to pick her up and stroke her. I hoped that was a winning move.

Felipe and Dora huddled together with their neighbor, my advocate. They motioned me over. I transferred the cat to the arms of the oldest girl who took her inside as Dora laid out terms for my staying in their madhouse.

"You can stay in the girls' room. You have to share our bathroom. It will cost you a hundred American dollars in advance."

"Thank you! I will take it, sight unseen."

"It is just for you?"

"It is for me and my husband." I motioned to Gilberto to come along. He acted like an overgrown pre-schooler with a new lunchbox as he toddled over carrying my pack and big straw bag. His friends cheered. He turned and bowed. The beagle added his bark to the Hallelujah chorus.

Toys and baby gear cluttered the living and dining rooms. The kids glared at us.

"Wait one minute while I make up the bed," Dora said. "The girls will sleep with my husband and me tonight." She turned to the pouting oldest girl and her three sisters and warned. "Not a peep of complaint!"

So this tall, skinny kid and I got to bunk in with a family of eight plus a cat and dog. They invited us to watch TV with them, but we said we were tired, washed up, and settled into the double bed in a small pink bedroom with ruffled teddy bear print curtains and piles of stuffed animals on shelves. Gilberto clambered onto me as though I were a boogie board. With no desire to be squooshed to death, I slowed him down and took over. He was receptive and even grateful, and although it went quickly, I stayed in my body and had a quality orgasm. We fell asleep together sprawled out naked and uncovered in the airless room.

I woke up to giggles and warm dog breath near my face. The panting, tail-wagging beagle and all the children except the baby lined up around the bed, the kids wide-eyed, stifling laughter, and pointing to our private parts. Blanquita sat at the foot of the bed leisurely washing herself. I grabbed the pink top sheet and pulled it over both Gilberto and me, which disturbed Blanquita, who shot me an indignant look and jumped to the floor. It hadn't occurred to me that there was no lock on our door.

"Holy shit, go away, all of you brats!" I exclaimed. "I paid good money for this room, and it's supposed to be private."

"What's going on?" mumbled Gilberto, rubbing his eyes.

"You're sleeping in our bed," whined the biggest girl. "We don't like you here."

"We're even because we don't like you here either," I said, clutching the sheet. "Now *vayanse*, shoo, or we won't leave, and then you won't get your room back ever."

As they scurried out, Dora apologized from the other side of the door and rebuked the kids. Everyone shouted, bawled and carried on. The yapper was at it again. Family chaos unnerved me.

How did this happen? I asked myself. What kind of life am I leading? I reject a 28-year-old Jewish lawyer who's a viable, serious partner and shack up with a maybe twenty-one or maybe eighteen-year-old kid in an overpriced madhouse I'm actually grateful to get. I'm losing it. Without even showering, I dressed and asked permission to call a cab. I refused repeated offers of free breakfast, but Gilberto accepted. I settled for a banana, and waited on the front steps for the cab. Gilberto, grinning non-stop like a peacock, called one of his friends and asked him to meet in front of the Isabella Hotel. I heard him merrily say that yes, he had an unbelievably fantastic time with the *gringa*.

– ∞ –

The holiday weekend ended. I checked into a decent, reasonably priced room across from the beach where I could sit in the window and stare at the sparkling expanse of blue. For four days I ate minimally and managed to keep my head out of toilets. In the clear, deliciously warm water, I swam, floated, soaked up sky, surf, sun and felt delighted and relieved to be alone. I thought about Miguel and Gabe, the state of the world, my family, the childhood friends I'd lost touch with. I remembered the last encounters with Daddy tearily. So much emotion. What was there about him that upset me so? Why couldn't I remember details of the spankings? There had to be more. The business failures? Partly, yes. There was something else, something I'd blocked, something so painful I'd buried it. Gabe would be able to help me. But I didn't want his help. I didn't trust him. Maybe I distrusted all men. Maybe I was destined to be a spinster.

One afternoon, I decided to take a serious swim. The beach was deserted and the water shimmered invitingly. I swam out until the beach was a distant speck and suddenly felt exhausted and winded. When I began treading water, a strong undertow snatched my legs and tugged me down. I'm going to drown, I thought as I swallowed a mouthful of salty liquid. That's impossible, I can't die, I haven't figured out how to live yet. I will not let this ocean overpower me! I mustered every iota of energy and unlatched my legs from the vise. I told myself, I know I can make it. I know I can make it. I did the breast stroke and side stroke and crawled and floated and repeated that mantra as the beach got larger and larger. On shore, I collapsed onto my towel. I was wheezing hard with a loud whistle and had to concentrate on breathing. I thought about my experience conversing with baby Eliza three years before. She was three, and I hardly knew her. I thought about all the loved ones I'd seen in the corner of the baby's room. I imagined them all surrounding me, pushing my breath in and out, in and out. I lay there until my breathing eased. With help, I had saved my own life. It was time to interrupt the pattern of self sabotage. As a true radical, I vowed to get to the root of my destructive behavior and learn how to live happily ever after.

Back in my room, I fell into a deep afternoon sleep. In my dream, I swam way out beyond sight of land and sank like Alice falling down the rabbit hole. Monsters drifted past. Strange, colorful razor-sharp fish bared teeth, nipped me and drew blood. One after another beefy, man-faced fish punched me with human fists in the gut and kidneys. I threw up again and again. A lovely mermaid blew kisses at me and fed me pills of many colors. Wounded, bleeding, woozy, bruised, I kept on sinking until I reached a bed of green and black seaweed in a sandy bottom. A homunculus with Gabe's face peeked out from behind a gorgeous pink flower and smiled. He held up a glittering diamond ring, a clock and a calendar. "I'm waiting," he said and then he sang a refrain. "You have to drown in order to swim. You have to die in order to live. Hit bottom. Hit bottom. Hit bottom. I love you." "No, I don't want to die!" I cried and struggled to breathe. I kicked hard, and sand filled the water until darkness and panic woke me up.

_ ∞ _

Back at the house on New York Avenue, I had messages from Osvaldo and Fabiana. I went out to call her back from a public phone.

"Listen *preciosa*," Fabiana said, "if you still want work, I think I have private English students for you. They're wealthy, stylish women who are going to love you. They want someone to go to their houses. You're a short bus ride away. There are three of them and they live just blocks from each other in grand houses. I didn't want to give an exact figure for what you charge, but I said in the vicinity of twenty-five dollars an hour. I think that's great for here. It's possible they would like you two or three times a week. What do you think?"

"I think I don't know how to thank you! You're magical! I owe you!

A day later, I was employed. Now I could think of moving. Maybe I'd forget about the Teacher Corps and just stay in Mexico. But even if I did return by fall, I still had three months leeway. I deserved a better place to live.

– ∞ –

THIRTY-THREE

At the American coffee shop, I saw a sign on the bulletin board for a roommate wanted by an American artist named Leonor who had a large two-bedroom, two-bath house to share in the area where I'd be teaching. I loved the name Leonor, knew it from Beethoven's Leonor overture. Rather than copy down the telephone number, I ripped down the sign, went to the public phone in the coffee shop, and called.

"Have another cup of coffee," Leonor said in a husky voice. "I'll come and meet you in twenty minutes. You'll know who I am because I look electrocuted, like I stuck my finger in a wall socket. I've been expecting you." She clicked off.

I hung up, wondering whether I'd heard correctly. Electrocuted? Expecting me?

Leonor Messinger was around my age, about my height, and had shoulder-length dark hair with frizzed, electrified layers that lifted and squared off in Egyptian fashion and was so dramatic it was probably the first thing anyone noticed about her. I understood electrocuted, smiled, and waved from my booth the moment I saw her scanning the place. Her other noticeable feature was her exaggerated hourglass figure – a tiny waist and ample hips and breasts straight out of the Gay Nineties era. Her lips were full and her gray eyes soft and kind behind granny glasses. She was wearing paint-speckled white jeans, a tucked-in purple, white, and orange tie-dyed tee shirt, dangling, artsy turquoise, amethyst and silver earrings, and no makeup. She greeted me with a hug, then plopped down across from me and ordered coffee. I liked the way her hands fluttered when she talked. Her nails were short and clean. Her personality matched her hair, electric and ebullient.

"My dad told me you were coming on a Friday. He just didn't say which Friday. For six weeks, I've been putting up my sign every Thursday evening and taking it down on Saturdays."

"Excuse me? Are you sure you're sitting at the right table?"

"Rowie, right? You called about the room?"

"Yes, but I don't know your dad."

"He knows you."

"Wait a minute. Am I forgetting something? I'm sorry if I'm supposed to remember. My mind is blank at the moment. I called you from this sign." I waved it, then had a twinge of guilt. "Sorry, I took it down."

"I thought you might. It's okay."

I nodded.

"My dad is kind of psychic. His name is Max. He said you were going to enjoy the piano. God, you're thinner than I thought. Let's share a pastry. How about cheese Danish?"

I was starving, but she was confusing me with this talk of her dad and the piano and psychic stuff. I didn't agree to share the pastry, but she ordered it anyway.

"Your dad lives with you?"

"Hmmm. Technically no. Just the piano. Max said you would love it."

"Okay, pardon me for being logical here, but if your dad – Max – is a pianist and you have his piano, does he practice at your place? How does that work?"

The cheese Danish arrived and Leonor cut it in two and pushed it to the middle of the table. I picked at it crumbs at a time. I heard people talking, dishes clattering and knives, spoons, and forks clinking. I waited for her answer.

She took a deep breath and lit an unfiltered cigarette. I lit up too even though I'd quit. She blew the smoke away and looked at me intensely.

"I want you to keep an open mind. I've been told you can handle what I'm about to tell you."

"You're scaring me, Leonor. Who told you about me? I never met you before in my life. Do you work for the American Embassy?"

She shook her head, rolled her eyes, and made a thumbs down sign.

"I'm originally from Des Moines. I ran away from home when I was fifteen because I wanted to paint. My dad had me found and brought me home. Max was a bank president then, filthy rich capitalist Republican, the whole nine yards except he was an atheist." She looked at a spot next to me as though someone were sitting there and apologized. Was she cross-eyed? "I didn't like him then. I don't think he liked me either. He was into solving every problem with money, so he bought me a sports car and sent me to an artsy boarding school back East. I was grateful and even graduated and went on to RISD." She pronounced it "rizdee" and I knew it was the Rhode Island

298

School of Design. "But, instead of finishing, I joined the Peace Corps. A couple of years ago, when I was in Guatemala, my parents and my sister were killed in a plane crash. I hadn't seen them in three years. It was a pretty big shock, to say the least."

The mention of Guatemala and plane crash in the same sentence sent chills through me. I felt a strange sensation as though gravity were losing its hold on me. I was on my way out of my body and had to clutch the table to stay put. I would have liked eating a dozen pastries, but instead I ate a crumb.

"Do you mind if I ask what plane crash?"

"My dad was an amateur pilot. It was a small plane he'd chartered for the weekend. They were going to Vail to ski. We're not sure exactly what happened. Some kind of mechanical failure. The bank wanted me to sue, but it seemed superfluous since I was the sole beneficiary of the whole estate, and it was bigger than I needed as it was. Anyhow, my dad didn't care one way or the other."

"Oh," I said, relieved that it wasn't Flight 304 but even more confused. What was she talking about? "I'm very sorry for you."

"The strangest part is that Max came to me right away. I saw him as clearly as I see you, and I knew what had happened before he told me in words. I hardly knew him when he was alive because he had no time for me – too busy making deals. But he's more than compensated. Apparently when he was alive, he used his intuitive talent in business for his own ends without paying attention to social injustices like disparities between rich and poor. After his initial shock at leaving the physical plane – no pun intended – he says he was sent to a kind of training school where he reviewed his life and saw suffering he had never allowed himself while he was alive. In earth time, it might have lasted a few seconds. Time there doesn't exist as we know it. From then on, he focused on remaking the world. He's been hanging around me ever since, when I let him, steering people he chooses into my field. You're one of them. You understand?"

"Not really," I said. "I'm pretty confused. You say all this as though it's an everyday occurrence. Makes me feel as though I stepped into a science fiction novel. Please don't take this wrong, but losing your family is a huge shock. Are you sure this explanation isn't just wishful thinking or your imagination?"

"I'm sure. I never could have imagined this stuff. I think I was more open to accepting it for two reasons. First, at the time, I was living in the boonies of Guatemala. The indigenous people who were my friends have these experiences all the time – not a plane crash, obviously, but any kind of sudden death. They accept the non-corporeal presence of their departed loved ones as a normal part of their reality. Secondly, precisely because it was so shocking, it blew open my receptive channels."

I stared dumbly, feeling as excited as though aliens had just landed outside the coffee shop window. "He's right about my loving the piano. My teacher was murdered when I was fifteen, and I haven't played much since."

I shivered. She reached across the table and patted my hand and pointed to my half of the cheese Danish motioning me to eat. I picked a few more crumbs.

"I'm sorry if I shock you," she said. "I forget most people don't relate to dead guys the way I do." She laughed and her hair seemed to laugh too. "That's why I'm seen as eccentric. If my folks hadn't left me some money, I'd be seen as nuts. But then, artists can get away with all kinds of shit. If I were an accountant or a doctor, I'd be certifiable, even with money. I'm careful though. Even my best friends don't know about this. The only reason I'm being up front with you is Max told me I could be direct. He said you're psychic and a baby whisperer. So, you talk to babies?"

I stared, speechless. Not only hadn't I told anyone about my experience with Karen's baby Eliza, but I wasn't even sure it had been Eliza's voice I'd heard and not my imagination. Worse, if these people, or whatever they were, knew about that, did they also know about my messed up eating secret? I felt paralyzed, frightened beyond anything I'd ever known, as though I'd just been impaled with a long voodoo pin, as though the cops had busted me and were handcuffing and body-searching me. Lies wouldn't work now, I knew intuitively.

"Breathe, for Crissake, Rowie," said Leonor firmly. "Relax. This is a good thing! This is destiny. Our lives are going to be so different now. We've been waiting for you."

Weakly, I said, "Oliver Wendell Holmes wrote something about creating a monster called Destiny by heaping together all our mistakes. I'm going to be direct and tell you I've made many mistakes and I'd like to avoid making more so that monster doesn't materialize. To be honest, even though I'm intrigued, what you're telling me is scary and a little hard to grasp."

"Oh Rowie, I'm sorry to have blurted so much out. I have such a big shoe for a mouth, I'm constantly sticking my foot in." She grabbed the check. "First things first. Let's get out of here and go see the space."

I nodded, still voiceless. What was I getting myself into now?

– ∞ –

She drove a new tan Volkswagen van with a bright pastel mandala painted on the front in pale orange, green, and lavender. She was singing and smiling as my mind sped chaotically. At least Leonor was interesting, I thought, and she had to be real to know about my conversation with the baby. Did that mean there was some invisible, disembodied spirit of a dead bank president named Max watching me when I thought I was alone? Like, right now?

Goose bumps rose on my arms. Bad enough my guilty conscience was at play. This sounded like a benevolent Big Brother...or Big Father. Creepy. I also had a disturbing feeling about that place on New York Avenue. After all, Osvaldo had stuck me there and never mentioned knowing Lupe or working for the embassy. Was it my imagination, or were they watching me too? Why would they be watching me? Would the CIA care that I threw up? Were American tax dollars paying for vomit police?

Rowena Gay Wine, you are under arrest for throwing up your dinner. Sentenced to eating a mountain of food and then having your mouth clamped shut. No, the CIA would think throwing up was an effective weight control technique. The Romans did it. Maybe there were still vomitoriums in the Vatican cellars. Or would the correct form be vomitoria? Sounds like a girl's name. I'm glad Mommy didn't name me Vomitoria. Rowena's bad enough. I like Leonor even though she's unusual. At least she didn't find me. I found her. Or did they 'bring me in' as she hinted. Weird. Are they controlling me? Edgar Cayce communed through the ether and healed people. Maybe I should keep an open mind. Still, all this straightforward, matter-of-fact talk about communing with ghosts unnerved me.

"Earth to Rowie," Leonor was saying. "Come back from wherever you are. We're home!"

– ∞ –

301

THIRTY-FOUR

It was an elegant, fairly new area with trees maybe fifteen years old casting patches of shade onto flowering shrubs and vines that draped themselves over fences, garages and rambling houses, some set back from deep, perfectly clipped lawns. Leonor's place was a two-story, peach shuttered, wide white frame, surrounded with banana trees, magenta bougainvillea, calla lilies, jasmine, and laid out with a gated brick walkway flanked by multi-colored roses. An L-shaped living room with stone fireplace was located off the hall to the left with an ebony grand piano in the el. To the right was a large dining room, with book-lined alcove study on one side and large kitchen and sun-room stretched across the rear. Upstairs there were two master bedroom suites and a guest room. I would have my own private bathroom again if I lived here.

Strange, sensually evocative, pastel watercolors of exotic flowers, very Georgia O'Keefe, hung all around. Instantly I wanted to live with them. That Leonor, their creator, happened to come with the package, was even better. I was in awe of her talent. It was nosy of me to ask about her love life, but I did anyhow. She told me she had a couple of intimate friends and also was having an affair with Jorge Limon, owner of a prominent downtown gallery, and well-connected, married father of one of her students. A bit of déjà vu for me after my experience with my roommate, Lynn, in Guatemala.

"It's not serious," she said. "I'm only sleeping with him for business purposes. I'm not in love with him. I like him though. We have great sex. In six weeks, we're going to New York together for a big show in his gallery there. He's a player on the world stage and expects to sell my work for upwards of fifty thousand. Max says it's part of the plan. Not for fame or wealth, but power to influence, a way to acquire a voice. I have other lovers, one here and another in New York I met a couple of years ago in Guatemala. He went home to get involved in the anti-war movement there."

– ∞ –

One evening soon after I moved in, neither of us had plans so we cooked a simple meal of pasta and salad and polished off a bottle of inexpensive California Chianti. It was the most normally I'd eaten and drunk in years. My stomach quavered, but I was having too much fun to interrupt, so I controlled the urge to toss dinner. We shared stories about our exploits with men and laughed at the many, uncanny similarities. After we'd cleaned up and put everything away, we hugged warmly. Leonor looked at me, smiled, and quietly began unbuttoning the front of my white cotton blouse. I was shocked and aroused, and even more shocked to be aroused. I trembled. She slipped my blouse off, caressed my shoulders, then reached behind my back, unhooked my bra, and slipped that off. I stood totally still, half naked, rooted to the spot, my heart and genitals pounding.

"But, but, but...I thought you liked men," I mumbled.

"Never instead of, always in addition to," she whispered. "My life philosophy."

I was stunned, excited, confused, full of food, fearing and loving the moment. My head fought my body and snagged my emotions.

"You're gorgeous," she said cupping my breasts with her hands. Gently massaging my nipples, she kissed me passionately on the mouth, found my tongue, and pulled me close to her. I kissed her back. The kiss felt wonderful, soft, deep, familiar, sexy. Then I froze.

"I've never done this with a woman," I stammered. "I'm in virgin territory here."

"That's wonderful. I'm honored, you adorable one," she said. "Every woman deserves to know these sweet pleasures. Come with me." She took my hand and led me into her bedroom. Under a violet, blue and gold watercolor of the most sexual iris I'd ever seen, we continued kissing and stroking each other. Her breasts were large, high and firm, nipples hard, belly curved and soft, buttocks round and full. I was panting with excitement, curious to know whether she would let me penetrate her with my fingers or whether she would stick some kind of dildo in me any moment. I said nothing.

She stopped suddenly, leaned on one elbow and looked at me. "God almighty, you make love like a man!" she blurted.

"I do? What does that mean?" I felt insulted and scared.

"What does it mean? Who knows? If I were good with words, I'd be a writer, not a painter. All I can say is, it's like you're not here. Not connecting. You're going through the motions of making love but it's like you're distant, not feeling me, just sort of using me to masturbate. I think that's what men do a lot. Such a tragedy. What are you feeling?"

I was on the edge of tears. I wanted to say no one else had ever complained, but I couldn't get any words out. I shrugged. She was right, I wasn't all there. But I hated feeling like a failure.

"Listen to me. Here's what I want you to do. Completely relax. Forget about what's happening next. No goals. Stop your thoughts and judgments. Be in the moment. Feel everything we're doing. Take your time. Breathe slowly and deeply. Stay in your body. This is very sweet. Don't focus on coming and genitals and nipples. Don't think. Feel me feeling you. Let's just kiss and play with each other's mouths and tongues for now. Maybe that's all we'll do tonight. Orgasms are great, we all love coming, but that's not the aim. This isn't a race to a finishing line. It's about exchanging loving feelings as well as pleasuring. When we're aroused slowly and totally, we can come over and over just from lightly touching each other. We can ejaculate too. Did you know that? At least ten percent of women squirt when they come."

"Yeah, I do that plenty," I said, shyly. "First time scared the shit out of me. I never talked about it with anybody. Most people think only men squirt."

"I know. Guys think their orgasms must be accompanied by ejaculation because they've been brainwashed – or maybe cockwashed. Not true. They can have multiple orgasms when they drop preconceptions of what's supposed to happen. Ninety-nine point nine percent of guys believe big friction and a little squirt make them Casanovas. Poor things. Poor world. Yugh. This is why we have wars."

"Why do you do it with men if you don't like it?" Was I whining? I hoped not.

"I didn't say I didn't like it, darling. I do what I can to teach them just as I'm doing with you. Look at our bodies together. What a turn-on! Do you realize most guys would give their left nut to be watching us right now? Is it any wonder men get turned on by naked women together? We're gorgeous. Guys are animals. All they want to do is look, rub, stick it in, spurt, smoke, and sleep. The young ones maybe start over again right away, like rabbits. Minimal hugging, nuzzling, licking, squeezing, cooing, palming all over, arms, legs, toes, neck, ears, eyes, belly, shoulders, all the subtle yummy stuff, pardon the expression, but they suck at it."

"And you're telling me I suck too." My instinct was to pull away, go far away. She was rejecting me and I hated it. I fought back tears.

"Don't go away, baby. I'm not rejecting you. Stick with me. We're meant to be together. We have a lot to learn from each other. I can feel you pulling away from me. Come back. Be with me. Just be in this moment. Loving is intuitive when it's connected to the heart. That's the secret. She whispered in my ear. "Pussy connects to heart."

"That's it? That's the secret?"

"Did you know it before?"

"Sort of. I may have known it, but I didn't act on it."

"You will, baby. You will. The biggest secret on the planet. Cock and heart connect too, but most guys don't get that either. Too damn much porn in the world."

"Do you get more excited by naked women or men in film?" I asked.

"Christ, this is the porn influence again. It's all objectification. All right, so there's a tiny element of titillation seeing naked men and women fucking and sucking - which we women rarely get to see. We should have equal access to that shit. I have a few gay friends who get that stuff underground and if you ask me, naked men are pretty ridiculous looking with that thing hanging between their legs or sticking out like a weed in a hedge. Not that I'm knocking dicks. As I said, I appreciate them when they're hooked to a heart, But honey, you know God's a woman when you look at a group of naked guys. If they could bend over and suck their own dicks, they'd forget about women and never leave their houses. I told you, most sexual experiences are mutual masturbation in disguise."

"Do you say that to your boyfriends?"

"Shit, yes. Maybe not so bitterly but something like that anyhow. I much prefer snuggling to fucking - which I think is true of most women. Men like it too, only most of them think snuggling is just a necessary step to getting to it. Don't you love the way they call it "foreplay" relegating it to an inferior place, so you know damn well the main act is what counts? My theory is there would be far fewer divorces if there were as much snuggling as fucking. Fewer wars too. By the way, I've trained a couple of nice guys I'll pass along if you don't mind a Mexican. One's American. You can take your pick or pick them both."

"Mind a Mexican? How can you even say that? I'm Jewish, and I'm not prejudiced. But why would you want me to meet one of your trained guys? Sounds like you're talking about circus animals." It occurred to me, if she and I were getting into a relationship, why would she want me to see somebody else? I guessed this wasn't a relationship, just a little experimenting.

305

She shrugged. I looked at a painting across the room. Swirling, orgasmic waves of violet, gold, royal blue, cerulean and dark and pale blue hibiscus. Leonor was a love artist too, I thought.

"So you make love with girls and guys, like, equally?"

"Is that a math question? I haven't kept count. What is your preoccupation with definitions? Harry was the same way."

No, I thought, couldn't be the same Harry. "Defining is good. It clarifies. Tell me about Harry."

"Harry Apple. He was my lover in Guatemala when we were in the Peace Corps. I disagree with you about defining. It doesn't always clarify. It sometimes stultifies."

I howled, interrupting her. "Hold on. It's a small world. I know Harry."

"Jesus, you know Harry?" She lit a cigarette.

I nodded, grinned. "We bumped into each other in the market in Guatemala City. Literally, we met by smacking into each other. We cracked up laughing and went back to my place for brownies. How the hell is he?"

"I hope he'll get over me in New York. He's been lovesick, buzzing me like a fly at a cookout. I had to promise I'd consider moving to New York if he went first to get him out of my hair. Max loves him – from afar. Harry followed me to Mexico and got the teaching job at the American school first. He was teaching history across the hall from me. I only teach there for the studio. I don't want to foul up my living space with paint smells."

"Small world. Harry Apple, I haven't thought about him in ages."

"Did you sleep with him?"

"Not even close. I was completely involved with Miguel. I thought Harry was cute, though. That wonderful giggle. That bright orange hair."

"He is cute. He's the one I mentioned who went to New York to get involved with the anti-War movement and start a revolution."

"No shit. Harry's a radical now? To think, I might have started him down that path!"

"I think he mentioned something about an American girl asking him to nose around. That must have been you. He did nose around. I helped him. What we found out shocked us. Violence in Guatemala is brutal and getting worse. A lot of it is stoked by U.S. fear of another Cuba. Our government doesn't seem to care how many people suffer and die as long as they're not white and as long as American companies can keep doing business as usual."

"I hadn't thought of it as a race issue. Are you aware of the enormous Civil Rights movement in the States? Have you followed Dr. Martin Luther King, Jr.?"

"Yes, and yes. It's hugely important, but I'm not convinced it's really helping the masses of poor people who have to live in ghettos. The capitalist system requires some people to suffer while others prosper. As long as Civil Rights as a movement stays separated from the anti-War movement, and they both stay separate from an economic analysis, they'll be allowed to exist. But when people start connecting the dots and see the root causes of suffering have to do with corporate profits and a perpetual underclass, that's when we're going to see repression and ultimately revolution. Just wait and see. I told Harry that."

"So you consider yourself a revolutionary?"

"I'm sympathetic, but I don't carry a gun. Just when I started calling myself a revolutionary, Max showed up. He exposed me to people like William James, Huxley, Gurdjieff, and Ouspensky. Now I call myself an artist and metaphysician. Max has coached me to see beyond what most of us see ordinarily, the reality behind what we usually call reality. We have to open up to cosmic energy, get off our butts and stop thinking in narrow ways. There's no doubt in my mind that people who long for social change and put their asses on the line are ripe for moving into higher consciousness. They may start with political movements just because they haven't been exposed to metaphysics, probably because religion has blinded them – or logic, another big blinder. 'If I can't see it, it doesn't exist' kind of thinking. Has anyone ever seen or measured love? Yet we know it exists. I'm optimistic about progressive movements and see them moving in the right direction. That's why I help out financially as much as I can, and after I'm filthy rich and famous, I'll be able to do more. But I'm smart enough to leave no paper trail. The CIA has nothing better to do than follow Americans they suspect of radical activities."

"Really? I think they might have been following me." I told Leonor the story of my anti-war leafleting, then Joe Bob's showing up at the Welfare Center, Osvaldo singling me out on the plane, finding me the place on New York Avenue where Lupe could keep an eye on me. I also made a note to ask her about her metaphysical ideas. I'd never even heard of Gurdjieff or Ouspensky. If I'd had to guess, I'd say they were Canadian hockey players.

"Sure, it's quite possible they want to make sure you're not going to Cuba or associated in some way with the Cuban revolution. This is why I don't leave a paper trail. Watch your ass for a while and don't let them co-opt you with some kind of tempting offer."

"It seems so stupid. All I wanted was to find Miguel. What a waste of taxpayers' money. What if I did go to Cuba? Would that be a crime?"

"Yes, it would. Cuba is an enemy, dearie. You'd have to stay there or come back and face jail." She grinned. "Unless no one found out."

"You've been to Cuba! What was it like?"

"A mixed bag. Good if you were very poor because things are better for you. Not so good if you were comfortable - which is why Miami is filling up. Personally I don't like Communism. Max leads me to suspect there are powerful forces in the U.S. and Europe who support it. You want to know why? Because it's good for those in power and in business to have enemies - especially if they're involved in making weapons. War is good business." She stood and stretched. "Enough of this talk of conspiracies and politics. How did we get off on this? Snuggle up closer, baby. Put your head right here on my chest. Good. I want to talk to you about something else. How much do you know about consciousness?"

What did I know about consciousness? How could I answer intelligently? I found myself searching for an answer.

"I don't know what I know about consciousness except, let's see, being alive and awake and sane and intelligent, that would be conscious. Being asleep would be unconscious although I suppose dreaming could be a kind of consciousness. Someone who faints is unconscious. I'm grasping here, Leonor because the truth is I haven't thought about consciousness as a topic. Tell me what you're getting at."

"I like the last part of your answer because it's truthful. You could have been even more truthful and said you knew very little about consciousness, but most of us don't like to admit we don't know something. It hurts our egos to admit we don't know so we try to fake it, and then we can't learn a thing. It's far better to acknowledge ignorance. An empty cup can be filled. A cup filled with shit has no room for wine."

I nodded and waited quietly. I had a feeling I was going to hear something important.

"Have you ever experienced an out of time experience, maybe with nature?"

I closed my eyes and knew immediately the answer was a resounding yes. "It happened in Guatemala overlooking Lake Atitlán. I couldn't remember anything about who I was with or how I got there. All I knew was soft jazz was playing, probably on a car radio – although at the time I just heard perfect background music. All around the circular inner slopes, pockets of wispy mist settled into vivid green hillside patches. Below stretched the lake, smooth and blue and quiet like the sky. A single canoe with one person in it began crossing the lake, and as it moved, a wake of green and turquoise spread behind it, rippling across the expanse of water, slicing it and traveling in perfect geometric patterns. A little girl came up to me and handed me a long-stemmed red rose. I didn't realize someone had to pay for it, but someone from somewhere did. I felt myself merge with everything in the scene. There was no separation. I was one with the breeze, the trees, mist, water, canoe, canoer, music, everything. Deep awe filled me. I was in the scene, and the whole scene was also in me. I existed somewhere beyond the ordinary. It's amazing that I remember the experience as though it happened yesterday!"

"That's it!" She squeezed me tight and we rolled over and over together.

"When I turned around, I saw the passenger car door was open, and my traveling companion behind the wheel waiting for me. I have no idea now who I was with. It doesn't matter. There were half a dozen others standing on the same lookout but I hadn't noticed them either when I was awestruck. As I slid into the car, the magic dissipated. I remember now, the guy behind the wheel asked me whether I liked the rose, and I realized he'd paid for it so I thanked him. And now I thank you for returning that memory to me. I'd buried it."

"Ouspensky had a similar experience on a steamer crossing the Sea of Marmora in Turkey in 1908, and he spent the rest of his life searching for a way to recreate it. That's a good example of higher consciousness."

"My cousin Ralph was involved in an experiment with LSD. Supposedly it gives people a higher consciousness experience."

"All of those guys, William James, Huxley, Ouspensky, they all experimented with substances. Mexican Indians use mushrooms."

"I had a rebirth experience after drinking too much wine a couple of years ago." I told Leonor about the culvert in California.

"Max tells me you're very gifted, Rowie. Powerful manifester, some important healing lifetimes, only you have old issues to deal with."

"Don't we all?"

"Welcome to the human condition. I'd say so."

"Do you know my issues? Am I, like, exposed?"

"I don't know your specific issues, no. But I know issues most of us have, like fooling ourselves, trying to appear to be what we're not because we're ashamed of what we are. Feeding the false self because we're terrified to examine our true natures, scared we won't measure up. We feel unlovable so we keep reinforcing the kinds of behavior which insure we'll be unlovable, and then when we're not loved, we feel sorry for ourselves and play victim. We fool ourselves into thinking we're powerful because we lie so well no one knows we're lying, except we know and we count. Lying, like cheating or stealing devalues us in our own eyes and cuts us off from our higher selves. Max has taught me that we all need a good strong dose of humility. We need to boldly admit our mistakes. I think that's one of the twelve steps of AA. If it isn't, it should be."

That long list of peccadilloes, which she seemed to imply we all shared, comforted me. Maybe I wasn't such a freak. Was it possible I was a normal human being? I sighed and felt great affection for her.

"Can I kiss you, Leonor?"

"Come up here, baby doll. Let's make love, womb-on."

"If you feel me tuning you out, bite my lip." I laughed.

"I'll devour you."

"I'll devour you back."

"Yummy."

– ∞ –

When we lay deliciously exhausted, Leonor wanted to talk again.

"I want to tell you about Diego. He attracted me away from Harry and they became friends. I adore him."

Again, talk of another lover and more confusion for me. "Why aren't you with Diego?"

"Both of them are too possessive for me to be with exclusively. I've come to the conclusion that some people are monogamous and others are not. I'm one of the nots. My ideal would be a group marriage." She inhaled deeply and looked dreamily toward her painting across the room. "An ever-expanding group of people willing to love each other limitlessly, in a world of peace and harmony. My utopia."

"I've heard of polygamy. What's it called when a woman has more than one husband?"

She rubbed my belly. "You and your definitions again, Ro-ro.' Actually..."

I interrupted her excitedly. "You called me 'Ro-ro.' Only my grandpa ever called me that. I love that."

"Cool baby. It came to me. As I was saying, actually, polygamy means more than one partner, husband or wife. Polyandry specifically refers to more than one husband. More than one wife is polygyny. I don't want to fit in a box with a label. I want to define my own way as I go. I'm sick of people imposing their systems of morality on me."

"Leonor, you're the most radical woman I've ever known."

"That's a cool compliment. Thanks, baby. Do you know who Frida Kahlo is? Maybe I should say was – because she died in 1954."

"Never heard of her."

"I'm going to work to change that in the world and, by the year 2000, in about thirty-five years, she'll be an international icon, getting the recognition she deserves. My friend, Diego's parents were friends with Diego Rivera, whom he was named for, and Rivera's amazing wife was Frida Kahlo. Most Americans know Diego Rivera but haven't heard of Frida even though her paintings are awesome. You must see them. Those two both had multiple lovers and agreed to accept each other anyway."

"They weren't jealous?"

"My Diego says they were jealous and fought all the time, even left each other a few times, but they eventually worked it out because they chose that level of independence. She had women lovers too. Frida is my role model."

"Wow," I said. "I had one female role model and she was a comic book character, Wonder Woman. She flew, she righted wrongs, she was beautiful, strong and powerful. A ten cent fantasy and I bought it."

"I liked her too. Big boobs. Small waist. I'm sort of built like her. Wish I were a superwoman, but I'm not. I've picked up the bad habits of Frida as well as the good. I drink and smoke too much, and I'm frustrated by the fucked up world. So I'm not as free as I may look. When I'm at school, working in my studio, I'm freer than anywhere else."

"You're freer than I am, that's all I know at the moment." I longed to tell Leonor how I ate and barfed, but the words got stuck. I was more embarrassed about my secret addiction than anything I'd ever done. It surprised me to see myself so fearful after our frank talk.

We spent the rest of the night together in Leonor's big bed, our legs, arms, and bodies entwined like macramé. On the one hand, I loved the warm, comfortable connection. But I woke up with knotted stomach wondering whether I'd now be labeled Lesbian and how I'd tell Mommy. Why did the thought petrify me when it could be a fabulous, satisfying moment of truth? No, it definitely wasn't about Mommy, it was about me and my fears. A binging, puking dyke. Freakier than ever. Two steps forward and one step back, that was the way I grew.

– ∞ –

THIRTY-FIVE

For the first time, I sensed my life unfolding. I taught three days a week, and on my off-days, drove the van to market for fresh produce, cooked, played piano for hours, journaled, and one afternoon dashed off a bunch of letters – to Mommy, Karen, Victoria, Harry and even to Gabe. I surprised myself by the flutter of excitement I felt when I sealed the envelope for Gabe. I didn't even know what I'd done with the three letters he'd written me when I was in Guatemala and which I'd been too scared to open. I was ashamed to tell him so I decided to let him think they got lost in the mail. What if he'd made demands? What if he'd scolded me? So I wrote him a chatty letter about Mexico, my students, the weather, and a hint of my friendship with Leonor and her strange ghost dad. I eagerly awaited a reply from him.

Leonor and I had a good time even though we mostly confined ourselves to snuggling. Occasionally, when I was alone, I fantasized an image of a beautiful combination of man and woman – with a face sort of like Leonor's, large firm breasts like ours and a penis like Gabe's, not too thick or thin, not too short or long, a perfect, gorgeous penis. Sometimes I imagined it was my first boyfriend Skip's penis, just the thought of which had scared the crap out of me so much I'd chased him away. What a little asshole I was! I'd know what to do with it now, I thought. Woohoo! Just imagining this got me so aroused I rubbed myself about half a second, and hot liquid spilled right out of me.

Occasionally, when Leonor went out evenings and didn't come home, I told myself I felt liberated. I was jealous but wouldn't admit it because it seemed babyish.

"G'night darlin'," she said, the first time she was leaving, right after dinner. She kissed me lightly on the mouth. "Got something going tonight, sweetie. You and Max can hold the fort. I'll see you after work tomorrow. Can you manage without the van in the morning?"

"Sure, we still have vegetables in the fridge," I said.

So she was staying out overnight. With which lover? How did her married boyfriend manage to fool his wife? I wondered whether the wife would like company. We could binge and throw up together. I'd teach her my techniques. Not!

I coped in the same old way, full of shame and loathing. It scared me to think if Max really existed, he'd witness me, but I dismissed such silliness. I managed to find something to stuff myself with, a loaf of bread and a box of stale crackers. I decided to welcome Leonor's leaving. With her gone, I could throw up in privacy. Leonor never said anything about where she'd been, and I prided myself on not asking.

– ∞ –

I hadn't thought about Osvaldo or Lupe in ages, but Lupe found me as I was leaving the coffee shop one afternoon and acted as though I were still her friendly neighbor. Leonor had forewarned me.

"Rowena, hi there," she said, kissing me on both cheeks. She wore a long black suede skirt, cashmere turtleneck and leather vest. "I'm so glad to see you. I have a fantastic offer for you. There's an empty apartment that just became available not far from the embassy. We need someone to occupy it, and I thought right away of you. It's free in exchange for living there."

"Not interested," I said.

"Did you hear me, Rowie? It's free!"

"Lupe, nothing is free. There's always a price."

"No really, this is free. It's empty."

"Why don't you move your clothes there? You could use it as a closet."

She looked not just disappointed, but desperate. "No, it's not for me. It's free, Rowie. No rent."

"Bye, Lupe." I walked to the van and took off. I was sure she knew exactly where I lived. U.S. tax dollars at work.

– ∞ –

The days flew by much too fast. Leonor made plans to go to New York. I got return mail from Harry, Mommy, Victoria, and Karen, and I wrote them back. Everyone seemed happy to hear from me. Why did that surprise me? The day Gabe's letter arrived, I took it to my room, lay across the bed and opened it carefully. My heart pounded as I read:

"Rowie,

Four years ago you left for your Central American adventure. You asked me not to write to you but I got your address from your sister Karen and sent you three letters. I waited after each one but got no response. I checked the address so I know it was correct. My mother passed away three months after you left, and it hit me harder than I'd expected. I missed you desperately, Rowie. I longed to put my arms around you and feel our beautiful connection. I hoped to at least exchange letters and perhaps phone calls. I reached out to you. Alas, you were not there for me.

I realize I said I'd wait for you. But life has to go on. Yesterday I received a light, cheerful letter from you, as though our four years apart meant nothing. I suffered, Rowie. You broke my heart. I won't pretend that didn't happen.

I'm not alone anymore. I just got engaged to a wonderful woman, a former student of mine. She loves me. We're getting married next fall. She's from Long Island. I have accepted a position at Nassau Community College.

You will always have a special place in my heart. I wish you a happy life. Gabriel"

My first thought, just before the tears flowed, was whether he'd given the new woman my ring. Second, I realized he said she loved him but he didn't say he loved her. Maybe he still loved me. He said I had a special place in his heart. He said that I broke his heart! How could I be that important when I felt like a nobody. Still teary, I tore open the letter from Harry. It was newsy, funny, and full of jokes and references to radical stuff. I felt drawn to him, especially because I smarted from Gabe's news. School would start in Philly in seventeen days. Did I want to return? What if I detoured through NYC and stayed with Harry? He'd invited me! I'd wait until Leonor returned from New York and I'd take off.

– ∞ –

The hardest part of my job teaching wealthy Middle Eastern women was dealing with the effects of the Turkish coffee each insisted I drink, small cups of thick bittersweet brew offered with light, sticky honey pastries. By the third stop, in early afternoon, waves of quivering passed through me. I was accustomed to hiding physical sensations and discharged the jumpiness by appearing animated, vivacious, enthusiastic, sparkling, spirited, and a live wire. By the time I got home, however, I was grumpy, moody, nervous and bitchy, slamming around the house.

On this particular day, as soon as I realized Leonor was at school, I changed into jeans and went out to buy binge food. I settled for warm tortillas since they were fast and accessible, stood at the kitchen counter smearing them with butter and scarfing them down with lots of warm tea. Still twitching inside

315

hours after throwing up, I dusted, straightened, and vacuumed the whole house, then started the dinner I'd planned, peppers stuffed with rice and vegetables and a toss salad.

I was in a foul mood when Leonor got home.

"Yummy, something smells good," she said, coming into the kitchen and pouring herself a glass of wine.

"How did your English lessons go, Teach?" she asked, as she nuzzled my neck and put her arms around me while I was preparing a salad.

I snapped. "Who gives a shit?" Then, when she picked up one of my sliced carrots, I smacked her hand and told her to stop picking and wait for dinner.

"Jesus, Rowie," Leonor said. "What the hell is going on with you?"

"I'm sorry. I drank Turkish coffee all morning and I think the caffeine and sugar affected me." I didn't add anything about eating a couple of dozen tortillas smeared with butter and throwing up.

"No kidding! When I drink too much coffee, I pop a couple of Libriums. Let me get them for you, baby." She went to her room and came back with a bottle of pills. "Here in Mexico, you don't need a prescription for this stuff. Take three. If you're going to drink that much Turkish coffee, you'll have to balance it out."

I swallowed three pills and continued making dinner. A happy cook and eager learner, I was mashing an avocado for avocado salad dressing, which I'd never made before. First time I made rice, I used too much water and it came out like chewing gum. Now I consulted Leonor's mother's cookbooks all the time.

As I finished meal preparation, Leonor was setting the table in the dining room. She loved candles, flowers, and pretty placemats. My head hurt. My mouth felt cottony.

"Rowie," she called, "The party's on for Saturday night and I leave next morning for New York with Jorge. You can invite whoever you want. This is going to be fabulous. I'm making lasagna and you can make salad. The maid will come in and clean Saturday morning."

I wanted to say I'd just cleaned and I'd be happy to clean again, but I bit my tongue. I had more important issues bothering me. We spoke between rooms.

"Leonor, I want to know exactly what your relationship with Jorge is."

"I told you we're business partners who once in a while, fuck."

Jealousy flared. How could she be so blasé about fucking him?

"So if his wife found out, what would happen?"

"Darling Rowena Gay – sorry, I looked at your passport when you left it out – I love your name. Did your mother and father know what "gay" meant when they named you?"

I felt myself blush. I hadn't left my passport out. It was in my dresser drawer. So Leonor was a snoop, but I wouldn't make a big deal out of it. Ironic that homophobic Mommy had hung Gay on me. "My mother blanches at the slightest hint of anything queer or homo. She thinks it's sick and perverted. She tried to turn me against my favorite teacher when I was in fifth grade, and when my piano teacher was murdered, she sort of hinted that he deserved it because he was like that. Remember when 'gay' was a respectable word for jolly and merry? You haven't answered me – what would happen if the wife found out? I'm curious."

She came in and put her arms around me from behind, rubbed her body against mine.

"First tell me whether you feel sick and perverted when we hold each other, or do you feel closer to jolly and merry, Rowena Gay?"

My stomach churned. My eyelids drooped. I heard echoes. I wanted to tell her I'd felt sick and perverted way before meeting her. "Leonor, I'm confused. I don't know who or what I am or what I'm doing with my life. You're different from anyone I've ever known. I love your uninhibitedness. But I feel jealous just thinking about you sleeping with this man."

"How would you feel about my sharing him? Would you feel better? Maybe he'll leave his wife and come live with us." She stroked my breasts as she leaned against me. Her gentle moves aroused me, but I wanted to stick to the conversation.

"Call me old-fashioned, but I'd feel unfaithful being with more than one lover," I said. I wanted to make up for slapping her earlier so I handed her a carrot stick over my shoulder. Instead of taking it with her mouth, she let go of me and held it in her hand. She was getting agitated.

"Who's influencing you, dearie? Religion? Mommy and Daddy? The neighbors? Your superego? Malarkey! Hooey! Crap! Diego Rivera and my heroine, Frida, had lots of lovers, and that makes sense to me. Why label it unfaithful when you can include everybody in the loving fun? My philosophy

317

is, forget everything you were taught as a kid about what's right and wrong, and start all over again. Definitely forget about the morality of school, religion, and parents. Go with your heart. I'll bet you knew your mom was full of shit when she kept you from your fifth grade teacher, right?"

"Definitely right. I hated her for that." How was I even talking with this cottony mouth?

"And when she said your piano teacher deserved to be murdered, you knew the shit was coming out of her ears, she was so full of it, right?"

"Oh, yes!"

"It's not her fault. People are so fucking influenced by external sources, they don't think for themselves. That's why the world is so fucked up with a few rich people on top and everybody else at the bottom of a pyramid. Those in power want it that way."

"Are you saying the Communists have it right?" I was crushing garlic for the dressing, and the whole kitchen filled with the smell. I smiled, happy to be able to smell right through the fog engulfing me.

"Hell, no. I've told you I'm no fan of Commies. Nobody has it totally right." She glanced quickly at the ceiling. "Sorry, Max."

"Not even him?" I deadpanned. She ignored me.

"From what I see, those in power always become opportunistic shits. We'll have to wait and see how Fidel does. I'm in favor of some sort of cooperative system, shared power, with local control and a small central government. Cuba is a miracle when you think of how the United States hasn't allowed any independent governments to exist because of business interests. If the Bay of Pigs had succeeded, it would have been similar to Guatemala. Look, Arbenz is a good example. He had begun his agrarian reform program in Guatemala to expropriate land from large traditional landholders and the United Fruit Company and redistribute it to poor peasants."

I told Leonor about my conversation with Leticia, the maid at the Nuñez's, and her father's experience getting land and then having it taken back.

"The funny part is that all the land chosen to expropriate was either underused or uncultivated. It wasn't exactly a land-grab either because Arbenz's program called for fairly compensating those he took land from based on tax assessments. But United Fruit had been undervaluing their holdings for tax purposes and wanted more money or they wouldn't stand for losing an acre.

They openly opposed Arbenz and tried to negotiate with him for more compensation. When he refused, the president of United Fruit, with the support of major stockholders – who happened to include the powerful Dulles brothers – John Foster D. was Secretary of State and his brother Allen was CIA Director – they hired a couple of big public relations firms. Boom, they demonized Arbenz as a Communist in a whole barrage of magazine and newspaper articles; boom, they organized United-Fruit-financed tours for journalists; boom, they developed a strong lobby among conservative members of Congress, and generally did a whole number on the American people at a time when the big bugaboo was the Communist threat."

Leonor made a scary face and clawed the air. She was very animated. It was like watching a movie. I was in a different space, on another planet, observing. So many words. Her mouth moved endlessly.

"Eisenhower's guys got Somoza in Nicaragua to offer his country as a base for the CIA to begin to organize and train an army. The United States ambassador to the UN, I can't remember his name – I'm thinking John Purefoy, but don't quote me – he was also a major stockholder of United Fruit, so he got into the act too. When Arbenz went to the UN to protest the impending plan to oust him, Purefoy said it was a regional problem so it had to be solved by a regional organization in Latin American like the OAS, which had already been lobbied by Dulles. The British and French UN ambassadors were not convinced by Purefoy's arguments, so the US blackmailed them by threatening to withhold support for their Suez Canal problem – a whole other story. Anyhow, it was a set-up most of Latin America saw right through, and there were huge street demonstrations and a wave of anti-US feeling that's still there.They pulled off the coup, forced Arbenz to resign, instituted a military junta, and returned the land."

"Why does the US have to be so greedy?" I asked.

"I suppose the answer has to be the capitalistic model. Listen, after World War two, the American government realized there were German Nazi scientists with lots of know-how, and it would be a shame to put them in jail and lose that resource. So the CIA came up with Project Paperclip, a plan to smuggle Nazis into the US. They ended up in pharmaceuticals, weaponry, NASA – good places for Nazis, right? We've all heard of Werner von Braun."

She pronounced his name in a thickly exaggerated German accent.

"You and my mom would love each other. She knows about this stuff."

"Cool, I'd like to meet her. So the line between the good guys and bad guys is pretty blurry. I hang out with a lot of people who call themselves *comunistas*, and they claim they're utopians, but I argue with them because it seems to me they spout the same old party line that sounds great, but doesn't work. I prefer creative, original thinkers, true *revolucionarios*. Like I see myself, baby, just as I tell you, I'm an artist, metaphysician, and radical thinker, and of course, a free spirit and passionate lover."

"And bisexual?" I added, bringing the conversation back to sex, which is where I wanted it. I was Wonder Woman again, and a great Italian chef flying in low clouds, coming in for a landing, preferably in bed, ready and eager to suck pussy at last. My lover's voice droned on.

She banged on the counter with her fist. I jumped, and my insides quivered with startled overtones. "Please, please, please, no bourgeois terms from Mommy allowed. I definitely don't want to be limited to bi. I'm sexual with people who turn me on, and for all I know I might feel sexual with a tree or a house or a car, or, well, you already know I sexualize flowers in my work. Maybe I'm tri or quad or quint sexual. Maybe I'm poly sexual. I prefer plain old sexual. I go for simplicity. By the way I'm doing a painting for you. I think you're going to love it."

"That's exciting. Can I see it?" My lids flopped. It was getting harder to keep my eyes open. Maybe I took too much Librium?

"When it's finished, lady, and not before." She nuzzled my neck again. I turned around, and we began smooching.

"What should we do first, make love or eat dinner?" she asked as we both got aroused.

I grunted, moved my pelvis against hers, washed the garlic off my hands, rinsed my furry mouth. Fuzzy, foggy, flying, I weaved in and out of my body as we waltzed to her room. That's it, I was a weaver! In bed together, I was the warp, strung across a loom. She wove the weft into hearts, diamonds, Wonder Woman's whip, crown, boots, more hearts, pushing down the woven threads with a reed, Leonor's colors, painting me, weaving me gold, lavender, turquoise, orange, a lotus, an iris, sensual flowers bursting. We bilocated to her shower. I stood behind her and couldn't keep my hands off her back and buttocks, curved like a fine stringed instrument, a soapy classical guitar. We slithered together like sweet hot buttered corn and ended up back in a soft place that seemed to be her bed. Had we really left? More weaving, two Wonder Women, flying high, remembering, smelling aroma from Italy. It was

Tuscany. We put white chef's aprons over our naked bodies and sat with candles and placemats and salad and stuffed peppers and wine and Nina Simone. Loveliness. I was smashed.

The phone rang just as we finished dinner. I had devoured a whole stuffed pepper, salad with avocado dressing, and a couple of glasses of wine. I imagined the dinner calling from my stomach, begging for escape. "Release me now! Release me," the food called.

"Answer the call, sweetie, please," Leonor shouted from the kitchen. "My hands are wet. Please answer the call."

My drugged brain assumed she meant I should answer my stomach's call. I materialized in my bathroom, with no consciousness of getting there or of leaving the door not just unlocked, but wide open. This was familiar land, toilet land, my childhood country, Tizzathee, the land I sang about as a kid in "My country Tizzathee, sweet land of liberty, of thee I sing." This was my nation, my abomination, the one place on earth I chose to inhabit, again and again and again. I kneeled next to the toilet, gagged a couple of times, then helped it along with my fingers.

"Rowie, what are you doing?"

I looked up at her. Spittle hung from my lips and fingers, drooping eyes red, glands swollen, nose stuffed. I had been throwing up on and off since I was twelve and, except for nosy little Victoria's eavesdropping outside closed doors, this was the first time I'd gotten caught. Head throbbing, I came to. What could I say? I felt scared, busted, guilty, wheezy. Could I speak the truth?

"This is the fucked up, crazy thing I do. I'm addicted. I've tried to stop hundreds of thousands of times. You're the first person to see how disgusting I am. I will move out in a few minutes, soon as I clean up. Sorry. I understand if you hate me."

"Move out? Hate you? No, baby. I'm so sorry. I didn't know. Now it all makes sense. Tell me about it. Tell me your true story. I promise I won't reject you. I love you. I'm your friend."

In slow motion, I did the usual hand, mouth, nose, latrine wipe-up. She watched. Without secrecy, the bloated power of my ritual lost its hold. I felt stupid. Leonor took my hand and led me to the white living room couch beneath one of her erotic, multi-hued irises. We were still naked except for our aprons. She sat on an ottoman right in front of me with my feet in her lap, lit cigarettes for both of us. Without a word she faced me, smoked, waited. To speak I had to drag my tongue across rough macadam in my mouth. I began nodding out.

"You've had a little too much Librium, honey. I'll get you a little upper and you'll wake up." She vanished and reappeared. "Here, take these. Just a low dose of Dexedrine. I live on this stuff." I swallowed two with water and told my story.

I barely had energy for the short version. Spankings. Fights. Psychological war zone. Fear. Tiny crowded apartment. Lies. Grandpa's funeral, my broken heart, stuffing food, accidentally discovering purging, going back for more. All those years, creating pain from stupid choices, fat to thin, the shrinks' approval, never seeing my body, the whole pathetic summary took up little more than minutes. Not hard since it was the same basic pattern repeated gazillions of times with just a few details changed. What a pathetic, dumb, and boring story, I thought.

"We'll lick this together!" she said, lighting up again. "Here's what I think. First of all, you have to be serious about kicking an addiction or else you could get in trouble. If I quit smoking right now, I'd probably drive into a tree. That's just how self-destructive I am. I know I have to learn to love myself more and then I'll be able to kick smoking. So I guess the question is whether you are ready to give this thing up. If you are, I'll do everything I can to help you."

"I would like nothing more in the whole world than quitting, but to be honest, I'm terrified."

"If you're serious, I'll bet we could adapt the AA program for you. For all we know, there's already an eaters' anonymous group. We'll get a copy of the 12 steps".

"Leonor, you can't plan my life. Before I agree to do any 12-step program, I have to see what it's all about."

"I'm not planning your life. You're overreacting. That's part of your defense system.

"You don't understand. I've had it for almost 15 years. It's part of me like a close friend."

"Or enemy."

"Yeah," I said. "I'm probably my own enemy. What do I do with that?"

Leonor's eyes looked up and she held her head still. "Max says you heal."

"And Max is never wrong?" I asked in my smart-ass way. She ignored me and began to channel in a deep baritone voice.

"Miz Wine, you heal in stages. Defenses are a normal human reaction You developed your present food pattern to survive in childhood. It brought you pleasure and gave you a way to cope with emotional pain. It also isolated you, causing pain. Now that you're no longer a child, it's even more burdensome. When the pain outweighs the pleasure, Miz Wine, you'll be motivated to change the pattern. It'll be a process you'll learn from. The caterpillar sheds its skin many times before forming the chrysalis. With each turn of the spiral, you may feel you're repeating the same pattern, but you will have made progress, however small. Stop judging yourself. Daughter, darling, don't you judge you either." She smiled and her voice returned. "Okay, Daddy, I get it. Rowie, did that make sense?"

"Yes, thank you," I said. "Very odd, but I think your ghost father got through to me."

– ∞ –

THIRTY-SIX

When Leonor left for New York, the house felt eerily empty. I wandered around, opened and closed the refrigerator and cupboard about ten-thousand times without eating anything, then settled on the couch. In stillness, I sensed my breathing. How good it was to be alive! How interesting life was! I wondered what it would take to heal. I called very quietly, almost in a whisper, "Max? Are you around?" Nothing.

I had the urge to go to the piano. I played a few scales, then improvised a jazz version of "Row, Row, Row Your Boat." In a flash, I thought, if life really is a dream, I want to wake up. I played a little wake-up ditty on tinkling high notes, then dramatic final chords. That got me going, and I played for hours.

When Leonor called with the exciting news about her successful opening, I told her I had news too but it could wait. She'd sold seven paintings and gotten positive reviews in the *New York Times* and the *New Yorker*. She was going to spend an afternoon with Harry so I sent regards. In the next couple of days I said goodbye to my students, left Leonor a note, and took a cab to the airport. I planned my departure for a time when she'd be safely airborne. In order not to leave a trail, I bought my ticket with cash just before taking off. At the last moment, I had decided instead of going straight to Philadelphia, I'd stop off in New York.

– ∞ –

I called Harry from the airport.

"Harry, it's Rowie! I'm in New York for a week. Jesus, it's hot as hell. I just flew in from Mexico on my way to Philly. How's it going? How are you?"

"Hey, twin sister! You've forgotten what New York in August is like, huh? Mind over matter. Think cool. This is so amazing. I saw Leonor a few days ago and we talked about you. I'm good. Doing important work. I'm so glad you caught me. I'm working at home today. Come on over! You can crash at my place. No strings."

Harry lived in a fifth floor walk-up in the South Village. The temperature was in the 90's with high humidity and, besides wheezing, I felt like a rag by the time I shlepped up his stairs with my bags. Harry was shirtless and whiter than I remembered. His hair had expanded into unbrushed, moppy orange frizz that gave him a couple more inches. There was a little orange frizz on his chest and chin also. He was cuter than I'd remembered, straight nose, a few freckles, round green eyes with slight corner crinkles, even teeth, proportionate shoulders. He grinned, grabbed my bag, and led me inside.

The door opened directly into a narrow kitchen, which was bright and very warm. A whirring fan blew hot air around. Taking up most of one wall was a huge claw foot bathtub. Above the tub was a large poster of Che Guevara with the word "*Venceremos.*" Next to the tub was a single white porcelain sink with exposed galvanized pipes beneath. A wooden crate filled with cleaning supplies sat under the sink on the worn floral linoleum floor. A metal toothbrush and cup holder combo was attached to the wall next to the kitchen sink.

I sat in a rickety wooden folding chair at the red Formica table and whispered a request for water, which he brought right away in a jelly jar. My white cotton blouse, although sleeveless, was sticking to me and the blue flowered dirndl skirt wasn't far behind. I would have liked a shower, but I didn't see one. There was no shower curtain around the tub.

"Hey, kiddo, you look terrific, but you're out of shape. You have to live in a walk-up to stay fit. How about a nice tall glass of iced coffee?"

"Black, thanks," I croaked. He nodded. I knew strong coffee would ease my breathing, even if it gave me tremors. He had made coffee ice cubes and now dropped them in what looked like mayonnaise jars, then poured in black coffee from a pitcher in the fridge. He added milk and sugar to his. He sat across from me at the kitchen table in the only other chair, metal with ripped gold vinyl padding.

"So," he said. "You and I share the same lover. What is the world coming to? I'll bet that was the last thing you imagined when you were with Argentine Macho Man."

The mention of Miguel in that tone scuffed my ego, but Harry had such a disarming laugh, I forgave him for disparaging the memory of the great love of my life. I wasn't ready to get into the humiliating details about the abandonment so I said nothing.

I pointed to the Che poster, spoke slowly. "You weren't kidding in your letters. You really have become a revolutionary."

"By any means necessary," he said. "The war is an atrocity that capitalism requires. As I wrote, I have you and Leonor to thank for setting me straight."

"Leonor setting someone straight. That's funny," I said.

He reddened. "Well, let's say setting me on the revolutionary path where I belong. You told me to nose around. I did. I'm happy for the opportunity to thank you in person. I consider you a special person in my life."

I nodded a thank you, and thought, somebody else considers me special. Doesn't special mean retarded?

"Now, will you please tell me what's going on? I just saw Leonor and she said you were about to embark on a whole new life."

"I hope so," I said. What the hell did she tell him?

Holding eye contact, arms outstretched, he stuck his neck forward and bounced it one rung at a time down an invisible ladder toward his chest. New York Jewish body language meaning, so, c'mon, elaborate already.

I couldn't speak. Until that moment I hadn't realized how hurt I felt. Instead of crying, I laughed. "Do you happen to have a cookie or doughnut?"

"God, I'm being a shmuck." He smacked his forehead. "Why didn't I offer you something to eat? I'm sorry."

He got out half a bag of marshmallows and an almost full bag of Oreos. Oreos! In a second, my bulimic life passed before me like a flipbook.

"Are you okay, Rowie?"

I shook my head. I wasn't feeling okay.

"Would you rather have peanut butter and jelly? P,B, and J sandwiches are basically what I live on. I have some frozen peas too."

"A spoonful of peanut butter and a few peas will do. No bread. No jelly."

"You're easy." He warmed up the peas and spooned peanut butter into a small dessert dish.

"Could I wash up?"

"Yes, of course. I'll get you a towel and washcloth. If you'd like, I'll run you a bath. I'll even clean the tub first."

"I never saw a tub in the kitchen before." I washed my hands and face in the sink, stuck my head under the faucet to cool off. "Very efficient." He handed me the towel and washcloth.

"It takes some getting used to. When I have company and I bathe, it feels like Roman baths Very social."

"I don't remember my Roman life," I mumbled, my brain echoing "vomitorium" over and over. He had no clue.

"I'll go into the next room and give you privacy to change," he said. "The toilet is in the little closet in the corner. Lucky it's not in the hall. I pay thirty-five fourteen a month rent for this place, so that's why I put up with the stairs and the tub in the kitchen. It allows me to do political work full time and live off savings."

"Thirty-five a month! With a roommate that would be seventeen and change!" I winked. He winked back.

They were the winks heard round the world. With those two winks we both knew our destiny. No words needed. The destiny, however, would be on hold for a while.

After the peanut butter, peas, and bath, I changed right there in the kitchen into a Marilyn Monroe style halter top white sundress, wrinkled, but my only change except for a couple of tee shirts and a pair of jeans.

There were three rooms in the apartment, lined up next to each other along the street side of the building. He had fixed up the middle room as an office with an old desk, couch with famous Guatemalan blanket thrown over it, dusty Navajo rug and loaded wall-to-wall bookshelves. The bedroom had a large bed the width of the room, chest of drawers and more bookshelves. Each room had a dirty window to the street, no curtains.

I walked into his office. He had the desk set up with his back to the window so he faced the room. He whistled when he saw me.

"You look great!" he said.

"Thanks. Can I lie down for a while on your bed? I don't want to disturb your work."

He grinned. "No problem. Make yourself comfortable. *Mi cama es tu cama.*"

"Cute."

He came in and lay next to me. I noticed a few freckles on his shoulders.

"What do you think of Leonor's ghost?" I asked.

"I don't know what you mean."

"Max, her father."

"He died in a plane crash. Her mother and aunt too. It was horrible. I was with her when she got the news. I went back to Iowa with her."

"Yes, I know. But didn't she tell you about Max's ghost?"

"You're kidding, right?"

"No, I'm serious.

"I honestly don't know what you're talking about."

"Strange she didn't mention it to you." Very strange, I thought, but I didn't want to obsess over it. What the hell? Did it matter at the moment? I was in a bed with a cute man. I had a few peas and a bit of peanut butter in my stomach and I was fighting to make that okay. "It doesn't matter," I said. "People are either into that stuff or they're not. I'll tell you another time. Now I want to tell you I thought you were adorable from the moment I met you in the market." I stroked his face. He stroked my hair.

"I was pretty taken with you, too, but I knew it was the wrong time."

We gazed into each other's eyes and a strong magnet pulled our lips together. It felt good to be in New York, close to someone I was convinced was familiar and safe and, like me, hot to trot. Unlike Leonor, Harry couldn't have cared less if I traveled to Mars and back while we made love. I didn't go that far, just out the window, through the Village, and straight over to the river.

– ∞ –

I loved Harry's tenement heaven. Knowing we had the same exact birthday gave me a sense of intimacy, sort of like relating to my alter ego. We were playmates and pals. We screwed in the bathtub, on the couch, on the Navajo rug, up on the roof with the Guatemalan blanket, in bed, and even in a sports car. Harry was minding his brother Freddy's red Corvette while Freddy went to London on business, and after he met his deadline next day, we tooled around Long Island in style, stayed at a bed and breakfast in Montauk and pretended to be rich.

"Maybe it's not so bad to have money," I suggested on the way home.

"Don't go turning bourgeois on me," Harry said, and turned up the Stones and drummed the steering wheel to "I Can't Get No Satisfaction."

"No, seriously, why shouldn't everyone enjoy nice things?"

"That's a different story. As long as no one is left out. Except rich people. They've had it good for too long."

"Maybe we have too many assumptions and prejudices."

"Speak for yourself. I'm not prejudiced."

"Maybe you're in denial."

"I like it that way." He grinned. "By the way, what's your secret? Leonor said you had a big one."

"Oh, girl stuff. Someday I'll tell you." After I murder her. Bitch.

"Feels charged. You're blushing and about to cry. Never mind. Please don't tell me. I probably couldn't handle it."

"Don't worry." I sighed. "Would you be tempted to move back to Mexico and all three live together – you, me, and Leonor and maybe another one of her lovers? It could be an amazing experiment we could write a book about."

He tapped the steering wheel. "This is where the action is right now. We have to use this war to raise the consciousness of the American people to the evils of capitalism. All that group marriage bullshit is counterrevolutionary. Although the time may come when we need a safe house, and that would be an option. I'm not kicking you out of my apartment, but if I were you, I'd stick with the plan for the Teacher Corps and moving to Philly. Sounds as though you and your sister have some catching up to do"

‒ ∞ ‒

My last day at Harry's, we arranged to meet Victoria at Fort Dix in New Jersey, and I'd go home with her in the Volkswagen bug she'd found for me. Harry and I took the Corvette, even though Harry thought it was counterrevolutionary and embarrassing. But I needed a place to store my bag during the demonstration, and I didn't think the bus was safe.

A gaggle of buses were parked and a few still pulling up outside the front entrance to Fort Dix. From the crowd, there were gasps, murmurs about fascism, and cackles at a sign above the gate: "Obedience to the law is freedom."

Harry called loudly with his megaphone, "If obedience to the law is freedom, then we are outlaws redefining freedom! Freedom is peace, not war!"

"Right on, brother," came the group response. "All power to the people!"

Victoria and I found each other in the crowd and hugged joyfully. I had forgotten how petite she was, and I had a flash of feeling immense and awkward towering over her. I introduced her to Harry. They grinned at each other. Was that a twinge of jealousy in my gut? Silly me, so insecure.

Everyone donned a variety of helmets, including some German army surplus numbers that briefly jarred me. Chanting and singing, around three hundred of us, braless women, bearded men, stormed onto the base with large Stop the War banners.

Looking like Hollywood versions of aliens, a surreal line of gas-masked soldiers with rifles and fixed bayonets met us in the middle of a grassy meadow. It was so green it could have been a golf or croquet course in another place and time. We stood our ground, inches from the sharp, gleaming spikes, and continued to thunder our songs and chants as a voice over a speaker warned us trespassers to leave immediately. Would these giant alien insects charge and kill us? We had brought leaflets explaining why we opposed the war. Harry moved first, impaling a leaflet on the bayonet of a soldier in front of him.

"All we ask is that you read this, brother," he said. The soldier, who appeared too young to drive at night, didn't move. We quickly passed leaflets across our front line and each of us followed Harry's lead. The soldiers, as still as robots, looked less ominous with the papers flapping on their bayonets. Chuckles waved through our ranks.

"Trespassers, you have three minutes to retreat," a no-nonsense voice crackled through the loudspeaker. "If you do not retreat, we cannot guarantee your safety."

"Mission accomplished," Harry called. "We can leave now. Back away, folks. Nice and slow. Back away."

All the way to the parking area, we chanted. "Stop the war! Bring the troops home! Hell no, don't go!"

Harry and I hugged goodbye. He seemed preoccupied. He had to write a report on our action for the radical news service collective he belonged to and it was foremost on his mind.

"I'll call you," he said. "Good luck in Philly. Find out what's happening there. Check out the *Free Press* and *Distant Drummer*. They subscribe to our service. Maybe you can write for them in your spare time. Bye Victoria. Good to meet you." They hugged also. Everyone was elated from the excitement of our adventure.

– ∞ –

THIRTY-SEVEN

The first day of the weeklong Teacher Corps orientation, about eighty of us, name-tagged, diverse by age and ethnicity, sat in rows of metal folding chairs in a huge gymnasium on the Temple University campus. After speaker introductions and a brief welcome from education and psychology professors, one of them instructed us to count off by nines and form nine circles. I pulled a nine and wandered among the crowd looking for other nines. In about ten minutes, we all found each other, dragged chairs into circles and sat, ready for the next instruction. None came. We sat in silence, fidgeting. What the fuck was going on? Maybe I was in the wrong place and should leave immediately. My stomach groaned. I needed a cafeteria and toilet, in that order. What was I thinking? Slap my wrist. I hadn't signed on for this weird shit when I chose to train to be a schoolteacher in the inner city. Damn.

I considered myself sophisticated and stylish in my all black outfit, a chic New Yorker in backwater Philly. I supposed Leonor would say my false self was at work fooling me. No matter. I was into it. Two male psychology professors, both wearing wedding rings, supposedly ran this operation. What would Gabe think of this? Shit, why Gabe? What would Harry think of this? Tall blond, thirty-something, Wes ambled around and listened wordlessly with a dopey toothy grin. Don, about ten or more years older, gray hair, glasses, pock-marked, long, horse face, appeared more serious as he roamed silently from group to group. The program administrators and several graduate assistants wandered around as well, listened briefly to pleas for directions, ignored each one, then moved on. None of them spoke. Shades of the Barnard Freudian shrink, Dr. Flatte. They must have taken the same course in psychological torture.

Slowly, hesitantly, people began addressing each other in our circle. We introduced ourselves, shared where we were from, a little about why we'd joined the Teacher Corps, and our expectations. I still felt frustrated, let down, and angry at the organizers for letting us hang directionless. But every group seemed to find its way and before lunch, we discovered that we were in the vanguard, experiencing an organic team-building gathering called a T-group straight out of Southern California. Through discovery, we were teaching ourselves a skill transferable to the classroom. Brilliant. But I didn't share how upset and insecure I felt with the lack of structure.

By next morning, we had separate group room assignments. Interacting within the group was starting to be fun. I had a lot to say. Our group "facilitator" – new term – was Professor horsy-faced Don who talked very little. Near the end of the week, with one day left, it occurred to me that I was the only remaining member who hadn't been attacked and dissected. Anxious, even desperate, I flirted with Horsy, and invited him back to the apartment.

One beer led to another and soon we were both naked, frantically having sex on our brown canvass couch cushions thrown on the braided living room rug, the coffee table pushed to the side. Professor Don Horsy, the psychologist, humped me and chanted non-stop to the rhythm of the humps, "Maladaptive, maladaptive, maladaptive" about fifty thousand times.

The grating voice kept me in my body but I was furious. Here I was acting out my second favorite escape, and he had to ruin it with his rhythmic psycho-babbling accusation over and over in my ear until he finally came with a roar the whole block probably heard. I ran my nails across his back, hard. Let him explain that to the little wife.

"You realize you will be the receiver tomorrow, don't you?" he verified.

I puffed on a cigarette and nodded. He found his glasses, gathered his clothes and pulled them on. He spoke quietly, but it sounded loud to me.

"You've been sitting haughtily with your elbow out, your two fingers holding your cigarette and you've offered advice all week, Rowie. People are sick of it even though your suggestions were insightful. Behind your back, they call you Miss Superior and they're going to get you tomorrow."

"What can I do?" I was terrified.

"You can listen and learn."

"I think I may be insane. You made me feel insane with that 'maladaptive' crap. Why did you say that over and over?"

"Now you're criticizing me. You're expert at taking the spotlight off yourself, Rowie."

"Well, I don't think it was appropriate. You made me feel bad."

I finished the cigarette and started returning the couch cushions to their place. He moved the coffee table back.

He softened a little. "I'm sorry. It's not that people dislike you. It's just the barrier you put up. You keep yourself isolated. You don't connect."

"I wish I knew how. I do the best I can." I brushed my wet eyes.

"I know," he said. "Maybe someone will have helpful feedback for you tomorrow."

After he left, I went to the doughnut shop on Chestnut Street, bought three dozen assorted doughnuts, then back home, ate two dozen in record time. I forced myself to drink glasses of warm water and it all came up easily. Victoria came home just as I flushed the toilet for the last time.

"Have you been crying?" she asked noticing my red eyes.

"Yes, I'm upset about the stupid group." That was easy, I thought.

"I smell sex," she announced, sniffing.

"I fucked the psychology professor."

"Cool. That should be an automatic A."

"Yeah, an A in intercourse, only it's not a real course. It's still orientation. He was chanting in my ear the whole time." I explained the 'maladaptive' scene.

"He sounds pretty maladaptive himself."

"No shit. I'm very scared about tomorrow."

"Everyone else survived, right?"

"Right."

"You will too." She saw the doughnut box and lit up. "Hey, Rowie, I'm proud of you. You got doughnuts and didn't try to scarf them all down and then puke!"

I managed a weak smile. "I still could."

"Don't say that. Just have one. I'll help you."

"No, thanks, I'd rather not. I don't know why I brought them into the house."

"The best addiction is screwing," she said as she bit into a chocolate, cream-filled puff. "Not fattening, great exercise, and it feels so delicious."

"Speaking of which, Harry can't make it this weekend. I'm bummed."

"There's a party. Screw Harry. You'll have a better time without him."

"Victoria! He's my new boyfriend!"

"Uh...right. You just fucked your professor, but Harry's your boyfriend. Who are you kidding? Don't worry. I'll take you to a fantastic party."

"Come on. You know I didn't fuck the professor because I liked him. I had to do it. Anyhow, Harry and I don't have any kind of commitment. I like

333

him a lot and I want him to be committed. I'm disappointed he's not coming here."

I fingered a doughnut. Turned it over and over in the box. Licked my fingers. Picked at it. Victoria slapped my hand lightly. I slapped her back the same way. We grinned.

"Harry's probably staying in town for a date with a gorgeous revolutionary he can talk politics with as he screws her. He strikes me as a guy with a stick up his butt who never stops thinking of the revolution. I wonder whether he ever lets his hair down. Course he'd have to brush it first."

"You're being mean. He has a great mop of hair and I really don't think he's seeing anyone else. That was one of the things that bothered him about Leonor. No, he's staying in town to go to a lecture on Vietnam at the Washington Square Methodist Church."

"Square's a good fit for him."

"That's enough, Victoria. You're pissing me off."

"I don't care, as long as you come to the party."

"I don't know. I have work to do, and crowds freak me out. I can't promise. I think I love Harry. And I have to get through a group lynching tomorrow."

"Those are excuses and you know it. Fuck that group. Don't pay attention to them. It's all touchy-feely crap."

"Easier said than done. I have to be in the hot seat."

"Just listen to all the criticism and agree with everybody. Even thank them. They'll eat it up."

– ∞ –

Once I had adopted that attitude, the group meeting wasn't so hard. Everyone told me how I put on airs and acted superior as though I was better than everyone else, and they resented it.

"I'm sorry," I said. "You're right. I act that way on the outside, but inside I feel inferior. I think just the opposite, that everyone is better than I am. I don't like myself very much. It's an act to cover up my self-hatred."

I cried and people in the group comforted me.

"Thank you for pointing out my conceited behavior," I sobbed. "I will work on learning to like myself better."

I didn't mention anything about binging and purging. It wasn't so hard, and since it all sounded right to me, not an act at all, I decided I was definitely crazy.

I drove straight from the group session to the University of Pennsylvania psychiatric outpatient services.

"I need a therapist," I said to the receptionist. "I think I may be insane."

After a short wait, I got to see a young, handsome psychiatrist who I saw right away wore a wedding ring. The first thing he asked me was, "What was your nickname as a child?" The second thing he asked me was "So, Weena, how are you going to handle your sexual feelings for me?"

I stammered. "I wasn't aware I had any. Why are you calling me Weena?"

"It's therapeutic. Bear with me. You were flirting with me, Weena," he said. "You checked to see whether I wore a ring."

"I wasn't flirting but yes, I noticed your ring. I wondered whether you were single or married. Is that abnormal?"

"It's not uncommon for a woman to use sexuality in a controlling way, Weena."

"Let's say it's true," I said. "What then?"

"Well, Weena, I'd say you'd best have an older man therapist, a father figure you won't immediately associate with sex. Are you willing to explore your problems? Do you sincerely want to get better, Weena?"

"I do. Do you?"

"You use a sarcastic facade as a defense, I see. All right, then. Where do you live?" When I told him, he wrote a name and number on a prescription pad, tore it off and gave it to me.

"Call this doctor, Weena. His office is close to your home. He can help you. I can't."

I had no time to say anything about my main issues.

On my way out, I saw a bulletin board notice of an Eating Disorders Clinic there at the hospital, first meeting free of charge. A shudder went through me. A meeting was going to start in ten minutes. I copied down the room number, got on the elevator, and pushed the button.

I was the thinnest person of the half dozen in the room. One enormous girl asked me what I was doing there. Another massive girl told her to shut up, that thin people had disorders too and she knew it. I thought, if these people are attending the clinic and look like this, maybe I will look like this if I attend this clinic. Quickly, I got up and left. I half hoped someone would stop me, but no one did.

On my way out, I crumpled up the name and number of the psychiatrist referral and tossed it away. I stopped at the market on my way home and bought a big bag of junk food I sneaked into the house.

– ∞ –

THIRTY-EIGHT

Harry worked long hours with the Revolution News Service collective on the Upper West Side. My whole first year in Philadelphia, we saw each other weekends, either in New York or Philly. I got very attached to him. He let me drive Freddy's Corvette when it was around, and we buzzed up sixty miles to see Mommy and get a home-cooked meal. He and Mommy loved talking radical politics. She had just joined the Unitarian Church, and Harry laughed openly when she talked about it.

"I've found spirituality," she announced over strawberries and ice cream.

"Had you lost it, Pearl?" Harry quipped slyly, gulping a big mouthful. "You're a nice Jewish lady. Is Jesus going to be your personal lord and savior?"

"Oh Harry," Mommy said. "I know it's hard for a Jewish person to understand. But you, of all people, should. The Unitarians are moderate and peaceful. You can be Jewish and still belong there. They believe Jesus was a teacher of love. They go to peace marches too because Jesus would have. I'm happy to be part of such a group."

"Your chicken soup is delicious, Pearl. Your matzo balls are fantastic. Your strawberries and vanilla ice cream dessert is to die for, but as for your religion, I plead the fifth. There's no room for religion in my ideal world – Jewish or otherwise."

"Spirituality is with us, Harry," Mommy said. "It's here whether you acknowledge it or not. Dogmas mostly separate, but the reason I like the Unitarian church is the way they bring everyone together."

I said. "I'll reserve judgment, Mommy. You seem happy. I guess time will tell."

"Pearl," Harry said. "We'll have to agree to disagree. At least you have it right about the war. You're not connecting the dots though. Peace isn't the answer. Revolution is the answer."

– ∞ –

In the Teacher Corps we dived into elementary schools right from the beginning, working with small groups of kids, enriching their curriculum with math and reading games. I got a job teaching in an after-school center five days a week, and I helped Welfare mothers set up a support group and attended

337

their meetings regularly. I was busy with schoolwork, community work, teaching, demonstrations, talking on the phone with Harry, weekends of sex, toilets full of throw-up, a head full of confusion, and trickling news of escalating war. On April 4, 1968, came the sobering news of the assassination of Dr. Martin Luther King, Jr. Cities erupted in violence. Heartbroken, Victoria and I listened to the words of Bobby Kennedy, one of our articulate heroes, and we hoped, the next President. Some of his words struck me particularly hard. I rushed around and got things done, but all the while felt constant pain not just from the war but also from my addiction and the internal war it caused. Bobby quoted Aeschlyus:

'In our sleep, pain which cannot forget falls drop by drop upon the heart until, in our own despair, against our will, comes wisdom through the awful grace of God. What we need in the United States is not division; what we need in the United States is not hatred; what we need in the United States is not violence or lawlessness; but love and wisdom, and compassion toward one another....'

– ∞ –

Of course! I would pray again! God would help me to help myself. Mommy had found God with the Unitarians and I wanted to talk to her about it, but instead I criticized her behind her back and kept my distance. I didn't know five-year-old Eliza at all and had only heard through the grapevine that Karen was pregnant again. I had no interest in visiting anyone from my former life because I was horribly aware of being addicted. Shame dogged me. Hiding it was too much of a strain away from home – even at Harry's. In the two-and-a-half bath Philly apartment, I had worked out a method to carry on secretly. Only Leonor knew, so I dropped her completely right after sending a thank-you note for the gorgeous painting she'd sent me.

– ∞ –

Barely two months after Martin Luther King's assassination, on Wednesday, June 5th, as I drove to school in the morning, I gasped and had to pull over when I heard the news that my hero, Bobby Kennedy had been fatally shot earlier that morning in Los Angeles just after winning the California Democratic primary. He had pledged to end the war in Vietnam if he were elected. Are all the good guys getting killed? I wondered. What the hell is going on? Who's next? Is my self-hatred related to these events? Shaken, I managed to get to school where those on my team hugged and cried together. Two of the young men on my team, Ned and Billy, had joined the teaching program to avoid the draft and a third, Grant, belonged to the Black Panther Party. We were all horrified together.

Victoria and I moved even further to the Left. We were angry. We worked hard at our studies and partied hard in our free time. Our social circles included friends of Grant's from the Black Panthers who had set up breakfast programs and preschools for poor children in their communities.

As part of my Teacher Corps work, I taught in a North Philadelphia elementary school and helped Welfare mothers to organize, pulling together various groups of activists. Both Victoria and I made many friends and had a few quickie romantic affairs from that group. I still felt attached to Harry, but last time I'd stayed with him, I found a pair of black bikini underpants – not mine. "Sleeping around," the philosophy Mommy had preached to me half my life ago, suddenly made sense.

By the time Richard Nixon was elected President the following fall, the North Philly Welfare rights groups were strong and independent and no longer needed outside help from someone like me. Keeping lines of communication open, I left the African-American community and transferred to a poor white area, Kensington, where alcoholism, spousal and child abuse, unemployment, poor nutrition, and cooties raged.

I worked even longer hours, teaching, taking classes, playing piano and guitar in assemblies, running an after-school center, and going to evening meetings.

With other members of my team, I helped set up a night school in the neighborhood. In preparation, we walked around and interviewed people in the community to find out what courses they'd like, and then we opened our school. I taught writing and music. We also had classes in history and citizenship. Working with poor people who struggled to pull meals together, I felt more ashamed than ever of my habit of binging and purging and began to see it as a product of middle class privilege. But I still couldn't stop. I just added another layer of guilt.

At parties, like just about everyone else, I'd regularly hook up sexually with someone new, and it wasn't unusual for a small audience to gather. Open sex was everywhere. I bought a powder blue eyelet outfit for summer, hip-huggers and top, completely see through, which I wore to parties with nothing underneath. I'd become an exhibitionist, taking literally the new mantra, "If you've got it, flaunt it." I liked feeling powerful and desirable, and I especially liked shocking people. It was a little like insulting Daddy and getting away with it.

– ∞ –

Due a rest after collecting our Masters Degrees, Victoria and I moved out and headed for the beach. Our furnished waterfront beach house on Harbor Island wasn't swanky, but had two bedrooms, sweeping ocean views, and a nice deck on the beach. We befriended young lifeguards and soon were entertaining them together, a pair at a time, a foursome in bed, swapping partners but keeping it strictly hetero.

My friend Alan, a pharmacist from Philly who had been in the Teacher Corps, came for the Fourth of July weekend with his pal, Terry, who, sight unseen, Victoria volunteered to "cure" of gayness when she heard he wanted to try with an understanding woman. Terry and Alan were small, thin men, Alan dark, Terry blond, both sweet, gentle and shy.

Before Victoria and Terry went off to her bedroom to try this social experiment, the deal was that Terry would teach us how to levitate a table. The four of us sat at our round teak dining table, lights low, hands spread, pinkies touching. Terry said a blessing, asked for the most benevolent outcome in a sweet voice. Then, shy little Terry, in a shockingly booming deep voice shouted the order, "Rise, table, rise." We waited. Then he commanded in even stronger volume, "Rise, table, rise!" We felt a rumbling, then slowly the table rose up onto two legs.

"Good table," Terry said, as though he were talking to a dog. "Good table. Now, table, we are going to ask you questions, and we would like you to answer one knock for yes and two knocks for no. Is that acceptable?"

The table clunked down and shot straight back up.

"Thank you. Now, show us what 'no' looks like, please table."

The table clunked twice.

A shiver ran through me. Was this a trick? How did this work?

"Okay, who has a question? Rowie, would you like to contact someone from the other side?"

"What the hell? Yes, I would like to contact my grandfather Eli Fine."

"He's my grandfather too," Victoria added.

"Calling Eli. Table, will you please let us know when Rowie and Victoria's grandpa Eli is with us."

Clunk.

"Is Grandpa Eli with us?"

Clunk.

"Rowie, what is your question?"

"What should I eat to be healthy?"

The table began clunking quickly. Terry stopped it.

"Wait, please, table. If you are spelling out the answer, please knock once for A, twice for B, three times for C, and so forth through the alphabet."

As the table clunked down and up, we counted the clunks together until we had the answer spelled out. The answer was, "Eat greens."

"That's it?" I asked. "Do you have any other message for me?"

Yes! We counted clunks again. The message was "Stop. Sanctify. Harmonize. Cherish yourself."

I almost fainted. Tears rolled down my cheeks.

"What is it, Rowie?" Alan asked. "Are you okay?"

"I've heard the damn message before, without the last part. I've never gotten what the hell it means. I get the feeling I have to totally change my life."

Terry asked, "Does Rowie have to totally change her life, Gramps?"

There was no answer.

"Table," he asked in his commanding tone, "Does Rowie have to totally change her life in order to carry out her grandfather's message?"

The table clunked once for yes and then spelled a word I had never heard before, a-v-a-t-a-r. Then it stopped.

"What's a vatar?" I asked.

"Get the dictionary," Terry said.

"We didn't bring one," Victoria said. "Rowie, call Harry and ask him to look up vatar."

Terry said, "You can call later when the reading is finished. Let's go on with other questions."

Victoria asked shyly, "Will the experiment Terry and I are going to try be successful?"

One clunk. Yes!

Terry said, "We have to define 'successful.' One person's success may be another's failure, and vice versa."

341

Victoria exchanged glances with me, looked skeptical. She asked Terry, "Terry, what would success mean to you? What expectations do you have?"

"I expect to find out whether I can have sex with a cute and experienced woman, which you are, Victoria. If I find out, that will be success."

"Oh, okay, that's interesting," she said. "I'm ready when you are. This table stuff is intense. I've had enough. How about you, Ro?"

"I could do this all day. Let me ask one more question. Can I do what Terry does, facilitate levitation?"

The table clunked a definitive yes.

"In that case, Alan and I will go to the beach while you two go and play in bed. I'll try this table game myself later."

"It's a group activity, Ro," said Victoria. "You can't do it yourself."

"Can I levitate the table with one other person, like Victoria?" I asked.

The table clunked once. I whooped a hooray, still keeping my hands on the table.

"You have good rapport with the table, Rowie," Terry said. "You definitely have the gift."

"Don't we all?" I asked.

"I don't think so," Terry answered. "Someday we all will, but not yet."

"I will ask directly. Table, can anyone who wants to, relate to you with good rapport?"

Clunk. Clunk.

I was impressed, although skeptical.

Terry thanked the table and the entities for helping us, and the session ended.

– ∞ –

We went out for seafood later and made jokes about levitating the restaurant table. We toasted to success. Terry had been able to have intercourse with Victoria, his first pairing with a woman, and they both felt proud and happy about that, even triumphant.

"But I admit I was scared," he said, "and I still think I'm gay."

– ∞ –

After the boys left, I wanted to work with the table, but it seemed big and awkward to me. My eyes alighted on our lightweight metal TV snack tray table, and I knew I wanted Victoria to help me try levitating that because we could manipulate it faster and carry it anywhere. We sat across from each other with our fingertips touching. I did as Terry had, asking for a benevolent outcome and then, in my most dramatic voice, called for the table to rise. It lifted right off the floor instantly to about chest level and I asked it to drop a couple of inches so we would be more comfortable. It dropped slightly. Victoria and I asked questions about all sorts of things. I wanted to know what a vatar was and what Stop, Sanctify and Harmonize meant. We didn't have a tape recorder and couldn't take our hands off the table to take notes so we had to remember. I called Karen and asked her to look up vatar and avatar in her dictionary. I hadn't spoken to her in forever and she acted as though it had been a day or two. She put Eliza on and the talkative little one kept repeating avatar in a questioning tone.

"Okay, I've got it," Karen said. "It's avatar from Hindu, a god coming to Earth in bodily form."

"That's our reminder, maybe from Max!" I said, enthusiastically. "When I was in Mexico, I learned that each of us is a sliver of God, completely whole in ourselves but bigger and more powerful when we merge because there's more God. I'm a better person when I remember that. It may be related to Mommy's thing the Unitarians teach. Thank you, table!"

Both Victoria and I decided we were meant to explore spirituality and understand unity. While our pursuit of pleasures of the flesh was a good thing, we were to ease off because we'd gotten out of it what we were meant to. Now we could stop living lives of hedonists and find out what love was. I'd been trying to find love all my life.

Out of the blue, I wondered what Gabe would think of levitation, was tempted to call him but didn't dare. It was as though he'd become more attractive to me since he was no longer available.

Next time I levitated the table, it clunked out Max's name. Max spoke through the table in an accepting and loving way.

"Greetings, dear Miz Wine," he said. "It gives me great pleasure to speak with you again. You are a beautiful and loving being. As is your sister."

"No, I'm not," I said. "I'm fucked up. I curse too much and I'm promiscuous, and I still abuse ... that is, I eat too much."

"You are a magnificent soul," he said

He didn't scold me for anything even though I felt I deserved to be scolded for continuing my escapist, self-indulgent journey.

We asked about the future of everyone we could think of. Max told us Ralph was going to marry a Japanese woman, become a Buddhist monk and write books about Eastern influences on Western culture. Our mother was going to find a soul mate at the Unitarian Church and remarry happily. Karen would have two more children with Jon, a girl and a boy, then divorce and move to California with her allergist and have a son with him too. Eliza and her sister would be lawyers. The first boy would be a teacher and the second an actor. Victoria would marry an African revolutionary, have a daughter, move to Nairobi, and write sexy best-selling thrillers. I was going to write a book and a musical comedy, both about love and food. The show would be a hit on Broadway and teach people about the nature of personal reality. No word of marriage and children. Leonor would marry a new man and have a child prodigy. Alan was going to die of a horrible illness gay men would get. Terry was going to have a child with a dancer. Nixon was going to end the war in Vietnam, but there would be other, terrible wars to come.

I asked how accurate these predictions were and learned they were only possible realities of this moment and there were infinite other possible realities. We could choose our paths. What we do in every moment creates the future. If we think in limited ways, we reap limited results. Clunk, clunk, clunk, clunk, clunk, clunk. Hour after hour after hour. Victoria got tired before I did so I decided to try levitating alone. The table rose! I stayed up until dawn asking questions. At two in the afternoon, I woke up, had coffee, and started again. Victoria was amazed that I could levitate the table alone.

"Stop extremism," the table spelled out to me. "Devilish entities enter if you persist. Go to the beach."

Victoria panicked. "I think it's too late," she said. "I have a bad feeling."

"Just a little more and I'll stop," I insisted. "I know there's an important message. I can feel it."

The table spelled out b-o-d-y d-e-a-d w-o-m-a-n i-n w-a-t-e-r.

"You were right. Oh my God," Victoria said. "We attracted murder. We have to call the police."

"And tell them what? That our table told us about a woman's dead body?"

Victoria paced. "We'll have to ask the table what to do."

The table spelled out p-r-o-w-l-e-r.

Victoria made sure the door was locked. "This is it," she said. "I'm calling the cops."

"Hey, remember, we're not supposed to like cops. We call them 'pigs' now."

"At this moment, they're our friends. I'm calling and telling them I heard a prowler and want them to check around our house. That'll do for now."

Ten minutes later, a very tall, broad, fortyish man with freckled skin, red crew cut and bulbous nose dressed in a blue shirt, dark blazer, and Superman tie, rang our doorbell.

"Kevin Kelly, Harbor Island Police. You girls called us because you heard a prowler? Mind if I come in?"

He showed his badge and we let him in. I worried that the table might rise of its own volition and freak him out, but it behaved. He sat on the couch. We sat in small easy chairs. He opened a notebook.

"Nice tie," I said. He stroked it, grinned slightly, and cleared his throat.

"I'd like you to give me the names of everyone you know on the island, including who you've dated since you got here, what your activities have been. I want to know about any suspicious behavior you might have observed. Anything could be a clue."

Victoria and I glanced at each other. How could we tell this guy the truth? We'd slept with almost every lifeguard on the beach and spent the last 18 out of 24 hours conversing with spirits and a table. Suspicious behavior? They'd haul our butts off to jail or a loony bin if they knew. How were we going to keep from laughing hysterically? I was afraid to look at Victoria.

"I'm feeling sick to my stomach," Victoria said, hand over her mouth and rushed off to the bathroom.

"I'm sorry, I have to help my sister," I said. "Could you just keep an eye on our house? Maybe we were imagining the prowler. We'll call you if we see or hear anything suspicious." I went to the door and held it open.

Kevin stood up, closed his notebook hesitantly. "Are you sure? Because I can wait."

"I'm sure," I said. "Thank you for your prompt attention. I have to go to my sister now. I really like your tie."

Right on cue, Victoria made loud gagging sounds. How ironic, I thought. He walked out the door, still protesting.

We were so busy fooling with the paranormal that we missed the Woodstock festival. When summer ended, with no particular plan except the table's advice to move to New York, Victoria went to stay with her old Bennington roommate, and I moved in with Harry temporarily.

Harry's downstairs neighbor was moving to California, and Harry was feeling cramped with me around, so we concluded a perfect arrangement was for Victoria and me to take over the vacating apartment. It was bigger than Harry's place, originally a two-bedroom, dark as a cave even in broad daylight since all the windows opened to an airshaft and brown cork lined the walls, but the forty-two sixteen a month rent made up for the darkness, and electricity would substitute for sunlight. Who could resist? Everything was falling into place effortlessly.

The bathtub in our kitchen had a custom cover that converted into a countertop, a little low, but better than no counter at all, and someone had taken down a wall and merged one of the bedrooms into an enlarged living room. I slept on a hi-riser in the living room and Victoria got the bedroom. Harry and I were sleeping together again in his place, so I agreed I didn't need a bedroom of my own.

– ∞ –

Harry was still with Revolution News Service, a group structured as an egalitarian collective. RNS put out a weekly packet of news and graphics from a progressive point of view. Victoria got a job working as an assistant editor at Grove Press editing S & M books that freaked her out, but she loved the avant-garde feel of the place and it was just a short walk away. She was connecting with artists and writers and as long as she didn't have to get into bondage herself, she intended to have fun and learn what she could, maybe even get into analysis or therapy.

I thought about teaching, but it seemed easier to go back to the Welfare Department once again. I dressed professionally and wore my long hair in a neat bun I fixed with two big barrettes. I made home visits to the Lower East Side. Nothing had changed about the system. The job wore me out.

– ∞ –

THIRTY-NINE

One warm fall day, my hair in a tight bun, dressed in a fashionable professional frock from Bonwit Teller and matching sandals, I sat in the stifling living room of a dilapidated tenement even older than ours, interviewing a twenty-two year old mother named Delia Vega. Delia, toothless, wept as she recounted in Spanish how hard it was to feed and clothe her five kids on a Welfare check. Duh. The kids, two sets of twin girls and a boy, all under five, were stark naked, giggling non-stop, sitting bunched together on a thin gray carpet engrossed in their play with toys that were obviously delighting them. As I sat demurely, I felt something brush against one of my sandaled feet. A cat in the house? If only. I bolted up in shock. A large brown rat was sniffing my bare toes. My heart banged against my chest. From my standing position, I realized that the kids were playing with half a dozen live, tiny pink squirming creatures. Baby rats! I had handled baby mice in the country when I was little, but now, in this setting, I was horrified. There was no way I would sit down again. Delia took the opportunity to lead me into the kitchen where she opened the cupboard to let a trillion cockroaches rain into the sink. I shuddered. Swiftly, I instructed Delia to protect the kids, speak to the landlord and get the place cleaned up. She had no phone and didn't know where to find the absentee landlord whose only address was a post office box. I jotted down the address and agreed to follow through and call the Health Department. Still shaking, I high-tailed it out of there and down the smelly and rickety staircase.

When I walked through the front door of that hellhole, I got yet another shock. I found myself trapped inside a semicircle of men ringing a bloody fight, one sweaty, angry man wielding a broken beer bottle, and his opponent brandishing a switchblade. I froze. Someone yanked me out of there. It was a couple of hours before quitting time, but I headed straight home. As a radical, I told myself it was capitalism that created the conditions I'd witnessed on Avenue B.

Later that night, in bed with Harry, I told him about the afternoon experience and my radical take on it.

"Your analysis is right on," he said earnestly as he ran his fingers through my waist length mop. "I'm proud of you, Rowie. You could write about this for RNS. I wish you'd consider joining the collective. We need people like you."

"I like being needed," I said. "What's the pay?"

"Thirty-five a week plus lunch and dinner."

"A week? I gulped."

"A revolutionary doesn't count hours," Harry pontificated. "This is more than work. It's a commitment to change the world. It's a way to spend your time meaningfully. Dedicating yourself to the Movement is finally admitting you're serious about smashing capitalism. You won't have to dress up and wear make-up and conform to bourgeois morality anymore. You'll be on the road to real freedom! Don't you want to contribute to getting out from under the racist, oil-soaked, fat cat monopoly capitalist system, Rowie? Isn't it time to take a stand?"

"Yes, I'll do it!" I said, pushing him so hard he fell over backwards. I leapt on top of him. "You've convinced me! I'm going to have a new life! Thank you! Thank you! Wait till I tell Victoria. I'm so excited!"

"Great," he said. "Would you mind getting off me and making me a P, B and J? I'm starving."

_ ∞ _

A few weeks into the new job, on my afternoon off, I strolled around the Village, my thick wavy hair loosely hanging over my thrift store army jacket. I leaned against the fence at the little park at West 3rd Street and Sixth Avenue to observe the basketball hunks, mostly young, dark-skinned men who I imagined as regal, dancing Watusi tribesmen, graceful, high-jumping, and great fun to watch. Our revolution will free these guys, I thought, so they can work at anything. No more racism!

One of the towering players, Moffat, winked, smiled, and nodded at me. I nodded back. I was flattered, especially since I wore no make-up, not even lipstick. When he asked me out for coffee, I shortly found myself sitting across from him in a café on McDougal Street. His face gleamed with sweat, dark eyes roamed over my curves.

"What kind of work do you do, baby?" he asked. He dumped sugar and cream into his coffee, tasted it and added more of both as I watched silently.

I didn't like the 'baby' but I let it pass. He took a big bite of his first jelly doughnut of three, offered to share. Not even tempted, I sipped black coffee.

"I work as a writer for an alternative news service," I said, omitting details. "I got home at six this morning. We get the weekly packet of news and graphics out Friday nights and stay as long as it takes so I sleep in Saturday mornings and get the rest of the day to play. I get every other Sunday off too. I used to be a caseworker on the Lower East Side, but I just started doing this work because it has meaning. I'd like to change the world. How about you?"

"I'm a cop," he said.

"For real? You don't act like a cop." I was tempted to grab one of his doughnuts and was relieved I hadn't automatically spurted out he didn't act like a pig. Could this guy be another Joe Bob, investigating me? No, he wouldn't have said he was a cop if he really was. I sipped water. Now I was on guard.

"I don't advertise it."

"Are you undercover at the basketball court?"

"If I was, I wouldn't tell you now, would I?"

"You're no cop. You're shitting me."

"Yeah, I'm shitting you. Right. I dig you, baby. You stay around here?"

"Not too far."

"Got an old man?" He started on the second doughnut. I sipped more water. The place was noisy. Was Harry my boyfriend? I'd play it safe.

"A boyfriend? Sort of."

"Chick like you could make good money. How much you bringing in now?"

I laughed. "Thirty-five a week plus lunch and dinner sometimes."

"I could set you up, baby."

"Are you saying I could be a hooker?" I lit a cigarette to hide my fear.

"Not on the streets, baby. High class. Upper East Side all the way. Nice apartment of your own. You got to be a college grad like yourself to get the classy clientele. I'm talking judges, doctors, businessmen. They would dig you!"

"Thanks, man, but I'm not into that. I've got principles." I blew smoke up.

"Think about it, baby. It's an opportunity. Work for ten years and you'll retire. I know a chick who's an artist. She paints, man. This gives her time to do what she digs. All you'd have to do is fix your hair, put on a little make-up, dress up nice, maybe lose a few pounds..."

"Lose a few pounds? You think I'm fat?" I coughed and took another sip of water. He called me fat! And what was wrong with my hair?

"To make the big money, you have to look like a model. You're close."

"I have to go now. The answer is 'no.'"

"I bet you do it for free all the time, don't you, baby? I'll bet you like it, too. You're a classy broad. Great knockers. Let me walk you home. No hard feelings, okay?"

I had never felt so petite before. Walking with Moffat, I felt like a two year old with my daddy. I didn't want him to know where I lived, but I worried he might think I was racist if I said anything, so I let him tag along with me. If he hadn't made the crack about losing weight I would have considered sleeping with him, but that turned me off. Bastard had some nerve. I had measured myself that morning as I did every morning. I knew my waist was an inch and a half bigger than the ideal. What was I supposed to do, cut it off? All along the way home, Moffat high-fived one after another guy, each of whom eyed me like a tasty lamb chop. At my front door, I said goodbye and thanked him for the coffee. I thought I heard someone climbing the stairs behind me, but I didn't look, just hurried on up, unlocked the door quickly, let myself in, locked and bolted it.

Victoria was in her pajamas engrossed in a novel. I got her attention long enough to tell her about the encounter and call girl offer.

"Hey, if I were you, I'd think about it," she said. "This could be your meal ticket. Moffat's right. You could get a fabulous piano and work on your music all day instead of going to that silly Movement job. You're supposed to write a musical comedy, remember?"

"That doesn't mean my life should be a comedy. You do it if it sounds so good."

"I didn't get the offer. I'm too short, and I'm not as pretty as you," she said.

"Would you stop saying that, please?" What the hell did it mean to be pretty enough to work as a hooker? Was that something to aspire to? My sister was encouraging me to be a call girl! What could be more counterrevolutionary? We were bright, well-educated Jewish girls, granted, a little mixed up, nevertheless, we could succeed at anything we intended. We'd better get a grip. I felt myself sinking lower and lower, losing control. The dark apartment reminded me of our childhood home. Harry, upstairs was the source of light just like Grandma and Grandpa had been. I was stuck in hell again, only this time I'd chosen the place myself.

– ∞ –

The war in Indochina raged, the anti-war movement gathered momentum, the women's movement was taking off. I was stressed, still binging and purging. My shadow dogged me with every lie. I'd been working at RNS for a few months when all eight women decided to meet regularly as a consciousness-raising group. I found myself analyzing my life through a new lens. I thought I'd understood oppression of minorities and sympathized with the plight of underprivileged people but had never considered women an oppressed group.

Lightning struck in the middle of a group meeting as I realized the high school yearbook quote assigned to me, despite all my early accomplishments was "There's a woman behind all great men." That was the best they could come up with? I saw more obviously than ever Mommy's main goal for her daughters had been to marry us off to the right man even though she'd been one of the first people in the entire world to work with computer applications. Men ruled the world! How could I have been so blind? When Daddy got me instead of a son, he unleashed his anger on me as though having a vagina deserved punishment. Would he have hit a son as much? To think that I'd worried about being labeled Lesbian when I was with Leonor. Maybe I would be happier giving up men for the sake of the Women's Movement.

At home I looked in the mirror and said the word. "Lesbian. Lezzzzzbyun." It sounded like music to me, every bit as lovely as "huzzzz-band" used to. I smiled and blew my image a kiss and giggled. Whether or not I loved a specific woman wasn't as important as the possibility. Leonor had been right about forgetting everything we'd learned and looking at the world with fresh eyes. Beginner's mind, she'd said the Buddhists called it. I'd have to dump the brainwashed contents of my mind and begin anew trusting myself.

So, if the word lesbian sounded lilting to me, how about the word god? So many associations. God as Mind, Word, Protector, First Cause.

Interesting, but all in my head. More importantly, in my gut, I hated that everyone always talked about God as a He. In Mexico, I had discovered a baby god-seed inside myself and now I had to beware not to throw that puppy out with the bathwater. At Lake Atitlán, I'd felt interconnectedness with everyone and everything that hit me viscerally, cellularly, heartfully. I didn't want to call it God, but I didn't want to dismiss it. I'd try various terms – Goddess, Universe, Great Spirit, Higher Power – until I found one that worked.

– ∞ –

At the office, I wrote and edited articles about the women's movement, labor, Latin America. All the stars of the Left passed through our offices, from Abbie Hoffmann to Jane Fonda. I covered the takeover of a church in East Harlem by the Young Lords, a Puerto Rican revolutionary group, and the breakfast programs of the Black Panthers. Pushing thirty, Harry and I were the oldest members of the collective, which was mainly comprised of kids from eighteen to twenty-five.

I didn't levitate one snack tray or table, nor did I speak of it. I wore an army jacket and jeans every day. I threw out all my bras and let my moppy hair grow as thick, long, and wild as it wanted to.

One day, in my journal, in my own version of revolution-speak, I wrote about my addiction:

"Forty-thousand children die of starvation on our planet daily, yet I have to admit, shamefully, that my life has become unmanageable because I am powerless over food."

I continued with the thoughts that *"...the craven capitalist society, through advertising and the media star system, objectifies and dehumanizes women. Refusing to be sexual objects, some women fatten themselves in hopes of becoming invisible, but they are then objectified in a worse way, as objects of derision and disgust. This leads to self-deprecation and the spiral of eating as self-punishment, thus fattening and hating themselves more.*

"There's a human element in each of us starving for love and attention. Ironically, media brainwashing leads us to believe we can obtain love and attention if we buy certain products and conform to a prescribed image. Thin models pose with cars, trucks, toothpaste, furniture, cigarettes – you name it. Society's concept of beauty isn't natural for many women – a Barbie body measuring thirty-eight, seventeen, thirty-eight! One day, probably by the turn of the century, if we haven't had a revolution by then, surgeons will have technology to lop off fat from one place

and put it back in another to create the perfect robotized body. But we haven't gotten there yet, and we can refuse to go there.

"In a just world, everyone will receive respect and be free to emphasize fitness and health rather than a cultural concept of the ideal body. But we don't live in a just world yet, do we? I found the perfect resolution to the contradiction by eating my pain away, but not holding onto the food. Overeating, followed by self-induced vomiting, is a product of the worst of capitalist culture, a world in which food is mass-produced, engineered for taste rather than nutrition, and intended to nourish profits rather than people.

"In fattening the bottom line, junk food has ended up fattening the bottoms of millions of people around the globe. As a twelve-year-old, I stumbled upon what I thought was a perfect solution, giving me an illusion of power and control. I could eat as much as I could stuff in, and by throwing it all up, shield myself from obesity. I had found a way to eat my cake and say slim too! How many other people suffer from this eating malady? I have no idea. As far as I know, I'm the only one, but maybe there are thousands of us doing it...."

Shyly, I showed the piece to Harry, expecting him to say something about how sorry he was that I'd suffered for seventeen years with this pathetic addiction.

"This is great," he said. "Put it out in this week's packet."

"Really?"

"Of course. It's original, creative, and a great story."

It was the first time I'd gone public. Everyone in the collective except Harry congratulated me on my courage and agreed the piece should be in the packet. Still, I imagined they looked at me in a new, suspicious way as though I were different and freaky. In a couple of weeks, when our subscribers' publications started arriving, I found more than thirty of them had picked up and featured my article, several on their front page. *Great Speckled Bird, LA Free Press, Rat, Berkeley Barb,* one after another, all over the country. Estimating a readership of about fifty thousand per paper, higher in large metro areas, I had admitted Step One of the Twelve Steps to about a million and a half people!

Victoria was flabbergasted and angry that I'd been secretly binging and purging all those years.

"I'm furious at you, Rowie. I should have watched you more closely."

"You couldn't have stopped me. Maybe I still do it."

"Rowie, that's unbelievable! It's disgusting. Does Mommy know?"

353

"No, and don't go blabbing to her, please. I'll deal with it in my own time."

"That could take another seventeen years at your rate. Remember what the table said about Mommy helping you when you least expected?"

"The table also said I wouldn't have to ask. She'd show up...with her new husband. Well, she isn't married. We can't trust that levitation stuff, Victoria. It's too weird."

"I don't know. I heard Ralph is engaged to a Japanese woman. I think she's a Buddhist so maybe he's on his way to fulfilling the prediction."

"I'm mad at Ralph for never writing to me. It's weird that you're closer to him than I am now."

"You lost touch with all your old friends, and now I know why. I think you need a therapist, and I'm going to bug you until you go. You could go to Gene. He's great."

"Please don't ask me to go to your therapist. I hate therapists. Every single one I've gone to has been an asshole. Except maybe Gabe and he was a kind of asshole but he wasn't my therapist."

"Gene is not an asshole. He's decent and helpful. Maybe you should go find Gabe again. Maybe he's divorced by now. I always thought you'd marry him. I think you should get help before you kill yourself."

"Don't bug me, Victoria."

– ∞ –

The week after my article came out, letters to the editor appeared, mostly sympathetic except for one letter from an irate black woman who said I had some nerve complaining about throwing up when I was lucky to have enough to keep me alive. I agreed with her, wrote back that was the craziest part of the addiction, but did she know of any addiction that made sense? I had never felt so empowered. I had no more secret to guard, and thought I was on my way to an easy final cure. But I didn't stop.

– ∞ –

Victoria was sleeping with Forrest Nicholas, a forty-year-old poet she'd met at Grove Press who liked tickling her with a peacock feather. Forrest escorted her to an endless round of loft parties with other writers, painters, actors, wannabes, and young editors like her. Many of them experimented with multiple drugs and lovers and most of them had therapists, including Victoria.

She talked more about her therapist, Gene, than her lover, Forrest, who, she thought, smoked and drank too much and whom she would have dumped except she had no intention of sacrificing her arty-party ticket.

"I'd like to have a few boyfriends," Victoria announced as she chopped onions on the bathtub lid and I sat on the chipped white stepstool we'd rescued from the trash. She was six inches shorter than I, and the countertop worked comfortably for her. She was making spaghetti sauce for a rare Saturday afternoon dinner together. Harry would probably join us. Victoria's eyes teared. She sniffed. "Gene says I may be obsessing over sadomasochistic sexuality to overcompensate for my feelings of chthonic powerlessness, but I think my whole problem is that Forrest is a dick and I need more than he offers me. I don't think monogamy is natural."

"Sounds like bullshit. Do you really want a boyfriend for every day of the week, Victoria?"

"Maybe not that many," she said. "I'm not looking for the seven dwarfs. Just, say, three good ones. An artist, an athlete, and an intellectual."

"Which one will cook?"

"All of 'em."

"And how will you feel about their other girlfriends?"

"Do they need other girlfriends? That's the part I'm not sure of."

"Aha, there's the rub! I'm exactly the same. But I can sort of imagine sharing a man with a woman I love. A true ménage a trois."

"Like you and me sharing a guy?"

"I don't know. That could be tough since we don't want to be lovers."

"What if I slept with Harry?"

"I don't know," I said, my heart flip-flopping. "I suppose if I were occupied with another fabulous guy of my own, I wouldn't mind. No, I'd probably still be jealous. I might want to kill you."

"Don't worry. It's all hypothetical. I may be a sex addict but I'm not a scumbag. Will you open the can of tomatoes, please? I'm making a nice dinner, for eating, not barfing. You're not really doing it anymore, right?"

"None of your business, Victoria. I'm dealing with it, period." I opened the tomatoes, changed the subject. I hadn't lied, and it felt fabulous. She made a face, and I didn't care. "You know, Victoria," I continued, "you would probably adore Leonor. She would welcome you if you wanted to vacation in Mexico or even move there. You'd love her just as you love this awesome painting she did just for me." I thought, Go far away, Sis. Go far away from me.

"I've always felt the painting was incredible, the most erotic flower painting I've ever seen. Maybe I will consider going to Mexico. Maybe I could hook up with a Mexican revolutionary instead of an African. Hmmm." She smiled slyly. "By the way, you're not fooling me by changing the subject. I'm going to watch you after every meal."

Bitch! What was I doing living with the vomit cop? How had I agreed to this? Why did I have to go and write that article?

I felt trapped, went to pee. A loud knock on our apartment door startled us. It wasn't Harry's knock. Victoria interrupted vegetable chopping to answer the door.

"I was just leaving," I heard her say, as I flushed and walked out of our little bathroom. In walked Moffat, followed by three other dark-skinned giants.

"Hey, baby," said Moffat. "Hope you don't mind. I brought my buds from Detroit to meet you. They're in town for a police conference we were at all day today."

"You really are a cop?"

"I told you, baby. Show your badges, dudes." They pulled out wallets and flashed shiny metal.

"Do you even know my name, Moffat ?"

"Hey, a rose by any other would smell as sweet, right?"

"I'm Rowie. How did you find my apartment?"

"I got ways, baby." He grinned. Shit, he must have followed me up when he walked me home. I had heard footsteps.

One by one, they introduced themselves. Joe, Roy, Tom. Moffat was looking around. He walked into the back bedroom.

"Mattress on the floor. Come here a minute, Rowie. I want to talk to you."

I went, mesmerized and apprehensive. He grabbed my arms hard, then patted my hair, enfolded me like a big burrito, laid me down, pulled down my jeans and underpants, pulled up my sweater, spit on his fingers and put them inside me. In a flash, I was out the window and flying west toward the river. While I zoomed up over the Hudson like a superhero, part of me heard Moffat speaking softly, musically, sweetly, saying flattering things about my breasts, pussy, legs, lips, hair, telling me I was beautiful, I was desirable, he'd wanted to fuck me since he saw me by the basketball court, he wanted to work with me, he could set me up. I watched the scared woman who was me the same way I had watched the little girl receive blows so many years earlier, the same way I watched the rape in Guatemala, only before I had to stay on the ceiling to see, and now I was both on the ceiling and outside in the sky, soaring higher and higher, faster and faster, through the ionosphere, passing airplanes, passing clouds, now rounding the Arctic Circle and heading South, and yet I was also up by the light switch, watching this big, strange man on his knees manipulating my body in a dark dungeon of an apartment I should have left before even moving in. He pulled off his pants, stroked his immense penis, entered me and began immediately humping. Tears rolled out of my clenched eyes but not a whimper escaped . I watched from above as both man and woman came loudly and saw my painful grimace. Moffat pulled out and stood up. I covered my face with my hands and rolled over into fetal position. The other three men crowded round watching. Wall to wall giants. Could I smite them from another dimension? I flew down to attack Moffat, and ended up passing right through him into my body. Another one had pulled off his pants and had a hardon ready. I immediately popped back out through the wall.

"I'm next," he said. It could have been a bank line.

"Go for it, man," said Moffat. "Sweet white poontang."

"Hey," I said, briefly back in my body, reaching for covers. Was this a nightmare? "What's going on?"

"Don't play dumb, baby. You know you want this as much as we do."

I was wet, slippery and scared. With no effort, I fled my body again, in a sudden burst, like ejaculate, and was borne aloft like a kite untied in the breeze. I surveyed the scene. There I was, limp, weeping, pale and pathetic under a gleaming dark muscular body riding me like a stallion in a squalid little room. Number three followed similarly. I kept mumbling stop, but they didn't stop. The fourth man had all his clothes off and took his place above me. He rubbed my nipples with his huge open hand. I thudded into my body to confront him.

"Please," I begged, low. "Please don't. I can't take anymore. I think I will die, and you'll all be responsible." I kept pleading and crying. Snippets of music from changing FM stations blared. He felt sorry for me. The others had gone back into the living room and were chatting and smoking, blasting Marvin Gaye's "Heard it through the grapevine."

"We'll just pretend," he whispered. "I won't do anything."

"Thank you." Tears flowed. I ached, body and soul. How could this have happened? Marvin Gaye sang, "Just about to lose my mind." Me too, I thought, me too. Gang-raped by cops. Black cops. Oh no! Am I living out a crazy racist stereotype? But then I remembered all the positive sexual experiences I'd had with black men, especially my darling Nigerian lover, Moiseh, from college days. If only he were here now. At least Harry is around to comfort me.

Later, as they filed out of the apartment, Moffat reached down and kissed me on the forehead. "Hey, baby, you're a good sport. The offer I made you is definitely still on."

I quickly latched both bolts, attached the security chain and leaned heavily against the door. I sure wasn't going to call the cops. Where the hell had Victoria gone? I was numb. Dazed, I moved everything off the bathtub lid, the half-chopped onion, carrot, celery, parsley, knife on cutting board, potholder, dishtowel, emery board, shampoo. I started a bath and climbed in while the water level was low so I could adjust more easily to extra hot water. When I saw my bruised arms, more tears came. My vulva was tender and swollen. I could feel my bladder aching. I wailed.

Too sore for jeans, I'd put on my blue chambray skirt and Stop the War tee shirt. Purse in trembling hand, I knocked at Harry's door. I'd take him out for pizza since dinner got ruined. I'd get him to hug me for solace. Maybe I'd tell him and maybe not.

"Proud Mary" by Credence Clearwater was blaring, so I figured he didn't hear me knock and let myself in with my key. I noticed Freddy's Corvette keys, a couple of joints, and a sheet of acid tabs on the kitchen table. The song ended and voices from the bedroom emerged. Was that Freddy? I thought he was still in London. I stole into the office to listen more closely. My heart sank. They were love-making sounds.

My head throbbed. I couldn't resist peeking through the open doorway. Harry was naked, on top humping, his hands resting on bare legs split incredibly in a dancer's hundred and eighty degree angle parallel to the bed. The coos and moans were coming from Victoria.

"You fuckers!" I screamed. "Assholes, scumbags, traitors!"

– ∞ –

FORTY

I was possessed, irrational, blind. Storming through the kitchen, I picked up the car keys, joints and tabs, then slammed out and flew down five flights to the street. Freddy's red Corvette was parked halfway down the block. I jumped in, buckled up, and headed for the West Side Highway going uptown. At a traffic signal, I swallowed a couple of tabs and used the lighter to light a joint. I inhaled deeply. Fuck them all!

Where could I go? I had no friends in New York. Karen and Eliza were five hours away upstate. It would have to be my mother, the Unitarian. I would crawl back into the womb. Perfect. I inhaled again, gunned the Corvette, just missed sideswiping an Oldsmobile which honked loudly, and made my way onto the highway.

I crossed the George Washington Bridge in the dark, missed the turn onto the Palisades Parkway, and stayed on Route 17, the road my parents had taken when I was a kid. Maybe I was a kid again! I'd go to the Red Apple Rest! Fucking Harry Apple. Some revolutionary! This low car couldn't be real. I was in a movie scene! In movies there were crashes, so I would crash. My bladder ached. My pussy burned. I saw lights in the other direction, beautiful lights, blinking like stars, all heading to the evil city. The city held trouble and temptation. I would save these poor bastards behind the lights. I was Wonder Woman, and I could keep them away. It was my duty to stop them. I aimed the Corvette and swerved across the highway, jouncing through the center median. There was a loud crash of metal upon metal and then stillness. I slumped onto the wheel. My window was open. The engine was still running.

Suddenly an arm reached into the car. It groped for the ignition. I looked up. The arm belonged to a guy in uniform, a cop! I knew he was going to hurt me. He had to be Moffat's man! I would outsmart him. I bolted up, threw the Corvette into reverse and took off. It made a funny noise, but it ran. I hung a U-turn, zigzagged through traffic and headed away from the city. I'd get away from them all. Wonder Woman always won. I'd defeat them. I heard sirens. The fuckers were coming to get me again, but this time, I would escape. The chase continued. I crossed the median again, bumping through the grass. There were no cars on the road except mine and the pigs'. I vaguely saw cars lined up in the distance, a cop car with lights flashing like Christmas, blocking the road. Lovely lights beckoning me, trying to trap me with their beauty. Not me, I wouldn't fall for their tricks. Round and round we went. I knew I had to travel light to increase my speed, so I threw my jacket out the window, then my purse and the tabs and joints. Finally they had the Corvette trapped. I would fool them. I didn't need the car. I'd fly away! I stopped, leapt out and ran flapping my arms. The cops chased me on foot. No way would I let them get me. When they grabbed me, I fought, kicking, biting and scratching. I knew they were going to rape me, and I wouldn't allow it. It took nine of them to subdue me. They were big, but I put up a valiant effort. They cuffed me and forced me into the back of a car. They were transporting me to hell.

– ∞ –

Why was I handcuffed to a chair in an office full of cops? Was I a character in a book? Was I in a movie? People came and went, voices made no sense to me. I must have dozed because all of a sudden, Mommy was there, teary, with a strange old man at her side. Was that Grandpa? He was bald like Grandpa. Snatches of conversation echoed.

"No history of drug use. No idea who Frederick Apple is. Owner of Corvette. Not reported stolen. Miracle no one hurt. Passengers just shaken up. She aimed Corvette. Not under arrest. Remand to psycho unit."

I woke up in a room with other beds. A dormitory? Rockland State Hospital. Daylight. They had given me a shot. Everyone smoked tobacco. People wobbled, bent over, robotic. What film was this? Why was I weighted down? Did they fatten me for the kill? I had visitors, the nurse said. She led me to the lounge.

"Sweetheart, thank God you're okay," Mommy said through a haze of cigarette smoke, not hers. Patients looked dazed or hypnotized, parked in front of a TV with the volume turned way up. What kind of place was this? Mommy spoke, pointed to the old man with her. "Rowie, this is Chris. We met at the Unitarian Church. He's my dear friend. He's a lawyer, and he'll help you. He...uh....You tell her, Chris."

"Hi, nice to meet you, Rowie," the man who looked like Grandpa said. "Actually, I'm a retired lawyer. But I still dabble. What your mom wants me to tell you is that I've been a psychiatric patient. I'm a survivor. I'm sorry you're here, but I'll help you deal with it. Do you need anything?"

"I need to get out of here."

"We'll see what we can do."

"I'm not crazy. Why am I here?"

"It was here or jail. We thought this was a better alternative."

"They gave me a shot of something that's bulking me up."

"Haloperidol," said Chris. "It brought you down. Stiffens the joints. The sense of weight will go away, don't worry."

"What happened?" Mommy asked. "I never saw you like you were last night." I could see she'd been crying.

Chris added, "Did you have any kind of shock? I thought you looked traumatized, not just from the accident."

I knew there was something, but it was just out of range. I couldn't recall. I shrugged, felt vacant.

"I don't like you and Victoria living in that Mafia neighborhood," Mommy said. "I keep thinking you'll witness a gangland slaying."

My brain reeled. Mafia. Moffat. Victoria. Harry. I snapped into clarity, shivered. My body ached all over.

"Usually those neighborhoods are safest, Pearl," Chris said. "If you're the 'right' color anyhow." He had his arm around her shoulders. I noticed they seemed comfortable brushing against one another.

"I don't want to live with Victoria in that shithole anymore, Mommy. But I like my job. I'm doing meaningful work. I need to find another home."

"I have a studio apartment on the Upper West Side you can stay at for a while, Rowie. My daughter lives in the same building." He smiled at Mommy.

"Chris's daughter Mara is a Lesbian, Rowie. She's very nice."

A very nice Lesbian? Was I hearing this from my Mommy, Pearl Fine Wine, the homophobe?

"Chris is retired," Mommy went on. "He likes to putter. He's building bookshelves for me."

"I've always wanted to be a carpenter. Your mom is helping me fulfill a dream." He smiled, a sweet, beaming, radiant, toothy smile that erased the wrinkles around his mouth and crinkled the skin around his eyes. His front teeth protruded slightly. My Jewish Mommy belonged to a church and now had a boyfriend named Chris. He looked at me earnestly. "There are three conditions, Rowie. Your mother and I want you to promise to see a therapist. You could have killed yourself and others last night. There were five people in the car you hit and they all walked away. You must have a guardian angel. But you might not be so lucky another time. That's number one. The second is there will be no drugs. No pot, no acid, no drugs, period. The third requirement is no lying. We'll have Mara check in with you regularly, and you have to promise you'll tell us the truth."

"You remind me of my grandpa," I said to Chris with a smile. "Otherwise, when I first saw you I might have told you to go fuck yourself. But I'm glad I didn't."

"Lucky me," he said, smiling back.

Mommy scowled.

"No disrespect intended. I agree to all three conditions. I'm grateful for your generous offer. When can I get out?" I addressed Chris.

"You have to stay a week. They want to observe you. Behave yourself. Be compliant no matter how difficult. Tell them you'd like to try healing without the Haloperidol, that you are grateful for the dose that helped you and you don't think you need more. Legally, you can refuse medication. Meanwhile I'll speak to Mara and get the apartment cleaned and ready. I'll expect you to pay some sort of rent, whatever you can swing."

"Thank you."

"By the way, whose Corvette were you driving?"

"I don't know the guy. My, er...neighbor was watching it for his brother."

"They're both in for a surprise."

"How bad is it?"

"Let's leave it up to the insurance company to decide. You seem to be in remarkably good shape considering. Does any part of your body hurt?"

"I ache all over, but nothing feels broken."

"Good." He looked at Mommy. "Do you want to add anything, honey?"

So it was 'honey,' was it?

"Jonathan, Karen and Eliza send their love. Karen's very concerned. She's pregnant again, did you know?" Her eyes were moist. "I love you, Rowie." She hugged me. "I've missed you. I'm sorry." The hug was softer than usual. "I'll bring you chicken soup tomorrow."

We all laughed together at the stereotypical Jewish mother offer. Then I took a deep breath.

"Mommy, speaking of food, I have to tell you something very hard to say but I'm just going to say it. Are you listening?"

"Of course, dear. What is it?"

"Excuse me, Rowie," Chris said. "Are you sure you want me to hear this?"

"You're offering me a home, Chris. You might as well listen. Anyway I want to get used to saying this." I took a deep breath again. Words and tears flowed out together. "Mommy, Chris, I've been overeating and then inducing myself to throw up for more than fifteen years. It's an addiction and I'm determined to kick it."

Mommy paled. "It's all my fault," she said, and hugged me. She was crying along with me. "I remember when you first asked me about it, just after Grandpa passed away, I told you it was all right. I didn't understand what it meant back then. I'm so sorry, Rowie. I had no idea."

"It's not your fault, Mommy. Blame isn't going to help. I made some bad choices and I have to take responsibility. I'm scared shitless, but I'm determined to face this thing. Can I count on you to help?"

"A hundred percent, Rowie. I love you. I didn't know what love was back then. It's taken me years to begin to learn. I guess you'd call me a fucked-up mother."

I'd never heard her use the f-word before. We grinned. "No more than I was a fucked-up daughter, Mommy. Let's just do our damnedest to get through this." I was laughing and crying.

"Promise me you won't throw up my chicken soup," Mommy said, holding both my hands and looking straight into my eyes.

"I promise I'll do my very best to keep it down, Mommy. I want to be truthful. I honestly don't know how long it's going to take me to succeed at this."

"Fair enough. I can understand because food is a big issue for my women's group at the church, especially those of us who are Jewish. I have a feeling my own food *mishugas* got passed on to you. I'm so sorry, Rowie."

"Thanks, Mommy. I'm happy to hear you're in a women's group. But I'm confused that you're still calling yourself Jewish and you're going to church."

"I'm more Jewish now than I was before I discovered my spirituality. I love my Jewish roots more than ever. You never know where you'll find what you need. I strengthened my ties to Judaism at the Unitarian Church."

She smiled at me. We hugged again.

The announcement that visiting hours were ending came through the loudspeaker. I had to pee badly, felt sore and burning.

Chris held out his hand to shake mine, quickly changed his mind and hugged me. "I have a Jungian analyst I can recommend, Rowie. She's within walking distance of the apartment. She does deep tissue work also. I think you'll like her."

"It's a possibility," I said. "I'm willing to meet with her. Thanks, Chris, for helping me, and for making my mother happy."

"Oh, and Rowie," Mommy said, winking. "Chris's apartment has a piano."

– ∞ –

Victoria arrived next afternoon. I greeted her coolly.

"I called Gene," she said. "He said I didn't take away anything valuable from you."

"Oh, well, if Gene says so, it must be true."

"It's not as though that was the first time Harry and I slept together. Didn't you know we'd done it in Philadelphia a few times too and when he visited at the beach?"

I felt stabbed. "No, how was I supposed to know? I trusted you and I trusted him. You're both fucked up. Don't you have any conscience?"

"Rowie, I come from the same crazy Wine family you do. What do you expect?"

"More, I guess. Maybe too much."

"How many tabs of acid did you take?"

"I don't remember."

"That was potent stuff. You're lucky to be alive."

"That remains to be seen."

"Are you getting laryngitis? You sound hoarse."

"I'm losing my voice. Maybe I've never had a voice."

"You're wallowing."

"Go away, Victoria. You're pissing me off."

"I'm waiting for Mom and her new boyfriend. We're having dinner together and I get to meet our future sister, the dyke. Isn't it wonderful that Mom is in love?"

"Yeah, peaches and cream. Victoria. I have to ask you to wait out in the lobby. I have nothing to say to you."

"Are you going to hold a grudge?"

"I don't know yet."

"Harry's freaked about Freddy's Corvette. Freddy could charge you with stealing his car."

"I'll deny it. Harry gave me the keys."

"Plus the tabs were worth a few hundred dollars. Why are you in a loony bin? You seem normal."

"Shut up, Victoria. Just go away now before I lose my temper. I'm already losing my voice." I coughed.

"Okay, okay, but I love you and I'll always be your sister."

"I suppose that second part is true. You'll always be my sister. I really want you to go away now. I don't want to be around you. I feel betrayed. You haven't even apologized."

"My therapist said..."

"Fuck your therapist and fuck you."

"Just tell me one more thing. What happened with Moffat and those dudes?"

"We had a tea party. Now, fuck off. Get lost. I have to behave myself here. Chris told me if they see me agitated, I'll be in fucking bad shape, maybe put in a strait jacket and drugged even more. I have a sadistic doctor who should be named Mengele."

"Sorry. Bye."

When Victoria left, I burst into tears. Why was I so mean to her? Why was I saying fuck so much? Why couldn't I act loving as I'd been with Mommy? After I peed again, I lay on my hospital bed, pulled covers over me, and silently cried non-stop. When the tears slowed, I entered a strange dead silence. I saw blue, then maroon, then an inky blue-black abyss and I was free-falling, tumbling and diving in fancy forms, weightlessly, gracefully, safely, alone, hurtling deeper and deeper into dark spaciousness, nothingness, the Void.

Suddenly, a movie of my life unfolded vertically, in 360 degrees, scene after scene. I saw myself conceived near the World's Fair in Queens, missionary position, born in Cornwall Hospital to a screaming mother unsure of how to cope with pain of childbirth. I saw my first few years go by, my Fine Wine parents in the background bickering, lashing out, wounding, fighting about money non-stop.

Over and over, I watched the negativity of their anger hit my solar plexus like an exploding ball of pain, moving up to stain my heart. I wanted to play with a gun like my cousin Ralphie, but my parents refused to get me one, said they didn't believe in violence. I made my fingers into a gun and played bang, bang instead. I saw Grandpa's smiling face as he ran his Singer, heard his music, saw me curled up on his lap, my heart straining to stay open. I saw five-year-old me smile for Daddy's Kodak in our backyard. I saw as he spanked me over and over and over, and over and over and poked me with his fingers, hurting and confusing me until I fled through the crown of my head, floated by the ceiling for a while and then took off, over rooftops and trees, awed by star-filled skies, soaring above snow, sleet, hail, torrential rain somehow making my way to connect with benevolent energies. I avoided my new baby sister's crib, frightened by her siphoning off attention I craved, but then I fell madly in love with her and we danced around the house.

My first grade teacher, large and unhappy, humiliated me. I wrote an elephant story I never finished, fabricated a long list of Christmas presents in second grade and recited them to the class. I saw myself chewing wax and spitting it into test tubes as part of the fluoride experiments in Newburgh. I saw Uncle Sidney and Aunt Bea criticizing me thoughtlessly, how big I was compared to other kids, how ashamed I was of my body and how I forgot my discomfort when I listened to opera on the radio with Gramps on Saturday mornings.

I saw my neighbors entice me with pornography and later proposition me. I saw my father coming naked to my bed and straddling me as I passed out into total denial. He was drunk and he sat on me and fucked me in the head and came in my mouth. I almost choked, and I swallowed it, salty and creamy and scary. I woke up and forgot it completely, had no memory. None. He did it a couple more times and I forgot those too, buried the entire scene with oceans of food: loaves of rye bread and tubs of butter, cake, cookies, calories galore, adding heft to my little girl body and a new talent for shooting off noxious gas at will that saved me from Daddy's spankings over and over in a switch to slapstick comedy.

Seders, lunches, dinner after delicious dinner at Gram's. Gramps waving from the maple tree outside South Junior and then his funeral. I was horrified by my uncles' laughing during *shiva*, so upset I stuffed my stomach with noodle pudding, then excitedly stuck fingers down my throat and threw up. It was as though I were shooting myself with the toy gun fingers.

Flying stopped. I became an outlaw, miserable inside, presenting a happy face to the world. I saw the moment when I punched the TV set and the anchorman flinched. Bells rang, lights flashed like a winning slot machine. I smacked Daddy across the face and freed myself from his power.

With my first boyfriend Skip appeared rainbow colors, hearts, flowers, sunshine, happiness, fear, happiness, fear, happiness, fear, back and forth. I turned greenish brown and toxic as I sent him away. Pearl gloated. As I lay in my hospital bed, years unfolded like pages of a flip book. Ira, Sy French, Pierre, Barnard, Lydia, Sarah, graduation, Ralph, Govinda, California, Ceil, Tommy, Cuban missile scare, Gabe, Guatemala, Enrique, Nick, Lynn, Ricardo and the rape, Miguel, Harry, missed plane crash, baby Eliza communicating with me, more bells and lights. The Village apartment, Joe Bob, Mexico, Leonor, Max, my students serving me Turkish coffee, Harry again, Victoria, Philadelphia, Martin Luther King, Bobby Kennedy, funerals on TV, antiwar banners, loud, screaming anger, sex, sex, sex, rolling naked with one after another stranger, still with the happy face, leaping out of my body as it participated in orgasmic exchanges.

Here were Moffat and his pals humping me in the dark back tenement room, Victoria and Harry, desperation, licking a couple of Orange Sunshine tabs, gunning the Corvette, aiming it at a two-toned green Pontiac across the median, too dark to see the color with my eyes. I heard the crash, felt the car careen off the road, saw a uniformed arm reach in to turn off the ignition. I saw traffic stopped in both directions as police cars chased me.

I watched transfixed, gripped with the realization that every scene in my personal movie formed me. Flow charts passed before me, maps showing roads not taken, still existing in a less material, less dense dimension. Once I was a grown-up, at any time, I could have chosen an alternate path. Outcomes could have been different if I'd chosen differently. Now and for the rest of my life, I could make choices consciously and carefully. I would choose a wise guide.

Fascinated, I continued watching the movie as it entered unfamiliar places, possible futures. I ate fresh vegetables and whole grains, smiled, no throwing up. I saw millions and millions of girls and women around the world and some men too, sticking their fingers in their throats and purposely doing what I had done. It was called bulimia. Dancers, skaters, gymnasts, college girls, entire populations of dormitories throwing up. Doing it to stay thin, because thin was so in. There were special treatment centers for eating disorders, meds to change the brain.

More sunshine, a place in the country, cooperative, peaceful sanctuary in a pastoral setting, welcoming a young girl, a smiling, middle-aged woman in a long tie-dyed caftan – the woman in the caftan was me! I wore a wedding ring. The man standing with his arm around me was an older version of Gabe. His first marriage had ended in divorce. We ran a collective healing center. We produced workshops, books, plays, interactive games, and films. I had written several of the books myself. One was called *The Skinny*. It was the story of my life. The tape rewound.

Maroon silence replaced pictures. Then scenes continued, a variety of possibilities.

The middle-aged woman in the caftan wasn't me anymore, she greeted me! I was old, worn, unhappy, stick thin, no rings, bent over, holding a giant bag of potato chips. I fell into her arms at the door.

There was a sign coming into focus; a group of women at the sanctuary held the sign as a homemade banner. It said, "Row, row, row your boat. Your boat will go where you lead it to go, if you know how to row, Ro-ro."

– ∞ –

FORTY-ONE

When I opened my eyes, a stranger with a kind face appeared in the doorway of my hospital room. He looked a little like Chris, and a lot like Grandpa in the old black and white wedding photo that had sat in a frame on my grandparents' bookcase. Had Chris stepped into a time machine? He had hair now. Olive complexion, wire-rimmed glasses on clear brown eyes, broad nose, sensual lips. Grandpa in that photo wore a three-piece suit, tucked broad tie, gold chain to pocket watch. This man looked to be young middle-aged, corporate in conservative dark suit, striped silk tie, ecru shirt. He carried a black and white composition notebook like kids used in elementary school, like I used as journals years ago. Was he a teacher?

"I'm delighted to see your mood has shifted, Miz Wine," he said, smiling broadly. "What happened?"

I smiled back. "I just saw a fast forwarded movie of my life and found out I've had quite a mixed ride so far. I've stretched a tough childhood into an unnecessarily tough adulthood. I'm ready to make more careful choices."

He nodded. "How do you feel?"

"I feel a little heavy and sad, but happy to be alive."

"Your story is heavy and sad, so your feelings are appropriate. Happy to be alive is a good place to begin each moment." He pulled up a chair next to the bed. "How did you land here?"

"Smoothly," I said. "From a rocky beginning, I landed smoothly, except for my voice, which as you can hear, I'm losing."

"I'm glad you landed smoothly, that's wonderful, Miz Wine." His voice, in contrast to mine, sounded like Mario Lanza's. Soothing, mellifluous.

"I've brought you presents," he said.

"Presents?" I croaked. My voice grew progressively weaker. I knew my sore throat and disappearing voice related to the scene I'd buried for so long, the agony of Daddy's sexual invasion. I knew the bulimia and casual sex were defenses I'd built because I didn't feel worthy to receive food or love. Sadness and hope engulfed me.

He handed me a small black and white pen and composition notebook with a matching design.

"My daddy had a fountain pen like this," I whispered.

"I know," he said.

Even whispering was a chore. The composition notebook looked blobby and Rorschachian. With tears in my eyes, I managed a joke.

"Am I supposed to look at the inkblots and tell you what I see?"

He laughed delightedly and shook his head. "You think you've lost your voice, but there's a spiritual law that says you can never lose what's really yours. You've found your voice a number of times in your life, and each time you freed yourself a little bit more. Your true job in this lifetime is to find freedom and love. You've focused on negativity. We've sheltered you from physical effects of your addiction. You must now feel those effects. Your physical voice won't return until you've strengthened your unique personal voice. In this notebook, the first of many, you don't have to write words, Miz Wine. You can write music or draw pictures, whatever you choose. You know how knights of old righted wrongs? You, my dear, are a righter. You may look upon your childhood as a mastery school. You managed to master the art of survival. Now you must begin to live and thrive."

I nodded.

"If I may, I believe one reason you landed here has to do with your talent as what I will call a riter, r-i-t-e-r, a shaman, who performs ceremonies. Your culture has few outlets for transformative voyages into alternative realities and for the most part has created a punitive system, misidentifying spiritual crises as mental illness. There was an aspect of ceremony to what you enacted on the road with this car crash. You did something similar in California on wine. Don't try to talk. You'll get skilled at ritual and ceremony in time and you'll be able to stay sober and enact them, for yourself and others." He smiled.

"Then there's rider, r-i-d-e-r which sounds similar, one who rides the crest of reality, choosing carefully what to create. Yes, you'll learn that as well. It's in the lesson plan for you."

This man was other-worldly, so deeply kind I was feeling my heartbeat shift slightly. When I opened my mouth to say something else, there was no sound. Zero voice. I wrote in the notebook with the new pen: "Who are you? What lesson plan? What's your name?"

I handed him the open notebook and pen, forgetting for a moment he could talk to me.

He accepted the notebook and pen, read what I'd written, and wrote something quickly with his left hand. Then he closed the book, clipped the pen to the cover, patted my arm, and vanished.

He had written, "Stop, sanctify, and harmonize means remember to give thanks and love. You're Love ingesting Love and blessed by Love. Be grateful!" He signed his name 'Max Messinger.'"

Max!

The first thing I wrote was a bar of music.

Next, amid a torrent of cleansing tears, I began my story.

– ∞ –

APPENDIX

Rayni Joan's Seminal Newspaper Article: June, 1970

About the Author

The author of **The Skinny** is Rayni Joan, who grew up as Roberta Joan Weintraub in Newburgh, New York during the 1940's and 50's. During a critical period in the early 1970s, she was part of the Liberation News Service collective, where for $35 and 10 free meals per week, she researched and wrote news and feature articles.

It was during this period that her ground-breaking feature article, "Women, Fat of the Land" appeared widely throughout the U.S. It was June, 1970, and Ms. Joan became the first public confessor to the then unheard of habit of binging and purging, later diagnosed in the 1980s as *bulimia*. Although the word and the fact of "bulimia" were largely unknown at the time, her compelling story containing her stunning confession was picked up by and published on the front pages of dozens of alternative weekly newspapers, where it struck a chord with more than a million women readers - a chord that resonates to this day.

Although her public confession was a major turning point in her life, it nevertheless took Ms. Joan seven more years to kick the habit. Today, she shares her wisdom and experience in a tranquil setting with a select few

Ms. Joan is now Director of the Center for Increased Consciousness, and lives near the beach in Santa Monica, California, with her husband, writer Robert Moskowitz.

– ∞ –